MEMORIES

MEMORIES

by
Spencer Ash

Aventine Press

© August 2004, by Spencer Ash
First Edition

Without limiting the rights under copyright reserved above, no part of this publication may be reproduced, stored in or introduced into a retrieval system, or transmitted, in any form or by any means(electronic, mechanical, photocopying, recording, or otherwise), without the prior written permission of both the copyright owner and the publisher of this book.

Published by Aventine Press
1023 4th Ave #204
San Diego CA, 92101
www.aventinepress.com

ISBN: 1-59330-203-7

Printed in the United States of America

ALL RIGHTS RESERVED

*This book is dedicated to my incredible three children:
Avalon, Ryan, and Marina.*

I would like to thank Doctor Rodney Redelsperger for all of the medical information he gave me. He made the book possible.

CHAPTER ONE

Death lurked in the motionless air, searching for a prey. It was like a starved, cunning predator that had been wandering through a barren wasteland, void of any suitable game, for a long time. It hung weightless like an ominous invisible cloud, and smiled warmly as the pickup quietly rolled down the dirt path and stopped. It merged into the gentle wind and rustled through the leaves as Nick shut off the engine and stepped out of the cab. It had found its prey. Like an old friend waving hello, it swayed back and forth in the tall grass—a sign of fair play—to give fair warning, and even though he looked in its direction, he didn't even give it a second thought. He just stood there for a moment, wearing dark-shaded glasses and smiled at it, then took a deep breath, filled his lungs with the clean mountain air and was happy to be alive. Little did he know the fate that would soon befall him. Death softly floated past the truck, to the river beyond, gently caressing the side of his cheek as it went, and then beckoned to him from the sun-speckled water's surface.

He unloaded the kayaks from the back of the pickup and brought them, one at a time, to the riverbank. Allie brought the accessories. Nick turned and watched as she divided the paddles and deck bags. She looked great in the new wetsuit he bought her, but then again, she looked great no matter what she wore. Even with all the tragedy that had happened in his life, he was a lucky man. After putting on their lifejackets he helped her into the cockpit of her *Breeze* and then climbed into his own. She smiled and pulled out into the calm water. It was a cloudless summer morning.

The water rippled as Death gracefully glided through it, like a beautiful unseen swan, making no special attempt to conceal its path, and then softly dissolved into the side of Nick's kayak, gently rocking it as it went. It oozed upward and thinned out until it saturated every inch of the boat. It smiled as Nick cinched up his suspenders and became off balance, almost capsizing in the calm water. This would be an easy kill.

By the time Nick had finished suiting up, Allie was floating about fifteen feet away and playfully splashing the water with her oars. He had taught her how to kayak last year, and this morning he had taken her away from a comfortable warm bed to this cold and rough river to go kayaking with him. Shirtless, he pulled out, toward her. He was lean and extremely handsome. Even after five years of marriage she never tired of looking at him.

Her thoughts drifted back...

They had met six years ago in Oregon. She was unhappily attending a crazy college get-together at the invitation of a close friend. Normally she stayed away from this type of thing. It wasn't that she didn't like to have fun. She just didn't care for the stupid ways most people conducted themselves at these wild college parties.

Sitting on the floor next to the fireplace in a relatively calm room, she was repeatedly hit on by one of the over-confident, over-intoxicated, macho college flunkies. After turning down several obscene propositions she decided enough was enough and rose to leave. Disappointed by her obvious lack of good taste, her newest male admirer stood in front of her, blocking her path. He looked like a disorientated beer-guzzling Neanderthal. She stepped to one side. He matched her step. She asked him to move, but he did not. Instead he leaned in close, and with alcohol-polluted breath, slobbered below her ear and down her neck. Immediately, she pushed away and tried to run, but he lunged at her and brought her to the wood-planked floor. He dropped his beer and pinned her down, slobbering all over her face and neck. She screamed repeatedly, but no one seemed to care. The party just continued on around her as if nothing was happening. His saliva rolled across the surface of her skin seeping into her left eye and through the corner of her mouth.

She squirmed and kicked, but it did little good. He was as large as a gorilla and at least ten times as strong. He ripped at her blouse, popping off the top three buttons and exposing her bra. With both her wrists pinned to the floor he lowered his stubbly face to her breasts. She closed her eyes and screamed. A small group of wide-eyed, grinning kids gathered to watch the fun, but no one came to her aid. His hot wet breath passed through her thin bra, but just before his mouth connected, he released her and flew up into the air.

She opened her eyes and saw Nick for the first time. He was extremely good-looking and strong. He was wearing a black leather jacket and close-fitting blue jeans. His long dark hair had been pulled into a tail and hung down beneath the red and blue colors of his rebel-like bandana. He held the confused aggressor like a rag doll and twirled him around as he cocked his fist. Then, with seemingly super human strength, he hit him, lifting him up off the ground and back against the wall. Nick waited as his opponent slowly came out of his daze. Then instead of running in fear as she thought he would do, the Neanderthal came to life and somehow sobered up. He reached behind his back and mysteriously produced a harmless plastic handle, and with a flick of the wrist a blade snapped into place. Standing in a half-crouch, he skillfully wielded his weapon with his right hand while inviting Nick to come closer with his left. Allie pulled her blouse closed and slithered back, over to the far wall, next to the fireplace.

Nick kept his distance and matched the Neanderthal's crouch. More partygoers slowly gathered to watch as the two men danced around each other. The would-be rapist lunged forward and sliced through the air, missing Nick by mere millimeters. Petrified, Allie pressed her back into the wall and slowly rose to her feet. As she watched the event unfold she was struck by an odd revelation. Both men were tall, but the Neanderthal was taller, and Nick was weaponless, while the monster held a knife. The bizarre thing about it was that Nick's eyes held no fear.

She looked closer. He wasn't hiding it or merely trying to be macho. He just wasn't afraid. The beast on the other hand, who clearly had the advantage, seemed to be filling with fear by the second. Nick's ice blue eyes were calm and solid. She wasn't sure, but it even looked as if a smile hid just beneath his somber look. The man with the knife soon began to tremble and sliced again. Nick quickly moved to one side, and the blade struck air.

Someone stopped the music, and the crowed began to chant. Allie couldn't understand it at first. It sounded as if they were all saying something weird like *eye sman*. As they chanted, more and more fear worked its way into the Neanderthal's face. The chanting grew louder. *Eye sman! Eye sman!* Then she understood. *Iceman!* They were chanting Iceman.

"Iceman! Iceman!"

A bead of sweat developed on the Neanderthal's forehead and slowly trickled down the side of his face. He jabbed again and missed. Then, almost as if Nick had decided that he was through doing this silly dance, he quickly dropped to the floor and extended his right foot out in front of him, to the Neanderthal's right. In one smooth motion he shifted his weight, spun around, and knocked the giant's feet out from underneath him. The gorilla fell smack on his side and hit the floor with a thud. Almost instantly Nick was standing over him, pressing the full weight of his boot into the man's wrist, forcing him to relax his hand and release the blade. The chanting stopped and the room quickly fell silent while everyone watched. Nick carefully withdrew his boot and then softly nudged the knife across the floor. For a few intense moments he coldly glared down at the pathetic drunken fool, then slowly turned away. Just as the Neanderthal was letting out a sigh of relief, Nick spun back around and rammed his right boot hard into the man's ribs, completely knocking the wind out of him. The crowd all winced in unison.

Afterward, Allie decided she should hang around a while and at least get to know the mysterious rebel in the leather jacket—a jacket that he later shared with her as they talked the night away. The next morning, before daybreak the magic continued. He took her to breakfast and was able to show off his artistic talents and play Romeo, by skillfully drawing a heart on nothing more than a paper napkin. In jest he told her that it was *his* heart and that she should handle it with extreme care. She kept the napkin and still has it to this day.

Before he took her home she found out why everyone had been chanting the words Iceman. It was a subject he didn't like to discuss and for good reason. Both his parents had been brutally murdered three years earlier in a botched up robbery gone bad. The killer was never caught, and the incident changed the way he looked at life forever. It left him cold and angry inside. He had acquired the nickname *Iceman* because of his seemingly unshakable demeanor.

Over the next few months they spent more and more time together, getting to know each other better. She would share her dreams with him and he would tell her about his past. He grew up in an upper middle-class neighborhood and had the best parents anyone could hope for. Whenever the subject of his parents came up he always started out happy, but as the conversation progressed, somehow, his happy demeanor always turned into rage. Instead of withdrawing from him, like others had done, Allie embraced him. What wasn't to embrace about him? He was an amazing man who had gone through a nightmare that would make most people crumble. Several times, she tried to imagine how she would have dealt with such a traumatic event if it had happened in her life, but just couldn't fathom it.

Soon they were married and with her love, Nick slowly let go of the *Iceman* and started becoming Nicholas Chadwick again. He had recently decided to go back to school and finish his law degree. To celebrate they had come here, to West Virginia.

Now, as he paddled out toward her, she cocked her lovely head, coyly smiled and then, at just the right moment, splashed him. It wasn't a little splash either, a soft sprinkle of love. Oh no! It was an all out assault that caught him totally by surprise. The icy water shocked his body, stung his eyes and blurred his vision. By the time he recovered and decided to get even, she had already made her way to the main current and was being whisked down the river. Determined, he paddled after her. She looked over her shoulder and giggled. He wasn't far behind and was closing fast. She paddled harder, although she knew it wouldn't do much good. He was a lot faster than she was and much more skilled. The current was smooth and fast as he pulled up alongside her.

He grinned a confident grin and took aim, but then, just before he could return her splash, they were swept apart.

Her smiling face disappeared around one side of a large rock while he was pulled around the other. He emerged first and was already a good twenty feet ahead when she rounded the bend. He turned and looked over his shoulder. She just humbly smiled, waved, and shrugged her shoulders. Her smile was contagious and he couldn't help but to return it. The water calmed and he slowed his kayak, allowing her to catch up. Before long they were nearly side-by-side again and this time he didn't hesitate. He splashed her, but it had little affect. They had already been swept through more than a thousand yards of river, and she was already used to the water. So much for revenge! She was just about to splash back when something abruptly knocked into the bottom of Nick's kayak. At precisely the same moment, the current shifted a little and before he knew it, his kayak had flipped. Allie held her splashing position and waited for Nick to roll back out of the water.

Below the surface, as Nick tried to execute the *Eskimo roll,* a terrible pain shot through his side. After knocking the kayak over, Death circled Nick's body like an eel and sunk its deadly fangs deep into his flesh. It bit down hard and locked its jaws in the form of an unsuspected muscle cramp. The rapids began to grow stronger and something rushed by, dangerously close to Nick's head. Death grinned. Clinching his teeth and ignoring the pain, Nick forced the maneuver and rolled up out of the water. Allie splashed.

Angered and unwilling to give in so easily, Death used the uncertain rapids and Nick's own momentum against him, forcing him to continue the roll and plunging him back underneath the icy river. Death was a bulldog and the pain in Nick's side intensified.

Above the water, Allie nervously looked ahead. The river would soon divide into two separate waterways. She and Nick had always taken the one on the right because according to Nick the one on the left held a dangerous rapid called *Devil's Twist* and was impassable. They were on the wrong side of the river as the current sped up. If they didn't get over soon they would be forced to ride through the left channel.

With the rapids building and the pain in his side growing, Nick gave up on his roll and decided to exit his kayak. He pulled the front strap on his spray skirt, but incredibly, instead of releasing him, it snapped. Death was laughing at Nick.

"Nick!" Allie screamed as they drew closer to Devil's Twist.

Suddenly, Nick understood. Death was in the kayak with him, calling to him, laughing at him. Death had unfairly claimed his mother and his father and now wanted him, but he wasn't ready to go just yet, and Death wouldn't find him as easily claimed as his parents had been. In spite of the growing pain he grabbed the sides of the kayak with both hands and struggled free. Moments later he resurfaced, gasping for air, with powerful torrents exploding all around him. Miraculously, the muscle cramp was gone. Death must have stayed in the kayak, which was now moving down the river just in front of him.

The current was stronger here and growing. It slapped him, pulled him under the water, and knocked him hard against unknown structures. He was helpless, as it shot him up above the surface, and then pulled him back again. It whipped him around huge rocks and over dangerous falls as he struggled to get a fix on where he was. He knew that Devil's Fork was quickly approaching, a dangerous division in the river, but wasn't sure which stream he was in. If he wasn't in the right one he would be forced into a deadly rapid called Devil's Twist.

Devil's Twist was a section of river that bottlenecked to less than thirty feet across and featured a dangerously long drop onto several jagged rocks. No one ever attempted to cross it. On the rare occasion that someone missed the right channel, they would almost always find their way to shore and carry their vessel around the fall. The few poor souls who missed the right channel and were unable to make it to shore never survived the drop.

Desperately looking around, still trying to figure out which channel he was heading for, Nick spotted Allie. She was a couple of kayak-lengths ahead of him. Through the crashing waves it looked like she was paddling toward the left. They must have already passed the right channel and now she was trying to get to shore. With all his strength, Nick followed suit.

Allie was pulling away and making much better progress than he was. Even though he was working with all his might, he seemed to be doing little good. It was all but impossible to swim. Like a small toy boat, the rapids decided his direction. They pulled him this way and that way, sometimes pulling him closer to shore, but more often not. His kayak was no longer ahead of him. The river had pulled it out into the main current, quite a distance to his right. Perhaps he was making better progress than he thought. He kept stroking. Suddenly the river shot him up almost completely out of the water, and he saw Allie. She was nearly to safety. He saw the bank. It wasn't far off.

Plunge! Back down, underneath the surface. Then suddenly, a spike of pain shot through his side. It felt like a long, sharp ice pick had just been jabbed into his back, tore its way through muscle and tissue, and then poked out through the front. Unbelievable! Somehow, Death had left the kayak, swam up stream and found him.

Death was determined!

So was Nick!

Feeling the relentless desire that Death had to claim him, only made Nick push himself harder. Death wouldn't win! Not today. Or would it? Nick took a breath, and at the same instant the river slapped him square in the face. Water filled his mouth and some of it found its way to the back of his throat and down into his lungs. A dozen microscopic bombs went off, all at once, inside his chest. He coughed, gasped, and spat, but somehow managed to keep swimming. For an instant, he saw the bank then white water exploded in front of him, obstructing his view.

Then, Death grabbed the ice pick at both ends and tugged hard, pulling him back into the clutches of the river. Ignoring the pain with thoughts of his parents, Nick swam on. Allie screamed—or did she? It was hard to tell with the blasting rapids. Something hard smacked into Nick's shoulder. Whitewater exploded in front of him and then he saw the bank again. It was extremely close this time. Death, not Nick, would have to accept defeat today. While kicking for shore, his shin slammed hard into an unseen rock beneath the water. Pain entered his leg and worked in unison with the one in his side.

He was now at the bank but unable to get passed the menacing rocks without being torn to shreds. He glanced down river, at the edge of the falls. It was only seconds away.

Desperate, he decided to risk it and reached out for the rocks but was bounced back into the current and whisked around them, disallowed any opportunity to latch on. Undaunted, he reached for them again and this time grabbed onto the slimy face of a large boulder. His body jerked to a sudden stop, but the fast-moving water continued to pull. The roaring tone of the rapids changed and he knew he was just dangling on the edge of the fall.

He could hear the pages turning as Death's trophy book opened. Death dipped its quill into the inkwell and prepared to record his name. Infuriated, Nick all but leaped out of the water and clawed at the bank. His hands met clay, but the powerful current still sucked at him, pulling him back down. His scraping and clawing only delayed the inevitable. Death pressed its pen to the paper and laughed. Nick's fingers transformed into iron hooks. They dug into the soft clay and slowed him down but didn't stop him. The soft earth continued to give way underneath his fingertips and he inched toward the roaring fall. His already exhausted arms grew numb and felt as if they were about to be ripped from their sockets, but still he held on. Perhaps it was his imagination or some trick of the water, but he felt the river underneath his feet drop away, and he was sure that he was inching over the edge. An instant later, the river under his calves dropped away as well. He was about to go over, and there was nothing solid to grab onto.

Death was going to win after all. Damn it! His imminent death only enraged him more, but with nothing left to do, he thought of his parents again and prepared to join them. Then, Death gently reached up and slowly peeled back the clay under his fingers, causing it to give way and Nick was violently pulled over the falls. But miraculously, at the very last moment, his hand gripped something solid and his body jerked to a sudden stop. A perfectly round handle hid just beneath the surface of the soil. He tightened his grip and reached up with his other hand, dug through the mud, latched on and pulled his body up. The thick root steadily oozed through the mud, but never broke. Already over the fall and dangling from the top, Nick slowly climbed up the side of the bank and out of the river. The pain in his side had gone away again. He had won at last. Death would have to find another victim today.

Once he was on solid ground he rolled over onto his back to catch his breath. He panted heavily and every muscle in his body ached. Even the smallest of movements hurt. He wouldn't be able to walk for a week. They would have to come and drag his ass out of here because he wasn't moving.

Then a faint scream filled the air! Allie? Immediately, he sat up. A moment later he was on his feet, running through bushes and jumping over brush. Beyond the passing leaves he saw Allie's kayak, but not Allie. It was upside down, against a fallen poplar. The once tall tree was extending perpendicular into the river. Water rushed around and underneath it. Allie must have used it to exit the kayak.

"Allie!" Nick's yell filtered through the forest as he looked around. Two odd-looking men stood beside a Cadillac Escalade less than fifty feet away. They were both in fine dress clothes and looked like they had made a wrong turn on the way to the board meeting. They stood expressionless, staring in Nick's direction. Nick paused at the oddity, but then quickly continued his pan.

"Allie!" He called out again.

After his panoramic view revealed no sign of her and his calls elicited no response, he felt a cold chill creep into his spine and looked back at the kayak. It had stopped only yards from the waterfall and violently strong water rushed around it, pinning it to the tree. Exiting from there would be a difficult task for anyone. One small slip and a person could easily lose balance, fall back into the rushing water and be pulled over the edge. Nick looked toward the falls and screamed again for Allie, then looked back at the kayak. Why was it upside down? He raced to the edge of the water and braced himself against the trunk of the tree. The kayak was only eight feet from shore, but the current was still overpowering. Fighting the undertow, he carefully made his way out to the boat. As he approached, his heart found its way into his throat as he saw a hand sticking up out of the water, tightly clutching a limb of the tree. Terror washed through his body.

"No!" He shouted and turned toward the men on the shore. "Call 911, quick!" he said, and then quickly turned around, inched deeper into the river and grabbed her hand. She grabbed back. The current was incredibly strong here. Nick slipped and was almost sucked beneath the tree. Under the water his feet shuffled and quickly caught solid ground. Running his hand across the kayak and under the water he felt Allie's spray skirt. It had already been pulled. She must have attempted to exit the kayak when she was sucked into the current and pinned. Death had indeed found another victim. Damn it! Nick braced himself, grabbed onto the sides of the kayak and pulled. It slowly released her legs, letting them flop back into the rushing water. Nick clumsily heaved the kayak over the log. He then tugged on her, softly at first and then harder. She didn't budge. She must have been stuck on something under the water. Several times Nick tried to submerge himself, run his hands down the length of her body and find whatever it was that held her, but each time he did, the current kicked his feet out from underneath him. Knowing that he was running out of time, he shifted his position to get better leverage, wrapped his hands around her waist and tugged again. Nothing! She didn't even budge. He looked back up at the men on the shore. They were closer now, nearly at the edge of the water. They must have called 911 by now, but weren't doing anything else to help.

"Help! Please!" Panic filled his face and tears streamed down his cheeks as he pleaded. Somberly, and with pocketed hands the men watched, but still did nothing. "Help! Damn you! She's drowning!" His screams echoed violently through the lonely trees.

Allie's hand gradually went limp and sank beneath the surface. Nick continued to pull as he watched the multicolored rays of light shining through the diamond on her engagement ring disappear into the whitewater.

He began to shake violently, and his face turned purple as he pulled with all his strength, but without success. He turned and looked at the two men on the bank and screamed at the top of his voice. "Help! She's dying damn it! Why won't you mother-fuckers help?" One man folded his arms and raised one hand to his chin, but still did nothing.

Nick stopped pulling, stopped shouting, and began to sob. Suddenly Allie's hand shot up out of the water and reached for the sky. Her fingers and wrist were stiff and tight. Then all at once her hand relaxed again and plunged back into the icy grave.

CHAPTER TWO

E ight years later and many miles to the West a mystery unfolded...

    A man stood in the pouring rain, dazed and confused with his eyes shut, wearing a black dress coat, white shirt and no tie, repeating one word over and over again, *run*. Even as he chanted, his memories were draining from his mind like water funneling from a sink. He shook his head, tightened his eyes and willed them to stop, to return, but soon even his name was plucked from him. He felt off-balance and out of sync with reality as the last of his most cherished memories swam out of reach. Although he was no longer able to recall his mother's name, his father's name or even any childhood dreams, he still felt as if he had lost something vital, something sacred. A single tear ran down his lean face, as he tried in vain to simply recall the day, the month or even the year.

    Slowly letting go of yesterday and bringing his attention into the present, he began to hear the patter of dress shoes smacking against a tile floor, just around the corner to his right. Suddenly, a terrible fear came over him. He had to run, and he had to do it now or *they'd* catch him and they'd hurt him. *They* knew how to hurt a person in unimaginable ways. However, as he stood there with his eyes shut, he could no longer remember just exactly whom they were or why they were chasing him. He opened his eyes and gazed onto the rain-filled parking lot, in front of him. Fear gripped him as he realized that he had no idea where he was, nor which way to run. He was staring into a vast open area featuring a handful of cars and pools of muddy water. The tall chain link fence, in the distance appeared to have a head of barbed wire and looked as if it encircled the lot. Something grinded beneath his black dress shoes. He looked down. The area of blacktop he was standing on was covered in broken glass. Directly to his right, beyond the shattered window, was a lightless office with quickly moving shadows inside.

"Number Nine…where are you?" He heard a familiar, middle-aged man's voice calling from within. "Come on back. There's nowhere to go." The voice was getting louder. He could not remember to whom it belonged, only that whoever it was, was dangerous-very dangerous. If he ran forward into the open lot, he would surely be caught before he reached the fence, and supposing he did make it, what then? In a race against time and feeling out-paced by unknown adversaries he quickly spun around and spotted a small security booth and a closed gate just ahead. The fence around the gate was covered in shrubbery and cloaked whatever lay beyond. Still continuing to repeat the word *run* he felt something brush against his sleeve, then heard glass shatter against a car door to his right. Turning toward the sound, trying to locate its origin, he felt something small and powerful rip into the tail of his dress coat.

Desperately willing himself to awaken from this bad-dream-turned-nightmare he quickly examined his coat. Everything seemed to move just a bit too slowly, and reality held a bizarre liquid quality as he spotted an oversized hypodermic needle dangling from the torn cloth. The syringe was filled with a translucent, bright green liquid, and almost glowed against the water-filled asphalt below. Being careful not to stick himself, he pulled it out of his coat and quickly looked to his left. Through the window he spotted a tall bald-headed man just coming out of the shadows. The man wore an expensive suit and tie and was carrying an odd looking large rifle. Panic-stricken, he ran as fast as he could. An ominous spirit saturated the overcast sky as he sprinted toward the gate, and although he didn't see it, lightning must have struck, because the gate exploded as he approached. The explosion was so powerful that it ripped the gate right off its hinges and threw it into the street beyond.

The face on the guard looked distorted and unreal as he ran past the booth and exited the lot. To his right, the quiet residential homes went on as far as the eye could see and to his left he spotted a busy avenue just a couple hundred feet away. Behind him he heard tires squealing, and he knew he'd never make it to the avenue, but he had to try.

"Run, run, run, run." They were going to catch him. There was no doubt about it, and when they did they were going to put him in a dark and evil place that he would never be able to run from again. Consumed with fear and still gripping the hypodermic needle, he sprinted toward the avenue. Out of the corner of his eye he glimpsed a partially opened security gate leading into a run-down apartment complex. It was on the other side of the road, but still much closer than the avenue. As his overly thin, lengthy body shifted directions and headed for the gate, a silver-gray, Toyota Camry pulled out of the lot and screeched to a halt. Two clean-shaven men sat in the idling car. The driver might have been able to double for Lurch on the Adams Family if it weren't for the menacing scar that began below his left eye, ran across the bridge of his nose and ended just to the right of his long flat chin. His passenger, although bald, was by far the better looking of the two and slightly resembled a white Montel Williams. Both wore black dress suits and sunglasses. They looked first to the right, then to the left. Spotting the man with no memories running across the road, the driver stepped on the gas and turned the wheel hard, while his passenger gripped the door handle and prepared to exit.

As the fleeing man leaped up onto the curb and ran across the grass, the Toyota skidded to a stop just behind him. The doors flew open and both men jumped out of the car and raced toward him. Literally less than a second ahead of them, he ran through the iron security gate and slammed it closed as he passed. It shut with a loud bang, nearly smacking into the face of his pursuers, and locked automatically. Without time to think, he ran up the stairs to the left and continued on around the corner, shoving the needle into his coat pocket as he went. In the process something else in his pocket pricked the end of his thumb.

A gunshot rang out behind him as he slowed down just long enough to withdraw the mysterious prickling object. He heard the gate swing open and slam into the thick iron screen as he pulled out a second hypodermic needle and a wadded up piece of yellow paper marred with red ink. This needle, like the fist, contained a bizarre green liquid, and he was sure the two were a match.

"You go that way. I'll take the stairs." A commanding voice echoed from below. "Remember, whatever you do, we have to take it alive. It's no good to Dr. Boris or anyone else if it's terminated, so only shoot to wound."

"Gotcha!" Another voice spoke with a rasp and was a bit overly enthusiastic.

As the men spoke, he instinctively took the two needles to the nearest door, door 211, and like a skilled thief, picked the lock. The speed and skill in which he accomplished the task more than suggested that this was an act that he had performed many times before. As the door opened he could hear heavy footsteps chasing up the stairs behind him. He stepped inside and pushed the door closed just as the baldheaded man rounded the corner. Keeping his hand on the knob and being as still as possible, he felt the floor shimmy as the man ran past and kept going. Then he carefully relocked the door, closed his eyes and let out a long, slow sigh of relief. Miraculously, he had gotten away, at least for now, but he wasn't out of the woods yet. He slipped the two needles and crumpled up piece of paper back into his pocket, and then turned to survey the room.

The musty, dark blue carpet covered the small living room, met with the kitchen linoleum and ran down the hall to the left. The furniture was stained and worn with age. Two half-eaten plates of food sat on a rickety coffee table across from a small, rabbit-eared television set and filled the air with a foul odor. After taking a quick look at the room and listening for occupants he stealthily made his way around the loveseat and down the hall. As he moved, he realized that for some reason he was no longer afraid. Somehow, he had been transformed into some kind of super spy. It was as if he had been expertly trained and practiced his whole life to do just this sort of thing. With all the skill of a professional cat burglar he started searching for money and anything else that might further his escape. He amazed himself at just how secure he felt as he walked through some stranger's apartment.

He made it to the master bedroom and quickly looked around. He searched through the chest of draws, felt under the mattress and rummaged through the various nick-knacks throughout the room. After finding nothing that could help his cause he turned his attention toward the closet. Opening the door he saw an array of women's clothing. On the floor were a few shoeboxes, women's sandals and two pairs of high heels. The overhead shelf was full of cardboard boxes that contained nothing more than old clothes and fake jewelry, nothing he could use. As a matter of fact the entire apartment turned out to be void of anything useful.

He ended his search in the kitchen and pondered his situation. As he did, he remembered the crumpled up piece of paper in his pocket. After retrieving it and while he was flattening it out, he saw a hand-written note in red ink. As he read it his palms began to sweat and he was filled with anticipation.

Your name is Alex Kendallman. You are running from extremely ruthless people who have been using you as their guinea pig for many years in a freakish experiment that has stolen your memories. Disappear! Start a new life, and whatever you do, don't go to the police, they're in on it, and so is every other government agency. Just run and don't look back, just run...

Alex stared wide-eyed at the note and for the first time since he entered the apartment he became acutely aware of just how empty it was. He felt lonely and lost. He didn't understand why he felt so sad. After all, now he knew his name and that was a lot more than he had known just five minutes ago. Not only did he know his name, but there was also someone else out there who knew it, perhaps the same someone who helped him escape in the fist place. He wasn't alone any longer! With this new revelation his spirits rose. Keeping his focus on the paper he moved to a chair between the window and kitchen table and quietly sat down.

After staring at the note for a few more minutes, he pulled the string and raised the blinds. The window overlooked a dumpster and the back of another building. The rain had lightened up a bit and the blue sky was now filled with fluffy clouds of various hues, ranging from ivory white to dark gray.

As he gazed out the window, he imagined what his childhood might have been like. Did he grow up in the country and go to a country school? Maybe he was born in a different place somewhere outside of the US, somewhere far, far away. He wondered what his mom looked liked. Was she tall or short, fat or skinny? Did she have dark blond hair like his, or did that trait come from his father? Maybe his dad was a shrewd businessman or perhaps a tough construction worker. He wondered where they were now and if they were worried about him, trying to find him. He took a deep breath and stared at the sky, then glanced at the note one more time before he carefully folded it up and slipped it into his other suit pocket. When he did, he discovered another small round object, like the syringes, only skinnier. Curiously, he pulled it out. His heart stopped and his spirits plummeted as he withdrew a red, ballpoint pen. Was he the one who had written the note?

Fearfully, he slowly unfolded the paper and stared at the letters. The scarlet writing took up less than half the page. He placed the paper on the table and brought the pen close, but for some strange reason he was unable to write. He wasn't weak and there wasn't anything wrong with his fingers, he just couldn't remember how to write. The pen dangled from his thumb and forefinger with the tip all but touching the paper. It swayed back and forth like some mysterious pendulum trying to predict the future. Things stayed like this for a while as he tried to remember just how to work the pen. Then suddenly it connected with the paper and began to produce little red marks. Not exactly sure whether he was moving the pen or if it was moving all on its own, he did his best to stay steady and copy the note word for word onto the lower portion of the page. In spite of his nervous state and the fact that he had no idea how to hold a pen, the two sets of handwritings seemed to be nearly identical. He must have written the note to himself. The room grew dark as a heavy black cloud rolled in front of the sun. Somehow, the apartment was emptier now than it had been just a moment ago and the world bigger, colder.

Anger and fear gripped his soul as questions ran through his mind. Who were the demons that had stolen his memories? And to what end? Why was he being hunted like some animal? And most importantly, where was he going to go? He had no memory and knew no one. He felt so afraid, so empty…so alone!

For quite some time he sat expressionless, nearly hypnotized by the newly formed drops of rain dancing on the window. His teeth grinded together and his eyes filled with water as a knot developed in the pit of his stomach. To have no memory is to have no past, and to have no past is to have no future. There was absolutely no one for him to turn to, and there really was no way of telling if anyone even cared whether he lived or died. The only true memory he had was of the current events and as far as he could tell he was nothing more than a runaway lab rat. The sheer thought of things was too immense for him to comprehend. He squeezed his eyes shut and forced himself to remember an event—any event in his past. He could almost see himself as a boy, running across a small sandy beach somewhere. He concentrated. Yeah, he could remember, but it was very faint. The sky was blue—no. He shook his head. It was green. Green? This couldn't be right. Make the sky blue! Okay, he could now see a blue sky again. That was better. The sand was white, yes that's right, and he was yelling, "Mom...Dad..." No, that wasn't right, not at all. He shook his head again. The more he focused on the mist-filled memory the more he saw it for what it was, a product of wishful thinking rather than a valid recollection of actual events.

The phone rang breaking the ever-deafening silence and snapping him back into reality, chasing away phantom memories that never truly existed. Startled, he stood up, and after another ring he blinked himself awake, refolded the note and returned it to his pocket.

"Hello, this is Ginger. I'm sorry I missed your call. Please leave me your number and I'll call you back as soon as I can. Thanks." The answering machine kicked on.

"Hey Ginger. It's Mitch. I'm running a little late. I was hoping we could make it 6:30 instead of 6:00. Call me on the cell-phone if you get the chance. If not I'll just pick you up around 6:30, 'kay? Bye." Alex looked at the digital clock above the stove. It was already 5:17. If this Ginger person had a date at six o'clock, then she would be walking through the door any moment and he still hadn't found anything to further his escape.

The pit in his stomach grew as he pondered the situation. As far as he knew, his pursuers had already searched through the complex and were now watching all the exits. They knew what he looked like and these clothes would be a dead giveaway.

He looked back at the clock: 5:18. With his eyes racing, searching for anything that might conceal his appearance, he quickly returned to the bedroom. He thought he remembered a large woman's coat near the back of the closet. With any luck it might fit him. He swung open the closet door and fingered through the clothes.

Although it was a soundless digital clock with no hands, in his mind, he could hear it ticking louder and louder as the second hand moved and time passed. Finding the coat, third garment from the last, he swiftly removed it from the hanger and pulled it out. It was large, and it indeed looked as if it would fit. However, when it was in the closet, behind the other articles, he wasn't able to see the color very well. It was bright lavender with pink ruffles.

Great! In order to avoid detection and have any chance of sneaking out of the complex, he would have to look like a *transvestite wannabe*, or at best an overgrown girl scout. Holding the coat in his left hand he searched through the clothes again. There had to be something else he could use, something a little less feminine. Starting from the left he slid each article of clothing across the bar one at a time: a bright yellow sun dress, a flowery pink silk blouse, a light gray pair of slacks, a black leather miniskirt. He kept looking but to no avail. Nearing the end, he saw a dark blue mini dress with black sheer sleeves.

Suddenly, a blinding flash of light and a loud boom exploded in his head. Everything went black and he was dizzily swirling down a long dark tunnel.

Voices echoed through the tunnel, "Number Nine? Where are you Number Nine? The doctor wants to see you, Number Nine." The voices morphed into white-stenciled words, and the words separated into nicely spaced letters that organized themselves alphabetically, and then dissolved into the blackness. As the swirling slowed and eventually stopped, a beautiful, slightly familiar jazz melody skillfully weaved its way into his head. The tune started out faint, as if it were almost imaginary, but soon took on substance as images overtook the darkness.

Somehow, he found himself sitting at a dimly lit table in a dark, upper class nightclub, next to a mildly attractive brunette with assuming green eyes. She wore an expensive gold necklace adorned with a diamond pendant, equally valuable gold earrings, accented in diamond studs and a dark blue mini dress with black sheer sleeves. *This must be a memory or something*, he thought as excitement filled his being.

He was sipping on a glass of seven-n-seven and carrying on a conversation with a young devious looking, dark haired fellow wearing a light gray pinstriped suit. Once again, everything moved a bit too slowly and seemed like a dream. However, this time he was unable to control his actions and could only watch from within as the scene unfolded.

"All right, here's how it's going to go down." He was surprised to hear his own voice. He had a heavy New Jersey accent and kept running his index finger around the edge of a nearly empty glass. "You, Tony and Franko are going to get there first. I want you to take the Dodge. Once you're there, go around to the back. The only thing holding the gate is a small chain." He paused and smiled at the young, scantily clad blonde approaching the table.

"Ready for another, Sugar?" She pointed at his drink.

"Nah!" He shook his head and bent his wrist, lifting his finger up off the glass. "I'm fine Sweet Cheeks, maybe later." She smiled and turned away. He continued his conversation. "There's nothing but a bicycle chain with a small padlock wrapped around the gate. Cut the chain and go to the back door. The old man's going to be at a fundraiser all evening. I want you inside, waiting when he returns. This has got to be a clean hit. And it's got to be quick."

Alex could hardly believe what he was experiencing. This was *his* memory, and he was planning a murder! No! Alex struggled with the new revelation as the scene continued.

"Once you're on the back patio, bust through the glass…"

"What about the dogs, Louie?" The brunette interrupted, while smacking on pink bubble gum.

"Sheila!" He responded loudly and slammed an authoritative fist on the table. After holding her gaze for a moment he continued in a condescending tone. "Let me handle my business… Okay? You have a hard enough time handling your drink!"

With eye-rolling, gum-smacking attitude, she demanded to be let out of the booth. "I gotta run to the little ladies' room." As Louie stood up to let her pass, a tall blond headed man, who had been sitting at the bar, got up off his stool. Sheila leisurely scooted around the table while Louie stood at the edge and held his hand out, hoping to speed her highness along. The young man from the bar nonchalantly reached under his coat and then turned to face Louie. Sheila stepped out from the booth aggravatingly slowly, glared at the wannabe mob boss, blew and popped a large pink bubble then turned to leave.

Two thunderously loud booms went off directly behind Louie. Sheila, less than five steps away, spun around just in time to see his chest bulge forward and his eyes open wide. For one chilling second he stared eerily at a corner of the ceiling and looked somewhat like an unstrung bow. Alex felt an intensely sharp pain shoot through his back and enter his chest. Sheila screamed and stumbled backward.

Alex fell to the floor of the apartment, letting go of the purple coat while Louie simultaneously toppled over the table in the nightclub. A blues song ended in midcourse. A horrified waitress dropped her tray to covered her mouth, letting several cocktails fall and shatter. The gunman coolly walked up to the booth, shot the other gentleman sitting with Louie in the face, then emptied one more round into the back of Louie's head, pulverizing it and splattering his brains across the tabletop. The waitress ran screaming.

Alex hovered weightlessly above, as Louie's body and the lower half of his head oozed off the table, hit the corner of the booth and flopped onto the hardwood floor.

The assassin dropped his gun and ran for the door.

The nightclub was in a panic.

Someone shouted "Louie's been shot! Call an ambulance!"

"Oh my god!"

"Quick! Get help!" Screams echoed, glass shattered, people ran.

Two more shots rang out, creating even more panic, and the gunman, halfway to the exit, stopped, dropped to his knees then fell face first onto the floor.

Alex held two points of view: he stared blank-faced and lifeless at the bedpost in Ginger's apartment and at the same time floated up, passing seamlessly through the club's ceiling and into the night air. He was filled with a strange and wonderful calmness as he hovered above the rooftop. In one view, the bedpost began to fade, letting the image of the nightclub's roof dominate Alex's vision. He still had no control over his actions, but for some strange and unknown reason he didn't care. All was peaceful. All was calm. He floated forward past a scurrying rat and several ventilation units until he reached the edge of the roof. It must have been cold out, as everyone on the sidewalk below wore big heavy coats and thick warm mittens, however he wasn't cold at all.

Like a slow-moving breeze, he gently glided down from the rooftop and for a few ghostly moments, strolled carelessly around the city, floating in and out of shops, up and down avenues and in and out of homes. Then out of nowhere, a terrible fear saturated him-nothing like the fear he felt earlier in that unknown parking lot. This was stronger, deeper. A fear that consumed his consciousness and gripped his soul. He felt himself struggling as his course changed. He couldn't tell whether he went up, down or in some other direction. All he knew was that he was moving quickly and wherever he was going wasn't good. His speed increased and he found himself rapidly moving down a long dark tunnel. He felt isolated and abandoned and his entire being filled with fear as his final destination quickly approached. A mild hissing sound came from every direction. His speed increased, the hissing intensified and the hopelessness he felt grew stronger. Every wrong doing Louie ever did flashed in Alex's mind. I'm sorry, I'm sorry his soul cried out. The hissing grew into humming and the humming into buzzing as the tunnel narrowed and his speed accelerated. He clawed, scratched and scraped at the unseen, unfelt and for all practical purposes nonexistent walls of the tunnel. The buzzing escalated into blaring and the blaring intensified. Then at the brink of madness, a blinding flash of light came from everywhere and nowhere simultaneously, consuming the darkness. As the white cloud slowly evaporated, Alex found himself staring once again at the round wooden bedpost. He was lying on his stomach and slightly drooling with his right cheek on the carpet. He lay there, dazed for a few moments, then the answering machine kicked on.

"Hey Ginger, it's Mitch. I'm running a little bit late I was hoping we could make it 6:30 instead of 6:00. Call me on the cell-phone if you get the chance." As he listened, he wondered why Mitch was calling again and why he was repeating his previous call almost verbatim. "If not I'll just pick you up at 6:30, 'kay? Bye." As the long beep-tone sounded Alex realized what was happening. Mitch wasn't calling again. Someone was in the kitchen replaying the message. Disorientated, he lifted his head and wiped his slobber-filled cheek.

"Hey Mitch." A woman's voice came from the kitchen. "It's me, I just got in. Where ya at?"

Weak and tired from his trip out of Hell, he rolled over and pushed himself up.

"You're pulling in now?" His head thumped and he lost his balance as he raised to his feet his. The room swayed and he pushed off the approaching wall to keep his balance.

"Well, then let me get off here so I can hurry and get ready." The room was small, with absolutely nowhere to hide. Gradually regaining his equilibrium, he slowly reached down and snatched up the pretty pink coat. She hung up the phone and started shuffling down the hall in Alex's direction. He looked around the room again then rested his eyes on the window just above the dresser. As luck would have it, it was directly across from the open bedroom door. He froze as he heard her walk up to the very edge of the bedroom, stop, take a few side steps and then close the bathroom door. He let out a sigh of relief as he abandoned the window idea and quickly slipped past the bathroom, through the living room and soundlessly out the front door. Outside, he put on the purple coat with bright pink ruffles and tried to walk inconspicuously to the stairwell.

As he walked down the stairs, in drag, he passed a slightly rugged looking man smoking a cigarette and heading in the opposite direction. The man's gray windbreaker hung down and covered the top of his tight-fitting blue jeans. He seemed to be in a bit of a hurry, but slowed down long enough to take a good look at Alex. He kept on ogling and even turned his head after Alex had passed. At the bottom of the stairwell Alex could still feel the man's eyes upon him. He looked back just in time to see the man turn around and continue his ascension. Just before the man turned, however, Alex caught a glimpse of the iron-on name-patch attached to his coat, "Mitchell." Mitchell? Could he be Ginger's boyfriend, Mitch? The more he thought about it, the surer he became. He probably recognized Ginger's coat and that's why he kept staring.

As he approached the entrance gate his heart rate accelerated. The gate was slightly ajar with an extremely damaged latch that looked as if someone with super human strength had punched it from the outside. He stopped about fifteen feet away and stared, remembering the gunshot he heard earlier while climbing the stairs. What if the men chasing him were out on the street, waiting? Maybe, after conducting a thorough search in and around the premises, they reasoned that he was hiding in one of the units, waiting 'til nightfall. That would make sense. The people chasing him, whoever they were, surely knew his unique talent for opening doors. They probably knew more about how he thought than he did. If they did indeed know him better than he knew himself then they would certainly be waiting for him just outside that gate, waiting for him to step through, waiting to nab their *guinea pig* and take it back to the dark deep abyss, where they kept it.

Scanning the courtyard for another way out, he spotted Mitch and some lady rounding the corner at the top of the stairs. They were walking quickly and looking around carefully, as if they were searching for something. He didn't have to guess what that something was, he knew. After Mitch passed him on the steps he must have told Ginger about the stranger wearing a purple coat like hers. Ginger probably looked through her closet, found her coat missing and decided to go with Mitch to look for the man in drag. Alex thought about running to the rear of the complex. If he did, they would certainly spot and chase after him, causing unwanted attention to be drawn his way. For a moment he thought about just going through the gate and taking his chances.

Just then Mitch spotted him, got Ginger's attention and pointed. As she looked in his direction, Alex bolted toward the back of the complex. Tossing his cigarette, Mitch leaped from the stairs, skipping the last four steps and ran after. Another iron gate guarded the rear of the apartments and Alex sprinted toward it with Mitch right on his tail.

Without thinking about who might be waiting on the other side, he ran up, pulled it open and jetted into the alley. Mitch was fast and got to the gate just as Alex was leaving it. Without slowing, Alex turned to his right and sprinted toward the busy boulevard.

Mitch followed one step behind, almost close enough to grab the perverted burglar who had just been inside his girlfriend's apartment. The alley echoed with the sounds of tennis shoes and dress shoes slamming hard on black asphalt as Mitch reached out to snatch the coat that Alex had already halfway removed. The tip of his fingers grazed the surface of the coat as he barely missed his target. Alex could feel Mitch's presence right behind him as he reached the busy street.

He had one arm completely out of the coat as he ran directly into high-speed traffic. Mitch kept pace as a blue minivan swerved to miss the two brainless idiots jetting out into traffic. Mitch reached out for the coat again. Crossing the last lane of the avenue, Alex paused, altered his course and kept going as a screeching Mustang skidded to a stop. That was all Mitch needed. He grabbed onto the coat, which still wrapped Alex's left forearm and jerked hard as he came to a stop, spinning Alex violently back into traffic. Alex spun around, out of control, broke free of the coat, hit the front passenger's corner of an idling firebird and rolled over the hood. Mitch now had the coat and was finishing a spin of his own. Alex completed his roll and landed feet-first on the asphalt.

Without looking behind himself to see where Mitch was, Alex kept going, now running down the middle of the road directly into oncoming traffic. Mitch wasn't going to let this sick son-of-a-bitch get away. Somehow, he had gotten into Ginger's apartment. He might even have a key and if he did then Ginger wasn't safe. Mitch chassed after him. Alex ran in front of a quickly approaching bus crossing over the last lane and up onto the sidewalk again. Trying to avoid hitting the man running across the street, the bus driver, a heavyset black man, widened his eyes and slammed on the brakes. Alex barely cleared the front of the bus and sprinted down the sidewalk toward the corner.

At the last minute Mitch changed his course as the crazy pervert ran in front of a bus, nearly flattening himself. Mitch put his palms out and pushed off the side of the bus as he ran along its length. Once he cleared the end of the bus he spotted his prey running toward Foothill Boulevard. The slinky bastard seemed like he could run forever.

Although he was fast in short sprints, Mitch wasn't much when it came to long distances. His breathing was heavier now, his heart pounded faster and sweat poured down his face. He kept going but soon found himself falling further and further behind. He rounded the corner onto Foothill, saw his target shrinking in the distance and reluctantly gave up the chase. His chest felt like it was on fire. With sweat pouring from his head, he placed his hands on the knees of his blue jeans and looked like he just might hyperventilate.

Alex thought his pursuer would never stop. Almost out of breath, he ran into the parking lot of a bowling alley. Halfway to the door, he looked over his shoulder. Mitch wasn't there. He slowed to a jog, ran up to the double glass doors and stopped to catch his breath. He leaned up against the brick building and watched the far end of the parking lot, waiting for Mitch to round the corner. Night had just fallen. The sky was a black canvas, salted with tiny pinpoints of white. There was no moon in the sky but the parking lot's overhead lamps kept the area well lighted. Alex waited and watched. Soon he had regained his breath and with no Mitch in sight, walked into the bowling alley.

CHAPTER THREE

Theodore Connelly, the second, was standing in line at the small donut shop, patiently waiting his turn to order. He was a tall, good-looking man, in his early thirties and wore an expensive silk suit with matching tie. He stood behind two other customers. A large, heavyset man in his late thirties, with a jolly warm face and thinning blond hair, wearing a thin white t-shirt, blue jeans and brown heavy-duty work boots stood at the counter holding his already filled white bag and waited for the young oriental woman to hand him his coffee. Directly behind him and just in front of Theodore was an upstanding young man about fifteen or so with dark brown hair styled into a buzz cut, wearing an oversized coat, baggy pants and tennis shoes. He was looking over the contents of the display case through dark-colored glasses, holding a skateboard in one hand and a five-dollar bill in the other.

"Looks good, doesn't it?" Theodore asked with his hands in the pockets of his slacks and a newspaper tucked nicely underneath his left arm. The boy kept perusing the pastries and said nothing. The heavyset man took his coffee and thanked the clerk as the teenager stepped up to the counter. He pulled one earphone out of his right ear, revealing a faintly blaring, musical banging and ordered a cream filled éclair, two old-fashioned donuts and a hot chocolate.

As the clerk grabbed a small square of wax paper and a set of tongs, Theodore smiled briefly, closed his eyes and said, "Mmmmm! Éclairs are my favorite." The boy turned his head, lowered his shades and looked oddly at the stranger, then without replying, turned back to the counter and waited for his order.

"That sure looks like a nice skateboard." Theodore continued to try to break the ice. The teenager rolled his eyes as the hot chocolate machine stopped. The young lady grabbed a lid, fastened it to the steaming cup and set it on the counter next to the plain white bag.

"That'll be three-eighty-eight please." He handed her the five, took his change, dropped his board to the ground, grabbed his purchase and rudely rolled past Theodore to the exit.

Theodore kept a smile on his face and watched through the store window as the young man rolled down the sidewalk and then vanished behind the wall.

"May I help you?" The lady asked.

"I think you can!" Theodore replied over-enthusiastically as he turned his bright smile away from the glass. "Mmmm, I just *love* donuts, don't you?" he asked with a warm look and a twinkle in his bright baby blues.

She half-rolled her eyes, shook her head and repeated the question,

"May I help you?"

He took a deep breath, scrunched his eyebrows together and cocked his head. His expression was one that said *shame, shame on you*. Then he paused for a second and changed his attitude back to his naturally cheerful self. "I'll take an old-fashioned please, and a tall cup of coffee!" The clerk turned and filled his order. He paid the lady, took his cup and bag, then found a seat next to the window.

He set his coffee and bag on the table, reached under his left arm, took out his newspaper, opened it and sat down. The front page featured a bizarre story about a local serial killer who had been collecting his victims' heads after he murdered them. Theodore believed in the positive powers of the universe and he was determined not to let this world get him down. He flipped right past the story, went directly to the cartoon section and read Garfield. He laughed as he set the paper down and opened his bag. He reached inside, removed the donut and carefully made a plate out of the paper bag. He carefully took a bite of the donut, set it on his neatly positioned paper plate and picked up his coffee. After pushing down the protective tab he sipped his cup and reached for a napkin, dabbed the corners of his mouth and then resumed his reading. Dagwood was a blast and Dennis the Menace was even better.

This was what life was about, not pain and suffering, murder and violence, hatred and malice. No, that was what everyone else focused on, and they wondered why they were so unhappy. But not Theodore, no Theodore Edward Connelly was upbeat, positive, happy. He finished his donut, laughed his way through the rest of the funnies and gulped down the last bit of his coffee. He scooted out of the booth, brushed the few crumbs off the table into his cupped hand and tossed them, along with the Styrofoam cup, newspaper and paper bag into the trashcan by the door and walked outside.

The sun had set more than an hour ago and Theodore had work to do, but he decided that work could wait and he would drive by mother's house first.

He was ashamed of himself, as he wasn't able to go by and visit her as much as he used to, because of how busy he had become recently. He walked through the parking lot, took out the remote control to his Lexus and pressed the button. Three cars away on the left, the headlights flashed as the hi/low tone sounded. Theodore got into the car, turned the engine, and pulled onto the boulevard. He kept the Lexus at a nice thirty-three miles per hour, a full two miles under the posted speed limit. The laws were there for a reason, and he *always* obeyed them. He drove through the city smiling at everyone he passed. *If you see someone without a smile, give 'em yours.* That was Theodore's motto.

He turned off the small road onto the long narrow driveway just before eight o'clock. His headlamps illuminated the back of the shiny red Mazda that he had bought for his mother four years ago last June. She wasn't able to drive anymore but didn't want to get rid of the car because it had come from her precious little Teddy. He switched off the ignition, got out of the car and went around to the back porch. He didn't knock, he had a key, but most of the time, as in this case the door was unlocked. He called hello as he stepped through the back door and into the kitchen, where a large pot of simmering stew filled the air with a mixture of delicious aromas ranging from onions to garlic with the dominating smell being beef.

The house was silent except for the loud *tick-tock* sound coming from the decorative pendulum clock hanging on the wall beside an older model, single door icebox.

"Well looky who's here...it's my Teddy." An elderly woman's voice trembled through the air from beyond the kitchen. Theodore walked up to the small white stove, which was scratched and dented with age. He picked up the long wooden spoon next to the stainless steel pot, leaned over the stew and took in a long, deep breath through his nose.

"Mmmm!" he said as he closed his eyes and shook his head, "That smells so good, Mom!" He opened his eyes and was just now dipping the wooden spoon into the pot when a tiny wrinkled-faced woman with gray hair and gray eyes entered the room behind him.

"Teddy!" she shouted in a shaky, high-pitched yet commanding voice, "Put *that* spoon down immediately!"

Without completing his taste test, Teddy obeyed. He shook the thick sauce from the spoon and returned it to the paper towel as he turned around.

"Mama!" He said lovingly while holding his arms out and tilting his boyish head to one side. They kissed their hellos and walked slowly, arm in arm, through the small archway into the living room, which was filled with furniture from previous eras. The few electronics were big and bulky and looked more like decorations than anything else. The stereo, which played old 33s and 45s and even 78s as well as AM and FM, was encased in wood and sat on the dark green carpet. It was the size of a home office desk and was beautifully crafted. The TV was designed before the invention of the remote control and featured a turn knob rather then a push button pad. The dark brown walls made the room look even smaller than it already was, and were covered in a multitude of religious paintings. He slowly walked with her as she held his arm for balance, to one of the aqua colored, over-stuffed chairs next to the heavy, dark blue drapes.

After seating her, he took the matching chair on the other side of the table lamp. They visited for the next hour talking about the moral decay in America, the breakdown of the family unit, and the blatant disregard for honesty and truth. They expressed the common belief that they shared about the deterioration of the country, the lack of moral values, the shameful way in which the young women dressed these days—and Teddy would be wise to keep his eyes shielded from such things. They talked about the fact that every politician today had an agenda, how most church leaders couldn't and shouldn't be trusted, and how the world was no longer approaching, but rather was living in the end times. They agreed on just about everything.

The few things Teddy saw differently than his mom—and they were few—were quickly reevaluated and brought into their proper perspective when she started to talk about what happens to pagans, whoremongers and heathens who fail to stay on the straight and narrow path. She had a way of reminding him just how *real* Heaven and Hell were and just how easy it was to unknowingly slip into a pattern of backsliding and hence end up in Hell.

"And Hell is real you know! And it's not over in a day, a month or even a year. No Sir…Hell is forever!"

Most of the people alive today would surely find themselves begging and pleading as God unforgivingly cast them into an endless sea of never-ending fire. But Teddy's fate would be different. He would not have to suffer the endless tortures of fire and brimstone. He would not be a wretched outcast, to forever be without God's mercy. As long as he heeded the truth and listened to his mother he would someday walk on streets of gold and have rewards unimaginable!

"How's your promotion Teddy?"

"It's good Mom. I'm saving souls and making money."

"That's good son. I'm so proud of you! I always knew you would do good."

Teddy raised his eyebrows and smiled as he said, "Speaking of work Mom, I really should be going. I have quite a bit to do tonight."

"Oh Teddy, but you just got here. Do you have to go?"

"I'm afraid I do Mom, but I'll be back soon. I promise."

"Will you be saving souls tonight?" she asked, hopefully.

"Oh, I hope so Mom! Now, I really have to go." With that statement he rose and walked over to her chair. She smiled and said, "Well, if it involves the Lord's work, then I guess you should go." He bent down to kiss her as she stood up.

"I have to stir the stew," she said as they walked into the kitchen together.

"Mmmm, that smells so good Mom."

"Well, Teddy it'll be ready by tomorrow, if you want some."

He kissed her goodbye again, said he might stop back in tomorrow, but if he couldn't for her to save him some for another day. He walked out as she picked up the wooden spoon and began to stir. She stared at a small painting above the stove and listened to the Lexus start up and pull away as a tear left her eye and ran down her face.

"My boy," she said, then closed her eyes, "Lord watch over my boy!"

Teddy felt good inside as he pulled away from his mother's house. She always knew right from wrong and helped Teddy see the truth. His thinking was always clearer after visiting with Mom.

Teddy drove down the boulevard thinking about where he should start his night. The last few weeks had been extremely slow, with the exception of the night before last. That night Teddy had found a lost soul in one of the strip clubs in the red light district, downtown. He had originally driven down there the night before last hoping that the Lord would use him to save the soul of one of the lost exotic dancers. However, when he got there the sight of those half-naked, barely clothed, nasty, immoral women repulsed him so much that he just could not find the strength to be an effective witness. He almost gave up and went home when he caught the eye of one of the young men watching the nearly nude lady dancing around the pole. He walked over to the young man and commented on the beauty of the female body, hoping to build some common ground before he began to witness. It worked, but not quite the way he had planned. The boy had mistakenly thought Teddy was looking for someone that he could pay for a blowjob. Before Teddy was able to tell the kid that that wasn't the case, the boy agreed. The young man went willingly with Teddy back to his house in San Dimas where Teddy was able to give the boy the greatest gift of all, eternal life.

Once again Teddy found himself cruising through the red light district. The avenue came to life with lights advertising sin in every possible form: *XXX girls, Daddy's Bar and Grill, The Silent Adult Fun Club.* On every corner Teddy saw sin: young women soliciting sex, young men selling drugs, muggings, winos. He thought he even caught sight of a handful of men brutally raping a young girl. However, he drove past the alley a little too quickly to be able to be sure.

It was nearly nine-thirty and Teddy felt uncomfortable driving around this type of area in his new Lexus. He almost turned it around and went home when he felt the spirit of God rivet his soul, and he knew he had to be here. There was a person here who needed Teddy, well the Lord working through Teddy anyway. There was someone here Teddy could help, someone he could save from the eternal flames of Hell. Teddy stopped at the red light and watched the crowd of people cross the street. Was it the fat man in the ball cap with the brown corduroy coat? Or the young woman beyond the corner wearing a very small, black leather miniskirt? Or perhaps it was the tall lonely guy standing in the parking lot of Kim's Topless Bar, smoking. The light turned green. Teddy drove on looking left to right, watching for a sign from the Lord. Iniquity and unrighteousness were everywhere! It was more than appalling. It was revolting. As he drove, Teddy wondered why God let this area and others like it to continue. Why didn't He destroy all the terrible places in the world as He did Sodom and Gomorrah? The blocks were short and soon Teddy found himself waiting at another light. Teddy studied the sea of endless traffic lights ahead of him. It looked as if the district of sin went on forever.

"Hey baby." Teddy heard a strange woman's voice coming from the passenger's seat of the car. Startled, he turned his head to find a sleazy dark-skinned woman leaning on her elbows, in the window.

"Got plans for tonight?" Her lips were full and painted rose-red. Her hair was dark and ratted up, with stiff tight bangs dangling down in her eyes. She wore way too much makeup on her face. Her eyelids were green and her lashes were caked with mascara, which made them look abnormally thick and long. Her shoulders were bare except for two thin spaghetti straps, which held up a nearly sheer tightly fitting top.

Didn't she know that he had work to do? Didn't she understand that the Lord's work was at hand? Teddy was angered and appalled that she had no regard for his personal privacy, but he still maintained his warm, pleasant demeanor.

"I'm busy, thanks." He smiled politely.

"Ok sugar." She ran her hand along the doorjamb, as if to say I can touch flesh just as sweet and just as soft, if not softer. "But if you change your mind," she smiled and raised an eyebrow, "I'll be right here and I'm looking for a big strong man like you," her smile turned innocent, "to take me away."

Disgusted and repulsed, he was about to pull away when he caught a glimpse of her necklace. It read, *Be my teddy bear.*

It was a sign from God!

In the middle of the street, with drivers behind him honking, he shifted into park, stretched his hand out over the vacant seat beside him and said, "Um, taken away? By a big strong man like me?" He gulped.

She was just turning away as he spoke. She stopped and leaned back into the window. She stared at him for a second, and then pointed at him, extending and retracting her hand with every word she spoke. "Just... like... you..."

He knew what she was, and he knew that she was only being this way to earn a buck. His stomach soured at the thought of how she conducted her life day in and day out, but it didn't matter, the Lord had sent her to him so he could save her soul, and if he had to capitalize on her perverse, greedy obsession in order to do the Lord's work, then so be it. He smiled as his confidence grew. "Get in!"

With horns blaring behind them, she excitedly opened the door and took the seat next to his, revealing a tight black miniskirt that looked to be a size or two too small, and dark fishnet stockings, which he could see was attached to a garter belt underneath her miniskirt. "Where to?" she asked as he shifted into drive and pulled forward.

"I thought we'd go back to my place."

With her head bent over her lap, fixing something down around her ankle she turned to face him. "Your place?"

"Yeah, is that okay?" he asked with warmth and empathy as if to say is there a problem with going to my place?

"Well," she said while sitting up in her seat, "I don't usually go home with the guys I entertain. They usually...take me to a motel or...something." She shook her head and seemed a little uneasy.

"Don't worry," he said confidently as he turned onto Azusa Avenue, heading north, leaving the red light district, "everything will be okay. I promise." He looked at her and, seeing she didn't have one, gave her a smile.

"Look, I don't know...maybe we should just go back," she said while looking out the window like a lost puppy.

He smiled quietly and drove on.

"I mean, I'm sure your place is nice and everything but...I..."

Without turning his head to acknowledge her, Teddy reached under his coat and pulled out his wallet as he entered the onramp to the 10 freeway. Still looking forward and merging into traffic he pulled out a crisp, new, one hundred dollar bill, which he held up with his right hand. "Here."

She looked at the bill for a second.

This was what she worked for. This was what motivated her to ride into dark alleys and go into sleazy motels with guys she didn't know. This is what made her give her body away without reservations to strangers.

Still she hesitated. Even she had her standards. One of the things she never did was leave the red light district with a first time customer. Another thing she didn't do was go to the *client's* home, at least not until she knew him well enough.

Still, this *was* a hundred dollar bill and they hadn't actually done anything yet. She contemplated.

"Just take it," he said warmly as he smiled her way, "This should cover the first ten minutes. I'll have you back to work in a couple of hours."

A hundred dollars every ten minutes? Was he joking? For two hours, that was twelve hundred bucks! Twelve hundred bucks for two short hours! She looked at Teddy; he was a fairly cute looking guy. Whatever kinky, perverse things he wanted to do to her, couldn't be that bad. But what if he was some sick-o who got a thrill out of picking up working gals and torturing them to death? Or, what if he was that guy in the newspapers? The one who kills his victims and then, for some twisted reason, removes their heads?

Teddy patiently held up the money as she struggled with her thoughts. He looked innocent enough. Twelve hundred bucks! Finally, she decided to decline his offer and have him take her back, but right before she opened her mouth she changed her mind and snatched the bill from his hand. He smiled.

"See there. Was that so hard?" He merged onto the 210 Freeway. She still wasn't sure she was going to go into the guy's house, but she reasoned that the money would at least pay for the drive. "I'll give you another one when we get to the house."

She pulled out a small black change purse from a tiny zipper pouch in the side of her skirt and stuffed the bill inside.

"All I really want is someone to talk to tonight." Normally, he could not lie, but when it came to lying in the name of God, the Holy Spirit gave him the power. "I've never picked up a hooker before." He paused for effect, looked ashamed, and forced a single tear to flow from his eye. "My wife left a couple of weeks ago and I've been feeling really lonely lately."

He had never been married. His mother told him that God had a higher plan for his life and it did not involve a wife. These were the end times and Teddy was a soldier of the Lord.

He continued his lie, "I was on my way home from work when you came up to my window back there…you were so pretty. I just…."

She didn't know what to believe. She had learned to read just about anyone, and her friends referred to her as a human lie detector because she was so good at spotting lies. And now things didn't feel *exactly* right, but they didn't feel totally wrong either.

"I married her right out of college." Teddy continued to spin his web of deception. "She was the most beautiful thing I'd ever seen and she was the only woman I've ever…." He coughed. "You know...been with."

At this point he was only half-lying. He *had* dated a beautiful woman in college and almost married her, but once his mom had found out that they had shared a bed together and were planning on getting married, she sat him down and reminded him about the sin of fornication and said the only way he could atone for what he had done and be accepted back into the love of God, was if he called off the wedding and never saw her again.

He continued on with his lie. "I found out she'd been cheating on me for the last year or longer with some guy at her office." He looked away from her, out the driver's side window. "I just don't want to be alone tonight. I've got plenty of money." He paused as if he was struggling to find the words he needed. "Look, I know you weren't planning on being a counselor tonight but…"

As he talked she began to loosen up. Exiting the freeway and driving into the foothills of San Dimas he repeated how lonely he was, how beautiful she was and how he only wanted to talk.

It seemed safe enough she thought, and if he only wanted to talk, well then, she might be willing to stay even longer. After all, twelve hundred bucks was more than she made in three or four good nights. She could afford to take the rest of the night off after making that kind of cash. They pulled up to a cream colored home as he pressed the remote control attached to his visor. It was fairly large and sat far enough up the hill to overlook the city lights of San Dimas. He drove into the driveway as the garage door opened, then continued forward and switched off the engine as the door closed again behind them.

Illuminated only by the digital lights in the dashboard, he reached into his wallet, pulled out another hundred-dollar bill and handed it to her, then silently got out of the car and went into the house. She took the money and followed behind him. She walked inside with her five-inch high heels clicking on the ceramic tile. They went through the pantry, past the restroom and ended up in a beautiful, huge kitchen. The walls were covered in expensive religious paintings and small angelic figurines sat on most of the flat surfaces.

"Would you like a drink?" he asked, while opening a cabinet beside the big brand new double door refrigerator.

"What do you have?"

"Whatever you want." The shelves in the cupboard held just about every type of alcohol and mix on the market.

She walked up and stood beside him studying the liquor. "Do you have any orange juice?"

"Sure." He opened the over-stocked refrigerator, then reached in and pulled out a carton of Sunny Delight.

"I'll take some vodka and orange juice," she said as she walked through the large archway into the den. Her high heels sank a little into the plush white carpet. She sat on the velvet white couch and crossed her legs as he walked in with two drinks. She looked around the room and wondered what it would be like to be married to a man like Teddy and live in such a beautiful home.

"Here you go." He handed her the vodka and orange juice, and then sat down in the large vinyl chair next to the couch. After setting his drink on the glass tabletop and staring at her for a moment or two he said, "Oh I almost forgot," and reached into his wallet and pulled out fifteen more hundreds and handed them to her.

Her eyes widened and she almost spilled her drink as she reached out and took the money. Now it was seventeen hundred dollars, and just to talk. This was unbelievable. Wait 'til the girls downtown hear about this. If she played her cards right he might even become a regular. She would have to break through his boyish shell and somehow show him how good it could be to do more than just talk. She would have to give him a reason to come back for more. She'd have to get him into bed before the night was over.

"Tell me more about your wife." She inquired while sipping her drink.

They had a couple more glasses and talked for the next hour. Teddy didn't want to make her feel uncomfortable, for fear that she might want to leave before he got the chance show her the light and give her an opportunity to repent of her sins and accept the gift of eternal life. When the time was right he would coax her down into the basement where he had the Bible, his pulpit, *his tools*, and the ensuring device.

The conversation was going well and just as Teddy was about to ask her if she wanted to see a picture of his wife she said, "So Teddy got any place more comfortable than this old couch, like say a nice big bed that we could sit on while we talk? I promise not to bite."

"Well, I really don't want to go into the bedroom as that's where she and I used to," he cleared his throat, "used to…sleep."

"I see, well is there any other place we can go? Or does this big house only have," she touched her thumb to her fingers as she remembered the rooms she had seen and heard of, the bathroom, the kitchen, this room and his bedroom, "four rooms in it?" She spoke with playful sarcasm.

"Well, there's the guestroom downstairs, it has a bed." He said pretending to be nervous.

"Perfect!" She rose to her feet and tilted her head back, swallowing the last of her drink. She slowly walked over to him, set her drink down on the end table and then said with innocent wide eyes, "wanna show me?"

Ashamed at how much he enjoyed looking at her body, and still pretending to be nervous he set his drink next to hers and replied, "sure."

After rising to his feet, he led her through the den, passed the formal living room and into a storage area, where the door to the basement waited. He took out his keys, unlocked the door and switched on the light illuminating the stairwell. The door softly creaked open as he politely invited her to go first.

MEMORIES

Although the stairs were lighted, the basement was dark. She walked down the cream colored, wooden steps as he followed behind her. A silent prayer escaped his lips as she reached the bottom. She thought she heard him whispering, but wasn't sure.

"What did you say?" She smiled.

"Nothing, why?"

"Never mind." She shook her head and turned back around to face the darkness. The unseen room smelled strongly of bleach and other powerful disinfectants. This Teddy guy even kept his basement clean. Wow!

Teddy stood directly behind her, facing her back. "I have something I want to show you," he whispered warmly in her ear as he slowly wrapped one hand around her small waste, "but I don't want you to see it until I'm ready." His other hand joined his first at her belly and he slowly raised them, simultaneously, up the front of her torso, sending a sexual chill throughout her body. "So, I want you to wear this before I switch on the lights, ok?" As he spoke, he gently placed a folded silk bandana over her eyes. She felt a little nervous, but the alcohol had kicked in and she reasoned that if he were going to do anything violent he would have already done it by now. Besides, she really wanted him as a regular. He was her way to easy street. He fastened the blindfold to her head and tied it tightly in the back.

She heard a click. He must have turned on the light. He led her carefully through the room and onto a bed. He helped her sit, lifted her legs and leaned her back onto a pillow. She was nervous but also oddly aroused. She felt a metal surface under her neck about an inch wide. Maybe he was a little kinky after all. She smiled as he laid her right arm down beside her waist and then tightly fastened her wrist to the bed with a coarse leather band. Her sexual excitement rose along with her fear. She started to resist but then he reassured her with that soft warm comforting voice.

"Shhh, trust me," he said while touching her lips with his finger. She relaxed again while he continued to fasten her other arm and legs the same way. Then everything was silent for a second as she lay there on her back blindfolded and helpless. What was she, nuts?

"Teddy?" she asked as she heard the door shut and the lock latch. "Teddy?" she repeated as she heard his footsteps approaching the bed.

"It's completely soundproof in here, you know," he said as he fiddled with something above her head.

"Teddy, I'm scared. I want you to take me back."

"Awe now, now," he said in a warm sympathetic voice while unzipping the pocket of her skirt and retrieving the seventeen hundred dollars he had given her. "It's too late for that. You're here now, and the Lord is going to give you a chance to accept His love and ask for forgiveness for all those terrible sins that you've committed." He replaced the money into his wallet.

"What?" Her countenance changed from being mildly nervous to being starkly terrified. "What the Hell is going on?" she demanded while he removed her blindfold, revealing his smiling face.

"Do you know just how much the Lord loves you?" he asked pleasantly while walking over to a large metal cabinet a few feet from the foot of the bed.

She began to cry, "Please Teddy, please…let me go…"

"Awe now, I can't do that," he said warmly as he opened the cabinet door and pulled out a rolling tray. "The Lord brought you here…to me, so you can be shown the light and have the gift of eternal life." He rolled the tray over to the bed next to her legs.

"You're sick!" Her eyebrows bunched together in terrified unbelief. She tried to lift her head and strained to see what was on the tray, but couldn't. He stood beside her waist and looked warmly into her eyes. "Tomorrow is going to be a better place because of you. Do you know that? The Angel of the Lord has told me this."

She began to scream for help.

He kept talking in the same soft tone as if she were just lying there adoringly listening. "Not only is the Lord going to save your soul tonight, but he is going to use you to make this world a better place."

She kept screaming and struggling to get free. He paused, and with a look of utter confusion asked loudly and factually, "What is wrong with you, stupid woman?" His neck tightened and his head began to tremble. "Don't you remember? I said this room was soundproof?" He raised his voice even louder as his anger grew. "What? Did you think I was lying?" She stopped screaming and looked up at him, petrified, as his anger soared and his face began to turn red. "I don't lie! I am a child of the Lord!" He stood there for a moment, looking more like some wild beast than a man, and little beads of sweat began to pop out around his hairline. He blinked as she stared expressionless and afraid. He took a deep breath as he transformed back into the sweet calm guy that she had been talking with earlier. He smiled warmly at her and then removed his coat and tie, laying them neatly on a table beside the bed.

Is he going to rape me? She wondered. Then he rolled up his sleeves and lifted a book from the pushcart, opened it and began to read. Afraid to speak, she listened for more than an hour, silently crying from time to time, but always afraid. He read passage after passage from the Old and New Testament, adding his own personal excerpts here and there, excerpts which she was sure couldn't be found anywhere in the Bible. He read about fornication, adultery, sins and forgiveness. When he had finally finished he closed the book, set it back on the cart and asked warmly, "So, do you understand your sins and the way to salvation now?"

Terrified of saying the wrong thing and hoping that if she answered correctly he might be inclined to release her, she answered, "Yes!"

"Are you sure?"

"Yes!" She said with terror in her eyes.

Pleased with her answer and relishing over this achievement of leading a new soul unto the deliverance of the Lord, he drew near, bent down and whispered in her ear. "Before I walk you through the steps of salvation, I want to show you something, something amazing, a marvelous device that I created to ensure that those who God sends to me are guaranteed never to stray again. I call it the *Ensurer*."

She watched as he leaned over her head and pulled forward a tall metal device. He locked it in place, attaching it to the metal band underneath the back of her neck. She trembled with fear as she realized what it was. This psycho had constructed his own makeshift guillotine. Teddy reached onto the tray, grabbed the can of WD-40 and oiled the track.

He spoke as he worked. "I realized long ago that people are weak, very weak. Only a few of us have the strength to walk the straight and narrow day in and day out. See," he shook his head, "it used to be that I would share the good news of God's love with people and show them the way of salvation, but no matter how sincere their intentions were, they'd always backslide. Then one day I had a vision from God."

Barely able to breathe through the flood of drowning fear that permeated every fiber of her being, she listened as he continued his story.

"I was living at my cabin in Big Bear, just after I obtained my medical degree and found a wounded bird. It took three weeks but I finally nursed it back to life. The day finally came when I was going to turn it loose and let it fly a way. I took it from the cage and carried it to the door. But I tripped before I got there and landed right on top of the fragile little bird, snapping it's frail little neck in two." His eyes brightened and his face beamed with enthusiasm. "Don't you see?" He shook his head and blinked his eyes. "I had saved the bird and immediately killed it." He paused waiting for her acknowledgment and approval, but she gave neither. He continued. "You see? I killed it! I killed it, before it could fly away." He reached for something off the pushcart as he spoke. "It was a sign from Heaven, God was teaching me how to ensure the salvation of those he sends to me." His smile widened, his back straightened and from her deathbed he looked like some deranged self-glorified psychopath.

Her stark fear changed to a sudden urgency to get out, to escape, to somehow get away. She remembered him ranting about the room being soundproof, but she no longer cared. She screamed at the top of her lungs

"Help, please! Somebody help me!" She squirmed her arms and legs, trying with all her might to get free, but without success.

"Once I walk the wicked through the steps to salvation, I send them home to be with the Lord, before they have a chance to fly away." He flapped his arms like a bird and then stuffed a gag into her mouth, wrapped his silk bandana around her head and tied it tightly.

"So now, let's make you ready for the Kingdom of God, shall we? I will say a few verses from the Good Book and you repeat them in your mind and accept them into your heart." As he quoted the scriptures she released muffled screams of terror and continued to squirm violently, like a frail animal caught in an inescapable snare. When he finally finished he said, "There, now you're ready to be sent home, but before we launch you into eternity, God has instructed me to do something special with you, something that will help the world become a better place. You should feel honored. Out of all the souls that I've sent home to be with the Lord, none of them have been able to give as much of themselves to the world as you are going to give tonight."

Her heart rose when she understood that he wasn't ready to release the blade just yet. Realizing that her screaming and struggling were probably doing her more harm than good, she stopped and went after a new approach. She looked up at her tormentor with despairing, pleading eyes. Perhaps, somewhere inside of this monster there was still a piece of him that was partly human, a piece of him that she could appeal to. Her eyes begged for mercy. Her face pleaded for sympathy.

Mistaking her sudden calmness for an acceptance of her fate, he looked into her eyes, placed his open hand softly upon her forehead and said warmly, "There, there, see how much the Lord loves you?" As she stared into his deranged eyes, she wondered how she could have ever been duped by a psycho like him. After holding eye contact for a couple more seconds, Teddy calmly walked over to the pushcart, grabbed a pair of bolt cutters and said, "Now we better get to work. We have a long night ahead of us."

What was he doing? She was unable to raise her head far enough to see. He picked something up off the tray. He looked at her and smiled as he grabbed her right hand.

"Now this is going to hurt *quite a bit*, but that's okay, it's *supposed* to." He grinned. "Just stay focused on those beautiful streets of gold. You'll be on them sooner than you think, and this will all be over. You know, in many ways I envy you." He smiled proudly. "I even have this gun. I call it my ticket to paradise." He chuckled. "At times I can almost hear the good Lord calling to me, telling me it's time to cash it in and come home. What a glorious day that will be."

As petrified as she was she couldn't help but to agree with him. It would be even better if God called this psycho home right now, before he had the chance to send her there. She felt him isolate her pinky finger, and then wrap something sharp and cold around it. She didn't know exactly what he was doing, but she had a pretty good idea it wasn't good.

Teddy held the bolt cutters in place, paused for a second and then ever so slowly tightened his grip. Her finger instantly swelled up like a small water balloon. Thin lines of red liquid began to appear where the sharp metal surface met the tightening flesh. Teddy could hardly contain his excitement as pain shot up, through her arm and into her neck. He squeezed harder. There was a momentary pause when the blades met bone and then her finger snapped off completely. For an instant blood sprayed forth like cola from a punctured soda can as the finger dropped into a waiting metal dish. She screamed in pain and in fear, remembering what he said.

"We have a long night ahead of us."

CHAPTER FOUR

Over twenty-five hundred miles east of San Dimas, California in a small, dark cabin in the Appalachian Mountains of West Virginia a computer burned late into the night. A dark-brown haired man in his mid thirties, wearing a flannel shirt and blue jeans, sat awake, sipping on coffee and searching through the Internet for information on serial killers. The cabin was small, just one bedroom, a kitchen and a bathroom. The computer tower sat underneath a small wooden desk in the corner, next to an old iron wood burning stove. The man worked in the dark at the desk in an old folding chair, perusing one site after another. Every inch of the walls was covered with news articles, and except for the occasional Gummy Bear wrapper or stray Gummy Bear, the floor was crowded with piles of papers. The headlines were all basically the same.

Serial Killer Puts Louisiana City on Edge!

Oklahoma City Women in a State of Panic!

Gun Sales Up 60%!

Fear Grips Austin as Killer Goes Unfound!

San Francisco no Longer Safe!

The current heading on his computer screen read *Los Angeles' headhunter still on the loose*. The article stated that twelve bodies have been discovered in the past four months and the lead detective on the case, Detective James Garvey, wasn't any closer to solving the case now than he was when the first body had been found.

"This is the most puzzling case Los Angeles has seen in a long time. There seems to be no link between the victims. It's as if the killer just pulls their names out of a hat." The article quoted Garvey, and then went on to say that the first person found was a middle-aged housewife from one of Los Angeles' upper class suburbs. The second was a ninety-three year old man who lived in the slums of El Monte. The third was a heavyset waitress from Anaheim. All but the seventh victim had the same twisted thing in common. The killer, for some sick unknown reason, collects their heads!

Illuminated only by the light from the screen, the man clicked the mouse and scrolled down the page as he read. Then he picked the cell-phone up off the desk and dialed information. The automated system came on and he obtained the number to the Los Angeles Police Department. The digital clock in the corner of the monitor read 2:28 AM, *that would make it 11:28 in LA*. The last thing he wanted to do was come across like some wacko when he called Detective Garvey. He had already been labeled that a few times before with other law enforcement agencies throughout the country.

"Hello, LAPD how may I direct your call?" A young woman's voice came across the line.

"Yeah," he cleared his throat. "My name is Nicholas Chadwick and I'm looking for Detective Garvey. Is he there?"

"Is this about the case he's working on?"

"Yes it is."

"Sir, Detective Garvey has requested that all leads pertaining to the case go through the toll free tip line or be e-mailed in. I have the number and e-mail address here if you want it."

Nick turned away from the monitor and bent over, resting his elbows on his knees. "Is there anyway I could just speak with him, really quick?"

"No sir. I'm sorry, not if it's about the case. We've just been bombarded with calls. And although we are extremely grateful for all of the help the public's giving, it's becoming quite overwhelming, but I assure you we are working *every* lead. If you have a tip that you think we can use, *please* call our tip line."

It was silent for a moment, he couldn't think of anything to say. He had a desperate desire to get in touch with Detective Garvey, but the words he needed to get through escaped him.

"Would you like that number sir?"

He thought in silence. What he had to say wouldn't be taken well third hand. It would be difficult enough trying to convey what he knew directly to the detective.

"Hello? Sir? Are you there? Would you like me to give you the 800 number?"

A young girl in her mid teens came out of the bedroom as Nick told the lady, "No thanks," and hung up the phone.

"Burning the midnight oil again, huh Dad?" she asked with sleep still lodged in her eyes.

"Sweetheart, what are you doing up?" Nick glanced back at the computer clock.

"I couldn't sleep, at least not with you in here making all this racquet."

"Racquet? What racquet? I thought I was being quiet."

"Oh daddy, this is a *one* room cabin! My bed is on the other side of *that* wall." She rolled her eyes and pointed at the wall directly to his right.

He looked sheepishly. "I know sweetie. You're right." He motioned for her to come over and sit on his lap. She came to him in her white and pink cotton pajamas, took a seat on his knee and looked at the screen.

"Daddy, You've gotta stop doing this. She's gone! You've got to let her go." She looked into her father's eyes. All was silent for a few moments as she stared deep into them with love and empathy. Instead of acknowledging her gaze he returned it with shock. "Let go?" He shook his head and blinked his eyes in disbelief. "What if it was you? When would you want me to let it go then?" He scrunched his eyebrows together and tightened his stare.

"Daddy?" She shook her head as her eyes filled with water. Her expression changed from empathy to pity. She looked back at the computer screen and then suddenly came alive. She grabbed the mouse and sucked up her tears. Her eyes widened as she swiftly clicked and read. The pity for her father swiftly turned to apprehension. Looking at her father with distrusting eyes, she asked, "We're not moving again, are we?"

"Well, sweetie…"

Her look intensified as she stood up and said sharply, "NO! I'm not going!"

"Now honey…" She snapped away and burst into tears as he gestured toward her.

"I just made new friends. Daddy, it's not fair! I *don't* wanna do this anymore. Please Daddy. Please, No!"

"Ah sweetie." Tears also filled his eyes as he rose from his chair and moved toward her.

"No, no, no. I *won't* do this, I won't! Not again!" She stormed into the bedroom and slammed the door before he could make it to her. He heard the lock engage, and then muffled sobs filtering around the edges of the door as he stood in the darkness.

After a moment, he book-marked the current page and shut down the computer. The cabin was quiet except for Lisa's whimpers, which were quickly dying. He walked over to the cabin door, opened it and stepped out into the warm West Virginia darkness. He looked up into the night sky, slipped his hands into his jeans and held back the tears.

It had been eight years since he had lost his Allie, but he could still see her face as if it had been only yesterday. As he gazed up at the few stars peeking through the clouds he wondered what life would have been like if she hadn't have been ripped away from him. He slowly walked over to the door of the RV as one small tear escaped his eye and ran down his face.

He went inside, removed only his boots and lay down on the foam mattress next to the half-sized refrigerator. It would be hours before he would fall asleep, but he didn't want to make any more noise inside the cabin. A single photo was pinned to the thin wooden panel next to his bed. The face of a beautiful young woman with dark hair and green eyes smiled softly at him as he stared at her, lost.

CHAPTER FIVE

Teddy stood in a small forest of ingenious medical devices, brought about by the scientific boom of the twentieth century. All of which were designed, in one fashion or another, for the purpose of prolonging life for as long as humanly possible. He looked down on his newest *sister in the Lord.* How sweet.

On her back, naked, and in a semi-state of shock, she stared up at a blurred basement ceiling, just a hum above unconsciousness. She would have slipped even deeper into her physiological collapse if Teddy had not been so patient and possessed so much knowledge about the human body and how it reacts to pain and massive amounts of blood loss. Even with his vast understanding of biology and all of the medical tools he employed, he knew he would not be able to keep her conscious much longer. Alive? Maybe. Awake? No. And what good would she be if she were not alert and able to understand everything that was happening to her? Although he didn't know why, the angel of the Lord had specifically told him to keep her aware of what was happening to her, and he never questioned the word of God.

Her strength had been totally sapped from her body. Around her waist, a strap held her tightly to a blood-soaked bed. Several crimson medical wraps and sections of gauze were thoughtfully and securely placed on and around various parts of her body to stop excessive bleeding and reduce shock in an attempt to keep her alive and aware just a little while longer. Teddy was amazed that she had stayed awake this long. The chemicals that the angel had given him were unlike any he had ever seen in medical school and more powerful than any that man could have created. Teddy stood in awe.

Both of her legs had been surgically amputated and placed in a metal pan beside the bed, for her viewing pleasure. They were not merely whole legs, simply removed from her body with a single stroke, but rather, they were in parts. There were several independent toes, a severed foot, and an independent calf. He had taken her apart a piece at a time, patiently tending to each open wound and keeping her alert, stopping her from fading off into some secrete hiding place deep within the recesses of her mind. The only limb still attached to her torso was her left arm. It lay lifeless, receiving an intravenous drip of miracle medication. It was, itself, missing all five fingers, which were in a smaller pan, placed next to the first, with all the separate pieces of her right arm.

She began to drift off into unconsciousness as she had been doing periodically throughout the night. Teddy picked up the smelling salts from the tray, on top of the pushcart and said in a twisted parental tone. "Now, now, you can't fall asleep. We're not done yet." He held it under her nose, and her eyes swam back into reality once more as she remembered where she was and just what was happening to her. She wondered if God had sent her to Hell and if Teddy was just a demon or the Devil himself. This must be Hell, she thought, because she could not imagine a place more tormenting, more painful, more hideous and more evil anywhere else in the universe.

"Please," she whispered so faintly that it was nearly inaudible, "please kill me."

Teddy picked up her fingerless hand, which no longer held any sensation, and thought *how sweet*. She wanted him to send her home to be with the Lord. He knew that once she had been given the opportunity to accept the greatest gift of all, she would see things in their proper perspective, and he was right. Not only did she see things the *right way,* but she couldn't wait to be sent home and be with the Lord.

"Soon," he said softly as he patted her unfeeling hand, "soon."

He checked her IV and pondered for a moment, then said with an impish grin, "Now don't you go anywhere while I'm gone." He winked and then walked in the fading light, to the far end of the basement, where he opened a huge metal door and vanished beyond the threshold. A couple of minutes later he returned carrying a metal container, just a little larger than your average milk crate, and a clear bag of liquid. He sat the box on the cold concrete floor at the head of the bed and opened it. It was made of thick stainless steel on the outside, a cushioned rubber padding on the inside and featured a built-in cooling unit. He placed it in such a way as to catch her head once he released the blade of the guillotine. He smiled.

Then he changed her IV bag, and began speaking as a grade school teacher might to a small child. "See, this is why we left this arm. We needed some way to keep these chemicals flowing into you, well what's left of you anyway." He smiled and winked again. "The chemicals we've been pumping into your blood thus far have only been designed to keep you awake and alert. The angel tells me however, that this chemical will not only keep you conscious, but will also turn on certain signals in your brain that have already shut down. See the brain has this defense mechanism. Whenever the body starts to experience more pain than it can it can handle, it turns off its ability to feel. This heavenly sent chemical, however, given to me by the angel himself, reverses that process and allows the body to feel much more pain than it otherwise could. Now, I know what you're thinking, and believe me, with all I know about medicine, I had a hard time accepting it too, but if the angel says it will help you to feel pain again, well then, it will help you to feel pain again!" His eyes widened and his smile grew from ear to ear.

After making sure the IV was operating correctly and releasing the proper amount of liquid, Teddy reached into the tray on the pushcart and said in a more serious tone, "now even with the powerful medicine we have dripping into your arm, we'll still have to hurry through this last part, because the body itself just cannot continue to function for very long after we do what we are going to do to you now."

With that Teddy took a battery operated, electric bone saw and, starting at the center of her stomach, just below her rib cage, using extreme care, he steadily cut through the middle of her torso, straight up along the center of her chest, being extra careful around her heart, and stopping just below her throat.

She could not believe what was happening to her. How could she be living through such an ordeal? If it weren't for the intense amount of pain, she would have been sure she was trapped in some sick nightmare, but she wasn't. She was being dissected alive! She had gone numb long ago, as her body went into shock from the trauma of being diced up before her very eyes. Every spot on her body had lost its ability to feel. She thought she was unable to experience pain any longer. She was wrong. The pain she felt from the bone saw was beyond excruciating. She didn't understand how she was able to stay awake, much less alive through this hideous and evil torture session. She longed for death, but still it did not come.

She cursed modern medical science and the wicked life extending devices it brought. She cursed the men and women who invented the hideous machines and the drugs that now prolonged her torment. Impossible as it seemed, her pain intensified a thousand-fold as he reached into the center of her freshly sliced chest with both hands and with a grunt of effort, pulled it open. It didn't give much and produced a bone chilling, cracking sound and released thick gobs of blood onto her chest.

With deep-red hands he stood in awe as he watched pools of blood bounce around her ever-slowing heart. The angel of the Lord had truly given him chemicals and skills that defied reality. Hopefully, in the future, God would allow him to send others home in much the same way as he was sending her home tonight.

"Isn't God amazing!" he whispered as he stared wide-eyed at the spectacle before him.

The drugs could no longer hold her back as she started to fade into an irreversible state of collapse. She crept up to the very brink of unconsciousness and death, slowed only by a tug of war with the menacing chemicals dripping from the clear plastic bag into her arm. Knowing he didn't have much time, and wanting her to see and feel the cold, smooth blade as it sliced through her delicate neck, Teddy quickly moved around the bed to release the blade. He placed his hand on the palm-sized lever and paused.

"See how much God loves you," he said and then pulled the switch. The blade dropped with a swoosh, and her head tumbled into the box.

Thank God she thought as the blade finally extinguished the unbearable pain. Teddy quickly closed the lid and set the controls to steadily lower the temperature until its interior became a cool 31 degrees Fahrenheit, exactly as the angel had instructed. Then he looked back at her picked-apart body and was glad to be an ambassador of the Lord. He returned the metal box to the room beyond the light, at the other end of the basement and locked the strong metal door. He was tired but he knew he could sleep in as late as he wanted tomorrow, so he began to clean up the mess.

CHAPTER SIX

Alex stared up into the night and followed a layer of steadily moving, ominous looking clouds as they slowly traveled across the sky. He was leaning back, against a concrete wall in a pile of recently discarded cardboard boxes. Wrapped in an old burlap sack, he recounted his day and struggled to remember anything more. The earliest memories he could recall were the dream-like ones he had this afternoon, in that rain filled parking lot. He remembered repeating the word run, however he couldn't remember when he had begun to repeat it or why. He tried to press his memory beyond that point and into his past. He tried to recall how he had gotten there in the first place. He tried to simply reach one second further into his past than his current recollection permitted. Nothing!

No matter how hard he tried he could not remember anything before that moment. It was as if some strange power of the universe had just brought him into being right then and there, as if he had no past and his entire existence began at that very moment, just a few hours ago. Still feeling the uneasy knot in the pit of his stomach, he thought about the events after his escape from the parking lot.

He was ashamed of himself for snooping through some strange woman's apartment, but really he had no other choice. He was just trying to stay alive and get away, right? The knot in his stomach grew as he wondered just what kind of a person he really was. When and if he ever got his memory back would he find out that he was nothing more than a two-bit thief and wannabe murderer?

He pondered the note that he had found in his pocket and compared it to the flashback, or whatever he had had in Ginger's bedroom. Things just didn't seem to add up. In the *memory* everyone called him *Louie*, but in the note that he had written to himself, he wrote his name down as *Alex*. Was he lying to himself, trying to keep himself from remembering a terrible criminal background? If that were the case, didn't Louie die? And if Louie was dead, then how could he be Louie? In the flashback, not only did everyone call him Louie, but also deep inside himself he remembered feeling as if he really *was* Louie, whoever Louie was.

So what then, did Louie die and become reincarnated as Alex? He shook his head. That was too crazy. Was it possible that Louie survived and somehow changed his identity into Alex?

It seemed like nothing made any sense. A gentle breeze rustled his hair as he thought. He was tired and could have easily dozed off, but dared not sleep for fear they, whoever they were, would find him. He repositioned himself, trying to get as much comfort out of this visit behind the supermarket as possible. The night grew cooler and the infrequent drops of water he felt indicated that it just might rain. Fitting, he thought as he pulled some empty boxes on top of him and continued his pondering.

What about that strange event in the bowling alley? After being sure Mitch had given up the chase, Alex went inside and sat down in an empty booth near the entrance. While regaining his breath, he tried to organize his thoughts and puzzle though his situation. However, the bowling alley seemed unusually loud. Every time he tried to focus, he found himself distracted by all the voices he heard. He remembered thinking how odd it was that the voices were louder than the heavy bowling balls bashing into their waiting pins.

As he was pondering the peculiarity of these louder than normal voices a young lady approached his booth carrying a small notepad and pen. She wore a nametag, a bowling alley uniform and asked if he wanted anything to eat or drink. Alex was starving, but had no money. Then something odd happened. Just as the waitress was turning to leave, Alex heard her say, "He looks cute, but he sure smells bad."

"Excuse me?" Alex questioned.

The waitress turned back and said, "Yes?"

After a brief pause he asked, "Didn't you just say something?"

She looked puzzled. "No, why?"

He stared at her for a moment. Then as he was getting ready to say *never mind* he heard her say, "What a psycho." The phrase took him by surprise, but the odd thing was, her lips never moved!

He stared at her with a very puzzled look on his face and said, "What? How did you do that?" He wondered if she was a ventriloquist who liked to play with people's minds.

Her expression took on a queer look as she asked, "Are you okay?" then continued to say, without moving her lips, "This guy is weird."

"What?" he asked as he quickly stood up. "How are you doing that?" He was frighteningly anxious and she was worried that he just might do something to hurt her.

"Doing what?" she responded while cautiously backing away.

Full of confusion, he remained beside the table as she continued slowly backward. Her words kept coming but her mouth never moved. "I hope he doesn't hurt me. Christie, this guy is definitely, *not* your type." She kept her eyes on him as she went. "Oh God, I hope he's not that psycho from the papers."

Although her voice faded as she retreated, it still seemed louder than it should have been.

Without saying anything to him, and still talking to herself, she turned around and disappeared through a swinging door into another room.

Alex looked around the bowling alley at the different people. He peered closely at everyone. They were all talking. Some were talking to others, and some were talking to themselves, but most, however were talking without moving their lips! He found that when he focused, he could *tune in* and hear one voice better than another.

He concentrated on a couple sitting three booths down from his. They were talking and sipping on soft drinks. He watched the guy's lips move as he said, "I'm really glad you decided to meet me tonight." Then he watched in amazement as the guy closed his mouth and said, "God I want to get you into my bed and fuck the Hell out of you." The statement was so odd for a public place and it came across so clear and loud that Alex flinched when he heard it.

Was he actually hearing what people were thinking? That's impossible! How could that be? As he was pondering the question he heard a man's voice directed at him. "Excuse me sir?"

He turned around and saw the waitress standing with another gentleman. The man's nametag read *assistant manager*. "I'm going to have to ask you to leave, sir," the man said with an agreeable yet firm smile. He could tell that the guy was nervous, not because he looked that way, but rather because, in some way, he felt it.

He looked at the waitress, whose thoughts were so loud, they almost sounded like she was shouting them. "Weird guy! Why is it that all the good-looking guys are screwed up in some way? It must be some bizarre universal fact!" She smiled pleasantly.

Alex shook his head in amazement as he accepted the unbelievable fact that he was indeed picking up the thoughts that people were thinking. He looked back at the manager and not wanting to cause any unwanted attention to come his way, obediently left the bowling alley.

For the next few hours he aimlessly wandered the streets, trying to make some sense of his day, occasionally picking up the thoughts of strangers as they passed, until finally, he found himself here in the back of the grocery store. He was tired, scared, and hungry, but mostly, confused. What was he, some freak of nature? What did they do to him, the evil people his note spoke about?

Alex opened his eyes and was startled by a bright hot morning. Unknowingly, he must have nodded off somewhere in the night. He moved a piece of cardboard off his face and shielded his eyes from the blinding sun as he looked around. Squinting, he noticed a garbage truck turning the corner at the far end of the building and coming his way. He stood up, untangled himself from the burlap sack, dusted his clothes off, and tried to work out the kink in his neck. Still squinting, he staggered away from the dumpster.

He walked around to the front of the supermarket and, as his stomach growled, thought of all of the ready to eat food inside. Tapping the empty pockets of his slacks, he turned away and moseyed down the block. He had no idea where he was going, nor did he know where he was. Not that it mattered much, for he had no frame of reference to compare it to. He was lost. No, he was worst than lost. To say he was lost would give the false impression that there was some place he belonged, some place he could call home, but he had no memory of a place like that. The world was big and he belonged nowhere in it. The morning passed slowly as he strolled along the busy avenue, in an ever-expanding ocean of loneliness, looking for anything that might help him make some sense of this bizarre reality he found himself in. As the sleep left his eyes he began to pick up the thoughts of those whom he passed once more.

Approaching a busy intersection he noticed a phone booth in the parking lot of a small convenient store and had an idea. He went to the booth, opened the phonebook, and flipped to the k's in the white pages. Karat, Kasier, Kata, Keadle, Kendra, Kendallman. He stopped. The name *Kendallman* called to him and took up almost half a page. He shook his head in disappointment and began to count how many listings there were. There were exactly seventy-eight different *Kendallmans in this particular phone book,* and no doubt, there were more in others. Since he had no idea where he was from, there would be no way of knowing which if any, of the many *Kendallmans* listed in the world, might be related to him. He read the first few listings, in their entirety, hoping to chance upon one that might jog something inside him and give him a reason to inquire further. None of the ones he read stood out any better than any others.

"He looks like he can spare a dime." A devious voice floated in from behind. He turned around and saw a tall slinky black man in dirty blue clothes approaching.

"Hey man, could you help out a brother trying to get something to eat?"

Alex looked at him and then heard his thoughts. "He's worth at least five bucks maybe ten!"

"I'm sorry, but I don't have any money."

The man came closer and his thoughts continued. "Whoa! What happened to this guy?" He hesitated, looked at Alex and said, "Come on man, just a couple bucks."

Alex shook his head and let out a half-chuckle as he said, "Why don't you use the twenty dollars in your pocket and buy yourself something? Huh?" He raised his eyebrows. "And while you're at it why don't you get me something as well? I'm starved."

"What twenty bucks man? I be broke brother, I haven't had anything to eat in three days. Come on man… help a guy out!"

"The twenty bucks in the front pocket of your jeans," Alex pointed with an all-knowing look of disgust, "and if you haven't eaten in three days as you say, then what exactly was it that you were doing to that hot cereal in the shelter this morning, huh?"

The eyes on the black man widened. He looked like a young child who had just been nabbed for eating the last cookie in the cookie jar.

"What are you some kind of FBI man or something? How do you know so much about me? You been following me, huh?" He decided to let Alex keep whatever money he had and to find another place to work his jive. "You just stay away from me! You hear me?" He shouted as he nervously crossed the street to the convenient store on the opposite corner. "Just stay away!"

Alex laughed to himself for a moment then turned back to the phonebook with a new purpose and looked up the address of St. John's Homeless Shelter. He memorized the address and went inside to ask for directions. The clerk was kind enough to write them down and explain, in detail, how to get there. On his way to the shelter, Alex thought about how he was able to use his unique ability to obtain the information he needed to find a place to eat and clean up. Maybe this weird ability of his wasn't so bad after all.

The shelter was close and Alex was there in less than ten minutes. As he approached, the chatter of voices in his head escalated until they sounded like the cafeteria of an over populated middle school. The place featured an entryway big enough to drive a couple Mac trucks through and still leave considerable amount of room on both sides. Inside, he found a humongous warehouse filled with a multitude of portable beds and a couple dozen folding tables with chairs. At the far end, along the wall was a short line of people from various ethnic and economical backgrounds waiting to be dished something to eat by a small group of volunteers standing just on the opposite side of four food-filled, folding tables.

Directly across from them, on the other side of the warehouse, Alex spotted a sign for the restrooms and six small showers built into the wall. Two were being used, which were shielded from view by heavy cloth shower curtains, three were empty, and one sported a sign stating that it was temporarily out of order. Alex looked around the shelter as he walked to the back of the food line and grabbed a cracked, yellow tray.

He couldn't shake the feeling he was being watched. He kept thinking about the people who were chasing him. He was fairly certain they weren't just going to *go away*. He remembered the note in his pocket. He wondered where he would look if he were one of the people trying to find him and he couldn't get away from the conclusion that they would inevitably, sooner or later, stakeout every homeless shelter within a fifty mile radius, maybe even a hundred mile radius.

He picked up a large plastic plate and put it on his tray. He felt claustrophobic as a heavyset woman smacked his plate with an oversized spoonful of lumpy mashed potatoes. He must have appeared more than a little paranoid as he kept looking out at the street for anything or anyone who looked a little out of place. He wasn't sure what he was looking for but he hoped that he would be able to recognize it if and when he saw it. The man cutting the roast beef must have known how hungry Alex was, because it seemed as if he sliced him a slightly bigger piece then everyone else's. Alex took his tray to one of the empty places at a table that provided him a clear view of the street. His special talent for picking up the thoughts of those around him afforded him a unique vantage point over everyone else in the room.

He could hear how unfairly the heavyset lady, assisting in the food line, was being treated by her, *no-good-for-nothing husband*. And how the young man near the showers couldn't stop thinking of that perfectly shaped little blonde that he had spied upon, through the crack in the back of one of the showers, the day before yesterday.

When he concentrated, he could even hear the thoughts of a man, out on the sidewalk, passing by. "This place is ridiculous, a sheer waste of time, money and energy! These people don't need food and a place to sleep, what they need is a good lesson in personal responsibility!" Alex shook his head in disgust as the man's self-righteous thoughts of indignation slowly diminished with each step he took away from the shelter.

Alex was touched by a young woman's prayer for her family. She thanked God for all the financial prosperity they had enjoyed up until now and asked him to help her husband, who was at this very moment, out diligently searching for another job. She thanked God for everything good in her life: her children, her husband and all the love of her friends. She prayed for the people in the shelter, that God would keep them safe in their time of misfortune and help them to regain their foothold in life.

Alex turned and listened to the thoughts a young, very pregnant widow, no more than 20 years old. Her husband had been in the wrong place at the wrong time and found himself in the middle of a gang shootout. She had no family and nowhere to go. Alex could feel and relate to her emptiness. She was afraid and alone in a huge incomprehensible world.

Sure there were those individuals who just liked to take advantage of the system, and there were those who were able to pull their own weight, but were too lazy to do so and could use a little lesson in personal responsibility. However, for the most part the people Alex found in the shelter were people who didn't want to be here. They were people who were hardworking, honest and reliable, but for one reason or another found themselves in a situation they did not want, nor deserve to be in.

As he listened to the hearts and minds of those around him, Alex found that most, if not all, of the volunteers, were now, or had been at one time, homeless themselves. Alex finished his food, with a new perspective on his own situation. He wiped down his tray and returned it to the beginning of the line where he had taken it from, then reached into his pocket and wondered what he was going to do with the hypodermic needles as he walked toward the showers. To his dismay, he found that one of the vials had shattered and whatever was in it had seeped out. He hadn't checked his pockets since he put the needles in them yesterday, in Ginger's apartment. The other vial seemed to be okay and felt as if it still held whatever chemical it had when he found it.

As he neared the showers, he noted a sign taped to the wall above several large cardboard boxes, which read, *free clothes*. Alex made a quick pit stop and rummaged through the articles of clothing. He found a faded pair of old blue jeans that looked like they might fit and a ball cap that proclaimed the ever-popular phrase *Just do it!* After looking through several shirts he chose one that featured a hyped up looking rabbit who seemed as if it could have easily belonged to one of the mafia families from the movie The Godfather. The caption read, *Welcome to Wonderland Alex.* Startled, he blinked and looked again, *Welcome to Wonderland Alice.* After catching his breath, he thought how fitting as he laid the shirt over the jeans in his left hand. He was also lucky enough to find a beaten up pair of tennis shoes that he thought should be a close fit. He walked over to the showers, where he found a barrel full of clean white towels. After grabbing one, he laid his new wardrobe on the concrete beside the stall and removed all but his slacks, and then stepped into the stall. Behind the curtain he finished undressing, dropped his last garment on top of the others and turned on the water.

It was hot and felt extremely good! As he focused on the warm water bouncing off his body, the voices in his head slowly changed from individual utterances to a single collective ambience of gratefulness. Alex closed his eyes letting the water hit his face and run down his body. Although he could not remember a single time that he had ever taken a shower he was more than half sure that none could've ever felt so good. He didn't realize how sore he felt until he started to enjoy the pulsating action created by that wonderful silver showerhead. After a moment of soaking in the comforting rain of warmth he pumped the soap dispenser attached to the wall and began to lather up. With his eyes shut and his hair full of suds, Alex felt the entire aura of the shelter change. The feeling of thankfulness that had engulfed the shelter just moments ago was now carrying an odd emotion of curiosity.

Alex quickly rinsed the soap out of his hair and off his face, as he began to focus on the individual voices again.

"Who are they?"

"What do they want?"

"Are they FBI?"

"Who are they looking for?"

Alex peeked out from behind the shower curtain and after a second of scanning, spotted a well-dressed man in a dark suit. The man was tall and had a face unlike anyone else's. It looked hideous and featured a scar that ran diagonally across it. He was standing over a heavyset fellow in a white t-shirt, who was sitting on one of the many cots in the room. The man was holding a square white piece of paper. He looked at it for a moment, then shook his head and handed it back. The man in the suit took it, turned around and handed it to a young black woman holing a small child.

Alex concentrated on what she was thinking. He was able to hear her thoughts a millisecond before she actually spoke them. It was almost eerie to hear her voice just before seeing her lips move. It felt as if he was watching a movie where the audio and video were slightly out of sync. "No," she shook her head. "No, I'm sorry I haven't seen him."

Alex continued to scan the rest of the shelter. There was another man with his own piece of paper, questioning more people on the other side of the room. Suddenly Alex was stricken with fear. They were at the far end of the warehouse-sized shelter, but they were quickly working their way toward him. He had to move fast.

Reaching down he scooped up his new set of threads and suit coat, which contained the only clues to his identity. After running the towel over his body, looking more as if he was performing some mysterious magic trick rather than drying off, Alex jumped into his recently acquired jeans and pulled the t-shirt over his head. Peeking through the curtain again, he saw one of the men questioning the meat carver. The man nodded his head and pointed in the direction of the table that Alex had eaten on. Alex slipped on the tennis shoes, which were tighter than he would've liked but under the circumstances, very tolerable, and with lightning speed, laced them up.

He removed the hypodermic needle and handwritten note from his coat and placed them in the ball cap. He dropped the coat to the tiled floor, closed his eyes and took a deep breath. After a brief moment he opened his eyes with a look of determination and confidently pushed back the curtain just in time to see the young pregnant woman pointing toward the showers. His immediate thought was to run, but if he did they'd spot him for sure. At present they hadn't seen him and didn't know he had a new wardrobe. Fighting the urge to move faster, Alex casually walked toward the restrooms. At the restroom door, he reached down, turned the knob and just couldn't resist. As he pushed the door open he looked over his shoulder.

The two suited men were now standing side by side next to the showers intently studying the shelter. One of them carried a small handheld radio in his left hand while the other held up Alex's recently discarded gray slacks. At the very instant Alex saw him, he saw Alex. He released the pants, letting them flop to the floor and took off after Alex in a dead run, while the other man raised the radio to his mouth and chased after.

Alex pushed open the door and bolted into the restroom. Directly in front of him on the left was a row of three porcelain sinks, across from them, four toilet stalls, and on the far wall, a window, halfway opened. Alex ran to the window and with his one free hand, tried with no luck to push it up. As carefully as possible, without slowing, he laid the ball cap on the windowsill and using both hands, shoved upward with all the strength he could tap.

The window released with a pop, slid up until it was fully open and smacked loudly into the upper sill. The opening was large and there was no screen. Alex snatched up his mystery-filled hat, bent over, and straddle-stepped through the window just as the bathroom door swung open and slammed into the wall.

Alex found himself in another alley. He managed to race to the end and round the corner before his pursuer clambered through the window. He sprinted across the street, to a row of small offices and went into the first door he came to. It was small and he vaguely caught sight of someone sitting at a desk opposite the door. From the outside looking in, the glass was dark and acted somewhat like a mirror. Alex looked beyond the white-stenciled lettering on the glass door and his heart pounded faster as the man chasing him came running out of the alley and stopped.

The man looked both ways and then for an instant appeared to be staring directly into the office at Alex, but then quickly looked away. He pulled out his own two-way radio. Talking, slightly out of breath, he turned and slowly walked down the street, carefully studying the area as he went. A few moments later a plain looking, dark-colored sedan pulled up next to him. He slowly did a final 360 then got into the car with a burst of angry disappointment.

"Can I help you?" A soft female voice floated up over his shoulder and into his ears. Alex was so caught up in what was happening outside that he had almost forgotten there was someone else in the room and the question startled him. He quickly turned around as the sound of squealing tires squeezed around the cracks and vibrated through the glass in the office door. A young shapely brunette sat at the desk with her hands together and her fingers interlocked. Her hair hung just below her shoulders and her eyes were an amazingly deep shade of green. She wore a soft cream-colored business suit that featured just a touch of turquoise, which drew her eyes out even more. She smiled with a look that expressed puzzlement more than warmth. Alex paused for a moment, captivated by her beauty.

"Are you okay?" she asked.

"Huh?" He jiggled his head. "Yeah…Yeah, I'm fine." His attention was divided between her and the street.

"Is there something I can help you with?" She asked, with obvious confusion in her voice.

Her desk was made of cherry oak wood and supported several items. Among them was a bronze nameplate, which featured the name *Mercedes Atwater*

"No thank you," he said oddly, "I…um, just stepped into the wrong office. Sorry."

He heard her think, "yeah sure." as she slowly nodded her head and hesitantly said, "Okay."

Alex turned and opened the door to leave, then read the name on the glass, which he had understandably overlooked on his race in. *Atwater Investigations.* He stopped and looked back at Mercedes, who was now curiously watching him and holding both ends of a pencil in such a way as to suggest she just might, at any moment, take a bite out of the center.

"You're a private eye?" he asked. He could hear the disappointment in her thoughts as she assumed he was either some diluted idiot, who had a bizarre conspiracy theory to tell her about, or a person who had a true need for her services, but no money in which to pay for them. Alex wondered just how she would react to a person who fit *both* of those categories.

"Maybe," she replied, not wanting to say yes and unwilling to lie, "Why?" Her teeth harmlessly bit the pencil.

Alex let the door swing shut and walked over to her desk.

CHAPTER SEVEN

Martha Rodman tossed the last piece of luggage into the backseat of a tan colored 1974 station wagon and shut the heavy metal door.

Nick stood on the dirt driveway next to the passenger's side window, looking quietly at Lisa, who sat coldly staring through the windshield. She was silently singing the lyrics to the pop song blaring through the headphones of a portable CD player as she painstakingly waited for Martha to get in and start the car.

"She'll be all right, Nick." Nick turned and looked at Martha, who was in her late forties and wore her dark brown hair up in a bun. It featured something like a knitting needle that stuck up in the back and made her look as if she had grown a single plastic antenna. She was overweight, but not fat. Her pale blue dress came down to the middle of her calves, and now, as in most cases, she wore sandals instead of shoes.

She was happy more often than not and radiated a somewhat carefree attitude most of the time. However, Nick was frequently surprised by her uncanny ability to *simplify* the truth and reveal it in such a way as to make it all but impossible to deny or continue overlooking. She possessed a *certain wisdom* that made her seem almost *magical* at times and then mysteriously she would fade back into her happy-go-lucky personality and pretend that nothing profound had been uttered.

She and Nick had met twelve years ago through Allie, and she was one of the few people in town who stood by him when Allie died. Even when he was a major suspect in the case, she never doubted his innocence. Nick was the type of man who always pulled more than his own weight. He never burdened others with his own troubles. However, on those rare occasions, during the first few years following Allie's death, when the weight of emotions became too heavy for anyone to carry alone, Martha was there. She was the only person that Nick felt that he could truly talk to. She had loved Allie almost as much as he had, and she also needed a shoulder to cry on.

Many nights they would stay awake and talk until sunrise. They would share memories of Allie's warmth and understanding, and how she often cared more about others, than she did herself. They would cry, remembering the many things Allie wanted to do with her life, but now wouldn't be able to. They would laugh as they reminded each other of various memories where she had brightened up their lives and brought the healing power of laughter to their souls. However, on most occasions, they would usually end up discussing the bizarre circumstances that surrounded her death. At first, Martha was just as interested in discussing them as Nick was, but as time passed and vivid memories faded into vague uncertainties, Allie's death seemed less and less like some weird conspiracy and more like the tragic accident it really was.

It wasn't that Martha wanted to avoid talking about what happened. Nor did she forget just how bizarre the events were surrounding Allie's death, but as Martha put it, "Thinking about the past is one thing, but living there is quite another. When we spend more time in the past, trying to work out its mysteries, than we do in the present, with those who really need us, well, then it's time to let go."

She had spoken those words nearly five years ago, after he and Lisa had returned from a trip to Tennessee. It was just one of the many trips that they had taken as he looked for answers to what really happened that day. As with most of his searches, the trip turned out to be a complete waste of time. It had taken more than three weeks, and Lisa missed school because of it. Nick dragged her along out of guilt, as he always did. He never spent nearly as much time with her as he should have and he thought they could catch up on the road. As usual, however, the trip kept him too busy chasing phantoms of the past and Lisa didn't get any more attention during the journey than she did at home.

Lisa needed a father and no matter what he did, nothing was going to bring her mother back. That was true, but he just couldn't let go as easily as Martha had. She wasn't there when it happened. She wasn't condemned to the memory that would haunt his dreams for the rest of his life. She wasn't the one who was with Allie when she died, yet powerless to save her. Fate hadn't given her the terrible memory of being in that cold, icy water, screaming violently and desperately for help as the two strange men stood emotionlessly on the bank, and did nothing more than watch. Nick, not her, was cursed to remember every single detail of that terrible day. It was burned into his mind as if it had happened just yesterday. He could still feel his hands on her hips beneath the icy water as he struggled with all of his might to free her. He could still picture the strangers standing on the shore watching him. He was doomed forever to remember every little feature of their cold solemn faces, and rare was the night that he wasn't awakened by their haunting expressions.

His love for Martha was enduring, and he understood her need to let go. He understood everyone's need to let go, but he couldn't, at least not yet. If nothing else Allie deserved justice.

Martha's eyes held genuine concern as she said, "It's you I'm worried about."

Nick paused thoughtfully for a moment and then said confidently, "Don't worry about me. I'll be okay."

"I'm not worried about your trip to California, Nick." Her loving glare was all knowing.

He looked back blank faced, unwilling to express even the slightest emotion, not because he had none, but rather because he knew what she meant, and he knew if they began to debate it, he didn't stand a chance. She stared into his eyes as if trying to send some kind of mental wake up call into his brain.

"I'll be okay," he repeated as he widened his eyes, sounding and looking a lot like Lisa did whenever she wanted to do something that she knew was wrong. Martha stared back silently, letting the quiet truth speak for itself. After a few intense seconds, Nick could no longer take it and shook his head. Martha wasn't sure if he had given her an eye-roll or just quickly looked around before letting his eyes fall on Lisa.

Lisa still sat looking forward, doing her best to hold back her feelings of anger, hurt and emptiness, nevertheless her eyes slowly filled with water.

"I love you, Peaches," Nick said with a crackle in his throat. She coldly sang louder, over his words, as the tears left her eyes and spilled onto her cheeks.

"If you need anything..." Martha spoke as she walked around to the driver's seat.

"I know Dottie." Most people called her Martha, but for some unknown reason Allie had always called her Dottie and Nick just followed suit. Martha pushed the button in with her thumb and pulled on the door while Nick walked around the front of the station wagon.

"You sure you don't need a ride to the airport?" she asked.

"No thanks, I'm just going to leave the truck in the long term parking."

Martha got into the car and started the engine while Nick walked up and pushed the door closed.

Feeling powerless and not knowing exactly how to reach beyond his emotionally clouded determination she said, "Nick, let me ask you something."

Nick listened but kept his guard up, sensing that she was about to throw out some *Dottie wisdom*.

"Would you want Allie and Lisa to live like this?" She looked around thoughtfully at the rundown cabin, which was more than a little overgrown with weeds as she continued, "all these years, if things were reversed?" Then she paused and met his eyes with so much warmth and compassion that they almost leaped out of her and became solid. Nick returned her gaze, bracing himself for a shot of the truth, determined not to let it get past his ears and into his soul, but she said nothing. She just continued to stare at him in silence for a while and Nick began to wonder whether there was more or if that was all of it. Then finally, when he had had all but lowered his defenses, she asked, "Do you think she wants *you* and her *daughter* to live like this?" She cocked her head and raised her eyebrows leaving it as a question for him to ponder, then shifted into reverse and slowly backed up.

Nick stood in silence as he thought, wearing dark blue jeans, a black shirt and brown leather boots. A breeze hit his dark-brown hair, shifting it across his forehead as he turned his attention to Lisa, who was determined not to look back.

The station wagon backed up, turned around and pulled away. Without moving her head, Lisa shifted her eyes to the side view mirror and stopped singing as she watched the image of her father shrink in the distance. Nick took a deep breath as the station wagon rode down to the end of the drive and turned onto the asphalt, disappearing around the corner. He stood there for a moment just staring at the empty section of blacktop, and then shifted his gaze to the dry dirt beside his feet. After another deep breath he reached into his pocket, pulled out his Gummy Bears and headed for his truck. He hadn't taken more than three steps when he heard a car quickly pulling down the driveway behind him. He turned back just in time to see Lisa flying out of the station wagon. She ran up and wrapped her arms around him, squeezing with all her might. Nick started to cry as he closed his eyes and held her close.

"I love you Daddy!"

"I love you *too* Peaches!"

"Be careful!"

"I will."

"I'll miss you!"

"I'll miss you too!" Nick held her close for a few seconds and then asked, "Hey, want a Gummy Bear?"

"Sure," Lisa smiled as she wiped her cheek with the back of her hand and accepted the little orange bear.

"Heck, why don't you just take 'm all?" he said as he placed the bag into her hand, and then closed her fingers around it.

"But Dad," she shook her head, "These are your favorite."

"Don't worry," Nick smiled, "I got an another pack in the truck. Now, get going. I got a plane to catch."

Nick watched as she got back into the car and rode away for a second time, then turned and continued on to his truck. He had woken up early and purchased his ticket online. Everything had been all packed up and ready to go before noon. His plane departed at 5:53 pm. He looked at his watch, it was 3:08 and it would take about an hour and a half to get to the Charleston airport. He had just enough time to run by Jimmy Hollenbeck's house and still make it to the airport an hour before takeoff. Jimmy was a young man who Nick paid from time to time to come out and do various gardening jobs around the cabin, and in an attempt to weasel his way out of the *Dottie wisdom* he would pay Jimmy to come over, clean the place up and maintain it while he was gone. He grabbed his shades from the visor, reached into the glove box and smiled warmly as he withdrew the new bag of bears, then started the engine and pulled away.

***

"Aunt Dottie," Lisa asked while turning her head and removing her earphones.

"Yeah sweetheart?"

"Why does he keep doing this?"

Dottie listened, considering the question.

"I mean…I know he loved Mom…and I know that some weird things happened to her after she died, but…" Lisa stopped in mid-sentence. She didn't quite know how to finish her question.

Dottie held the steering wheel in the famous ten-two position and tilted her head slightly to the left, patiently waiting for Lisa to reformulate.

"What I mean is, after all this time and finding no answers, it seems as if he would," she shook her head and squinted her eyes, "I don't know…let it go." She paused as Dottie nodded and reflected. "It tears him up inside and we're constantly moving from one place to another as he chases down what *he* calls *clues*, only to return here when he doesn't find what he's looking for. I don't mean to sound insensitive, Aunt Dottie. Allie was my mom as well as his wife, but no matter what answers he finds, it'll never bring her back nor change what happened."

Nodding her head in agreement Dottie asked, "How much do you know about what happened when your mom died?"

"Just what Dad's told me. I know about the strange men on the shore, the weird ambulance that took Mom away, how her body disappeared for three days and when it finally turned up, there was this weird huge hole in the top of her head, with most of her brain missing." Lisa made an icky face.

"Do you know whose idea it was to go kayaking that day?"

"No." She looked at Dottie puzzled, not knowing how her question tied into the conversation.

"It was your dad's. Your mom never really liked to kayak. They had only been to West Virginia once before and they stayed in that cabin where you and your father live now. Her death, itself, was just an accident. It wasn't the men on the shore that killed her or anything else bizarre. It was simply a freak accident. Her kayak flipped over and the current was too strong. She wasn't able to regain control and was sucked underneath the water, beneath the trunk of a tree. Your dad tried to pull her loose but wasn't able. He yelled for help but no one came. Those two men on the shore just stood there and watched, that's true, but they were not in the least bit responsible for her death. See, your dad still blames himself for what happened. I *think*, deep down inside, he feels that if he can somehow prove, at least to himself that the men on the shore purposely did nothing because they wanted your mom dead, for some strange reason, that only God and they know, then he'll have someone else to share the blame with. Not that he'll feel completely blameless, just that he won't place the blame entirely on his own shoulders anymore."

"But," Lisa looked puzzled, "Aunt Dottie, it's not Dad's fault that Mom died. I mean… he didn't kill her."

"I know sweetie. But to your dad, it's not so clear."

"I don't understand. Dad's not stupid. He's *got* to know that it wasn't his fault." Lisa shook her head and scrunched her face in confusion like only a teenager can do.

Dottie slowed the car, as they approached the tollbooth. "It's difficult for your dad. See, there was a time, just after your grandparents died and before he met your mother that he wasn't, in his own eyes, a very," Dottie paused, reaching for the right word, "*nice* person."

If Dottie were to be totally honest, she would have to tell Lisa things about her father that might demean him, in Lisa's mind. As it was, Dottie would water down the truth and tell her just enough information to help her understand why her father hasn't yet been able to let go of the past.

"What do you mean?"

Dottie pulled up to the tollbooth and dropped a quarter into the basket. "Well, your dad was really close to his parents and *his* dad always told him that *you only get out of life what you put into it*. So, your dad worked hard, got good grades and always played by the rules."

Dottie changed lanes and merged onto the off ramp. "One Friday afternoon he dropped by the general store that his parents owned and found that it had been robbed. His dad was dead and his mom was in critical condition, on her way to the hospital. When she died, upon arriving at the hospital, your dad snapped and his entire philosophy changed. Right then and there he decided that you *don't* get back what you put in and for the next few years he lived his life a little…recklessly. That is, until, he met your mom."

That was just enough information to help Lisa understand but not enough to ruin the image she had of her father. The truth is Nick didn't just snap that Friday afternoon and live a little on the reckless side for a while. He literally submerged himself in hatred and thrived on it! He had grown up in Bandon, Oregon and with the support of his parents, was studying to become a lawyer. When they were maliciously ripped away from him by the hands of a heartless crook, who got away with no more than fifty dollars and who would never be found or brought to justice, his whole world flipped upside down. Despite being at the very top of his class, he dropped out of law school, and hung out in sleazy pool halls and dangerously rowdy biker bars.

He turned so cold that he became known as the *Iceman* and for a short time, was one of the most feared men in the small town of Bandon. Only the meanest and bravest dared to befriend him and even to them he showed no mercy. The wonderfully intelligent mind that granted him the excellent grades in college also helped him to understand the ruthless rules of the street, and before long, few, if any played the game better.

He became a small time user and seller of many different drugs and if he wasn't in a fight he was usually looking for one. The money he received from his parents' savings and their combined life insurance totaled well over a million dollars but he spent none of it. To him it represented the death of his parents and the evil way in which life repaid them for all their hard work, honesty, and sacrifices. He wanted nothing to do with it! Still, understanding the foolishness of throwing it away, he locked it into a ten year savings plan, which now totaled over a million and a half and was more than enough to fund his search to find out what really happened when Allie died.

Lisa listened and for the first time began to understand. "See, your mom was one of the only people who was still able to see the true goodness that was hidden deep within your father. I didn't know your father back then, but I believe your mom brought out qualities in him that he didn't even know he had. Your dad loved your mom as much as any man has ever loved a woman. It's almost like your mom brought your dad back from the dead."

Dottie turned onto Sand Branch Road toward Curtsville. "See, so when she died it was as if your dad lost *all reason to live* again. He would have done anything just to trade places with her, and he blames himself for talking her into going kayaking that day. To be painfully honest, Sweetie, I don't know where he'd be right now, if he didn't have you in his life."

"Whoa!" Lisa sat silent for a half a mile or more then said, "I'm so ashamed at myself Aunt Dottie. I haven't been a very good daughter lately."

"Oh, Sweetie, it's not your fault, you've been doing the best you could under the circumstances."

"Yeah but…I don't know." Lisa continued looking out the window at the endless sea of passing green trees, and then asked, "How come nobody ever told me this before?"

"Well, *I* never said any of this before because I never felt you were old enough or needed to know. See, a person's past is not who they are and your dad is one of the finest men I know."

"I love Daddy, Aunt Dottie, I love him with all my heart."

"I know you do Sweetie, and he knows you do too."

***

The drive to the airport took less time than he thought. He parked his truck in the long-term parking and took his bags, which contained his handgun, to the check-in counter. After answering a few routine security questions and providing documentation for ownership and transportation of his gun, he found a seat in the waiting area and fired up his laptop to get a head's up on the layout of the LA area.

He had an up-to-date map program installed, but he didn't bother opening it. Instead, he connected, wirelessly to the Internet and used Mapquest's online services. He looked up the location of LAX and made reservations for a rental car. Then he looked up the location of the LAPD and the locations where each victim was found. The plane was on time and soon he was aboard, heading for California. He had a seat next to the center aisle and found himself sitting beside an older lady who had never flown before and just loved to talk.

CHAPTER EIGHT

With the exception of a few fluffy-white clouds the bright blue California sky was sunny and clear. Theodore drove his Lexus to an abandoned, Victorian style house next to a local park where God had instructed him to go and parked underneath a huge eucalyptus. The day was smiling on Teddy as he got out of his car and walked to the trunk with an upbeat rhythm in his step. He looked stylish in his newly purchased, pinstriped, gray suit and even though he had woken up much later than he would have liked, he still had enough time to drop by the cleaners and pick up some shirts, go by Wal*mart and deliver some film, stop by the dumpster and drop off a body and make it to the house before four. He felt good and did a half-step back as he hit the button on his remote, unlocking the trunk.

He spun around, performed a quick dance step that probably originated from Fred Astaire and softly began to sing one of the many songs by Frank Sinatra, then reached into the trunk and latched onto a stainless steel box with built-in temperature controls. He withdrew the box and softly danced his way, with style and grace, up onto the sidewalk. After setting it down, he looked up at the white three-story house with a curious look and wondered why the angel of God had chosen this particular place to reward Teddy for all his hard work.

A strange feeling flashed through his body when he thought he saw one of the curtains on the second floor sway. It looked as if someone had just been looking down at him through the dirt-crusted window and then quickly backed away. He looked closer at it, and after a moment of careful study, concluded it had just been a trick of the shadows and the curtain had never really moved.

He reached down, snatched up the box and continued with a song in his heart and a lift in his step around the yard, to the gate on the south side of the house. Using a key he had received from an angel of God earlier in the year, he removed the large padlock and swung the heavy iron gate inward. Teddy was very fortunate that God loved him enough to send the angel to him. Last year

God afforded Teddy the opportunity to bring salvation to someone who was unwilling to go with Teddy to his home.

After walking the fortunate young lady through the steps of salvation Teddy asked if she would like to be free of the worries of backsliding? He promised her a foolproof way to *ensure* her salvation. He said he had helped others just like her to *ensure* theirs. When she asked if he was a prophet, he smiled and told her that he was, but only one of many. She agreed to let him help her, but was still adamant about not returning with him to his home. Not wanting to risk losing her soul to the temptations of Satan, Teddy walked her to an out of the way area and, using the tire iron from his car, beat her repeatedly until he was sure her soul had left this temptation-filled world and went home. He still wanted, however to take her head and add it to the rest of his collection. Whenever possible he would collect the heads of those he helped find salvation to remind himself of the good gift he had given them.

Her corpse laid face down, on its stomach next to a pile of old wooden pallets in a small walkway in between two tall buildings. Teddy, now pouring with sweat, was violently jabbing at the back of her neck. He was using the sharp end of the tire iron, trying to cut through the last mound of flesh, connecting her nearly severed head, when someone, who must have heard her earlier cries for help, came to investigate. Teddy knew they would not understand so instead of risking being taken to jail or worse, sent to Heaven, before finishing his work here on Earth, Teddy left the woman's head and ran.

It was a week later that the angel first appeared to him. He told Teddy what a great job he was doing and how pleased the Lord was with his work. He acknowledged the misfortune of not being able to collect the young woman's head last week and told Teddy that God wanted to reward him for all his efforts. He said that it was unwise to send someone to heaven while they were in a public place and told Teddy that he should never take that risk again.

He also told him that God has decided to give him $5,000.00 every time he sends someone home. He told Teddy he would not receive his reward unless the angel could match the person's soul to the body they had lived in while they were here on Earth. The angel said that the best way to do that would be for Teddy to bring him the head of each person and let him take it back up into Heaven where he would then match it to the soul it belonged to. Once the angel was sure that Teddy was the one responsible for their salvation he would return the head to Teddy along with his monetary reward.

He gave Teddy detailed instructions on how to keep the heads preserved and told him where to take the first one. Teddy heard from the angel twice more after that, in which the angel had changed the drop-off location. This big beautiful house was the latest one. Teddy often wondered why a powerful angel of God would need to go through so much trouble in order to be sure that

Teddy was the one who deserved the reward, but he decided that it wasn't wise to question a holy deity.

The gate made an eerie creaking sound as he pushed it open and walked past. Everything looked just as it did the last time he was here, three days ago. He closed the gate and replaced the lock, then walked through an area that might have been a beautiful garden once, but now was filled full of dry dead weeds and hard cracked earth. He thoughtfully lifted his black shiny shoes over the brush, being careful not to harm any one of God's beautiful, delicate shrubs then made his way to the backdoor. Using another key provided by the angel he unlocked it and went inside.

The room, which was filled with dust and several tiny cobwebs was little and looked as if it had once served as either a pantry or small washroom. The baseboards creaked and sagged as he slowly walked into the living room, which held several unknown pieces of furniture covered in white, slightly soiled sheets. This room, like the pantry, was covered in dust and featured a countless number of old spider webs. Carrying the box in his left hand and pushing thick, grayish-white webs aside with his right, he happily grinned his way through the house, on a creaking floor, to the padlocked cellar door, which he entered with yet another angelic key.

The stairs crackled, popped and creaked as he carefully carried his box down into the cold dark cellar. The air was thinner here and he could faintly smell the musty scent of stagnant water as the soles of his shoes left the last wooden plank and tapped onto the hard concrete floor. In the dark, Teddy felt his way to a small table, set his box down and blindly searched for the oil lamp. Reaching around in the dark, being careful not to get splintered from the old wooden table, Teddy felt tiny, claw-sharp paws trot across the back of his hand.

Instinctively, he jerked back and knocked the lamp off the table. The smell of kerosene filled the air. After a moment on his hands and knees, searching through the dirt-filled floor, he found and lit the lamp. A flickering light bounced off objects throughout the cellar, casting creepy shadows onto wooden beams and cinderblock walls. Looking like a demon in a pinstriped suit, he adjusted the lamp and then held it up high as he glanced around this subterranean chamber. With the lamp in this elevated position the shadows shifted and took on a life of their own, creating an even more sinister look. Something startled him as it scurried out from behind an old wooden shelf filled with books that were probably written in another century. It scampered into a nearly shredded, overstuffed chair, positioned just underneath the entry stairs, which Teddy had just descended. After catching his breath and waiting for his heart rate to return to normal he smiled, shook his head and said, "It's just me Mr. Angel. I have done another good work and I have another gift for you."

After giggling with a demonic drool that would easily compete with any mad scientist's he wiped his chin, grabbed the box, and scuttled past various wooden crates and antique pieces of furniture to a horizontal deep freeze at the far end of the cellar. He sat his stainless steel container on the floor and placed the lantern on top of a nearby shelf. The freezer's lid was secured by a combination lock which he opened using a code he received from God through a dream. Maybe it wasn't a dream. Anyway, he lifted the lid, and his stomach fluttered as his vision focused upon another shiny metal box identical to the one at his feet.

He exchanged containers and relocked the freezer. Then suddenly the ceiling creaked as if someone was walking through one of the rooms above. Teddy froze and his eyes followed the squeaking wooden planks overhead. The sagging slowly moved from one position, stopped and then returned to where it had started. Creaking, crackling boards sagged left to right and then back and forth. Then the boards were creaking in two separate locations simultaneously. One went this way while the other went that way. One went fast and the other went slow. Then strangely, as if they knew right where Teddy was standing, they quickly moved, in unison to the spot directly over his head and came to a silent halt. Teddy could not be sure if people, animals or something else had been the cause of the movement.

Perhaps the angel was already here and couldn't wait to get the newly dropped off head that Teddy had brought. Or was it a demon that had sabotage in mind? The floor did not creak again and after a few moments of silence Teddy continued with his current task. He took the light and his newly acquired steel case back to the table. After sitting them down and offering a silent prayer of thanks, he slowly opened the box. Inside, the rotting eyes of a human boy stared aimlessly out of decaying sockets. Their gaze fell on Teddy's forehead. He shook the box and rocked the head, until the boy's eyes were looking into his own. He smiled, remembering how he had helped this youth find salvation, just last Tuesday. Teddy grabbed it by the hair and lifted it up out of the box revealing a fat, plain white envelope. He replaced the head, shut the box and opened the envelope, which carried fifty one hundred dollar bills. He didn't have to count it. He knew God would not short-change him and even if God did, who was Teddy to argue with God? Teddy stuffed the envelope into the inside pocket of his coat, switched off the lamp and left, exiting the way he had came in. Teddy was surprised to find that all the locks were still in place as he made his way out of the house. If anyone, any human, that is, had been in the house while he was in the basement they had not come in through the same doors that Teddy had. Now, outside of the house, full of life and happy to be alive he placed this new box into his trunk, got into his car, started the engine, and began to hum as he pulled away.

CHAPER NINE

From the chair behind her desk, Mercedes used hand gestures as she exaggerated every so many words and spoke in a *matter-of-fact* tone. "Okay, let me see if I've got this straight. You claim you can't remember anything before *yesterday*. There are strange men *with guns* in business suits chasing you. You're having memory flashbacks of *somebody else's* memories, and, as if all of that wasn't already enough, you say you can *hear the thoughts* of those around you." Mercedes paused, looked Alex squarely in the face and with an air of superiority and a *get real* attitude continued, "Mr. Kendallman does that sound like a fairly accurate summation of your situation?"

Alex's heart dropped as he listened to just how insane his story sounded. Even though he knew it must have come across strangely when he told it, somehow it seemed even worse when someone else repeated it. If he did not absolutely need her help, at this point he would have probably told her he was only joking and that one of her friends had sent him to her to have a little fun and this was nothing more than a harmless prank, but as it was, he *did* need her help. He needed it desperately. Alex took a deep breath and half expected her to throw him out as he said. "I know it sounds bad but-"

"Bad?" she interrupted, "No Mr. Kendallman, this isn't bad. Bad would be someone coming in here saying they were on the mafia's hit list and didn't know why. Bad would be someone claiming that their spouse was having an affair with someone from another planet and wanted me to figure out which *planet that was*. No Mr. Kendallman, your story isn't *bad*. It's worse than bad, it's ridiculous." Mercedes leaned forward, thought a second and then changed her tone to a more inquisitive one. "Did Ramsey send you here? Is this one of his sick practical jokes? Because, if it is, he has really outdone himself this time and sunk to a level that even I didn't think he could. And if you're here, trying to make me feel stupid, it's not working. The only reason I'm here and not at the bureau is because of Ramsey's stupid ego. I never cheated on any test in my life."

"I don't even know who Ramsey is."

Mercedes inhaled, closed her eyes for a moment then exhaled and said, "Okay Mr. Kendallman—if in fact that really is your name—thank you for dropping by. I would appreciate it, very much, if you would leave now."

Alex stood up and beamed with sincerity, "Please Ms. Atwater, this is not some joke and I'm not crazy. I really do need your help."

"Have a nice day Mr. Kendallman." Mercedes looked at the door, raised her eyebrows, and gestured.

Thinking quickly Alex said, "Wait, I can prove it to you." He paused, reached for her attention, then peered into her mind and enthusiastically said, "Your thinking that there's a crazy man standing in front of you right now!"

"Bravo!" she said arrogantly as she picked up the telephone handset. "Now I suppose you'll say that you *just* read my mind." She shook her head in unbelief.

Feeling nervous and as if he was in a race against the clock he blurted out, "Now you're gonna call the cops!"

Acting as if she were in utter amazement she said, "Very good Mr. Kendallman, perhaps you should market this strange ability of yours." Mercedes dialed the number to the local police department.

Alex was surprised at how difficult it was becoming to convince her he could actually read minds. Everything she was thinking was so obvious it didn't take a mind reader to figure out. Even though he was able to pick up her every thought he knew no more than any other observant person would have.

Without removing her eyes from Alex she spoke into the phone, "Yes, my name is Mercedes Atwater and there is a strange man causing trouble in my office. I've asked him, *several times,* to leave but he refuses." Directing her words at Alex she said, "I'd leave now, if I were you." Then she returned her focus to the phone, answered some questions, gave out the address to her office, then said thank you and hung up. "The police are on their way." She raised her eyebrows.

Feeling desperate and not knowing what else to do Alex anxiously said, "Please Ms. Atwater, let me prove it to you... Think of a number in your head, any number."

Alex sounded like a cheap rip off artist, posing as some mystical fortuneteller. Mercedes thought *what a psycho.*

As quickly as the thoughts entered her mind, Alex repeated them, "What a psycho! You're thinking what a psycho." How stupid, obviously she's thinking that.

This guy is too much. Mercedes raised her eyebrows, shook her head and slightly grinned.

Feeling even more desperate now, Alex continued to repeat her thoughts without thinking. "I'm too much! Your thinking, *I'm too much*"

"Mr. Kendallman please, the game is over. The police are on their way."

Alex had no idea how impossible it could be to prove to another person that he could really read minds. Not sure he was going to be able to persuade her before the police arrived and remembering what his note said about not being able to trust them, Alex walked over to the door, grabbed the railing and racked his brains, trying to think of a way he could demonstrate the reality of his ability.

Alex stood in silence at the door, as the clock ticked, contemplating whether to leave or continue trying to authenticate his claim for help.

"You know, I'm not an expert in these matters, but I don't believe they'll have their sirens on when they pull up. I don't think you'll receive any warning. I'm not sure. If you're going to leave, you'd be wise to do it now."

Still holding onto the door railing, Alex felt time slipping by as he rubbed his head. He waited, hoping Mercedes might think of something else. Something that had nothing to do with what was happening here. All he needed was one unique thought, no matter how trivial—something he would have had no way of knowing. Every single thought she had, however pertained to this current situation. Nervously waiting for her thoughts to change and becoming increasingly anxious to flee, Alex could feel the clock ticking even faster. The cops were on their way. Still looking at Mercedes, Alex pulled the door open. The sun had changed position in the sky and the office was instantly filled with a bright beam of golden light. Feeling the intense pressure of the imminent arrival of the long arm of the law, Alex lingered, desperately searching for a way to gain her confidence, but still nothing came.

A squad car rounded the corner two blocks down and Alex decided to give up and leave. With crushed hopes, he stepped across the threshold, out onto the sidewalk and let the door swing shut behind him. As the glass door swung closed Mercedes reached down to scratch her leg and felt a run in her stockings. Aggravated, she wondered where she could have gotten it. She didn't remember seeing it this morning before she left the house. Rubbing her leg, she ran through her day. Just then the door abruptly swung open and Alex rushed back in.

"Your couch!"

Oh no, not more of this.

Alex continued, "The two back legs of your couch broke this morning, and you left your house late because of it, a little after eight." He spoke quickly. "You ran by your friend Clark's house and returned some CDs... Um..."

Alex shook his head as he continued, "Barry Mannilow, Billy Joel and Neil Diamond. Then you stopped in at Applebee's for a late breakfast. You had the..." Alex anxiously rattled off his words, "Shrimp Caesar Salad... You drive a red Porsche."

Mercedes eyes tightened as she curiously asked, "How do you know all that?" She tilted her head and her face filled with enlightenment. "Have you been stalking me?" If she wasn't going to press charges a minute ago, she was definitely going to now. Even as the door swung inward, undoubtedly being opened by one of the city's finest, Alex continued, desperately, "You have a run in your stockings, just above your ankle. You didn't know it was there until just now!" Alex pleaded with her, "And you never moved from behind *that* desk, so there's no way I would have known that."

A tall broad-shouldered policeman walked in just as Alex was finishing his sentence.

"Excuse me Ma'am, Sir." The policeman touched the tip of his hat. "We just got a call from a Mercedes Atwater, saying she was having trouble with an uninvited visitor."

"I'm Ms. Atwater"

"Afternoon Ma'am" The policeman smiled with large hands on an oversized belt. "And is this your unwanted visitor?"

The door swung open again as another officer entered the room. Alex felt his Adam's apple swell and the palms of his hands dampen as he waited for Mercedes to reply.

"Everything okay, Don?" The second officer asked.

"Yeah, I think this guy's just causing a little trouble here for the young lady and needs to be escorted downtown."

Just as Alex was preparing to run, Mercedes, still rubbing her nylons, spoke, "No! He's okay. He's not the guy I called about. Uh... that guy left just after I called you guys."

Suspiciously, the first officer asked, "Can you give us a description of what the man looked like?"

"Yeah, sure. He was about..." she looked at Alex who stood around six feet and continued, "oh, say five-five or so. He was balding...um...he was a heavyset guy."

"I see. And did he try to hurt you in any way?"

"No. He just wouldn't leave, that's all."

"But he's gone now?"

"Right! Like I said, he left just after I called."

Alex knew that neither one of the officers quite believed her. They didn't exactly suspect Alex, but they didn't feel like Mercedes was being one hundred percent honest either.

After letting out a sigh of resignation, the taller officer said, "Okay," then looked curiously at Alex, but continued speaking to Mercedes, "if you need anything else Ms. Atwater, just give us a call." He looked back at Mercedes, smiled, tipped his hat again, and left with his partner.

As the glass door swung shut, Alex remained motionless except for his eyes, which slowly shifted from Mercedes to the door and back again. Mercedes continued to run her finger over the tear in her nylons, and the next few seconds that passed seemed like an eternity as they just looked at each other in silence. Finally, in a breath of relief Alex said, "Thank you for believing me."

"Who said I believed you? I just wanted to find out how you knew I had a run in my stockings."

"I told you."

"Yeah, I remember." Mercedes shook her head then squinted at Alex. "Okay swami, tell me," she paused for a second and thought, "what am I thinking now?"

"You're thinking about your father, Donald Atwater," Alex said softly and then corrected himself, "No! You're thinking of the oil painting of your father that hangs in his office."

She shook her head in amazement. "How do you do that?" She stood up, walked around the desk, and sat on the edge. "Okay... what about now?" She peered curiously at Alex as if trying to see his mysterious power at work.

Without even a hint of concentration, Alex rattled off a nine-digit number and then said, "I believe that is your social security number."

Mercedes' pencil dropped out of her hand and onto the floor as her mouth slowly fell open.

After a brief moment Alex asked, "So, does this mean you'll help me?"

Still wide-eyed and apprehensive, Mercedes slowly nodded her head and then softly, but firmly demanded, "On one condition."

"What?"

"Promise me, you won't do that again."

"Do what?"

"Read my mind."

Alex shrugged. "I have no control over it. I hear thoughts just like you hear words."

Her nod accelerated and she spoke faster. "Fine! Then, try not to listen!" She raised her eyebrows and paused, "Deal?"

Alex's face looked as if she was asking the impossible, but he nodded anyway. "Deal!"

"And one more thing. Since it's obvious that you have no way of paying me, when this thing is all over and you're safe, you'll give me the rights to promote your story in any way I want for advertising purposes."

"What do you mean?" Alex looked confused.

"I mean after I solve your case, you allow me to promote it in order to get new clients."

"You mean you want to use me like some kind of freak show?"

"No. Nothing like that, but if your strange ability is any indication of the magnitude of this thing, then something tells me that this is going to be the case of the century, and if people know that I was the one who helped you solve it, then I'll never have to worry about getting clients again. So," she paused and looked him firmly in the eye, "that's my offer-take it or leave it." Her voice was confidant and her expression sure, but Alex could hear her thoughts as she anxiously and continuously repeated two words in her mind, *take it.*

"Okay, sure." Alex shook and then nodded his head.

Then the room fell oddly silent for the next few second as Mercedes just stared curiously at Alex. Even when she finally bent forward and retrieved her pencil, she didn't stop looking at him. She slowly moved past him to the door, locked it, reversed the open/closed sign and only glanced away long enough to make sure that no one could see in through the blinds.

Her never-ending gaze slowly began to get to Alex. The audible silence was one thing, but what really bothered him was the emptiness in her mind. It seemed to be teetering on some sort of indecision, as if she wasn't really sure that she was looking at another human being, but rather some unique, indescribable *something*, a something that she couldn't quite fathom.

"All right," she said finally, surprising Alex with the word out of nowhere and breaking eye contact as she returned to her chair, "Let's start from the beginning." Alex was surprised at the quick turn in her thoughts. She was confident and sure as she continued. "Tell me again, everything you can remember since yesterday in that parking lot."

They sat on opposite sides of her desk for more than an hour as Alex recounted the last eighteen hours of his life. He told her as many details as he could remember and provided her with his two syringes and mystery note. She couldn't help but to raise an eyebrow more than once and found it just a bit difficult accepting the story exactly as he told it, but as he began to recount his memory of *being* Louie, something inside her stirred. She wasn't sure what it was, but something about that part of his tale stood out more than any other. As he described the nightclub, she was filled with a strange sense of déjà vu and had him take his time, recalling every little detail. The more he spoke the more it pulled at her, as if he were describing a place that she had been. She sat forward and tried to imagine the place as Alex went through the layout of the bar, the atmosphere, the music.

"Can you remember the name of the place?"

He thought for a moment. "I believe it was Peppino's"

Mercedes looked as if a light bulb had just came on in her head and she excitedly repeated, "Peppino's? Wait a minute." She swiveled her chair and opened the top drawer of a half-size filing cabinet. After thumbing through a dozen or more files, she stopped, pulled one halfway out and silently read, then quickly removed it altogether from the cabinet, closed the drawer and slammed it down onto the desk. "Here we go!"

Mercedes pointed into the file at a news article titled "Blood Bath", and began to read. Alex drew closer and followed along, silently.

"Suspected small time mafia boss, Louie Ventino, was shot and killed yesterday evening while having drinks with friends. Louie and long-time girlfriend, Sheila Rotelli, arrived at the nightclub a little after eight o'clock. The couple was joined by suspected hit man David Winters around 8:45 pm. They had a few drinks and talked for the next hour. According to witnesses, at approximately 9:52 PM a tall blond haired man, later identified as Billy Marcus, AKA Bad Boy Billy, approached Louie's table carrying a modified Colt Python Elite with a six-inch barrel and unloaded two bullets into Louie's back. Billy then shot David Winters and pumped one more slug into Louie's head before running for the door. In the confusion someone managed to shoot Billy before he was able to make his escape. Billy is currently under tight security in the ICU ward of Saint Paul's Medical Center. He's not expected to make it through the night."

Mercedes stopped, looked up, and said, "He died that afternoon."

"I was there!" Alex suddenly came to life. "I was Louie!"

"That doesn't make any sense! This just happened three days ago, and Louie's dead."

Alex shook his head and couldn't believe her statement. "It doesn't make any sense? What are you saying, that the rest of my story does?" Suddenly their roles were reversed and he was the one with the *get real* attitude in his eye.

"Good point," she winced, thought for a minute, and then suggested, "Maybe it would help your memory if we went to Peppino's and had a look around."

"Yeah, I think you're right," Alex said as he shifted his gaze back to the news article. "But isn't it a crime scene? I mean can we get in there?"

Mercedes smiled, scooped up the note and syringes, and grabbed the newspaper, then said with a sneaky grin of confidence, "Oh yeah, we can get in there."

Mercedes locked up the office and they made their way around back to her Porsche.

"Wow! It's even prettier than you pictured it."

"Prettier than *I* pictured it?" Mercedes started the engine and hit the hardtop release.

"Yeah, I mean the image I saw in your head earlier. This car is *way* prettier than you think it is."

"Oh is that right?" Mercedes made a queer face and smiled curiously as she slipped on her sunglasses and drove the Porsche out onto the main drive. The wind rushed through their hair and Alex held on tight as she kept the car at least ten miles over the posted speed limit.

Alex was sure he wasn't the only one Mercedes frightened half to death as they weaved their way in and out of the dense California traffic. Several times he thought he heard horns blaring as they nearly sideswiped an unsuspecting motorist. However, Mercedes kept the Porsche going just a little too fast for him to be sure.

"How far?" He shouted over the wind.

"Not too far, but we have to make a quick stop first."

Mercedes worked the stick shift with one hand and turned the wheel with the other as they accelerated around a corner. She cranked the radio up and made an extra effort to keep her thoughts on the current pop song blaring through the speakers. If Alex wanted to read her mind he would have to work his way, sifting through the lyrics of Uncle Cracker. While singing along with the radio she turned her smiling face toward Alex, lowered her sunglasses and winked. She was beautiful, brilliant and on his side, and for the first time since yesterday, he didn't feel so alone. He laughed, shook his head, and made a careless gesture with his hand as they turned into the parking lot. Mercedes drove the Porsche into a stall and parked next to a plain black van with government plates.

"I'll be right back." She got out of the car, letting it idle with the radio still playing and darted off toward the building before Alex could reply. Reaching down, he lowered the volume and watched as she crossed the blacktop, in heels, and disappeared through a reflective glass door featuring white-stenciled words, which read Federal Bureau of Investigation, Employees only.

Alex puzzled Mercedes' relationship with the FBI and tried to keep his anxiety low. However, a sense of vulnerability steadily crept into his thoughts and began to grow. He had a friend now, or at least the makings of one, and for a while the world hadn't seemed so huge. But now, sitting alone in the Porsche, with the top down and the world looking in, Alex began to feel nervous. What if the people who were looking for him chanced across this area. He would have nowhere to run. He remembered the note warning himself not to go to the authorities for help. He no longer had that note. He had given it along with the syringes to Mercedes, and she had taken everything into that building, the FBI building. Could she possibly be working for the FBI? Maybe she was one of the people who were looking for him. His thoughts began to run wild as his anxiety grew. Perhaps the men who chased him from the homeless shelter saw him go into her office. Maybe, that's why they gave up so quickly. That would explain why she didn't want him reading her mind.

Alex shook his head and blinked as his face turned pale. No, she couldn't be working for them. He had no idea who they were but he knew she couldn't be one of them. It wasn't possible. They were evil and she wasn't—or at least he hoped she wasn't. Just then Alex heard a man's voice coming from behind him in the distance. He turned and looked over the backend of the car. His anxiety escalated and he could hardly believe his eyes as he saw the baldheaded man, who had chased him from the parking lot yesterday, coming his way. The man wasn't alone either. He was walking with a group of men. They were all pretending not to notice Alex, no doubt waiting for just the right moment to pounce.

As they drew closer a dark-colored sedan swiftly entered the parking lot just in front of the Porsche. It was the same sedan his pursuer had jumped into just outside of Mercedes' office a couple of hours ago. Alex was surrounded. It would do no good to hide; they already knew he was there. Mercedes had lulled him into a false sense of security and lured him into this trap. Alex quickly rescanned the area; there was nowhere to run, and the men were closing in, heading directly for him. The sedan pulled up and parked a few stalls away. Alex repositioned himself and crouched, with his shoes on the leather seats as he prepared to leap out of the car. He had no idea which way he would run. All he knew was that he must. Waiting for an opportune moment to flee, he watched as all four doors of the sedan quickly and simultaneously opened. Four solemn-faced men dressed in dark suits got out of the car. To his surprise they didn't even look his way, but rather all walked toward the building. Alex turned and looked back at the group of men approaching the Porsche from behind. He could now hear their thoughts. They were all laughing and discussing last night's football game. He looked closer at the tall baldheaded man and realized that he wasn't the one from the parking lot after all, just a good look-a-like.

With his heart beating fast and little beads of sweat developing around his hairline, Alex shut his eyes and let out a sigh as the look-a-like and his associates passed the Porsche on their way to the building. He shook his head and laughed a sigh of relief. The moment was quickly shattered, however, by an abrupt voice, immediately followed by the opening of the driver's side door.

"Jamiss me?" Mercedes smiled as she sat down and shifted the car into reverse. Her smile quickly faded, however, into a curious frown as she asked, "Why are you standing on my seat?"

"Oh, sorry." Looking like the kid trying to sneak away from Sunday service, Alex sank back down into his seat as the Porsche pulled out onto the street and sped away.

On the way to Peppino's Mercedes pressed the button to replace the top and briefly told Alex how she had always wanted to work for the FBI. She had enrolled in the Special Agents division a year after graduating from college, studied around the clock and passed the entry exam with flying colors. During the sixteen weeks of training, hers were the highest marks at the academy. It wasn't that she was the most talented or even the most intelligent, just the most determined. A few of the male cadets respected and admired her, but most of them resented her for outdoing them. She told Alex how someone had tampered with the results of her last test and made it look as if she had been cheating. She had never cheated on anything in her entire life, but the phony evidence suggested that she had been cheating since the very day she enrolled. Her graduation was put on hold, pending a full investigation, during which time more evidence was found implementing her even further. She fought the allegations all the way to the United States Equal Employment Opportunity Commission. In the process, she used what she had learned from the academy, mixed with her own special magic and uncovered evidence that would prove her innocence. She was able to find specific facts pointing to a cadet in her class who just couldn't handle being *outperformed* by a woman. Also, the evidence strongly suggested that this cadet wasn't working alone, but in fact had help from someone deep within the FBI. After months of investigation and deliberation the day finally came for her to present her evidence. The evidence was strong and would've unquestionably proven her innocence.

However, on her way to the proceedings she received a strange phone call from a man who wouldn't identify himself. He commended her for her persistence and dedication but said he just couldn't allow some spoiled little brat bent on revenge to degrade the Bureau with her hearsay. She told the man on the other end of the line where he could go and that she didn't respond well to *Gestapo* tactics. The man just laughed and told her that the FBI had been very busy lately investigating certain members of her family and found some very interesting and incriminating facts about her father.

Mercedes stepped on the gas and accelerated through a lingering yellow light. "I Knew the evidence was bullshit but... my father is a very influential man. His image is extremely important and the accusations alone would've seriously damaged his career. So, instead of going to the proceedings, like I probably should have, I drove around and racked my brains for an hour or so. Finally, I decided it wasn't worth fighting for. If it were only about me, I would've gone as far as they wanted to take it, but they were willing to bring Daddy into it. Sleazebags!"

The corner of her eye filled with water. "Shit! Shit!" She slapped the palm of her hand on the top of the steering wheel. "I had no idea how far they would go, so I," she wiped at the corner of her eye, "I let it go." Mercedes breathed in deeply and ran the car even faster over the top of a small hill. Alex held on tightly and his stomach dropped as he fully expected the car to go airborne; it didn't.

Still looking straight ahead and still accelerating, Mercedes continued. "Later, Daddy found out what I did and like he always does, became my safety net and bailed me out." She let out a sigh. "See, Daddy never liked the idea of me joining the Bureau, and when this whole thing was finally over he had hoped that I would choose to go into something else—something that wasn't quite so dangerous." She chuckled. "But, I was so damn angry with the FBI that I decided to open up my own private investigating company. I guess some shrink would just say that I was trying to prove something. I don't know." She paused for a moment and shook her head to avoid the truth. "Anyway, typical Daddy, even though he hated the idea, after he seen that I wasn't changing my mind, he funded the whole thing, and Atwater Investigations was born. I'm not that great at marketing," another laugh escaped her, "so I don't get very many clients." She shook her head and narrowed her eyes as if she was intently looking at something beyond the road in front of them, "but Daddy just keeps sending me money. I try to give it back, but he never takes it, the damn fool!" Suddenly, her voice changed and she seemed to be talking more to herself than to Alex. "I wish that just once he'd let me prove that I can take care of myself."

Still holding on for dear life with an iron grip, Alex patiently waited as Mercedes gathered her thoughts.

"Anyway, I found out a little later that the man who had called me that day was none other than John Ramsey, the department head here. So," she raised her eyebrows, "every once in a while, when I need something, I threaten him with the evidence I had dug up about the Bureau." She smiled and said with a devilish grin. "As long as it isn't too terribly much, I usually get what I want."

As the Porsche pulled into the parking lot of Peppino's, Alex couldn't wait to get out and stand on the non-moving, non-accelerating pavement. Walking up to the entrance, Alex was overcome with the strange sensation that he had been here before. He couldn't attach a memory to it and he wasn't totally sure if it was real or if his mind was somehow playing tricks on him. The doors of the nightclub were locked and yellow police tape blocked the entrance.

"Ramsey said he'd have someone meet us here and let us in." Mercedes glanced at her watch as she spoke.

Alex slowly turned and surveyed the area. "I've been here before." He backed away from the building, looking up at the roof. "I remember this. I remember this!" He spoke faster and exhilaration filled his words. "I remember it from the vision or the memory or whatever it was that I had in Ginger's apartment." He paused and thought for a second as his eyes raced and his excitement grew. He almost stuttered as he continued. "I remember floating down off the roof and," he turned around and continued to point, "crossing the street." His eyes narrowed. "I floated into that jewelry store over there!"

Alex walked to the edge of the parking lot, Mercedes followed. "This is the place. Yeah, this is it!" He placed his palms over his temples and for a few seconds looked as if he were trying to keep his head from turning to jelly and dripping away. "I hung around in there for a moment or two then I floated through the back wall. There's an alley on the other side." Suddenly, he became oddly quiet as fear overtook his excitement and he began to realize that his memory of Louie had indeed been true. The thought of how coldly Louie had planned someone else's death sent icy chills into his shoulders and chest. He and Louie had been one and the same and Louie had been a monster. Just as he was wondering what kind of a person he really was Mercedes spoke and interrupted his thought.

"Looks like our locksmith is here."

Alex turned around and blinked himself out of his trance as a dark colored sedan pulled into the parking lot. It looked nearly identical to the one he had seen pull into the FBI parking lot. He lowered his eyebrows and curiously asked, "Is there some kind of mandatory rule which states that all FBI agents must drive the same type of dull, dark colored car?"

"Yeah, I think there is," Mercedes said convincingly and then smiled. "That's one of the good points about not being able to join the Bureau," A devilish grin flashed through her eyes, "I like my car."

They walked back to the entrance where a tall gray-haired man, wearing a dark gray suit waited holding scissors and a set of keys. He snipped the yellow tape and inserted the key into the lock. He turned the key with his right hand, but securely held the door closed with his left. Mercedes pushed forward expecting the door to open. It did not. The FBI agent stood still, expressionless as she bounced off it.

"Number one." Still holding the handle with a firm left hand and raising his right index finger just below her nose, he spoke in a deep, slow, authoritative voice. "Don't touch anything. Number two: you were never here. Number three: if anyone unexpectedly shows up while we're inside, I will deny letting you in and say I just found you snooping around, then I'll take you in for questioning and when we finally decide you don't know anything about the case, the FBI will turn you over to the police who will then book you for unlawful entry and trespassing." He paused and calmly entered into a brief staring contest with Mercedes.

After a few moments of nerve-shattering silence Mercedes' anger boiled and she raised a hand to her forehead, clicked her heels together and sarcastically said, "Yes sir, commander!"

Unmoved by her childishness, he continued his authoritative glare for a few more seconds, letting there be no doubt who was in charge, then pressed down on the thumb release and slowly pushed the door open.

Mercedes had just shoved her way past Mr. God-wannabe and crossed the threshold in front of him when he spoke again. "You got twenty minutes."

She stopped and quickly did an about-face, "Bullshit!"

Amused by her cute bout of aggression, he raised an eyebrow and almost smiled, but said nothing.

"We got an hour!"

"Not according to what I was told."

"Well then you were told wrong!"

A contemptible mockery of compassion flashed through his eyes, as he coolly repeated, dragging out each word, "You've got twenty minutes." His eyes stayed with hers for a half a second longer, then shifted down toward his wristwatch as he coldly said, "nineteen."

Mercedes' stare lingered for a second or two more, then realizing she was losing time, she silently shook her head, turned back around and continued into the darkness. Alex followed the FBI man, being sure not to get too close, although he could read his mind and ascertain there was no *immediate* threat, he still didn't know if this man was friend or foe. He tried to peer into the man's head but all he was able to find out was this guy, Robert, didn't want to be here and felt it was a waste of his time and talent. He was also able to see that even though Robert had never met Mercedes, he fully believed her to be a spoiled little rich girl who had attempted to cheat her way into the FBI. He also believed she had a grudge against the Bureau for exposing her as the dishonest little cheat she was.

They entered the building at 3:22 pm. The bright yellow-orange stream of sunlight that followed them in and the pink neon sign hanging on a distant wall were the only lights in the club. Robert rotated the end of a pen-sized flashlight as Mercedes unsuccessfully felt around for a light switch. After a moment or two Mercedes took the lead as they made their way through the darkness, passing a shadowy set of booths on the right and what was probably a set of restrooms on the left.

"Alex, anything look familiar?" Mercedes asked, but there was no answer. She stopped, turned around and said louder, "Alex." Robert was behind her and she couldn't see past his handy dandy, standard issue, blinding pocket light. "Alex," she said one more time in a voice almost loud enough to be a yell. Just then the lights came on.

"Over here." Alex's voice came from behind her, further inside the club. Puzzled, Mercedes turned back around and kept walking. They entered an open area, skillfully decorated in a jazz theme from the 1940s. It was about half the size of a high school gymnasium and was divided into several smaller sections. There was a fairly large, varnished, wooden dance floor, a pool area featuring a half a dozen fairly expensive red felt tables. There was an area marked off for darts, with ten or more dartboards, a stage with built-in hookups for various musical instruments. In the center of the room was a large circular, high-polished, oak, liquor bar surrounded by stainless steel barstools with black leather seats. Alex sat at the bar, holding and intently studying a napkin.

Mercedes' heels and Robert's dress shoes tapped echoes through the edifice as they walked across the open dance floor and approached Alex from the left. "I didn't see you pass me," Mercedes said curiously.

"I didn't pass you," Alex replied while still staring at the napkin, "I took a shortcut."

Mercedes walked up to the stool next to his as Commander Dickhead lagged behind. "So then you're starting to remember things?"

Alex put the napkin down and then oddly stared up at the different types of glasses hanging overhead. The lights of the empty nightclub shimmered off the glasses as if they were crystal. Alex was silent for a few seconds, all but mesmerized by the tiny droplets of light. He slowly moved his head and watched the bright multi-colored beads change position and dance around the glasses' edges.

Mercedes glanced curiously at Robert, who stood at a distance, obviously unimpressed by Alex's bizarre change of state. Then suddenly, just as she was turning back to look at him, Alex spoke. It was loud, quick, and startling, and Mercedes flinched as he all but shouted the name Ernesto.

She stepped backward for a moment, not sure what was happening. "Alex, you okay? What's going on?" she asked cautiously while holding her chest and waiting for her heart rate to come back down to normal.

Alex didn't respond and for a minute or so seemed oblivious to anything else in the room besides the iridescent glasses. His eyelids gradually lowered until they were only half open and his breathing became shallow and rhythmic as his focus on the glasses intensified. He spoke slower and softer now, in a slightly deeper tone, "Ernesto." His lips stayed parted slightly and his eyes continued to gloss.

Robert, still at a distance, watched with increasing curiosity as Alex approached catatonia.

"What's going on? What are you doing?" Mercedes asked as she cautiously took the stool next to his.

It seemed as if either her question or perhaps just her voice itself broke the spell. He still focused on the glasses above, but his posture definitely began to change. Confidence weaved its way through his entire body as he sat up straighter and his shoulders widened. His countenance changed as well and a cold-hearted smile slowly took control of his face. Suddenly, he appeared to be chewing on something, perhaps gum. His voice became even deeper and now carried a trace of a New York accent. "I'm trying to relax here, lady." He turned and looked boldly into Mercedes' eyes, then asked with a self-assured grin. "You're new here, aren't you?"

Although it was still Alex sitting on the stool beside her, his expression, posture, and facial muscles had changed so dramatically that if she had not been here to see it happen she might have mistaken him for someone else.

"Alex, it's me, Mercedes." She said uneasily.

"I'm sorry, Baby." He turned to face her, studied her eyes and face carefully, and then cocked his head as he said, "You must have me mistaken for someone else." His grin extended into a boyish smile as his face brightened. "My name is Billy." He popped his gum. "Can I buy you a drink?"

Mercedes' eyes widened and she found herself unable to speak. She swallowed hard and slowly withdrew her hands from the bar as she remembered the newspaper photo of Billy Marcus. Incredibly Alex had somehow transformed himself into a dead man. It wasn't that he was just acting differently—sure that was part of it—but he actually looked like Billy Marcus.

Alex turned away from Mercedes and spoke to an unseen person behind the bar. "Hey, Ernesto!" He motioned with his hand for someone to come over. "Ernesto, I wanna buy the young lady a drink." Alex turned back to Mercedes with a slight rhythm in his body as if he were listening to a smooth jazz tune that only he could hear. "What do ya want, Sweetie?" Mercedes could almost hear the gum popping as Alex chewed.

"Billy?" Her voice crackled as she asked curiously. "Billy Marcus?"

"Yeah that's right, Sweetie. See Ernesto, *everybody* knows me." Mercedes felt her stomach drop as a silky blanket of fear gently wrapped her body. She had no idea what was happening. Billy Marcus was dead. Bad Boy Billy was dead. Nevertheless, she found herself afraid of Alex. "C'mon, Sugar, what do you want? The man's waiting." Alex looked at the ghost behind the bar.

"Um... I uh... I gotta go to the little ladies' room. I'll be right back." Keeping her eyes on Alex, Mercedes slid from the barstool and slowly made her way back next to her good pal Robert, who was mildly curious and slightly confused.

"Look lady, I don't know what you and your freaky boyfriend want with this place, but whatever it is you better get crack'n. Time is ticking."

"Shhh!" She gestured, and for the next few minutes they watched Alex sitting alone at an empty bar in a deserted nightclub talking to an imaginary bartender and having an imaginary drink. He stayed to himself and kept checking what might have been a pocket watch as if he didn't want to be late for an important meeting. Mercedes and Robert were standing in front of a booth almost directly behind him.

"Eight minutes," Robert said in a bored, intentionally loud voice.

"Shhh!" Mercedes repeated.

Although Robert made no attempt to quiet his voice when he spoke, Alex seemed not to respond. It was as if he was no longer a part of the *here and now* but rather belonged to an invisible world deep within the recesses of his mind. Robert shook his head and sat down with a half-grin, as he watched Alex play *pretend*. Then suddenly, Alex turned and coldly looked over his shoulder, directly at Robert and seemed to maliciously peer deep into his eyes. The act was so unforeseen and the look so malevolent that Robert couldn't help but to feel a cold chill run down his spine.

Mercedes watched as Alex stood up, off his stool and started to leave. Then, as if he had forgotten something from the bar, he turned around, but instead of walking back over to his seat, he moved toward Mercedes and Robert. Mercedes backed away as Alex approached. Robert, now slightly more intrigued, sat motionless and watched as Alex methodically drew near, reached underneath an invisible coat, and pulled out an invisible handgun. Although Alex gripped only the air and Robert was armed with a real live standard issue hand pistol, he still couldn't shake the eerie feeling that hovered just at the nape of his neck. Alex glared at Robert with evil eyes—cold and committed—the eyes of a man who had no soul.

Robert had been with the FBI for many years and had been involved in countless altercations with extremely dangerous men, however he had never seen someone with eyes as malevolent as these. Alex came closer and pointed his imaginary gun straight out, aiming above Robert's head, as if his target wasn't Robert, but something else, something unseen. Then, with a blank stare, Alex squeezed an imaginary trigger twice. Twice he flinched as if he was experiencing the kick of a real live gun. Although there was no reason to believe that this invisible gun would make any noise, Robert was almost shocked when it didn't. Then, Alex drew closer still and from less than two feet away he took aim again, this time directly at Robert's face, dead center between his eyes.

Pretending not to be afraid, Robert casually reached under his *real* coat and gripped his *real* gun as a small trickle of sweat rolled down the right side of his face. Alex fired again. Like before, there was still no sound, no loud boom and Alex wasn't being dangerously aggressive, however, Robert still blinked and gasped as the imaginary bullet left the imaginary gun in a trajectory straight for the bridge of his nose. Then, without missing a beat Alex calmly took aim at the empty tabletop and fired one more shot.

Basking in the murderer's spotlight, Alex looked around with a grin of confidence and an air of invincibility, then turned and ran through a crowded room, toward the door. Halfway there, however, he fell to his knees. It was as if an unseen, major-league baseball player had mistaken his back for the home run baseball. Alex's head jerked back, then his knees gave in and his face landed, nose first with a real live crack on the hard wooden floor. Alex lay lifeless and didn't move, neither did Mercedes or Robert.

After a moment Mercedes stepped forward and cautiously approached Alex while Robert rose from the *death booth*, finally removed his gun from its holster and followed behind. He was careful not to get too close to the psycho on the floor.

"What the Hell just happened?"

"I'm not sure," Mercedes said slowly as she moved in and knelt beside him. "Come on help me get him to my car."

Robert, still holding his gun and keeping his distance, scrunched half of his face, letting Mercedes know she was somewhat out of her mind.

"Come on, whatever it was, it's over now. Besides, I'm pretty sure he's all out of make-believe bullets, and you just might earn your Eagle Scout patch."

Robert carefully walked up, then reluctantly put away his gun and grabbed Alex's left shoulder. Mercedes took his right, and together they dragged a lifeless Alex through an empty building.

CHAPTER TEN

"Do you like fried okra?"

Nick graciously smiled but said nothing as the airplane's landing gear connected with the runway. He didn't get very much time during his flight to think about his arrival in Los Angeles. His travel itinerary took him from the Yeager Airport in Charleston, West Virginia to O'Hara's International Airport in Chicago where he had just enough time to catch the connecting flight to Los Angeles.

When he boarded the plane in Charleston his seating arrangement found him beside Gertrude, an older lady, who was on her way home after visiting her grandson. Nick is one of those special individuals in life who, even without trying, always seems to emit a certain type of confidence. Regardless of the situation or frame of mind life finds him in, Nick is always naturally secure with himself and his surroundings. As with many people who have had the opportunity to meet him, Gertrude immediately took a liking and before long he had learned what must have been close to her entire life story. By the time they landed in Chicago he knew where she was born, all about her first and second husbands, all about her children and grandchildren. But most importantly he learned how useless and unimportant she had begun to feel lately. During the last ten years or so all of her family members had moved away and she now found herself living alone. No one hardly called any more and when they did it was usually because they needed something, and that something was almost always money.

Her grandson had invited her out to West Virginia for a week. But after she was there he seemed to have little time for her and soon she felt lonely and unwanted. Although he wasn't sure why, Nick had always had a soft spot for the underdogs of the world, the weaker, simpler people, who for whatever reason found themselves at a disadvantage in life. More often than not he found himself in difficult situations brought about by an inability to walk away from someone in trouble. Even when he had a reputation for being the *Iceman* he still could not turn his back on someone in need. Perhaps it was an unconscious attempt to redeem himself for not being there to save his parents when they died.

They were givers—givers who, themselves, started with nothing—less than nothing. Through sheer will and hard work they were able to create a small business and purchase an average home. They gave Nick everything they never had. They were caring and giving people who spent very little money on themselves. Through blood, sweat, and tears they managed to save up and send Nick to law school. And just when it looked as if life might start rewarding them for all of their hard work, they were viciously and brutally murdered.

No Dad you don't get back what you put in. You get whatever crap life decides to toss your way. You get what others *don't* want. You get whatever you can take, and whoever isn't fast enough, strong enough, smart enough or talented enough gets the leftovers. They get taken advantage of. They get pushed around. They get screwed! They definitely do *not* get back what they put in!

Whatever the reason, Nick had a soft spot. He especially cared for the elderly and the very young. They were often the most vulnerable prey for the vultures of the world. When Gertrude thanked him for being so kind and friendly and then asked if they could sit together on the flight to California, he knew he shouldn't, but even though he tried, he just couldn't say no. From Chicago to LA he was sure he learned more history than he had learned all through school. Halfway through the flight he realized what a terrible mistake it was to have said yes. He could almost kick himself for being so softhearted at times.

Nick was the sort of man who could tackle almost any challenge. If Gertrude had been a six-hundred-pound gorilla with an attitude there wouldn't have been a problem. He could handle a six-hundred-pound gorilla. He had smiled and patiently listened to Gertrude's life story nearly the entire flight. Every now and then he tried politely to let her know that he had some very important studying to do before they landed. However, the words never quite came out right and when they did she seemed to become so hurt and lonely that before long Nick found himself inviting her to tell more about herself.

Nick could almost feel freedom when the captain announced their final descent.

Although the plane shimmied and bounced from touchdown Gertrude continued without interruption. "My grandson sure loves fried okra, especially with my homemade recipe. Would you like my homemade recipe?" She smiled wide and made a mmm, mmm sound.

Nick's spirits rose as the plane slowed down and taxied on its way to the LAX terminal.

"No thank you," he smiled.

Gertrude frowned sadly, as if Nick was rejecting her along with the recipe.

Nick politely smiled and tried looking past her, out the window to estimate how far they were from the terminal.

She slowly tilted her head as her eyes drooped, like a lost puppy dog.

Nick could see her sadness out of the corner of his eye. Uncomfortably, he looked at her, bobbed his head, in some sort of an awkward, *I'm okay-you're okay* motion and respectfully smiled again.

She tilted her head back the other way and looked as if she might just cry, but said nothing.

Nick's eyes shifted back to the window and then to the central aisle in the airplane, away from the abandoned old grandmother. She sighed a sigh of loneliness. The plane slowed. She sighed louder. Nick wondered if the captain had lost his way to the terminal. She shifted in her seat and softly moaned. Finally, overwhelmed with guilt, Nick uncontrollably turned and blurted out, "I'd love to have your recipe." Strangely, a smile found its way to both of their faces as the plane connected with the terminal. She reached into an oversized purse and found a pen. The *unfasten your seatbelt* sign came on and everyone stood up—everyone that is except Gertrude and her newly found family member.

"Now just let me find some paper." She searched through her bag as the passengers began to exit the plane. "I know I have some paper in here somewhere."

Nick smiled courteously and nodded his head as the last group of people shuffled on past.

"Ah! Here we go." She pulled out a quarter size spiral notepad, bound at the top, flipped it open and with an unsteady hand began to write. After writing 'Grandma's fried okra' at the top she stopped, looked up at the overhead baggage compartment, and whispered to herself. "Now let's see what was the..." Unconsciously, the end of the pen found its way to her thin, pink lips as she thought. Before long the flight attendant came by, checking the seats for forgotten luggage and personal items.

"We've landed sir," she smiled, "you can exit now."

Nick stood up with a smile and genuine warmth for the flight attendant.

"Now young lady, Nicky here wants me to write down my fried okra *secret* recipe for him. Do you really want him to miss out on something like that?"

Nick's smile faded and he sank back down, blank-faced as the flight attendant said, "Well the plane isn't scheduled to leave for another forty minutes. As long as you don't take too long, I guess it'll be all right."

"Great! Now let's see... where was I? Oh yeah!"

Four pages and fifteen minutes later Nick hurriedly exited the plane, claimed his luggage, and made his way to the car rentals where a pre-ordered Ford Mustang awaited. It had been thoughtfully picked out and didn't come cheap. It was a gray, two-door, fully loaded, GT Premium convertible. This wasn't Nick's first trip to a distant place searching for answers to his nightmares. In the past he had found one of the most important things to have in a new town was a reliable car. He needed something strong and fast, that he could maneuver quickly and easily, yet inconspicuous enough so it wouldn't be readily noticed or remembered.

After putting the two large luggage bags into the trunk of the car, Nick got in and set his laptop case on the leather seat beside him, then started the engine and flipped on the air conditioner. The radio came on, playing a depressing jazz tune. Nick quickly flipped through the stations and found KLOS Classic Rock.

The setting sun cast an amber glow over the lot of shiny, multicolored, metallic cars. He retrieved his sunglasses from the laptop case, slid them over his eyes, and then breathed in slowly and deeply. For more than a minute, he just sat there, studying the surroundings and taking it all in.

Nick had been here before, maybe not California, but *here* just the same. On countless occasions he had journeyed to distant lands hoping to find something that would end his sleepless nights, only to return home, seemingly more lost than when he had left. This time something was different. He couldn't exactly put a finger on it, but something was definitely different. He sat there, on the gray leather seat, with the *new car* smell filling his nose. The stereo was playing '*Live and Let Die*' by Guns-N-Roses as monster jumbo jets roared overhead. Somehow, in some way, he knew he would find the answers that he was so desperately searching for here.

Then, suddenly his eyes tightened slightly as if a switch of determination had clicked on in his head. Consumed with a renewed sense of faith he broke the silence by saying, "Let's do it," and shifted into reverse. The tires all but squealed as they gripped the blacktop and pulled the car out of the lot, straight for the Los Angeles Police Department. The drive took less time than he thought and the traffic wasn't half as bad as he imagined LA traffic should be.

He pulled into the bustling station right at 9:00 pm. The department was large and it took a little over a half an hour for him to navigate his way through all of the *not* so helpful administrative personnel. Before long he found himself standing in an area off limits to the general public, on the second floor, in front of an empty desk. A door waited just beyond the desk with opaque glass and etched lettering that read J. E. Garvey, Homicide. Although there were voices coming from the other side of the door, the room in which Nick now stood was empty. He paused, staring at the etched lettering for a moment and organized his thoughts.

He needed Garvey's help and had little to give in return. As he stood there, getting ready to enter, his memory played back several occasions in which he wished he had made a better first impression. He remembered being escorted out of the Oklahoma Police Department, just nine months after Allie died. He had participated in a heated yelling match with a young female officer who refused to let him through to the homicide division.

There was also the time he was asked to leave the station in Philadelphia under similar circumstances. Then, there was Detective Reynolds, of the Miami Police Department, who boldly laughed in his face after he told him how he thought the detective's current case might in some way be connected to what happened with Allie.

And he'd never forget being telephoned by the FBI last year. He was told, in no uncertain terms, to stay out of official police business. That was the result of some unwanted investigating he did in Baton Rouge. That case, like all the rest, turned out to hold absolutely no answers for him. They all ended up being nothing more than very expensive wild goose chases. Wild goose chases, they were, but in vain, they were not. In every situation Nick learned something new that made him a little better the next time around. He learned little tricks like being able to navigate his way around a police station after hours without being thrown out. To say that he didn't like cops much would be an understatement, and he had learned enough to get the answers he needed without the help of those already working on the case, but it just made things a lot easier if he had it.

He learned several different methods the police used to get inside the mind of a serial killer in order to catch one. He also learned how critical it was to make a good first impression. It was crucial not to come across like some wacko when meeting a new detective. Nick looked at his watch: 9:41. It was late. He pondered the possibility of checking into a motel and returning in the morning, but quickly dismissed it. He wanted to get a motel as close as possible to the serial killer's current activity and he would have to find out where that activity was before he could get the motel. Nick walked around the desk and quietly reached out for the doorknob.

"May I help you?" A deep male voice came from behind. Nick turned around as a blue uniformed officer approached. Nick was slightly startled, but didn't show it. Keeping his distance, the officer hovered his right hand over the handle of his gun. "I haven't seen you before. What are you doing up here?"

"I'm looking for Detective Steve Garvey. Is he in there?" Nick asked confidently as he innocently pointed toward the door.

"Do you know Detective Garvey?"

"Um… No, I don't. I wanted to talk to him about the case he's working on."

"Do you work for the department?" The officer looked at him suspiciously.

Reluctantly, Nick again said, "No." He could feel the situation quickly turning sour.

"How did you get up here?"

"I don't know. I was just looking for Detective Garvey in homicide and I ended up here." Keeping his hands out where the officer could see them at all times, Nick asked, "Is there a problem?"

The officer calmly drew his gun and radioed in an unidentified individual in homicide, then politely said, "Sir, please step away from the door and put your hands on your head."

Nick knew enough about the police not to argue and besides, arguing wouldn't do anything to help his situation look any better. Reluctantly, he slowly moved away from the door and followed the officer's orders. "I'm sorry officer, I was just trying to get to Detective Garvey. Did I do something wrong?" Nick played stupid.

The officer cautiously moved in, locked one handcuff over Nick's right wrist, and brought both hands down behind his back. Nick shook his head—so much for a good first impression.

The officer snapped the second cuff over the other wrist as the door to Detective Garvey's office swung open. A man in a heavy light brown corduroy coat entered the room. He was in his late fifties and his light blond hair was short, thin, and stringy. He was wearing glasses, holding a piece of paper, and reminded Nick of an older version of the character Joe Friday from the television series Dragnet. He was carrying on a conversation with a short, heavyset bald man in a white shirt and skinny black tie. They must have been unaware of anything happening in the outer office, as their conversation abruptly halted when they saw Nick in cuffs and the officer re-holstering his gun.

"What's going on?" asked the man in the corduroy coat.

"I just found this man here getting ready to enter your office."

"Detective Garvey?" Nick asked.

"Yes?" Replied the man in the corduroy coat.

"I know this looks bad, but I just wanted to talk to you about the case you're working on."

Detective Garvey squinted curiously. "Do I know you?"

"I don't think so. I'm new in town, just arrived."

"That's funny you look awfully familiar." Garvey removed his glasses, came closer and studied Nick's face. "I don't know where, but I'm sure we've met before. You say you just arrive here, in Los Angeles? From where?"

"West Virginia"

Garvey tilted his head. "Hum?" He shook it. "No... No, I've never been to West Virginia. First time to LA?"

"Yeah." Nick nodded.

"Hum?" Garvey shook his head again. "Damn curious!" He replaced his glasses on his head and frowned, "What do you know about the case?" Before Nick could answer, Garvey continued with apprehension, "You're not some crackpot who can see the future, are you?"

"No sir, it's nothing like that."

"Hum? Well, I don't suppose you're the killer, come to turn yourself in?"

"No sir."

"Well then, do you have some critical piece of evidence that I need to know tonight, like who the next victim is or when the next murder will take place?"

"No."

"I see. Well, come back tomorrow, during normal business hours. I'll see you then." He headed for the door with his pudgy little companion following.

Nick wasn't about to make things any worse than they already were. "Okay, yeah, good, tomorrow..." he said as Garvey was walking away. "What time?"

Garvey stopped at the entrance to the hall, turned around, and thought for a second. Nick adjusted his arms to relieve some pressure from his left wrist bone.

Garvey took a deep breath through his nose, pushed up his chin, and nodded assertively, "Why don't you drop by around eight-thirty."

Nick nodded, "Eight-thirty, thanks."

Garvey stood there for a second longer, silently studying Nick's face again, then repeated, "curious," before he turned and left. After being asked a few questions and having his driver's license ran through the system, Nick was given a warning and then released.

It was nearly midnight by the time he found a motel and checked in. He didn't bother unpacking. He was sure he would be out in the morning. He carried in only one suitcase containing everything he'd need for tonight and tomorrow. Even though it was late and he had a big day ahead of him, he knew he wouldn't be able to sleep and remembered seeing a pool hall about a half a block away.

The night was cool, but not too chilly. He threw on his black leather coat and dropped his gun down the inside pocket. Because the night was clear and the club wasn't far, he decided to walk. It would do him good and besides, if he took the Mustang he would have to go light on the booze, or risk driving under the influence. And after the day he had he definitely didn't need a drink restriction. He had already made a bad first impression with Detective Garvey and he had no intention of making it worse by being stopped for a DWI.

Ten minutes later he walked into the tavern wearing his light brown cowboy boots, dark blue jeans and an unzipped black leather jacket with a black button up shirt underneath. The place was small with a wide, unvarnished, wood-planked floor. Three aged pool tables sat near the rear and a beaten up antique jukebox stood over in the corner, filling the room with *Thunder Rolls* by Garth Brooks. Business was slow. Two guys were drinking bottled beer and shooting a game on the far table while an elderly man sat at the bar, nursing a glass mug. The bartender would have made a lumberjack look small, with broad shoulders and bulky arms. His shaved head was waxed clean and his goatee, although presentable, was slightly in need of a trim.

He wore a tight fitting white t-shirt over his large chest, and a pack of cigarettes had been rolled up in his sleeve, creating a square bulge on his left shoulder. The old man, his only customer at the bar, wore tennis shoes, faded jeans and a flannel shirt. He looked as if he had been here too long, drinking for days. His movements were sudden and wobbly, suggesting that he just might fall from his stool at any moment. Nick walked up to the bar and ordered a tall mug of Miller Genuine Draft.

Thunder rolls and the lighting strikes

This was Nick's kind of place. After grabbing a stool, he introduced himself to the old man and bartender. It's been one Hell of a day he thought as he brought the beer up to his lips. The bartender looked at the old man as Nick passed the halfway point without coming up for air. After Nick downed the entire glass with his fist drink the old man insisted on buying his next one.

"Anybody who can drink beer like that is a friend of mine," he slurred with a smile.

"Thanks." Nick didn't argue.

"So, young man," the old guy continued to slur his words, "you're not from around here, are ya?"

Surprised, Nick said, "No, how did you know that?"

The old man took a sip of his beer. "Your accent, silly." He swayed, and began to fall off his seat, but kept talking. "I'll guess Oklahoma, or Texas."

"Nah, I'd say North Carolina." The bartender chimed in with a surprisingly deep voice, which went along perfectly with his large build. He handed Nick a new mug.

Shocked at how much his accent must have changed in the few years he lived in West Virginia he asked, "You can hear an accent in my voice?"

The bartender laughed, as did the old man, who somehow defied the laws of physics better than the leaning tower of Pisa. "So where ya from?"

"Well, I've spent the last few years in West Virginia. But I was born in Oregon."

"What brings you to LA?" the bartender asked.

Nick stopped and thought for a second. He looked at the old man, who seemed to be paying a considerable amount of attention in light of the fact his eyes were half shut and glossy. The bartender stood behind the counter smoking a cigarette and running a dishcloth in a circular motion on the bar as he listened.

"Just thought I'd soak up some of the California sunshine." Nick smiled and held up his mug in salute then took a swig.

The bartender took a drag on his cigarette, turned his head and exhaled smoke from two giant lungs, and then rather confidently said. "Nah, I don't buy it."

Nick bunched up his eyebrows in a curious fashion then took another swig, but said nothing.

"You're a man on a mission." Nick's look of curiousness increased. "You're after something, aren't ya?" The bartender smiled, raised his eyebrows, and took another hit of his cigarette.

"What makes you say that?" Nick asked, now intrigued at how perceptive the bartender seemed to be. The old man snored then jerked and began moving his mouth as if he were remembering the taste of something he ate. With eyes half open he looked up at his nearly empty glass.

"Hey Roger, I think I need some more beer or something."

"I've seen your types before. Guys like you are hard to mistake. It's in your eyes. It's in your walk. Hell, it's even in the way you drink your beer. What is it—revenge? An old girlfriend? An ex-business partner?" The bartender gave Ned a refill as he spoke. "Whatever it is, it's all over you like white on rice."

Nick took another drink. "I'm that easy to read am I?" The music stopped and the bar became quite.

"Well, let's just say..." The bartender rinsed a glass as he spoke. "If you had it written right across your forehead in big red letters, it wouldn't be any clearer."

Nick was beginning to feel like an open book.

Crack! One of the two men playing pool broke a rack just as 'We Are the Champions' by Queen, came on the jukebox.

Someone shouted, "Yes!"

Nick, the bartender and even Ned turned to look as the man from the table continued, "Eight ball on the break!"

"This place get any busier?" Nick used the distraction to change the subject.

The bartender nodded. "On the weekends the place is wall to wall."

Nick took another swig of his beer.

"Did ya hear the news?" Ned slurred.

Nick finished his swallow and looked at Ned as the bartender went to serve the three gangster looking gentlemen who just entered the bar and approached the counter. Two were tall and slinky and wore hairnets. The third was shorter and muscular and wore a dark brown fedora. They were all dressed in dark baggy clothes and looked sorely out of place.

"There's a headhunter loose on the streets of Los Angles." Ned's eyes widened as he drug out the word loose.

"Really?" Nick looked intrigued.

"Yep! I wouldn't kid ya 'bout a thing like that." Ned turned his head all the way to the left and then all the way to the right, then took another drink.

"What do you know about this headhunter?"

"Some freak." Ned sprayed as he spoke. "I don't know. Some whacked-out serial killer."

The bartender finished serving shots to his new customers and returned. "You talkin' about the headhunter?"

"Ned was just telling me."

"You mean you haven't heard?" The intuitive bartender raised a skeptical eyebrow.

"I heard something. What's the deal?"

The bartender shrugged his shoulders. "Some twisted maniac serial killer who gets off on collecting the heads of his victims." He took another drag, then chuckled. "Only in LA."

One of the hoodlums went over to the jukebox.

"They found another body this evening."

Nick's ears perked up, and like white on rice, his interest was all too obvious. "Really?"

The three hoodlums slowly made their way around Nick and Ned, paying extra close attention as they passed, then found a seat with a good view of the pool game.

"Those guys look like trouble," the bartender said and made no secrete about watching them sit down. A staring contest nearly ensued between the one in the fedora and the bartender. But at the last moment the antagonizing thug lifted his chin, cracked a grin and turned to look at the game. Nick had hung around their types long enough to know something was up. These guys weren't here to soak up the country atmosphere or to listen to redneck music. Hopefully it was nothing more than a meeting spot-a place to do a quick drug deal or something similar. Yeah right! This wasn't a drug deal. These guys were sending up smoke screens. They weren't really interested in the game, they were scoping the joint out: a quiet night, no one around, easy cash. Nick became acutely aware of the weight in his coat pocket as the bartender took another puff.

"You said they found another body?"

The bartender looked back at Nick and continued. "Yeah, but this one was different from the others." Nick listened. "It was a girl. She was found stuffed in a bag at the bottom of a dumpster, in West Covina, a little after five today." The bartender made a sour face and seemed reluctant to continue. "Apparently she was mutilated and then dissected."

"What?" Nick set his mug on the counter.

"Sick huh?"

Nick said nothing.

"Yeah! She was chopped into little tiny pieces and slit from here to here." He ran his finger along his torso, from the top of his jeans to just below his chin. "And get this. They think she was alive the whole time."

Nick's face froze and his interest grew. "Alive? How?"

"They found some weird drug in her system. They think it might have been able to keep her alive while she was taken apart."

Nick felt a chill run through his spine and for a moment all but forgot about the three new guests in the bar. "What was the name of the drug? Do you know?"

"Nah. They said the name on the news tonight but I don't remember it. It was some kind of new experimental drug. I believe they said it was fairly expensive."

Nick thought a minute and rattled off some names of different drugs used in preserving tissue and stimulating the nervous system. The bartender wasn't sure but didn't think any of them were right.

"Wait a minute!" The bartender lightly slammed his dishrag down on the counter. "You're after the reward money aren't ya?"

"Reward money?"

"Yeah!"

"Yep! That's it, he's after the reward," Ned said while still defying gravity as he rocked.

"There's a reward?"

"Yeah, one of the victim's families put up a hundred thousand dollar reward for information that leads to the capture of whatever freak is doing this."

"Wow!" Nick sipped his beer.

"And now the FBI, The LAPD and several other surrounding police departments have upped the ante by offering a reward of their own. At last count, I think it was up to a half a million dollars or more."

"Tell me more about this girl. Where exactly did they find her?"

"You *are* after the reward, aren't you?"

Nick smiled, shook his head, and assertively said "No! I'm not!"

The bartender laughed. "Sure! That's why you're so intrigued about all this, because you're *not* after the reward."

'We are the Champions' ended as the two pool players were exiting the bar. The bartender waved and said goodnight. The song Cop Killer, by A.N.I.M.A.L., pounded its way through the bar's speaker, which amplified the presence of the out of place gangsters, who were now shooting a game of their own and reacting to the beat of the music.

As Nick was finishing his second glass of beer, the bartender set a fresh mug in front of him and lit up a new cigarette. "On the house Nick."

"Thanks. So tell me more about this girl."

"Not much else to tell. They haven't identified her yet and as usual there were no witnesses."

"West Covina?"

"Yeah! Damn! Good luck! I salute you! Hell, I'll throw in a reward of my own. If you do actually get the bastard all your future drinks here are free. How 'bout that?"

"Thanks." Nick smiled.

"Hey Dick breath!" Mr. Fedora aggressively stood at the bar, four stools to the left of Nick and held a small gun on the bartender.

"Throw me the keys to the bar!"

"What?" the bartender looked lost.

"Throw me the mother-fuckin' keys to the front door—now!" The lout raised his voice.

The bartender reached into the front pocket of his jeans. The thug gripped his gun with both hands and shifted his weight forward. The bartender withdrew a set of keys and tossed them over. The thug caught and re-tossed them to one of the other punks who was standing ready at the entrance. He snatched the keys out of the air and locked the front door.

With a confident grin Mr. Fedora continued, "Now, open the register."

The bartender despairingly shook his head and kept his hands out in front of him, being careful not to make any sudden moves, and slowly made his way over to the till.

Nick laughed, not all at once. He tried to suppress it at first. Then he gave in to a little grin and before long he was engaging in an all out guffaw that nearly threw him from his barstool. Unfortunately, laughing wasn't the best thing to do at the moment and Nick felt an intense blow to his ribcage, which completely knocked the wind out of him.

"Ain't so funny no mo', is it mudda fucka?" From the floor, Nick looked up at the menacing punk standing above and even though he was temporarily denied of breath his laugh continued. The thug stood over him holding a butterfly switchblade. "Shut the fuck up, mudda fucka." The thug pulled his foot back and threatened Nick's ribs again. Forcing his laugh to subside, Nick held his left hand up in surrender as his other hand held his aching side.

Ned took another drink as the bartender opened the till.

"Now back away!" Mr. Fedora commanded.

As the bartender moved away from the register the thug from the door leaped over the bar in one smooth motion and started removing the cash from the drawer.

The punk with the knife commanded Nick to stand up while Mr. Fedora had the bartender come out from behind the bar. While Nick was getting on his feet and the bartender was shuffling past the counter, Ned sat silently watching everything and calmly finished his beer. Nick stood up holding onto his ribs with the trace of a grin still on his face.

Mr. Fedora commanded everyone away from the bar and over to the far wall.

Ned wobbled off his stool and spoke to Mr. Fedora. "Can I have another beer, please?"

"Fuck you!"

The three men moved over to the wall as the last of the cash was removed from the drawer. Nick's hand secretly made its way from his wounded ribs to his inside coat pocket and even while he fought it, his grin grew. The cash collector flew back over the counter as Nick secretly gripped the handle of his gun.

"What is so funny that you just can't stop laughing?" Mr. Fedora asked.

Uncontrollably, a small chuckle escaped Nick's lips.

"This..." He laughed again, "This is a..." His laugh overtook him once more. Mr. Fedora, stone-faced, stood patiently waiting for Nick to stop laughing and come back down to reality. After a few more moments of laughter, Nick regained control of himself and started over. "This," he looked around with an obvious expression, "is a redneck bar!" With that the song 'Cop Killer' ended and the bar was silent for a moment. Then suddenly, Nick broke the silence with another bellow of laughter. Since laughter is contiguous and Ned, generally, a happy-go-lucky kind of guy was feeling pretty good already, he was easily swept up into Nick's chuckle. Feeding off each other, the laughter grew and the contagion spread. Before long even the thug with the knife cracked a smile and let out a small laugh of his own. Although there was nothing overly funny about Nick's statement and it could only make things worse for everyone involved, the bartender couldn't help but be caught up in the wave of hysteria that was consuming the room.

Mr. Fedora clearly did not see anything funny with this event, however the cash collector uncontrollably started to snicker as well. Now everyone in the bar was laughing except Mr. Fedora, who continued to stand there seemingly immune and becoming increasingly impatient. The laughter finally began to die and almost stopped, but then the thug with the knife pointed out the solemn face of Mr. Fedora and everyone was once again overtaken by a brand new wave of laughter. Mr. Fedora only grew angrier as the laughing continued which in turn added fuel to the flames like kerosene. Soon everyone was rolling and doing their best to remember the gravity of the situation.

After patiently waiting for what seemed like eternity, Mr. Fedora straightened his arm, aiming his gun for the spot directly in between Nick's eyes and said, "Laugh at this Dickhead!"

Bang! A gunshot went off and Mr. Fedora's eyes widened as blood poured from his neck. The laughter stopped as the thug dropped his gun and gripped his throat. Nick withdrew his gun and quickly snatched the other off the floor as the two thugs scrambled for the *locked* front door. Mr. Fedora, still holding onto his neck with both hands slowly fell to the floor, gurgling for help.

Nick threw his newly acquired gun to the bartender and fired a warning shot into the wall beside the two fumbling thugs who were desperately searching themselves for the keys. They both stopped simultaneously and turned around. The knife dropped to the floor and they both raised their hands in fear.

"Looking for these?" Nick dangled a set of keys.

"But… How did you…?" The bartender puzzled.

Nick grinned and then walked up to Mr. Fedora, who was now turning blue and drowning on his own blood. Calmly, Nick said, "should have laughed," then coolly stepped over him and approached the two petrified hoodlums. "The first person who lowers their hands gets the next bullet."

The bartender was already at the phone dialing the police while Ned, who was surprisingly sober and not wanting to wait for service, stood behind the bar helping himself to another beer.

CHAPTER ELEVEN

"So you're saying the two sets of writings are from two different people?" Mercedes sat in a dimly lit room in an armless black office chair, looking at a split-screen monitor. Two seemingly identical images of the word *powerful* appeared side by side. Both images were written in red ink on yellow paper.

"Well, not necessarily. If they are from two different people they would almost have to be identical twins. I would say they're more likely to be from someone with multiple personality disorder. Where'd you get this anyway?" Ernie Baxter was unquestionably infatuated with Mercedes and always got steamed up when she was around. He began to blush and become hot under the collar as his eyes kept shifting from the screen to her shapely legs and back again. Finally, he pushed away from the keyboard and rolled, in his office chair, across the tile floor to a larger monitor, which displayed the same image.

Ernie was a short thin man in his late twenties, who stood only five foot four and weighed less than one hundred and twenty pounds soaking wet. He wore dark thick glasses over his dark brown eyes. His irises nearly covered the entire surface of his eyeballs, leaving very little room around the edges for white. His stringy blond hair was dark and slightly greasy. It hung shoulder-length in the back and fell down around his face and over his glasses in the front. He was dressed in old tennis shoes, faded blue jeans, and a collared shirt with wide horizontal blue and white stripes that reminded Mercedes of the where's Waldo craze.

Ernie spent most of his time alone, here in the dark, staring at his computer monitors, typing code. He loved to write programs. Unlike others with the same interests and talents, Ernie could write a complete program from beginning to end with absolutely no help and when he was done there were usually very few bugs to work out. He could program in six different computer languages and even design whole new operating systems from scratch.

Before becoming totally consumed with computer programming, Ernie worked as a graphologist for the state of California's Criminal Research Division, where he studied many different handwriting styles. He learned more than just handwriting. He learned the psychology behind the way people thought when they wrote. He was able to tell if a person meant and believed in what they wrote or if they were just being deceptive. He could even tell if a person thought they were being honest, when in reality they were just fooling themselves. Eventually, he was able to spot even the best forgeries. He became one of the finest in his field and would often be called upon to testify for the District Attorney.

Ernie was good at graphology but he was even better with computers and before long found himself spending more and more time in front of a monitor and less time analyzing handwritings. Ernie found he could make good money writing programs and finally quit working for the state and opened his own business from home. Although he no longer worked in the field, he still enjoyed graphology and even wrote three very sophisticated programs designed to help analyze various aspects of human handwriting. The program currently in use wasn't the most sophisticated of the three but it was able to compare two separate sets of handwriting better than either of the other two. Even with the aid of the computer the differences were hard to identify and Mercedes was amazed at how fast Ernie was able to recognize and label them.

Ernie grabbed a half eaten cheeseburger that looked like it had been setting out for days and took a bite. He pecked on the keyboard as Mercedes got off her chair and walked over beside him. Ernie's feeling of uneasiness grew as the soles of her tennis shoes quietly tapped on the tile floor in his direction. The image magnified and enhanced as Ernie spoke with a stuffed mouth. "See here," he pointed with the pinky finger of a cheeseburger-filled right hand, "the incline of the *r* is about twelve degrees different from this one, and this *w* has a very tiny loop in it where this one doesn't."

Even though she could see the differences as he pointed them out she still didn't understand how they could indicate multiple personalities. Goodness, her own handwriting could be completely different from just one word to the next. If this was an indication of multiple personality disorder than she had to be totally insane. She thought a second then confidently pointed at the *o*. "And this *o* looks a little smaller than this one."

The corners of Ernie's mouth went up as he almost giggled but suppressed it. "That doesn't mean anything, people often vary the size of their *o*'s." Ernie tried to look macho.

"Oh." Mercedes hid her embarrassment.

Ernie snorted and a speck of burger hit the corner of the screen as an uncontrollable laugh escaped him, then looking a bit embarrassed himself, he said, "Don't worry about it, it's a freaky science." His head bobbed up and down as he snorted again and scooped the hair out of his eyes.

"So you're saying you think the same person wrote both of these statements?"

"Yeah!" he said confidently. "Well, no," he corrected himself. "Well, yeah!" he said again, then took the second to the last bite of his burger and in a muffled voice clarified, "Either the same person or some freaky set of twins."

Mercedes thought a moment as Ernie finished his sandwich and moved the hair out of his eyes once more. Ernie turned in his chair to face Mercedes who was standing with her hands behind her. She was leaning on the edge of a table and her weight rested on her palms.

"Thanks Ernie. You've been a sweetie"

Ernie's heart rate increased and his spirits dropped as he felt Mercedes getting ready to leave. When she had called him late last night and said she needed his help with something and asked if she could stop by this morning, Ernie almost choked on his answer and tangled up his words trying to say yes. It had been almost four months since he had seen her and he was all but certain she had forgotten about him.

She had sought him out and solicited his help in her last case. He was so overwhelmed with her beauty that he wasn't able to charge her, so before she left she kissed him on the cheek and softly whispered thank you in his ear. He thought of her everyday since. Girls like her never looked twice at guys like him, even if they did need his help. He had never before been kissed by someone so beautiful. Now she was getting ready to leave again and he wondered how long it would be until he saw her next.

"Um..." He fidgeted in his seat. Was she going to kiss him again? He would rather she wouldn't if it meant she was leaving, however the thought of it made the butterflies in his stomach morph into bats.

Mercedes smiled an angelic smile.

His eyes could not stop and rest on anything. He tried to look into hers but looked away almost immediately. He looked at the keyboard and then at the monitor and then at his fingers and then at her again. Finally, he looked at the screen in front of him and typed some keys on the keyboard.

"Is that...is that all you wanted...just to know if these were both written by the same person or not?"

"I don't know. Can you tell me anything about the person who wrote them?"

"Um..." He looked intently at the screen as he clicked the mouse and typed on the keys. "Like what?"

"I don't know, anything."

"Well…" Still staring at the monitor and clicking the mouse he said, "Whoever wrote this is real mental."

"What do you mean?" Mercedes pushed off from the table and knelt beside him.

"In the first statement he believes what he is writing but oddly, isn't too afraid."

Mercedes leaned in closer and opened herself up for understanding. "'Kay, and that means?"

He swallowed hard and stammered through his words. "Well… Um… Look, read it. If you were writing this to yourself and, let's say you believed it, as he did when he wrote it, wouldn't you be afraid?" After a second of silence he continued. "I mean look at it! That's scary shit!"

Mercedes nodded. "Yeah it is."

"Wouldn't you be afraid?"

"Yeah." The answer was obvious. She wondered if he was asking her a trick question.

"Well, whoever wrote this wasn't afraid when they wrote the top part."

"They weren't?"

"No!"

"And in the bottom part he wasn't sure if he believed it or not but…" Mercedes' face was inches away from his as they both stared at the screen. He stopped for a second and tried to recompose himself, doing his best to look macho at the same time, "he was very scared."

"So in the upper half he believed what he wrote but wasn't afraid, and in the lower half he didn't necessarily believe what he was writing, but was afraid?"

"Right."

After puzzling at the screen for a few more seconds Mercedes turned her head and looked directly at Ernie's profile. Ernie didn't notice at first and began to speak. "And he was more sure of himself when he first began writing the upper half but," he felt her eyes on him and became overly conscious of his face. He swallowed hard and his voice cracked as he continued, "As he wrote, his confidence slowly left him."

"Ernie?" Mercedes whispered.

Ernie took another deep breath and blinked. He tried to answer but wasn't able to speak. Mercedes smiled patiently. Ernie wasn't her type but it was obvious he had the *hots* for her. She wasn't attracted to him but she did think he was a very special person and considered him a friend. Lots of guys looked at her the way Ernie did but for some reason Ernie's attraction for her was much more flattering. He looked so cute when he got all fluttery over her. He finally answered in a very shaky and crackly voice. "Y-yes Mercedes?" He tried to turn his head and look at her, but she was so close and he was so nervous.

"Thank you again," she whispered and then gave him a peck on the cheek. His breathing deepened as he sat staring at the computer screen trying to swallow. "I have to go now…" His heart dropped. "But…" His heart rose. He was beginning to feel like he was on a roller coaster ride and just might be sick. "Would you do me a favor?"

Almost before she finished her question he blurted out, "Anything!" And then he realized how foolish and desperate he must have sounded.

"I need to know everything you can figure out about the person who wrote this. Would you keep the note and study it for a few days and give me a call when you got all you can?"

He nodded his head in a macho sort of way. "Sure, yeah, no prob." Realizing he was slouching he sat up straight in his chair and wiped the hair from his eyes. She still needed him. He still had a chance to show her the macho winning side of him. He would find out everything there was to know about this Alex Kendallman from these two paragraphs.

"Thanks again." She gave him another kiss. "You're my hero." She stood up as he narrow-mindedly stared at the screen and blazed through the keys. He had a mission—a single mission. He had been commissioned by an angel of heaven. Mercedes looked at Ernie and smiled to herself, *he's so sweet.*

It was a little before six-thirty by the time she left Ernie's. She got into a tan colored Toyota Corolla. This was her *low profile* car. Last year she decided a less conspicuous car would be a good thing to have standing by in her line of work. Using her phone she logged onto the Internet and navigated around to a password protected page that only she knew about. Before she had left her house this morning she focused her web cam on Alex and sent streaming video into this page. Alex and half of her living room was now on the Internet for anyone to see, anyone who knew her web cam was on, anyone who knew the web address and anyone who knew her ten digit password. The full color image downloaded into her phone. Alex was still on the couch where she left him. She pulled away from the curb and headed for her office as she dialed another number.

She had been on the go since five-thirty this morning. After carrying Alex out of Peppino's yesterday afternoon she took him straight to Saint Paul's emergency ward where his broken nose was reset and he was treated for a mild concussion. She checked him in as her brother, and since she wasn't able to provide the hospital with any of his identification he was treated for his immediate wounds only and then released.

Alex left the hospital in an eerie catatonic state, functioning more like some robot than a human. He was able to walk and was easily guided but that was about the extent of his abilities. His face was somber and his eyes never blinked. He didn't respond at all to vocal commands. When nudged from the back he would move forward. When pulled to one side he would change course in that direction.

She drove him straight to her townhouse in Beverly Hills. Once there she helped him to her broken couch. The couch was okay until this morning, before she decided it would looked better if it were moved back just a little. Its tall wooden legs went well with the western theme in her front room but when she scooted it back she must have pushed a little too hard because both back legs snapped and folded underneath it, first one and then the other. She remembered being so angry this morning. She had only had it a little over three months and for the little fortune she paid for it, it should have lasted long enough to be given to her great, great grand children. It seemed a bit trivial now.

She slowly waved her hand in front of Alex's face and back again. There was no response. She snapped her fingers. He didn't even blink. After trying several different things to wake him up she decided to leave him alone and move onto something else. She stood up and began to walk toward the staircase when she heard a faint noise coming from the couch. She turned around just in time to see Alex slumping over onto his side. He hit his head hard on the armrest and for a moment it looked as if the couch might topple backward, throwing him onto the floor behind it. It rocked once but then stopped.

The house was quiet except for the soft hum coming from the refrigerator in the kitchen, which somehow made the silence even more evident. She stood at the bottom of the stairs looking at Alex. He seemed eerie—almost too eerie. His feet were almost connected with the floor as if he was still sitting, but from the waist up he was laying. His arms and hands looked stiff like those of a corpse. His eyes were opened and expressionless. She hadn't remembered him blinking since his eyes first popped open in the emergency room. She wondered what was going on inside his mind—if anything was going on inside his mind. She stood there a few minutes more while a cold chill slowly worked its way into her spine. Alex still didn't blink. He didn't move. She wasn't even able to tell if he was breathing. The silence grew louder and she finally turned and went upstairs.

After freshening up she returned downstairs, sat down at her desk and ran the day back through her mind. She recapped everything from the very first moment Alex dashed into her office 'til now. She ran through her phonebook and quickly found Ernie Baxter's number, a techno geek who had helped her hack into a corporate mainframe on a previous case. She arranged a meeting early the next morning and then called a friend of hers who worked as a custodian for *Chryo-Plazz*, a local manufacturer of pharmaceuticals, who hooked her up with Louise Jennings, one of the lab technicians. Mercedes wanted someone to take a look at the weird green fluid in Alex's syringe. Mrs. Jennings was very busy and couldn't look at it then, but told Mercedes if she would bring it down right away she might be able to look at it first thing in the morning. Mercedes said she'd be right there, and using an old contact lens case from before the days of Lasik, took some of the fluid to Chryo-Plazz.

Mrs. Jennings was a tall bony woman and was wearing a light blue decontamination suit. A light blue latex glove covered her left hand and strands of dark hair poked out from beneath a blue hat that resembled a shower cap. She met Mercedes at the front entrance of the high-rise. The meeting was brief. Mrs. Jennings didn't smile. She briskly came out of the elevator, walked up, unlocked the glass door, and held out her hand. After an awkward hello, Mercedes handed over the contact lens case. Louise looked puzzled but accepted it and told Mercedes to call her in the morning, then abruptly went back upstairs.

Mercedes returned home a little after 10:30 pm. Her townhouse was on a quiet block in a middle-upper class neighborhood. As she turned the corner onto her street she noticed an unfamiliar car parked across the way from her house. There was nothing too particularly odd about that, but as she passed, she spotted two shadowy looking figures sitting in the front seat. After parking her car in the carport she casually walked back and tried to sneak a glimpse of the license plate. Unfortunately another car blocked her view and there was no way to get a good look at the number without being overly obvious. The odds were that it was nothing more than a couple of people sitting in their car, talking. Mercedes didn't give it a second thought.

Alex had fallen asleep on the couch and after a long relaxing shower Mercedes caught a few winks of her own. She woke up early and put on white tennis shoes, designer blue jeans and a light blue, sleeveless, v-neck pullover. She looked beautiful without makeup but always knew the right amount and color to go with any outfit. After putting her hair up in an athletic ponytail she checked on Alex who was still out cold. She picked up the phone, dialed Ernie's number, pulled a slat down on her Venetian blinds, and looked out the window. That's when her breathing momentarily stopped and her heart found its way into her throat. The car from last night still sat out on the street and still contained two unidentified passengers. One was eating a sandwich and laughing while the other was lowering a high-powered zoom lens camera. On the other end of the line Ernie's phone rang.

"Hello?"

"Hey Ernie it's me, Mercedes."

"Hi Mercedes, how are y-"

Mercedes cut him off. "Ernie, I'll call ya back." She spoke slowly as she stared out the window.

"Um Okay… Yeah. I um…"

Mercedes hung up, still gazing at the unknown visitors. They were two men in suits and she might have mistakenly thought they were FBI if they hadn't been in a white Dodge Intrepid. They were watching her; there was no doubt about it. She turned and looked at Alex, who was still out cold. If they saw her leave they might just let themselves in and if they did that, they'd find Alex. She thought a moment. Perhaps if they didn't see her leave and thought she was still here they would stay where they were. They obviously didn't know Alex was with her or they would have attempted to take him by now. Why were they watching her? How did they come to suspect her? The odds were they were just following every lead they had and since the last place they saw Alex was outside her office, she was now one of the many possibilities. She had no intention of becoming anything more than a possibility. She set up her web cam and wrote out a note with her number on it in case Alex woke up before she returned.

She figured she could run by Ernie's then stop in at her office and get back just before sunup. She wanted to get all the information she had on Louie Ventino and Bad Boy Billy Marcus. She climbed out of the back window and made her way to her Corolla, which waited out on the street, and drove to Ernie's.

Now, after leaving Ernie's, she was three blocks from her office and on her cell-phone waiting for Mrs. Jennings to answer. After six rings Mrs. Jennings picked up the phone, "Hello?"

"Hi. Mrs. Jennings? This is Mercedes Atwater."

"Oh yes Ms. Atwater, let me get to another phone. Can you hold on a second?"

"Sure."

Mrs. Jennings' voice was upbeat and she sounded much more enthusiastic than she had last night. Mercedes turned a corner and headed south on Main. A black van had been behind her for some time now and had turned onto Main as well. She wasn't sure, but thought she had seen the same van in her rearview mirror on the freeway. She was careful and knew no one saw her get into the Corolla when she left her house and there was no reason for anyone to have been watching Ernie's place. No, the black van wasn't following her, she was just understandably cautious. She approached Second Street and flipped on her blinker.

"Ok, Ms. Atwater?" Mrs. Jennings came back on the line.

"Yes." Mercedes replied.

"Where did you get this chemical?"

"It was in the possession of a client of mine in a case I'm working on. Why?"

The van's blinker came on as it merged into the turning lane.

"Ms. Atwater I can't talk over the phone, but this chemical," She paused and then lowered her voice. "This chemical is a very dangerous and complex substance."

"Really? What does it do?"

Whispering, Mrs. Jennings continued, "I don't know exactly what it does, but I do believe it was designed to be used on the human brain, to what ends, I'm not sure."

Mercedes watched the van in the mirror and changed lanes as she spoke. "On the brain? What do you mean?"

The van slowed down and seemed to linger in the distance, behind her.

Mercedes heard Mrs. Jennings take a deep breath.

"Let's just say I've never seen a drug like this on the open market."

"What do you mean, on the open market?"

Still whispering, Mrs. Jennings went on. "Well, about six years ago Chryo-Plazz was contracted by the government to help them perfect a chemical. Without saying what that chemical was used for, I can tell you that the sample you gave me has many similar properties."

"Similar properties?" Mercedes turned onto the street her office was on. "What does the chemical do?"

"I'd rather not say on the phone. Can you meet me somewhere tonight?"

"Sure. Where?"

"Do you know the Denney's off of Fourth and Bristol?"

"Yeah."

"Why don't we meet there?"

"'Kay, what time?"

"I should be off by five tonight. How 'bout we meet around six o'clock?"

"Six o'clock, I'll be there."

Just beneath the horizon the sun was climbing and bleeding a blackened-red crimson glow into the far eastern sky. It was just moments before daybreak and the sky was still dark. Mercedes pressed the end button on her cell-phone as she approached the long row of offices on her left. Hers was the third from the last. As she pulled into the turning lane, getting ready to park around back, she noticed a light shining from one of the offices toward the end.

She idled in the middle of the street for just a moment trying to see exactly which office it was. It looked like it could be hers. She wasn't sure. She turned her blinker off and instead of turning, pulled out back onto the street. She drove down to the end, passing her office along the way. The light *was* indeed coming from it. She slowed the Corolla and looked closely as she passed. The silhouettes of two men slithered along the blinds. They were going through her office. Shit! Who did these bastards think they were? Not too professional, that's for sure. If they really knew what they were doing the lights would be off and they would be using flashlights. She had half a mind to stop the car right there in the middle of the street and confront them.

Thinking about rummaging hands fingering their way through her files only made her blood boil. She slammed on the brakes. The car idled in the darkness. Looking to the left, at her brightly lighted office, she contemplated. What if she did confront them? Would they tell her anything about what was going on? Would they tell her anything she needed to know? She could park the car, sneak up quietly, and take them by surprise. She reached into the glove box and withdrew a small, 22-caliber pistol. With how unskilled they appeared to be, she was sure she could easily get the upper hand. As she thought, headlights appeared in her rearview mirror. A vehicle had just turned the corner a few blocks back and was now heading her way. Fear, like a gentle ocean wave, moved through the car and washed over her body as a familiar black van slowly drove by, to her right. It slowed down and looked as if it just might stop, but at the last minute accelerated. As it sped away she thought she noticed government plates, but the darkness kept her from being sure. Then, with her heart in her throat, she glanced back at her office just in time to see someone peeking through the blinds. The lights immediately went off. Shit! She pulled forward. She stepped on the gas. The car shot forward. And her heart became a jackhammer.

Maybe these guys were more professional than she thought. Maybe they were playing with her, like a cat with a canary. She returned the gun to the glove box and watched the red taillights of the van as it turned the corner a couple blocks ahead. Moments later she merged onto the freeway just as the crimson blood of the sun poured into daybreak. She logged onto the Internet again to check on Alex, who was still asleep on her couch.

On the way home she recapped the situation. She was working for a guy she didn't know, who wasn't going to pay her, and for all she knew could be some psychopath who just escaped from the mental ward. She had taken him into her house and left him there, alone. Unidentified and possibly threatening people were now stalking her. What was she doing? Why had she decided to take this job in the first place? Sure, Alex looked sincere enough. Sure, he seemed desperate and extremely afraid, but was that a good enough reason to put herself in this situation?

She *did* have to admit she was extremely intrigued by his strange ability to read minds. And danger was always an element in her line of work. She also knew *if* she—no—*when* she solved this case she would never have to worry about business again. This would undoubtedly be the most famous case in history. The strange man who could read minds. The man who had no memory and was being chased by God knows whom. Damn! She might even write a book about it when it was all over! She exited the freeway and turned south on Park. Has Alex always had the ability to read minds or is it a product of the experiments they did to him? Were they experimenting on him because he could read minds?

Maybe from some weird freak of nature he was born with this strange ability and someone found out about it, someone powerful—someone evil. Who were *they*? Who was behind all this and for what purpose? Was it the military or the FBI? Maybe it was the CIA or the Secrete Service. Whoever they were, she was fairly convinced they weren't the amateurs they appeared to be.

She parked the car back out on the street just as the sun was peeking over the horizon. Hurriedly, she walked around to the back window and climbed inside. Alex was still on the couch where she had left him. She walked over to the blinds. The Intrepid was still out on the street as well. She didn't like being watched, especially by people who were so cocky that they didn't feel the need to conceal themselves. She put her hand on the door handle and nearly opened it. She wanted to march out there and bluntly ask them what it was they wanted with her, but thought otherwise.

She tried waking Alex again but there was still no response. She walked back over to the blinds. Damn assholes! The archway to the kitchen was right next to the front door. She stepped through, filled the coffee pot with water, and added an extra spoonful of grounds to the filter. The aroma of fresh coffee quickly filled the air as water dripped through the machine. Mercedes went upstairs, got her own zoom lens camera from the closet, and took it to the window. Being careful not to be seen, she snapped six or seven quick close-ups of the two men in the car. The angle wasn't bad and she felt as if she got a few good photos of the driver, but because she was on the second floor looking down she wasn't able to get anything above the passengers' shoulders.

She went downstairs to the blinds next to the front door to get a better shot. She pulled down on one of the slats just in time to be photographed by the passenger. Pretending not to notice, she held the slat down a few more seconds and looked aimlessly out into the street. A moment later as both men looked away, pretending to be carrying on a conversation about something, she snapped two more quick shots and made sure to capture the passenger this time. As she zoomed in close, getting a clearer image of the man's profile, she couldn't help but notice how unsightly he was. His jaw, like his forehead, was long and flat and the color of his skin was pale and gray. A scar ran from just beneath his left eye, over the bridge of his nose and as far as she could tell, continued on down his right cheek. The corners of his mouth were naturally drawn down, making him look depressed, mean, and even evil. She lowered the camera and thought for a moment. Then, releasing the slat, she walked into the kitchen to pour herself a cup of coffee. She set her camera on the kitchen table and retrieved a cup from the cabinet. Who were they?

She had just finished with the sugar and was in the middle of pouring Half & Half from the carton into her cup when Alex groaned. She looked at him through the archway. His hand had moved to his head and was softly rubbing his temples. Mercedes quickly returned the milk to the glass shelf and closed the door. Just as she was walking through the archway into the front room, and with Alex's groans escalating, a loud, startling knock came from the front door. She jumped, accidentally spilling the coffee onto her sweater. She stopped, quickly composed herself and then looked through the security hole. The two men from the Dodge were now standing on her patio. Shit! They were both tall with large solid builds and wore dark reflective sunglasses. Now she was able to get a better look at the man with the scar. Her stomach soured and for a second she found herself unable to look away. He almost looked as if he was a walking corpse and the scar was much worse than when it had first appeared. It continued over the bridge of his nose, ran clear across his long gray cheek and ended just on the other side of his mouth. She looked at Alex who had just opened his eyes and was still moaning.

The layout of the townhouse was set up in such a way that anyone standing on the front porch, with the door open could easily see into the living room. To make matters worse the couch wasn't up against the wall like most others. It was in the middle of the room and unfortunately the first piece of furniture that normally caught the eye. If she opened the door now, they would undoubtedly see Alex.

Alex looked groggy and tried to sit up. Halfway into it however, he winced in pain and dropped his head back down onto the pillow. The men on the patio knocked louder.

Doing her best not to spill her coffee again, Mercedes raced to her computer desk and in the calmest voice she could muster yelled, "One moment please!"

"Ms. Atwater?" Another banging came from the door, this one louder than the last.

The unorganized surface was cluttered with various scraps, folders, and papers. She carefully but quickly scooted a few papers aside, set her cup down, then hastily produced a small key and unlocked the bottom draw.

Still noticeably sore, Alex looked around. "Where am I?"

Mercedes reached into the drawer and pulled out a small black pistol. "You're at my apartment and we're in a little trouble!" She spoke fast as she raced over to the couch and knelt down beside him. "Can you move? We need to hide you, quickly!"

Alex looked at Mercedes baffled, "Who are you?"

Another knock echoed through the house. It sounded as if the men on the patio might just bang a hole right through the door and open it themselves.

Although coming around, Alex still seemed to be in some sort of a daze and absolutely wasn't moving. Mercedes looked at him, closed her eyes, and shook her head, and then stood up and spun around. She raised the gun up and held it beside her head pointing the muzzle at the ceiling. Looking at the door she whispered, "It's show time," and then boldly called out, "Here I come!"

CHAPTER TWELVE

Teddy sat in his garage with a revolver in his lap, tapping his thumb on the steering wheel of his Lexus, and listening to the stereo. The car door was open and his left foot rested on the cold cement floor. He was still in his robe and barefooted. The engine was idling and the radio was softly playing gospel music. He had been here nearly an hour in the same position, impassively staring at the inside of the closed garage door. How could the Lord have let such a thing happen? Was He angry with Teddy? He squinted his eyes and slowly shook his head. Was the devil becoming stronger? These *were* the last days and the prophecies stated that in them Satan would be given ultimate power over the Earth for a short time. Satan was slowly growing stronger everyday and this was obviously an indication that his power was on the rise.

The Los Angeles Times lay on the seat beside Teddy and a full color photo of a white Victorian house dominated the front page. The headlines read *Police Move in on Freak!*

The article said that four teenagers had heard the old house was haunted and wanted to go exploring. They were planning on staying the night, but first wanted to scope the place out in the daylight. They arrived at the spooky old house a little before 3 PM yesterday afternoon. They scaled the tall iron gate and monkeyed their way through a slightly opened window into a bathroom on the second floor.

After exploring the second and third stories, the children reported hearing a car pull up in front of the house. One of them stated she looked out the window and saw a white Lexus parked out on the curb. Along with it, a man in an expensive gray suit, doing what she said, appeared to be dance steps on the sidewalk. He was carrying a medium sized stainless steel box and acted like a reject from the disco generation.

Fortunately, the ghost chasers had brought a high-powered camera. At first they laughed at the old wannabe dancer and only snapped a couple of shots so they could save their film for the ghosts. But the children quickly became nervous as the stranger had a key to the font gate and then to the house. The teens swiftly scrambled to one of the walk-in closets upstairs, but the visitor never came up. After waiting for what they said *seemed like forever*, they slowly came out of their hiding spot and crept about on the second floor. First they went to the window to see if the stranger's car was still there, it was.

Slowly as their confidence grew and the house remained silent they made their way downstairs, to see if he was still inside. There was no sign of him at first, but then one of them noticed the cellar door. It was slightly ajar and an amber glow of flickering light crept up from the basement. Realizing he was still in the house, they quickly ran back upstairs and waited, hoping he would soon leave. A few minutes later the muffled sound of a car trunk shutting came through the old crust-filled windows. The children looked outside just in time to see him getting into his car and pulling away. After they were sure he was gone, the teens went downstairs, broke into the basement, and found the head of the headhunter's latest victim, later identified as Michelle Brown of Cerritos, California.

"To think we were in the same house as that freak!" One of the teens exclaimed later to one of our reporters.

"Yeah it was really spooky, if that place wasn't haunted before it sure is now!" Another said.

"At first we thought he owned the place or something and was just stopping by to check on things. If we would have had any idea who he really was, we would have taken more photos."

Teddy had read the article three times and it bothered him, however it didn't bother him as much as the accompanying photos did. There were a total of four, and all in black and white. The first three, even though they were headshots, didn't bother him nearly as much as the last one did. The initial three pictures were of the back of his head and didn't show his face at all, however the last one was of the rear of the Lexus. It must have been taken as he was driving away. It clearly showed four of the seven digits of the license plate and he was fairly certain that one or perhaps two of the remaining three digits could easily be photo enhanced and cleaned up enough to read. It would only be a matter of time until they linked Teddy to the hooker and ultimately everyone else he had sent home to be with the Lord.

Teddy started tapping his foot on the concrete and softly humming to the gospel the song coming through the car's speakers. Perhaps this whole thing was a sign. Maybe this was God's way of telling Teddy his time on Earth was nearly over. Was the end already upon us and had God already turned the Earth over to Satan? Teddy let go of the steering wheel and gripped the butt of the gun as his humming seamlessly changed into singing. He sang softly and with conviction as he looked intently at the gun. It was shiny and clean. The handle was made of dark wood and comfortably fit his hand. The barrel was a bright and shiny stainless steel. The gun was well built and solid.

He felt the weight of it in his hand as he brought it up to his face. In the five years that he owned it he never once used it. He called it his ticket to paradise and always knew the day would come when God would give him a sign letting him know it was time to cash it in and come home. Teddy had long looked forward to this day. He had often prayed that God would shorten the time and call him home sooner. He held the gun up to his eye and looked down the long barrel trying to see if the one bullet he put in it was in the firing chamber.

He thought he had wanted this day to come more than anything but as he sat there in his car listening to the music and holding the gun he couldn't shake the tinge of fear that hovered over his shoulders and across the nape of his neck. He had hoped the good Lord's music would chase it away, but it did not. It only got worse. There was no way he could cash in his ticket while he was filled with fear. What would God think? Teddy wasn't afraid of God. He knew God loved him. He wasn't even afraid of dying. He wanted to go home. He hated this sin filled world. Teddy's fear came from the thought of sins he may have forgotten.

The only way one can be forgiven of their sins is to confess them to the Lord and ask for forgiveness. Teddy was afraid he might have forgotten one or two of the sins he had committed long ago. He was sure he had confessed all of them. But if he had forgotten even one he would burn in Hell for all eternity. His recent trips into the red-light district got him thinking about his younger days, about all those wicked thoughts that once ran rampant through his mind. He knew God loved him, that wasn't in question, but the good book states that the wages of sin is death. It doesn't matter how much God loves you, if you don't confess *all* of your sins you will surely burn forever in the hottest fire imaginable. He had only loaded one bullet into the gun. If it wasn't his time to go, God wouldn't let the bullet be in the chamber when he pulled the trigger.

A strange peace came over him and chased his fears away as the radio station began playing *Amazing Grace*. This was unquestionably a sign from God telling Teddy everything would be all right. He spun the barrel one more time, inserted the gun into his mouth, and joyfully pulled the trigger.

CHAPTER THIRTEEN

Mercedes took two steps toward the door, stopped, and squinted her eyes. Filled with anxiety, she took a deep breath and jerked her body as she voiced her thought, "Damn!" then turned around, walked back to the couch, and whispered to her catatonic houseguest, "Hold on, this might hurt a bit… and try not to make any noise."

Alex looked at the strange woman and wondered what she meant: *Try not to make any noise.* Then she bent down, placed her gun on the hardwood floor, grabbed the bottom of the couch and heaved it up and backward, so that the back of it was on the floor and its legs faced the door, forcing Alex to tumble off and onto the planks behind it. A soft grunt escaped him, but she was sure it wasn't loud enough to carry as far as the porch. Mercedes winced for Alex's sake then quickly pushed the couch back into place and whispered, "Now be quiet! Whatever you do, don't make a sound!"

She walked over to the door and glanced back at the couch as she tucked the pistol into the seat of her pants. Everything looked normal enough.

With Alex safely out of sight behind the couch and as the men began another pounding session, Mercedes cleared her head, tried to gather her wits, and then abruptly swung open the door.

"What in the Hell is your problem?" She blurted.

"Excuse me?" They hadn't expected her to be so brash.

Without waiting to hear what they had to say she continued. "Banging on my door at this hour of the morning? I have a half a notion to call the cops."

"I'm sorry ma'am. We're with the Central Intelligence Agency." The black-haired man, who wore an expensive navy-blue pinstriped suit, held up a black leather wallet, which flapped open, displaying identification. "I'm Agent Donaldson and this is Agent Young."

"CIA huh? Well what in the Hell do you want with me?" Mercedes paused, cocked her head and narrowed her eyes for a second then opened them wide as she only half pretended. "Oh my God! This doesn't have anything to do with me being kicked out of the FBI does it? Because if it does those bastards framed me!"

"No ma'am that's not our department. We deal with national security issues."

"National security issues?" Behind her, she was sure she could hear Alex's moaning floating up over her shoulders as she held the door at an angle allowing only the kitchen to be seen behind her. "Then what do you want with me?" She said trying to hide her anxiety.

"We have an urgent matter to discuss with you, may we come in?"

"Um…" Her thoughts immediately went to Alex as she struggled to gather her thoughts. It was unclear whether or not he was in a stable enough frame of mind to understand what was happening and it sounded as if his moans were getting louder. The hairs on the back of her neck stood up as she shook her head, politely smiled, and hesitated before finally stating, "My house is a mess."

"We believe the matter is too important to discuss at your door ma'am. It would be *best* if we came in and sat down." His smile was counterfeit and transparent, "It'll only take a moment."

Somehow, she had mysteriously transformed into one of the three little pigs and was now negotiating with the wolf for her life. Her knowledge of the CIA was little but if they were anything like the FBI then these two men had to be imposters. The identification said CIA, sure enough, but she wasn't convinced. Their suits were probably worth more than the average CIA field agent earned in a month.

Until now, Agent Donaldson—If in fact that was his real name—had done all the talking, while his evil-looking associate silently stood by, holding his own phony smile over the top of a dark, cold demeanor.

The so-called Agent Young stood an inch or two taller than his associate and his hair, although short, wasn't nearly as neat. His strong square face, although intriguing, was far from handsome and vaguely resembled Frankenstein's monster, and even though he was smiling, she could sense that there was something terribly evil about him. He had a slit for a mouth and his lips were pale and thin. His suit and matching shoes were both a colorless jet-black. And then of course, there was that scar. It was absolutely hideous and looked more like some weird birth defect up close. And although quiet, his presence was much more menacing than his talkative partner's. Even without seeing his eyes, which were hidden behind reflective shades, she knew he wasn't keeping eye contact with her, but was rather trying to peer past her into the house.

Slowly, he shifted his jaw, tilted his head to one side, cracking his neck, and then spoke. His voice was deep and raspy. His words were methodically slow and direct and even with his attempt to color them with artificial warmth, they still came out cold and heartless. "I'm sure your house is fine ma'am."

They had made up their minds. They were *going* to come in. She almost suggested that they get together later at her office but knew that she was already bordering on looking too suspicious as it was. If she didn't let them in right now they might just force their way in and start looking through her house as they pleased. She thought about it for a second. They couldn't possibly be sure that Alex had run into her office yesterday. She was probably just one of God knows how many leads they were following. If she invited them in and let them see that she had nothing to hide they would most likely go away and move on to their next lead. All she had to do was invite them in and play dumb for a few minutes. She could do that, but what about Alex's moaning. If they came in, would they hear it? She hesitated as she listened. For the moment it sounded as if the moaning had stopped, but she wasn't sure.

"All right then, come on into the kitchen. We can talk in there." Holding the doorknob with her left hand and indicating the way with her right, which nearly reached all the way to the edge of the archway, she left only one direction for them to go.

Immediately stepping forward, Agent Donaldson removed his sunglasses, said thank you, and walked into the kitchen while Agent Young lingered behind. His hesitation was awkward and obviously some kind of a control tactic. He breathed rhythmically and deep as he reached up and slowly removed his glasses, revealing deep sockets surrounded by dark skin. His eyes were an ugly shade of green and possessed an eerie, all-knowing glare, which seemed to look past the surface and into her soul. Keeping eye contact he calmly folded his glasses and slid them beneath his coat, into his shirt pocket. Mercedes wasn't easily intimidated and if he was trying to get under her skin with this *weak* imitation of a demon-possessed Dirty Hairy, he wasn't doing a very good job. A grin hovered at the edge of his expression and finally formulated into an evil smile as he stepped past her and joined his partner. The door swung closed as she followed them into the kitchen, being careful not to reveal the pistol in the small of her back. As she walked through the archway she noticed Agent Donaldson holding her camera. She had forgotten that she had left it on the table.

"Please, sit down." She gestured as she walked past the table to the coffeemaker.

"Thank you," they almost spoke in unison as they pulled out chairs and took a seat at the kitchen table.

"Into photography?" Agent Donaldson asked while examining the camera.

"Oh um... yeah! I'm a private investigator. A Camera comes in handy from time to time."

Donaldson nodded and set the camera back on the table.

"Cup of coffee?" Mercedes gripped the handle of the pot while opening the cabinet door and reaching for a cup.

"Yes please," Agent Donaldson responded politely while Agent Young just silently nodded once. She poured three cups of coffee. The awkwardness felt immense but didn't show as she skillfully kept the front of her body facing the table and her pistol toting back out of sight.

"Cream?" She raised an eyebrow as she opened the refrigerator.

"No ma'am." Agent Donaldson replied. *Dirty Hairy* just sat there and coldly shook his head.

"Sugar?"

"Just black is fine ma'am, thank you."

Mr. Young leaned back in his chair, crossed an ankle over one knee, and in a soft slow voice said, "No. Thank you."

The glass kitchen table was positioned up against the wall just below a blind-covered window, which if opened would present a bush-covered view of the street where the Dodge was sitting. Three chairs accompanied the table. *Dirty Hairy* took the chair right next to the archway and kept glancing into the living room while his partner had walked around the table, taking the seat opposite him, leaving Mercedes the spot directly across from the window. She couldn't see the couch from where she stood but was sure, this so-called Agent Young could. She handed the men their coffee and being acutely aware of the pistol in her jeans, pulled out her chair and sat down.

"What happened to your couch?" Agent Young asked while looking into the next room.

"Oh, that." The situation began to gnaw at her nerves, as she acted nonchalant and slightly depressed. "I broke it this morning." She sipped her coffee and changed to a more serious tone, trying to draw his eyes away from the couch. "So what's up?"

Agent Donaldson took a drink of his coffee and looked across the table at his partner, who returned his gaze. Cupping his hand around the warm mug, he then turned and looked at Mercedes. "What we're about to tell you is a matter of national security and must be kept secret."

"'Kay." Mercedes listened.

"That means you tell no one." Agent Young interjected and then smoothly shook his head only once, glaring authoritatively.

Mercedes turned from Agent Donaldson and looked at *Dirty Harry*, nodded her head, shrugged her shoulders and with the attitude of a defiant teenager emphasized, "'Kay."

Donaldson reached under his coat and pulled out a 5X7 photograph of a man's face. He laid it on the table and slid it over in front of Mercedes. The man in the photo was unknown to her and looked as if he was on some kind of drug. His expression was somber and his eyes were glossy. He had a queer looking smile on his face and his messy hair had obviously been cleared away from his eyes for the photo. It looked as if it hadn't been brushed in weeks. At first she didn't recognize him but then, like a ton of bricks, it hit her and she knew who it was.

"Have you ever seen this man before?" Donaldson asked.

It was a photo of Alex. He looked completely different in this photo than he did in person. He seemed as if he had lost all will to live. Mercedes looked at it trying to pretend to be unaffected by her sudden revelation.

"No…" She shook her head. "Why? Should I?" She looked up innocently, first at Donaldson then at Young.

Dirty Harry unfolded his legs and slowly leaned forward. "Look again."

His presence was powerful and ominous and she didn't like his attitude, but did what he asked anyway, and glanced back at the photo. It was Alex all right. She was beginning to think he was the man of a million faces. She remembered how his entire expression had changed yesterday in Peppino's. It changed so much in fact that he had looked like an entirely different person.

She shook her head again and assertively said, "No, I don't know him. Who is he?"

The two men were silent for a moment as she looked up and waited for an answer. She really wanted to hear what they had to say. Up until now, all she knew about Alex was what he had told her and that was very little. She listened as Donaldson gave her the details.

"He's a very dangerous international terrorist. We don't know how or when he got into the country. We discovered he was here about six weeks ago."

Her immediate reaction was to dismiss what he said altogether, but then she thought, what if they *really* were CIA. There was no real evidence that they weren't who they said they were, and if she were going to get to the bottom of things she would have to consider every possibility. She listened as he continued.

"We have some ideas but we're not sure why he's here. He likes to work as a hired mercenary for the highest bidder. We believe he's responsible for over three hundred deaths, five in the last two weeks. He loves to use explosives and has no problem killing someone with his bare hands."

If they were indeed CIA and Alex really was an international terrorist then why did he make up a story about losing his memory? The more he spoke the less she believed.

"We've been tracking him for several weeks now. He goes by many different aliases. We almost nabbed the bastard a couple of times but he always seems to get away. The general theory is…when he's close to being caught he finds someone who seems trusting and pretends to have problems with his memory. That way he doesn't have to answer any questions about his past and he appears to have nowhere to go. After things blow over and he feels safe again he goes back to business as usual. As far as the poor soul he duped into believing him, to be safe and cover his tracks, he conveniently gets rid of 'em."

She unconsciously perked up and cocked her head.

"He's *very* convincing."

Mercedes tried, but just couldn't picture Alex as a terrorist and if he *was* using her to escape from the CIA why was he still hanging around? He had plenty of opportunity to take off. And what about his strange mind-reading powers? They hadn't mentioned anything about that. She wasn't sure who Alex was, but she was fairly certain he wasn't some international terrorist.

Keeping an innocent face she asked, "What does all this have to do with me?"

Donaldson breathed out through his nose and tightened his eyes. "Where were you yesterday around lunch time?"

She looked confused. "I was in my office looking over some papers. Why?"

"Your office is about a block away from St. John's Homeless Shelter isn't it?"

"Yeah. Why?"

"Yesterday we chased this man," Donaldson pointed at the photo, "Through St. John's Homeless Shelter and down the alleyway behind it. We lost him just outside of *your* office."

These bastards weren't CIA, she was sure of it, and their story was becoming less and less convincing.

"I see," She nodded her head. "And you think he might have ran into my office and pretended to have…" She paused for emphasize. "Lost his mind! Is that it?" Her sarcasm was obvious.

"Did he?" Donaldson asked affirmatively.

"No!" Her face scrunched in aggravation and anger. "I never seen this man before in my life!" She surprised herself at how convincing she sounded.

Agent Donaldson turned to his partner, leaned back in his chair, held his hands up and raised his eyebrows, then exhaled in exasperation.

Agent Young caught Donaldson's look and coldly turned toward Mercedes. He puckered his mouth, sucked his teeth, and then leaned in close. He placed his large hand on the table less than two inches away from her ribcage and said in a voice, barely above a whisper. "Ms. Atwater, what exactly was it that you were doing in Peppino's yesterday afternoon?"

Her heart dropped and her mind raced. How did they know she had been to Peppino's? Had they been watching her? No. They would have busted in last night and taken Alex when she had left to go to Chryo-Plazz. Then how? She remembered the note Alex gave her. It said every governmental agency was in on it. Was Robert, the FBI agent who let them into Peppino's, in on it? In on what? What was it that everybody was supposedly in on? How could so many people be in on something so big and nobody know? What's going on? Who were these people? She began to feel the tension in the room rise.

"Ms. Atwater!" By his agitated tone she could tell that he had said her name more than once, although she didn't remember hearing it. Her head twitched as she snapped out of her thought and looked at *Dirty Harry*. His eyes were threatening and cold. They peered deep into hers. His face was less than six inches from hers and she could smell a foul odor on his breath. The metal of her gun pressed hard into her back as she dropped her right hand from the table and let it hang limp at her side.

"I asked you a question." His eyes were fierce and his imitation of *Dirty Harry* was transforming into something more menacing.

Her heart rate increased and the tension grew, as the kitchen shrank. She felt paralyzed and began to associate with the cat that just got caught for swallowing the canary. She swallowed hard and slowly leaned her head back away from his. There was only one way out of the kitchen and both Mercedes and Agent Young felt the presence of the archway intensify.

"I was just following a lead for an old client of mine. Why? What does that have to do with anything?" She was nervous and she knew they could see it. *Dirty Harry* sat back in his seat and quickly turned his head, cracking his neck again. She smiled and tried to act calm as she brought her hand back up to the table and reached for her coffee. It was no longer scalding hot and she took a long drink, nearly finishing it. Then she calmly stood up, pushing her chair back by straightening her knees, and stepped backward to the coffeemaker. Somehow, she felt safer here. Holding her cup in her left hand she grabbed the handle of the pot with her right.

Trying to act natural and lighten things up a bit, she asked, "Anybody want a refill?"

"No thank you." Agent Donaldson, still sitting back in his chair, casually unbuttoned his coat.

"I'll take some more." Agent Young said while unbuttoning his coat as well, revealing the shadowy contour of a shoulder holster. She brought the pot over to the table and refilled his cup as he moved his hand off the table and onto his lap, closer to his gun. She was less than three feet from the archway and could easily make it past him into the next room. If she spilled the scalding pot of coffee on him as she passed he would probably react slower and give her enough time to get out of the house; but what about Alex? Things weren't out of control yet. Agent Young sipped his coffee as Mercedes replaced the pot onto the burner.

Donaldson leaned forward and picked up the photograph. "Ms. Atwater, we believe your life is in danger and we're only trying to help you." Mercedes stood at the counter holding her cup, pretending to listen, but all she could think about was getting away. She was walking on thin ice and she knew it. She had been trained well by the FBI and knew how to handle herself in tight situations, but then again these weren't amateurs.

Dirty Harry stood up, sucked on his teeth again and smiled, "You don't mind if we have a look around the house do ya?"

"All right this little joke has gone far enough! I want you both to leave. Now!"

Donaldson stood up, "Ms. Atwater, I assure you this is no joke." His confidence was surprising. Things had changed from good cop/bad cop to bad cop/worse cop.

"Look, I don't know who you guys are. CIA, whatever! But I'm going to give you ten seconds to get the Hell out of my house before I call the cops." The telephone hung on the wall across from her between the stove and the archway, equal distance from herself and Agent Young. She looked at the phone. Young slowly shifted his eyes to the phone and then back again.

"Now Ms. Atwater, believe me, you don't want to do that."

She stepped toward the phone. He matched her step. The presence of the gun in her back intensified. She tried envisioning different ways to pull it out and get off two shots before they had time to respond, but just couldn't see it happening. No one spoke, no one moved. The tension in the air thickened and Mercedes' breathing became heavy. She took slow shallow breaths as her heart rate climbed.

She swallowed hard and coolly said, "Please…Just leave."

Just as Agent Young was in the middle of apologizing for being unable to comply with her request, the phone rang, startling everyone. Mercedes flinched, as the two agents appeared unaffected. She moved toward the phone. *Scarface* withdrew his gun and pointed it at her head. "Let it go!" His voice remained calm and soft; if the tension was getting to him it didn't show. The phone rang again. Mercedes could feel herself perspiring as she stared down the barrel of his gun, which was less than two feet from her head. On the fourth ring the answering machine came on.

"Mercedes, hey friend pick up." It was Ernie the techno geek. "I tried your cell-phone a dozen times or more."

"I should get this." Carefully, Mercedes slowly leaned toward the wall.

Dirty Harry extended his gun an inch or more, raised his eyebrows, and coldly said, "No you shouldn't."

Reverting back to her act, she asked, "Is this standard CIA procedure?"

"Shut up!" Agent Young was listening to the machine.

"I called a friend of mine in New York about the note you left here." Ernie continued, "He's a pretty good head shrink. He's got a real big practice on the East Coast. He said I could come and visit him whenever I wanted." He snorted. "Hey maybe we could go together some time or uh… something?" He cleared his throat. "Any um…" He cleared his throat again. "Anyway, I wanted to run this note past him and see what he thought of it." Her answering machine was old and only recorded for sixty seconds. She had been planning to get a newer one that would record much longer but never got around to it. She was hoping it would cut off before he said anything revealing.

Ernie continued, "After I read it to him he was so intrigued he asked me to fax it over. I told him I could do better than that and…" Trying to be macho, Ernie continued. "I e-mailed it to him. Cool, huh?" Agent Young looked at Donaldson confused. Donaldson had the *what a loser* look on his face.

Mercedes' leg wanted to twitch as she willed the machine to come to the end and stop.

"Any who, after looking it over he called me back very concerned." Ernie cleared his throat again and tried to deepen his voice to sound more *he-man*. "Very concerned." His voice crackled from low to high then back again.

The expression on Agent Young's face was full of confusion as if he was trying to puzzle through *geek lingo* and decipher what Ernie was saying. Mercedes could not believe that her answering machine was still recording. She was sure a minute had already passed.

"He said that whoever wrote it was probably delusional and more than likely had grandiose schizophrenia. He said the…" The machine finally clicked off. Mercedes felt a wave of relief wash over her as the room tension dropped a notch.

"What was he talking about? What note?" Agent Young still looked puzzled.

"It's a confidential matter." Mercedes replied with a cold glare as she slowly backed up. She moved away from the wall phone and toward the kitchen counter. Agent young relaxed his arm but kept her as his target. She leaned on her hands up against the counter, with the cold metal pistol pressing hard on the back of her right hand.

The phone rang again. Mercedes rotated her hand, placing her palm against the butt of the gun. Once more the machine clicked on.

"Wow! You sure do have a short recording time." Mercedes' shoulders slumped as exasperation and disbelief filled her eyes. "You ought to let me come over there and increase the memory on your answering machine. Oh um…what kinda recorder is it? It's not that old cassette type is it? Those things are ancient."

Agent Young turned and looked at Donaldson again and shook his head. "Is this guy for real?" Donaldson held his own look of confusion as he raised his hands and shrugged his shoulders.

"It might be better if we just bought you a whole new machine or something like that." Ernie cleared his throat again, getting ready to resume his macho routine.

Mercedes spoke up, "I don't appreciate you two eavesdropping on my personal conversations like this!"

"I said shut up…" Young raised an eyebrow and glared back at Mercedes.

Mercedes shook her head as she tightened her hand around the handle of the gun.

"As I was saying before your answering machine so *rudely* cut me off," Ernie snorted, "my friend in New York says that he thinks that the person who wrote this little note of yours is extremely mental and unstable. He specifically said that the part in the note where it says that some ruthless people had been using him as their guinea pig and has stolen his memories is a clear sign of…" The machine stopped again.

They didn't wait around for another call. Donaldson drew his gun and disappeared through the archway following Young into the front room as Mercedes withdrew her pistol and screamed for Alex to run. A second later she was at the archway looking into the living room.

Young's slacks were disappearing up the steps and Donaldson was standing behind the couch fiddling with the sliding glass door. Either he was blind or Alex was no longer behind the couch. He got the door open and ran into the back patio. Mercedes wanted to stay and search for Alex but there was barely enough time to save herself. She bolted for the door. The back patio was small and an instant later Donaldson was back inside. A gunshot went off and a hole exploded in the wall beside the front door. The living room wasn't that big and unless he was the world's poorest aim, that was a warning shot. Mere feet away from freedom, she stopped and held her hands out with the pistol dangling loosely from her right pointer finger.

"Drop it!" She heard Donaldson's voice behind her. Slowly bending her knees, she carefully lowered her gun-hand to just above the rug and let the pistol slip off her finger. Agent Young raced down the stairs as Mercedes stood back up, keeping her hands in the air.

"There's no sign of him upstairs," Mercedes heard him say as he aggressively approached her from behind. He grabbed her ponytail and violently jerked her head back, thrusting the mouth of his gun up under her chin. "Where is he?"

She wanted to answer but found herself unable to speak.

"I said where is he?" He pressed his gun deeper into her neck, all but cutting off her air supply.

She found the words inside her and somehow managed to push them through her restricted windpipe. "I don't know!"

Keeping his gun locked under her chin, he pulled her hair and forced her backward. Walking backward with a gun in her throat wasn't easy. She stumbled, losing her balance. Agent Young's firm grip on her ponytail nearly ripped the hair out of her head, but kept her from falling. He dexterously walked her around the western style coffee table and threw her onto the couch. As with Alex, it rocked once, almost fell over, but didn't. Donaldson stood behind it, between her and the sliding glass door and Young stood in front of it, still pointing the gun at her head.

Looking more like an aggravated Frankenstein's monster and less like *Dirty Harry*, Agent Young took a breath and used the back of his gun hand to wipe the trickle of sweat that was running down the left side of his face.

"Damn it!" He kicked the wooden coffee table into the couch, busting one leg and fracturing the top. It slammed into the couch hard. Mercedes hadn't expected it and was too slow to react. Its edge smashed into her leg just below her knee and she screamed in pain. Donaldson removed a handkerchief from his coat and gagged her. It wasn't necessary. She wasn't planning on screaming for help and if they could just refrain from losing their temper and inflicting unnecessary pain on her, she wouldn't be screaming again. He tightened his scarf. It was all but cutting into her cheeks through the corners of her mouth.

Young walked into the kitchen and returned with a steak knife. He grabbed the phone off the desk and ripped out the cord. Folding it in half, he cut it again, creating two long strands. He tossed them to Donaldson who secured her hands behind her back and tied her ankles together. After she was bound, Agent Young re-holstered his gun and Donaldson pushed her back onto the couch.

Agent Young walked over and picked her gun up off the carpet and set it on the desk next to the front door then took out his cell-phone and made a call.

Mercedes listened as he spoke. "Hello Sir, it's me…No, not yet. He's close. We almost got him………Atwater's………No, inside the apartment………… Yes Sir I know, but she made our cover, so we decided to go in without him. Do you want us to wait until he arrives?………It appears that way………We haven't found it yet but she called out to it telling it to run. It can't be far."

He looked at Mercedes and shook his head. "I don't know. I think she knows too much. He's supposed to meet us here at nine o'clock." There was a long silence as he turned around and faced the front door, listening into the phone. Mercedes wanted to say that she *didn't* know too much. Whoever was on the other end of the line was deciding whether or not Mercedes would die. She wanted to let Agent Young know, before he hung up, that she had no idea what was going on and there was no reason why they couldn't just untie her and let her go. Agent Young turned back around and looked into Mercedes' terror-filled eyes and said, "I understand," and then hung up, replacing the phone into his coat pocket.

He sucked his teeth again and cracked his neck. "Ms. Atwater you have two choices." He cleared his throat. "You can either give us the answers we require and we'll let you go, or," he paused, pushed up his chin, raised his eyebrows and slowly shook his head. Mercedes felt helpless. She pulled at her wrists, trying to get some space in between them, but the cords were too tight. "Now are you going to cooperate?"

She nodded.

"Good." He smiled as he reached down and brought the knife close to her face. She pulled her head back and widened her eyes as he worked the knife in between the handkerchief and her mouth. He hesitated as he met her eyes and held her gaze. His eyes were intense and his look was more than menacing, it was evil. Somehow he looked less than human. He looked demonic.

He cocked his head, speaking slowly and softly. "Now you've got *one* shot at this Ms. Atwater, any games," he brought his lips up to her ear, once again revealing the foul odor that resided in his breath and whispered, "and it's over. Do you understand?" He pulled his head back and looked into her eyes. She nodded as the terror within her grew. He carelessly sliced through the handkerchief, accidentally cutting the corner of her mouth. Bright red blood trickled down her chin, but she felt no pain.

They were going to kill her; there was no doubt in her mind. Agent Young's superiors probably told him to get as much information from her as he could, then get rid of her. The problem was, she didn't really know that much. Her only hope was to pretend that she knew more than she really did and pray that sooner or later they would let their defenses down, giving her a chance to escape. There was also the possibility that someone had heard the gunshot and called the cops. If she could keep them talking long enough maybe the cops would get there before they killed her. The cut at the corner of her mouth was bad and soon blood ran down her neck and flooded her shirt.

"All right let's take it from the top." Agent Young walked over to the desk, grabbed the computer chair and rolled it over in front of the couch. He twirled it around and straddled it, resting his elbow on the back. "What does he know?"

Mercedes breathed in and out rhythmically to calm herself down as she thought. She shook her head and said, "Not much! He can't remember much!"

Agent Young nodded, "Now we're getting somewhere." He smiled. Donaldson was now standing at the front door looking through the peephole. He had fired his gun earlier and they didn't know how much attention it might have stirred up. They felt fairly safe, as most people were either at work or still asleep at this hour.

"You called him Alex from the kitchen. Is that what he calls himself?"

Mercedes looked puzzled. What did he mean? Was he saying that Alex wasn't Alex? Agent Young became agitated at her slow response. "Where did he get the name Alex?"

Mercedes shrugged, "That's his name."

"That's his name? Alex? That's what he told you?"

She looked up and nodded.

"What did he say his last name was?"

She shook her head. "He didn't."

"Alex? Just Alex?"

She nodded. "What do you guys want with him anyway?"

"I'm asking the questions." Young shook his head and then paused. He had a question on the tip of his tongue but seemed reluctant to ask it. He shifted in his chair. Finally, he asked, "Has he displayed any unusual abilities?"

She looked at him and pretended not to understand. "What do you mean?"

"Has he demonstrated anything out of the ordinary?"

"Like what?"

Agent Young shook his head. "Never mind."

He looked at her for a second and thought. "Did he have any idea where he was going to go or what he was going to do?"

Mercedes' side began to ache with discomfort. She tried to sit up, but the cords around her wrists and ankles restricted her movement, making it all but impossible to change her position. She shook her head, "No."

"I'm getting tired of this. She doesn't know anything." Agent Young stood up and turned to Donaldson, who left the front door and walked over to the coffee table.

Even now he seemed friendlier than his demented partner. "What happened in Peppino's yesterday?"

She looked up at Donaldson, who continued in a caring sympathetic voice, "Did he have a flashback of some kind?"

Mercedes nodded.

"Whose flashback was it?" He waited. She didn't answer. "Was it Louie's?" He watched her expression carefully. "Was it David's?" He cocked his head and narrowed his eyes. "How about Billy's"

"She ain't gonna tell us anymore." Young said while peering into the street through the security hole.

"What did he say we were supposed to do to her?"

Agent Young turned away from the door, looked at Donaldson and grinned, "We get to *Teddyize* her." Donaldson matched his friend's grin.

"I'll get the box." Donaldson re-holstered his gun and went out the front door.

Teddyize me? What does that mean? By this time Mercedes had given up on the cops. If they were coming they would have been here by now. As she was wondering what *Teddyize* meant Agent Young walked into the kitchen and returned with a dishrag, which, without warning, he stuffed into her mouth as she began to squirm. He proceeded to secure another gag around her head as Agent Donaldson returned with a stainless steel box, a little larger than a milk crate. He placed it on the floor, in front of her. It featured three knobs on the side and what appeared to be some kind of a temperature gauge. Donaldson tossed a set of latex gloves to his partner and he slipped on a pair of his own.

The fear inside her was climbing as Agent Young smiled impishly and said, "Be happy, you're about to become LA's newest headhunter's victim."

Oh my God! Ever since the first reports hit the streets, she had believed that the headhunter was just one guy, one twisted and sick guy. It had never occurred to her that an entire organization might be behind the vicious murders. Her eyes grew wide and she began to jerk violently in a crazy attempt to get free. However, they weren't unskilled in binding techniques and although she bucked, shook and squirmed with all her might, her ties didn't loosen.

"We can't just remove her head, you know," Agent Young said with a smile.

"Why not?"

"Because good old Dr. Boris has started requesting that the company provide him with brain tissue from individuals who have had an intensely emotional death."

"So?"

"So Jackson programmed Teddy to start torturing his victims and take them apart before he kills them. Dr. Boris has even provided him with some chemicals that would keep Teddy's victims alive and awake through very terrifying and painful deaths."

"So?"

"So, Einstein, if we want this to look like *Teddy* did it, we have to do it, just the way *Teddy* would."

"I see." Donaldson widened his eyes. "So what did you have in mind?"

"I don't know." Agent Young began transforming into something more evil than he already was. "Chop her up first?"

"Hm?"

"We might as well, I mean she's going to be ran through the system like all the rest anyway. We'd probably score a few extra brownie points if we brought in some quality memory tissue. It might make up for not catching Number Nine yet."

"I guess you're right." Donaldson looked uneasy.

"Okay, let's see. What would Teddy do first?" Agent Young looked at his partner and with a wicked grin said, "Think like a psychopath."

Agent Donaldson held up his hand in a stopping gesture. "Sorry, can't help you there man. That's your department."

Agent Young's eyes looked deranged. "Hey, I'm not the psycho, Teddy is."

"Yeah, but you found him."

Mercedes couldn't believe what was happening and she seriously questioned her judgment about taking the case in the first place.

"No, no, no. Just hold on right there. I didn't find him. Jackson did. All I've done is sit back and admire the puppet strings."

Mercedes began to see her life replay in her mind. The fear inside her continued to grow as her eyes filled with water and her entire body began to tremble.

"Yeah, well it takes a psycho to know a psycho."

Agent Young didn't reply to the last statement. He just refocused the conversation to the business at hand. "I say we start with her toes."

"You mean you want to do this while she's alive?"

"Duh, where have you been? That's the way Teddy does it."

"Yeah but-can't we just kill her first and then slice and dice?"

Up 'til now Mercedes had all but tuned them out as she accepted the fact that she was going to die. But now as they started talking about cutting her up alive she began to feel with a brand new sense of horror.

"Now come on, where's your sense of fun? We have a golden opportunity here. How many other people do you know who will ever have a chance like this?"

Donaldson shook his head, "Nobody I know would want a chance like this."

"Just shut up and help me remove her shoes and socks. We'll start with her toes."

Mercedes began to turn pale and could barely breath. Where was Alex? How had he managed to pull himself together and sneak away without anyone knowing?

Agent Young reached down, grabbed her ankle and pulled it up fast, forcing her whole body to scoot across the couch.

CHAPTER FOURTEEN

As he was pulling the shoelace out of its bow, Mercedes jerked her body and managed to kick Agent Young in the face. The kick was hard and he stumbled back, releasing her foot in the process. Agent Donaldson couldn't hold back his laugh but did manage to keep it down to a little snicker. Earlier, Mercedes had tried to sit up, but could not. The cords binding her hands and feet had been too tight. Somehow, things were different now. She harnessed all of her strength and flipped her entire body over onto the broken coffee table. A large splinter of wood stabbed into her side as she tumbled off onto the floor, landing belly first. She'd never get away; nevertheless, she instinctively inched for the door. Agent young regained his balance and glared at Donaldson, whose smile was just fading from his face. He walked around and stood in front of the fleeing inchworm.

A look of disgust filled his face as he licked his lip and rubbed his sore cheek. "Little bitch!" He pulled his foot back and slammed the toe of his dress shoe hard into her face, just below the right eye. The pain was incredible. He must have shattered her cheekbone. Her vision blurred and she became lightheaded. She was swimming in a sea of dizziness as he reached down and took hold of her ponytail. He raised her head up and with his other hand, grabbed the waistband of her jeans. Like a small toy doll, he lifted her completely off the floor and heaved her back onto the couch. This time it not only rocked, but also fell over, throwing her off, onto the wood-planks, behind it.

With her cheek beginning to swell, Agent Young walked around the couch and knelt down at her feet. He grabbed her ankles and aggressively rotated her body, forcing her onto her stomach. He didn't bother untying her shoes this time, he simply ripped them off. Donaldson stood wide-eyed as Agent Young brought the steak knife up to her bare feet and began to grin. Mercedes tried to scream but it just came out as a muffled squeal, not even loud enough to be heard outside.

Something cold and sharp connected with the base of her pinky toe. The deranged smile on Agent Young's face widened. Just as he began to apply pressure to the knife, she squirmed again. Because he was kneeling and his hold on her was stronger than it was before, she wasn't able to push him away. However, the latex glove was slippery and the knife slid out of his hand, flew across the room and landed on the floor, in the archway.

He shook his head. "How in the Hell does Teddy do this? This is more difficult than I ever imagined." Not wanting to let go of her, he had Donaldson get the knife. As Donaldson was retrieving the blade an idea found its way into Mercedes' head.

Alex could read minds!

She remembered how he told her of his experience in the homeless shelter. He was in the back of the building, with a warehouse full of people and still managed to hear the thoughts of someone out on the street, walking by. She wasn't sure how far his ability worked but she decided to focus on him anyway.

Donaldson handed the knife to Young.

"She's like a bronco. Hold her still while I operate."

Donaldson's stomach soured as he latched onto her legs. Young brought the knife back up to her foot and reconnected it with the base of her toe. Still concentrating on Alex, she released a muffled shriek of pain as the demonic agent pushed the blade completely through and severed her toe. Blood oozed out from the stub as he marveled at the small ball-like piece of flesh rolling around in his latex-covered hand.

Like some wild animal, he looked up at Donaldson and grinned. "Look at it Haskell!" Mercedes was in too much pain and too deeply dazed to realize that Agent Young called Agent Donaldson by another name. "Oh my God! Isn't it exhilarating?" He shook his head and let out a quick, powerful breath. He was a madman.

***

Alex was outside, underneath one of the carports, trying to organize his thoughts. He had remembered going to Peppino's last night and having another flashback of some kind. However, it wasn't one with Louie's memories. This time he was Bad Boy Billy, the one who had shot and killed Louie. This experience was even stranger than the last. As he was slamming slugs into Louie he could clearly remember *being* Louie and what it felt like to be the one getting hammered. The death experience was much longer this time and seemed to go on forever. He hovered over Billy's body until the paramedics arrived. He floated in and around the ambulance all the way to the hospital. Once there, he lingered, in the intensive care unit that Billy was in, occasionally drifting into an adjacent room or floating out into the hall, but never going too far.

Sometime during the vision he briefly woke up in the emergency room of the hospital with Mercedes, but almost instantaneously blacked out again. He remembered Mercedes being there. He remembered hearing her voice. He thought she took him to her place but he wasn't sure. Then he remembered someone knocking on a door and a strange lady—or wait—was it Mercedes, telling him to be quiet. His life was in danger! The next thing he knew, he woke up on the floor. He was lying on his back and watching the helicopter blade spinning overhead, which gradually morphed into a ceiling fan. People were talking. He could read their thoughts. They wanted to capture him and take him to a dark, dreary place. Fear consumed him and he began whispering the word run. He got to his knees and with the catlike stealth he had displayed in Ginger's apartment, crouched behind the couch and focused on the voices in his head. Mercedes was in the next room with two men. His thoughts were cloudy and he wasn't sure what he should do. He focused on Mercedes. She was thinking about getting out of the house, about running past a man in a black business suit. She was pouring a cup of coffee. She looked at the door and thought about spilling the coffee on the man's lap as she ran, but decided not to. She didn't want to leave Alex in the house with them.

She wished Alex wasn't behind the couch. She wished he were outside. His reasoning wasn't functioning at its best and he thought that the best way to help Mercedes, and himself, would be for him to grant her wish and sneak away. Once he was safely outside she would be able to spill her coffee and run out to join him.

Now, as he stood in the carport, with a little clearer head he realized that his thinking had been tainted by his disoriented state of mind. Mercedes was still inside with two dangerous men and he was unsure of what to do. She had no way of knowing that he had left. Should he go back in after her? No. She was a professional. The FBI had trained her. She could take care of herself. If he went back in and tried to help, he'd more than likely, just get in the way. The best thing to do was try to locate her car and wait. Looking around for the Porsche, he heard her voice.

"Alex! Alex!" She was in a state of panic, a familiar state to him. "Help! Please! I need your help!" Not only could he hear her words but he could feel them as well. They were completely saturated in fear. Then a strange thing happened. For a few short, terrifying moments, he was looking out though her eyes. A familiar, sinister face grinned at her (grinned at him) with evil eyes.

A man, a wicked and horrible man stood over her with malice intentions. For some sick reason he was planning on slicing her up, alive!

Suddenly, his own fear began to fade until all he could think about was helping her. Looking out from the carport he saw more than a dozen townhouses. A moment ago he had no idea, which one, if any, belonged to her, but now, somehow, he knew exactly which one was hers. Not only did he know which one was hers, but somehow, he also knew precisely where in the house she was and more importantly, where her attackers were. For an instance he knew her house as well as she did. He thought about the gun on the desk. Overwhelmed with urgency, he ran to her door. Instead of reaching for the handle he willed it to open. A gust of wind swirled behind him as he extended his right hand forward.

Still grinning, Agent Young dropped the toe onto the floor and brought the knife up to the next one as the door exploded inward. It nearly came off the hinges and slammed hard into the wall. He looked up, saw Number Nine and dropped the knife. He couldn't believe his luck. Not only was he going to get to mutilate a live person today, but he had also found Number Nine. He reached under his coat for his gun as Donaldson turned to look at the door.

Number Nine stood in the doorway with his right hand stretched out in front of him. A bizarre wind rushed past him into the house, making his hair dance. His expression was cold and distant and his eyes were glossy and unfocussed.

Young gripped the butt of his gun and Donaldson reached inside his coat as the pistol on the desk took on a will of its own and spun around. With lightning fast speed, like a piece of metal being pulled by a giant magnet, it leaped off the desk and slapped into the palm of Alex's hand. He immediately and incessantly fired. A barrage of gunshots echoed through the house and out into the street as a shower of lead filled the living room. Four slugs immediately slammed into Donaldson, one in the shoulder, two in the chest and one in the left eye. Like dozens of little ketchup packages being squeezed at the same time, blood exploded out of Donaldson's body, splattered the walls and sprayed across Agent Young's face.

With open eyes he dropped the gun, hobbled backward and slammed hard into the wall. Young managed to pull his gun out and point it at Alex. But before he was able to pull the trigger, a bullet from Alex's pistol hit his hand and knocked the gun from it. It crashed though the sliding glass door behind him, completely shattering the glass, and landed on the patio outside. Even while the glass was still falling, Agent Young dove through the doorway and into the back yard. He landed on the concrete headfirst and somersaulted, head over heals, disappearing behind the wall.

Alex was sure he had hit the fleeing man at least once, maybe twice. And although the man had got through the doorway, he was unsuccessful in retrieving his gun. With the cold-blooded instincts of a trained killer, Alex calmly walked around the couch, keeping his gun-arm fully extended in front of him. It took him only a second to reach the doorway and gain a complete view of the backyard, however the man wasn't there. He must have scaled the wooden fence. Alex was sure he wouldn't get far before he collapsed. He turned and looked at Mercedes, who was still bound on the floor and barely awake. He blinked rapidly and began to shake. His shaking dwindled and his eyes swam back into focus as his hand relaxed, releasing the gun. It fell to the floor beside her feet. For a moment he looked confused and out of touch, then he gazed around the blood-filled room.

An open-eyed corpse leaned against the wall. He remembered shooting the man but had a hard time connecting his emotions to his actions. He looked back at Mercedes. The pinky toe of her left foot was missing and blood was slowing oozing out from the wound. He gently rolled her over onto her back. Her face was bruised, purple and black. Her shirt was soaked in blood. He picked the knife up off the floor and cut her ties. He removed the gag from her head as her eyes floated in and out of focus.

She tried to speak but her swollen face made it nearly impossible.

"Shh! Don't talk. I can hear your thoughts."

Her right eye was completely swollen shut. She looked up at Alex and thought, "I need to find my toe and put it in water. Maybe it can be reattached..."

Alex scanned over the floor, spotted it to his right and picked it up. He took it into the kitchen, found a seal-a-baggy, and after putting her toe in water, he grabbed some paper towels then returned to Mercedes.

As he applied the paper towel to her foot, securing it by putting her sock back on, she continued to think, "The cops will be here any second and we don't know whose side they're on. We have to get out of here. We have to find a place to hide, while we figure out what's going on."

"What do you want me to do?"

"Help me to the car."

He helped her to her feet as she held her side in pain. His frail body wasn't very strong and he had a hard time helping her through the front room.

"Wait!" she said as they reached the front door. He stopped as she leaned up against the wall.

Her thoughts filled his head. "We need his wallet and anything else that will tell us who he is." She pointed at the corpse.

After making sure she could lean against the wall on her own, he moved back over to the man's body and removed two wallets from his coat pocket. He shoved them into the pockets of his jeans and started back to Mercedes.

"My camera," she thought, "it's on the table in the kitchen."

He went and got it as well, then returned to her and they shuffled outside. A small crowd had already gathered across the street. Mercedes was getting heavier by the moment and Alex was finding it more and more difficult to hold her up. They made it to the carport and she leaned up against the wall.

"You'll have to drive, I can't see." She thought as she leaned up against the stucco covered wall.

Drive? He thought. He couldn't remember driving and was afraid he wouldn't know how. "I don't think I *can* drive."

They got to the car and she tried talking him through operating it. They bucked forward and slammed hard into the wall of the carport. They jerked back and stalled, then around to the street. They could hear the sirens closing in as they pulled out into the street and then stalled again.

"This ain't going to work," she mumbled. They stopped the car and he helped her to the Corolla, which was just a couple car lengths ahead. Doing her best to see, she drove them away from the curb as three black and whites pulled into the complex.

CHAPTER FIFTEEN

Raymond Hayward Jackson pulled the Camry up to the security booth and held up his identification. He had top-level clearance and was allowed anywhere in the building. The guard looked out the window, smiled, and waved him in. Raymond had a designated parking space on the fourth tier, but felt it was much too restricting. He liked being able to get away fast, incase something unexpectedly came up, as it almost always did. He parked in an empty stall just three spaces in from the security booth and got out of the car.

He was a well-dressed, tall, baldheaded man. He walked around and unlocked the trunk, retrieved his briefcase and whistled his way to the elevator. Even though he was running late he felt no reason to hurry. Everything was under control and he was sure that Number Nine would be caught today and business would resume as usual. He hadn't been as sure yesterday morning as he was today.

The day before yesterday he had been standing guard during a memory injection with Number Nine. Up until recently there had been no reason to have a guard. However, somehow Number Nine had started becoming more and more aware during the last few injections. It first began right after it was injected with the memory of a telepathic. During that session Number Nine was able to read all the minds in the room. God only knows what it found out and how it interpreted what was happening to it. After that injection the company wanted to see what would happen with the memory of a telekinetic. Dr. Boris and Mr. Davenport said it was incredible. Ray thought it was foolish. Number Nine was able to move small objects with thought alone. Over the next three months the company foolishly continued to feed telepathic and telekinetic memories into it.

Even though Dr. Boris would completely neutralize and erase the entire memory at the end of each procedure, during the next injection little fragments of memory from the last session would somehow crop up. They were *never* complete sets, only bits and pieces. Dr. Boris had predicted something like this might happen with a subject as pure as Number Nine. All was okay until last month. During an injection Number Nine was somehow able to keep its brain clear and hold the new memory at bay. Ray believed that's when it became conscious for the first time. It looked up, called Dr. Boris by name and demanded to be set free. Its restraints mysteriously untied themselves and Dr. Boris fell to the floor, suffering a mild heart attack. Number Nine nearly got away before one of the assistants injected it with memory neutralizer. It walked out into the hall and pressed the elevator button before its brain shut down, rendering it unable to think. It then collapsed on the floor.

After that Mr. Davenport didn't want to take any chances. He had Ray stand guard during all future injections. In any other case Ray would have taken the assignment as an insult. But with the awesome powers at work in Number Nine and with everything the company had at stake, he understood the importance of the position and felt honored by the job. Besides, the injections weren't every day. There might be three in a week at most and they only lasted a couple of hours. The company still needed Ray to do what he did best, what they hired him for, bring in new memory tissue.

During the last session with Number Nine everything went haywire. Ray was standing guard as Dr. Boris worked. Everything was going fine as they hooked up the IVs and started the recordings. Dr. Boris brought in the latest set of memory tissue. It had been acquired by Patterson.

Patterson was one of the newest members to the team. Ray himself had picked him out and trained him a little over two years ago. From time to time Ray had second-guessed his decision in selecting him, but overall he seemed to be working out okay. Patterson had some serious challenges with his interpersonal skills that made him a little unpredictable at times. But Mr. Davenport believed that it helped more than it hurt. He said Patterson's challenges were benefits that kept him focused and on task. Mr. Davenport saw Patterson as a motivated and loyal employee. Over the last few months Ray had come to the conclusion that Patterson had been a good choice after all.

Patterson had brought in three different sets of memory tissues that day. He had heard that there was going to be a hit done on a smalltime mafia boss. He organized a team and waited in the shadows. Luck was good to him and he managed to obtain three healthy memory tissues from the shootout, Louie Ventino's, Billy Marcus' and David Winters'. Dr. Boris successfully ran Louie and Billy's memories through Number Nine and recorded the results. However, in the middle of David's memory tissue injection, Number Nine opened its eyes and looked at Dr. Boris. The overhead lights quickly popped, one at a time, until everything was dark. Leaving the place illuminated only by the glowing computer monitors and the small self-lit control panels. In such an event, Ray's first priority was to sedate Number Nine. He had been given a tranquilizer rifle and three vials, containing memory neutralizer mixed with a fast acting sedative.

He raised his rifle and took aim at Number Nine, but before he could squeeze the trigger, his rifle flew out of his hands. It crossed the room on its own accord, slammed into the wall and landed on the white tile floor. He withdrew his handgun and a new vial, and then raced over to the restraining table, but Number Nine had already untied its restraints and fled into the control room. Ray chased after it. The control room was brighter than the last, but Number Nine wasn't to be found. It seemed as if it had vanished into thin air.

Ray searched frantically, but was unable to locate Number Nine until he noticed a faint glow, shining through the crack below the bathroom door. Inside, he found Number Nine oddly dangling a pen above a piece of paper. As he cornered it and slowly moved in he began to notice ink mysteriously appearing on the paper. Number Nine stood in the corner looking like a frightened animal. Ray kept a tight grip on his gun, pointing it in Number Nine's direction as he crept in closer. Number Nine wadded up the note and stuffed it into its pocket. Ray capitalized on the action and lunged forward. He stabbed Number Nine in the right arm but was immediately thrown up against the ceiling. Unfortunately, only half of the serum had been injected. Number Nine grabbed the syringe, pulled it out and stuffed it into its pocket, then ran underneath Ray, who was stuck to the ceiling, like a fly on flypaper. A few seconds later, the ceiling loosened its grip and released Ray. The drop was unexpected and he hit the floor hard, nearly knocking him unconscious.

Patterson and he chased Number Nine up to ground level, into the parking lot, and then out onto the street. They lost it in a rundown apartment complex around the corner. Mr. Davenport was furious and launched a company-wide search. Ray felt personally responsible and stayed up all night searching and researching homeless shelters, hospitals and police stations. There was no luck until yesterday. Patterson and Haskell had spotted Number Nine in St. John's homeless shelter and chased it to a row of offices where it once again, vanished. But then last night a little after eight o'clock something wonderful happened. One of the company's contacts at the FBI informed them that a Mercedes Atwater and an unidentified male friend had visited Peppino's yesterday afternoon. Ms. Atwater turned out to be a private investigator whose office happened to be amongst the row of offices where Number Nine had last been seen. Ray and Travis (another company man) had slipped in and looked through her office early this morning, while Patterson and Haskell kept tabs on her at her townhouse. Ray found no evidence of Number Nine at her office but did find a couple of articles about the shooting at Peppino's.

Now, Patterson and Haskell were outside of Ms. Atwater's apartment waiting for Ray. He had instructed them to keep an eye on her and wait for his arrival. When he got there, Haskell and he would go in and pretend to be CIA, while Patterson waited outside, watching the perimeter. They would ask some questions and tell Ms. Atwater that the man she is helping is really an international terrorist. They would convince her to turn him over to them. Then they would simply disappear. They'd have Number Nine and Mercedes would have the knowledge that she had helped her country capture a very dangerous criminal.

It was eight-thirty and he wasn't supposed to meet the boys until nine o'clock. Before he went to Mercedes' he wanted to stop in and personally assure Mr. Davenport that everything was under control and he would have Number Nine back in Dr. Boris' custody by the end of the day.

The electronic bell chimed and the elevator door opened. Ray stepped out onto the sixty-eighth floor of the *Trend Star* building, the tallest in a set of four owned by the *Biotronics Corporation*. He walked across the marble floor and into the plush outer office of Jonathan Davenport. The lady behind the counter looked up and said hello, but didn't smile.

"Hi. Is he in?" Ray asked.

She nervously nodded. "He's expecting you, Mr. Jackson."

"Expecting me? But I didn't tell him I was coming. Why is he expecting me?"

She held up her hands and shook her head. "And he's not happy either."

Ray looked alarmed as he walked past her to the large, dark, double oak doors. He straightened his tie and then walked inside.

The office was huge and obviously took up a corner portion of the building because the entire left wall and the one at the far end of the office were both made of glass and looked over the city. An elaborate oak desk sat in the corner where the huge glass walls met. Just behind the desk, a high-back leather chair faced the far glass wall. An original Van Gough hung to Ray's right. Antiques from various eras were strategically placed throughout the office. Ray closed the door softly and ran his hand down the front of his suit, double-checking the button at the bottom of his coat as he walked forward. He walked around the leather sitting area and stepped up onto the platform. He walked across the long putting green and approached the desk.

He cleared his throat. "Mr. Davenport?"

Ray could not see around the back of the chair as an elderly man's voice floated up over the top of it. "Raymond!" The voice was direct and sounded perturbed.

"Yes, sir?"

An old man's hand hung over an arm of the chair grasping a newspaper. "Do you have any idea of what a mess you've made?"

"Sir?"

The heavy chair slowly rotated, revealing an extremely handsome, silver-haired man in his late fifties, early sixties. His clothes were top of the line and gold adorned his fingers. He was very comfortable with himself and emitted a powerful air of confidence.

He lightly slammed the newspaper onto the desk, revealing the headlines. *Police Move in on Freak!*

The supporting photo took up nearly the entire page. It was a white Victorian style house.

"Isn't that your cousin's place?" His voice was solid and agreeably authoritative.

Ray leaned across the desk and picked up the paper. He gaped at the photo and turned to the article.

The old man leaned forward and interlaced his fingers. "You don't have to read it, Ray. I can tell you what it says."

Ray found the story and read silently as Mr. Davenport spoke. "The Monster..." He paused, nodded and cleared his throat. "...*Your* monster, was more careless than you thought he'd be. A bunch of *kids* with cameras managed to break into your cousin's house and photograph him coming and going." Mr. Davenport tapped his pointer finger on the desk. "I told you this one was unstable." Ray looked up from his paper in a blank stare. Mr. Davenport nodded again, slowly turning it into a negative shake. "Did you listen? No!" He turned his chair, stood up and walked over to the glass on the left side of the building. He clasped his hands behind his back and looked out the window as he spoke. "I don't suppose by some miracle you've managed to capture Number Nine yet."

Ray looked at Mr. Davenport. He stood, dignified, staring out of the glass at the city below. "No sir. But I will have it today. Mercedes Atwater is hiding it. I'm going to meet Patterson and Haskell in twenty minutes at her townhouse in Beverly Hills. I'm confident we'll be able to persuade her to give us Number Nine."

"Twenty minutes?" Still looking out the window the old man nodded. "You're going to meet them in twenty minutes?"

"Yes sir."

"How are you going to do that when Haskell is dead and Patterson is on his way to see Dr. Boris for *lead* poisoning?"

Ray's eyes shifted quickly as he thought. "What?"

"Was I not clear enough?" Mr. Davenport turned back around, looked sternly at Ray and then walked back to his chair. "Evidently, Haskell and

Patterson thought they could handle Mercedes without you this morning." He sat down and blinked in thought. "Well, I guess they were wrong."

"I told them to wait for me." Ray became anxious.

"Well they didn't and it gets worse. Apparently Number Nine has begun to tap his telekinesis. According to Patterson, Number Nine willed a gun to fly across a room, into its hand."

Ray shook his head in disbelief. "I can't believe they didn't wait for me. How bad was Patterson hit?"

"I don't think it's too bad. He says he was just grazed. I sent him to Dr. Boris anyway, just to be safe. He said Number Nine is calling itself Alex."

"Alex?"

"Alex! Do you know the significance of that name?"

Ray stood silently and Mr. Davenport glared.

"What happened to it and Atwater?"

"We're not sure. By the time the police arrived they had already gone."

Overwhelmed, Ray laid the newspaper on the desk and took a seat opposite Mr. Davenport.

"Do we have any idea where they went?"

"Not yet. But it's even worse than that. Haskell and Patterson had one of *Biotronics'* cooling systems with them and left it for the police to find!"

Ray looked confused. "So...there's no way to trace those boxes back to *Biotronics.*"

Mr. Davenport became agitated. "No? Why not? Can't they trace Haskell back to *Biotronics?* He's been found, dead, in the same house less than five feet away from the unit." He breathed in deeply through his nose, nodded and shook his head. "Now, if you couple that with the unit they found at your cousin's house, then Haskell is going to be linked to LA's headhunter, putting Biotronics in an extremely bad light!"

Ray stared at Mr. Davenport in silence, mortified.

"Raymond, that's not all."

Ray listened, not sure he wanted to hear any more.

"Nicholas Chadwick has just arrived!" He picked up the newspaper and flipped to another article.

City Thug is Gunned Down by Country Boy!

Ray took the paper and looked at the photo. It wasn't of Nick. It was a shot of Uncle Bob's Tavern. He shook his head and looked up at Mr. Davenport. "What's with this guy? Why doesn't he just give up?" He slapped the paper onto the desk again. "You should have let me take him out in that warehouse in Atlanta."

Mr. Davenport cleared his throat and nodded. "Maybe you're right."

"Is there anymore? Does it get any worse than this?" It was a fairly good day when Ray entered the office, but in less than ten short minutes it had turned into an incredibly horrible day.

"No, that's it."

"So what are we going to do?"

"We?" Mr. Davenport raised an eyebrow and looked across the desk. "*We* aren't going to do anything. *You* on the other hand are going to go find your little freak, Theodore, and turn him off." He cocked his head and glared at Ray, who nodded in agreement. "Then you are going to go find Number Nine and bring it home!"

"What about Chadwick? What if he starts snooping around with this new information?"

After a long pause he said, "Get rid of him."

Ray nodded and shifted his eyes to the desk. He swallowed, looked back at Mr. Davenport and stood up. Mr. Davenport said nothing, but kept eye contact with Ray while he stood up and turned around. Ray headed for the door. Halfway across the office Mr. Davenport broke the silence. "Haskell has always been a shady character and the company records will show that he was fired last week. If I were you I would collaborate that version of the truth."

Ray stopped and listened but didn't turn around then nodded and left the office.

CHAPTER SIXTEEN

The Mustang pulled into the police station at precisely eight-twenty-three. Nick got out, holding a paper cup of coffee from McDonald's and wearing his cowboy boots, dark blue jeans and black leather jacket. Even though he had gotten little sleep last night, it was more than usual. After the incident at Uncle Bob's Tavern he was pretty sure Detective Garvey would be reluctant to offer him any help.

The police showed up right at 1:00 AM and after questioning everyone and confiscating Nick's gun they arrested the two hoodlums and told Nick not to leave town. Nick walked across the street to the all night mini-mart, bought an economy size pack of Gummy Bears and then went back to his motel where he fell asleep around two-thirty or so. He might have decided to blow off his meeting this morning if his alarm clock hadn't already been set. It sounded at 7:30 am. After taking a quick shower, he threw on his clothes, loaded up the car, and paid his bill. He headed directly for the police station, making a quick pit stop at McDonald's. He went through the drive-through and ordered nothing but a black cup of coffee, something to wash down the Gummy Bears.

Now at the station, he walked up to a young, attractive, blond-haired woman at the counter. "Hi. I'm Nicholas Chadwick. I'm here to see Detective Garvey."

She smiled at him, "Do you have an appointment?"

"Yes ma'am." He sipped his coffee.

Her smile grew as she quickly ran her eyes over his body. "One moment please." She pressed a couple of buttons and spoke into the headset. "There's a Nicholas…" She looked back at Nick and covered the microphone. "What did you say your last name was?"

"Chadwick." He stood with his left hand in his coat pocket and held his coffee with his right.

She smiled again and spoke back into the phone. "Nicholas Chadwick here to see Detective Garvey." After a short pause she said, "Okay," pressed a couple more buttons, and smiled back at Nick. "He'll be right out."

Nick nodded, said, "Thank you," tossed a bear into his mouth and sipped his coffee again.

"So, how do you know the detective?" She asked. But as Nick began to answer, she held up her finger. "Hold on." Then she pressed a couple more buttons and said, "Los Angeles Police Department, how may I direct your call?"

Before she finished and could return her attention to Nick, the door behind her opened and a man carrying a manila folder, entered the room. "Is there a Chadwick here?"

Nick held up his cup and nodded.

"Come on." He waved the file in a follow-me gesture.

Nick looked at the lady, smiled, then walked over to the door and followed the man down the hall. They walked through the department, almost tracing Nick's steps from last night and ended up on the second floor just outside of Detective Garvey's office. The man rapped on the door.

"Come in." A voice came from inside.

The man opened the door and walked inside. Nick followed.

The first one to speak was Detective Garvey. He looked up from his work and pulled his glasses away from his face. "Ah... Mr. Chadwick. Please, sit down." He gestured with his glasses.

Nick took a seat in the hardwood chair across from the detective as the other man laid the manila folder on the desk. The man walked out and closed the door, shutting out the busy sounds of the department. Garvey looked back down at his desk, replaced his glasses and opened the file.

Nick rested his ankle on his knee and shifted his weight a little. "Detective Garvey?"

With his eyes on the file, the detective held up his hand. Nick paused, waiting for the detective's attention. A few moments later the detective looked up over the top of his glasses and said, "I understand you stirred up quite a ruckus last night."

Embarrassed, Nick nodded. "I'm sorry...I wasn't given much choice. The guy was... going to shoot me."

"Yeah." Garvey nodded, "That's what the report says."

Garvey looked back at the file. "Detective, I wanted to talk to you about..."

Interrupting, Garvey looked up and said, "I know what you want to talk about." Nick stopped and listened. The detective nodded again and continued, "I knew you looked familiar to me last night when we met." He shook his head. "But I couldn't place you." He leaned back in his chair, folded his hands over his stomach and slowly began twiddling his thumbs. "But then, after you left, it came to me. A little while after this case started I received a memo from the FBI. It appears you have a habit of getting in the way of these types of cases."

Nick uncrossed his legs and listened intently. The detective leaned forward and looked back at the file. "Albany, New Mexico. You got in the way and almost ruined the High Plains Strangler investigation. Austin, Texas. It says you called their station as many as five times a day. Chicago, Illinois. You were found inside a restricted crime scene after being warned repeatedly to stay out of their investigation."

Nick desperately wanted to say something in his defense, but there wasn't much he could say. He just sat and listened as the detective went on.

"Detroit, Michigan. Their department was running in circles trying to figure out what was your meddling and what were real clues. It goes on and on." Garvey turned the page. "Galveston, Texas. Hattiesburg, Mississippi." He shifted his eyes over his glasses at Nick and then looked back down again as he turned another page. "Memphis, Tennessee. Miami, Florida. New York, New York." The detective held a sheet of paper with one hand and gestured with the other. According to this report, it would seem that you've been almost everywhere in the country."

There was a moment of silence as the detective removed his glasses and tossed them on top of the file. Then Nick nodded his head. "Yeah, I've been all over." He paused, turned away from the detective and looked out the window. "And I've even gotten in the way of a few investigations here and there." He shook his head. "I don't know how to explain this to you detective, but eight years ago my wife died and some very strange things happened to her body afterward." He paused to keep from tearing up. "There were people there when she died, people that could have helped. But they did nothing!" He shook his head and repeated, "Nothing! Her body disappeared for three days and when she was finally found, we discovered that someone had cut through her skull and removed the top portion…" His eyes bunched up and he seemed to be looking not only at the window, but into the past as well. "And for some God-awful reason, removed more than half her brain." He looked back at the detective who sat unmoved by his story. "I can't explain how I know this… but most of the cases I've been following are somehow connected to what happened to my wife."

"Mr. Chadwick, I've been in this business for a long time. And one of the hardest things I have to do is look a decent human being in the eye and tell them we were unable to find the monster that killed their loved one and then watch their face twist in confusion and torment. I believe we, as humans, have a hard time accepting that sometimes there just aren't any answers. I'm not unsympathetic to your loss. The pain you've experienced must have been immense for you to have carried it around inside you all these years. But I've read your file and I know all about what happened to your wife *and* your parents as well. And I'm sure you desperately want to find a reason for what happened. You want to make some sense of the tragedy they went through. You want to-"

"Please." Nick raised his hand and stood up. "Spare me the lecture, Detective. I shouldn't have even come. I knew you wouldn't want to help." Nick turned toward the door.

"Mr. Chadwick, if you don't want to take my advice, fine. But make no mistake about it. If you're so much as *seen* near one of my crime scenes, I'll have you arrested."

Nick turned and looked at the detective, who was looking more and more like a 500-pound gorilla. "You can't do that!"

"Oh no? Weren't you involved in a homicide last night? Let's see, there were four witnesses. Two of them said that they were keeping to themselves, shooting a friendly game of pool and you provoked a fight. They said you told them that Uncle Bob's was a redneck bar and they didn't belong there."

"Oh come on! That's bullshit! Those guys were trying to rob the place! And the other two witnesses have an entirely different story."

"Oh yeah, that's right." The detective paused, then sarcastically asked, "Wasn't one of them a drunk?"

Nick stood bewildered. "You can't threaten me with this shit!"

"It's not a threat! Stay out of my investigation."

Nick turned back around and reached for the knob just as someone knocked. He opened the door and stepped aside as the short, heavyset man he had seen with Garvey last night, rushed past him. The man handed Garvey a green sticky note. Nick turned around and lingered just outside the door.

"It was just found."

The detective stood up and removed his glasses. "Where?"

"1123 Carolyn Court, Beverly Hills."

Garvey walked around the desk, slipped his glasses into his shirt pocket and grabbed his corduroy coat off the tree by the window. He started walking toward the door, where Nick was still standing as he slipped one arm into a sleeve. He walked forward, ushering Nick as he went.

He looked at Nick. "Mr. Chadwick, that's the last piece of advice I'm going to give you on this matter. You'd be wise to take it." He closed the door and with his companion, headed for the stairs. "C'mon Mr. Chadwick, I'll see you out."

Nick followed them back to the front desk. The blonde was on another call, but smiled and strummed her fingers through the air as soon as she saw Nick. Garvey and his partner disappeared through a back door. Nick walked out the front and then sprinted to the Mustang. He got in and opened his laptop. After connecting wirelessly to the net, he looked up 1123 Carolyn Ct. Beverly Hills, California. Almost instantaneously a map popped up, displaying the location. He then marked it as a destination point and pulled up the quickest route from the Los Angeles Police Department. Less than a moment later a point-by-point map was displayed on the screen. Distance: 12.6 miles. Travel time: twenty-two minutes. Pressing a few more buttons he downloaded the map and activated the global positioning system, then tied into Traffic Zone, a live traffic web-cam site. He activated *Starnav*, a little program he purchased last year. It followed the global positioning system and updated his computer with current traffic conditions every thirty seconds. If traffic began to congest along his course the system would automatically download the next quickest route, run it though Traffic Zone and if the new route were quicker it would display the changes as Nick drove.

Next, Nick pulled out a little black box about the size of a videocassette tape. It featured two suction cups that connected nicely to the windshield when he placed it on the dashboard. He flipped a switch on the side and a little green light came on, indicating that there were no radar guns pointing his way. As he slid his shades over his eyes, he turned the engine over and then backed out of the stall. The tires squealed slightly as he shifted gears and pulled forward out of the police station parking lot. Forty-five seconds later he was on the Santa Ana Freeway heading north. Almost instantly, traffic slowed down and nearly stopped. Starnav kicked in and within moments Nick found himself cruising down Wilshire Blvd. through Korea Town.

Sixteen minutes after leaving the station Nick was pulling up to a set of townhouses in a nice upper-middle class neighborhood. With any luck Detective Garvey wouldn't be here for another ten or fifteen minutes. There were a half a dozen police cars, an army of officers, uniformed and plain clothed, and a large crowd of onlookers. Nick pulled up behind a poorly parked red Porsche on the street, just outside of the complex, cut off the engine and studied the crowed. He wasn't sure what he was looking for. All he knew was that Detective Garvey was working on the headhunter case and for some reason he was on his way here.

He got out of the car and walked over to the crowd, which was being held back by two police officers and a long stretch of yellow tape.

"What's up?" he asked a young man in baggy clothes while popping a Gummy Bear in his mouth.

"I don't know. Some guy came home and found his girl with another dude. He went ballistic!" The young man repeated the gossip.

Nick carefully studied the plain clothed officers as they were periodically stopped and ID'd while crossing the yellow police tape.

The young man continued. "He drilled the guy with a semiautomatic, woke up half the neighborhood, then beat the fuck out of the chick. He dragged her out of the house and off somewhere."

Nick slowly shifted his eyes to the kid, popped in another Bear and then, chewing slowly, looked back to the townhouse. A uniformed police officer came out, ducked below the police tape and headed for the street where Nick's Mustang was parked. Nick left the crowd and followed, almost parallel with the officer, back toward his car. Beneath his shades he studied the policeman's uniform carefully. He approached the trunk of the Mustang as the officer walked up to the front, then turned and looked at the Porsche. The officer stepped off the curb and slowly circled the car as Nick walked over and stood in front of the Mustang.

"Is that your car?" The officer looked up and pointed at the Mustang.

"Yeah! Is it in the way?"

"Yep. I need you to move it."

"'Kay." Nick held up the keys, got in and cranked the ignition. After shifting into reverse he purposely let the clutch out too fast, causing it to stall. Immediately, he started it back up, pumped the gas a few times and then cut it off again. He shook his head, pulled the hood release and got out. "Something's wrong with the motor." After opening the hood he leaned over the engine and started jiggling wires. The officer curiously headed over. Nick smiled to himself.

Quickly scanning the engine for something sturdy to hold onto, Nick spotted and grabbed a motor mount. Locking his fingers in a tight grip, he pulled back hard, keeping a good fix on the officer's location. As the officer approached, Nick groaned and began to play tug of war with the immoveable piece of metal. Then, at just the right moment, he let go and fell backward, onto the officer, knocking him to the ground, with Nick on top. Instantly, Nick jumped up and apologized. Obviously angered and slightly confused, the officer reluctantly accepted Nick's apologies and demanded he move the car immediately or suffer the consequences of a tow truck. Nick nodded, closed the hood and tried the ignition again. Surprisingly, it started fine and kept running. Nick smiled and waved at the irritated cop as he pulled out and parked across the street.

After passing the officer and apologizing one more time, Nick confidently walked up to the police tape, ducked underneath and headed for the door of the townhouse. One of the officers guarding the crowd approached Nick, who quickly flashed his newly acquired badge and then entered the house. Once inside, Nick found himself standing in an ocean of cops. In front of him and to his right he saw a small desk and the latest in computer technology. The monitor was shut off making it appear as if the computer was off as well, however the green light on the tower suggested otherwise. The computer featured several common devices: a printer, scanner, modem. But the one thing that caught Nick's eye was the web cam. It wasn't facing forward where a person would normally be sitting. It was facing the front room and focused on a broken couch, which had been knocked over and rested on its back. The desk itself was a mess of cluttered papers. Nick quickly scanned through them, and except for the stack of business cards that read Mercedes Atwater Investigations and a nearly full cup of coffee, he spotted nothing that grabbed his attention.

Just beyond the desk, a narrow carpeted staircase went up to a second floor. On the other side of the couch, all the glass in a sliding glass door had been shattered. Just to the left of the couch a blood-soaked, one-eyed corpse sat staring at a busted up coffee table. Not wanting to look conspicuous by standing in the entranceway, Nick turned to his left and walked through the archway into the kitchen. Several pieces of evidence had been sealed in clear plastic bags and set on the table beside two half-full cups of coffee. Among them was a Smith and Wesson 9mm pistol, a Glock 31 (.357 caliber), two fully loaded, seventeen-round capacity magazines, and a 5X7 photograph of a man's face. It had a hole in the lower left side and looked as if someone might have used it for target practice. Nick studied the man. It wasn't anyone he remembered. The phone hung on the wall across from the coffeemaker. Directly below the phone sat an old fashioned answering machine.

Just as Nick was reaching down toward the machine, a man walked into the kitchen. He briefly looked at Nick and then went over to the coffeemaker. Nick waited, trying to look busy, as the man photographed several items in the kitchen and then left. Nick quickly opened the cassette holder, pocketed the tape and walked back into the front room. He desperately wanted to flip on the monitor and find out what information the computer could tell him, but it would be impossible with so many cops in the room. He walked over to the body. It wasn't smart to stay in one place too long and even less smart to hang around the corpse. Nevertheless, Nick quickly studied the body and counted three bullet holes in the chest. A few feet away from the corpse, a stainless steel box sat, opened. The inside was lined with a padded plastic material and the outside featured a set of temperature controls. It seemed to be some sort of portable refrigerator. After pivoting around and staring back at the web cam for a second, Nick stood up, crossed the living room and went upstairs, snagging a business card as he passed the desk.

Meanwhile, outside, a dark colored sedan with a magnetic siren on top zigzagged its way up to the yellow tape and stopped. Detective James Garvey and associate Mathew Grogan got out and headed for the front door. Upstairs, Nick found himself alone. He looked out the window, in the master bedroom, at the crowd of people across the way. A dark colored sedan, he hadn't seen before, sat just on the other side of the police tape. After pilfering through a few drawers and closets, Nick returned down the staircase. As he descended, his eyes caught glimpse of the tail end of an unmistakable corduroy coat.

In mid stride, he halted and turned around. Detective Garvey had managed to make it through the traffic and get here faster than he had anticipated. From the second floor, he quickly surveyed all the windows. A flood of cops and even more bystanders seemed to be outside each one. There was no way he could climb out a window and down the side of the building without being seen. He had no idea what kind of man Garvey was, but something inside told him he should take his threat seriously. He quietly walked back to the top of the stairs and listened.

"Yeah it's a match all right." Garvey's voice floated up the steps. "It's just like the one the woman's head was found in. Who's the stiff?"

"Don't know yet. He didn't have any identification on him. All we found was a photograph of a man's face in his pocket."

"Where's the photo?"

"On the kitchen table."

Nick inched down a couple of stairs, getting ready to make a quick escape the moment Garvey turned to go into the kitchen.

"Anyone we know?" Garvey continued, but didn't move.

"Not that we can tell."

"What's upstairs?" Garvey's voice changed and sounded closer. Nick quickly ascended back to the top step and around the corner to the right. He stood with his back flush up against the wall and listened.

"Not much. It looks like all the action took place down here."

"You geniuses already had a look around up there, huh?"

All was quiet for a second as Nick waited and listened. Then he heard faint, soft footsteps approaching from below. Garvey was coming up. Silently, Nick retreated to the bedroom, grabbed the cordless phone off the nightstand and ducked into the closet. Detective Garvey, followed by Grogan, hit the top of the stairs, walked up to the restroom and flipped on the light.

Scrunched tightly between various items and women's clothing, Nick hurriedly dialed the LAPD.

"Los Angeles Police Department, how may I direct your call?"

Being as quiet as possible, Nick formulated a rough, loud whisper. "I have Mercedes Atwater with me… Alive!"

"Excuse me?"

Thinking back and remembering the name of a neighboring street he passed on his way, he continued. "Tell Detective *James Garvey* to meet me at 1124 Sunshine Ridge in five minutes or she dies."

"I can hardly hear you sir, can you please speak up?"

"Five minutes-and tell him to bring my little metal box with him!"

"Sir?"

"Four minutes fifty-five seconds!" Click. Nick hung up just as Detective Garvey walked into the room. Nick wasn't sure if she was able to understand what he had said or not and he hoped that the front desk of the LAPD wasn't set up to trap every incoming call. If they were they would be able tell that the call came from Mercedes' house and not one on the next block.

"What do we know about this Mercedes Atwater?" Inside the closet, as stiff as a board, Nick heard the detective's voice moving through the room.

"Not much. She's a private eye. We're running her background now." Another voice filled the air, sounding as if it came from a man almost leaning up against the closet door.

When Nick first jumped into the closet he had little time to position himself. There were boxes on the floor that he crumpled as he stepped on top of them. He was a tall man and his neck was bent slightly as his head was wedged up underneath the overhead board. His back wasn't flush up against the wall. Something bumpy and hard was in the way. His legs were slightly bent with one over the top of the other.

Even though the position was awkward it hadn't felt this bad at first. Now he could feel a slight burning sensation beginning to develop where his right leg wanted to give way. If he could just shift his weight a little, he would be able to relieve some of the tension, however any movement, even the smallest, might call attention to the closet. His face tightened and he endured the pain.

"Nothing about this fits." Garvey's voice passed directly in front of the closet, heading for the window. "If it weren't for that little metal box I'd say this whole thing has nothing to do with our case."

"Yeah, I know what you mean."

"And these idiots! I hate them trampling through my crime scene. Sometimes I wonder how some of them ever made it onto the force in the first place." Garvey's voice left the window, came back, and stopped just in front of the closet door. Suddenly, with the pain in his leg still growing and now accompanied by an ache in the back of his neck, Nick was overwhelmed with the bizarre premonition that, any moment now, the door would swing open and he'd be caught. Then, almost as quickly as the feeling came, he forced it out of his mind. He just had to hold on a few more seconds and then the detective would go back downstairs.

"What's this door go to?"

"It's just the closet." A third man's voice floated from the distance into Nick's hiding place. Perhaps his premonition was true after all. The pain in his leg began to tighten up into a cramp. Nick bit his lip but didn't move.

"What's in it?"

"Nothing. We looked in it earlier."

"Yeah?"

"Yeah!"

"Like you looked through that van last year? The one we found that body in later?"

For just a moment everything was silent. Then the door shimmied as someone grabbed the brass knob on the other side. Nick was going to be caught.

The place was crawling with cops. It would do no good to run. Nick waited silently, as the pain in his leg flared into a full-blown muscle cramp. Just as the door cracked and light poured in, a cell-phone rang. The slightly opened door rocked as Garvey let go and answered the call. "Detective Garvey here."

Through the crack Nick could see the detective standing at the door, with his cell-phone to his ear. "What?" He spoke into the phone. "Five minutes? 'Kay, hold on." He looked up and moved away from the door, out of Nick's line of sight. "Give me something to write with—quick. 'Kay, go ahead, 1124 Sunshine Ridge. Got it! C'mon. Headquarters just got a phone call." Nick quickly shifted his weight as Garvey's voice faded down the stairs. A second later he opened the closet door and hobbled his way to the bed. The pain in his leg was excruciating. He quickly worked through the cramp by bending and extending his leg several times, then got up and walked out the rest. After wiping his prints from the handset, he replaced it on the base and then looked out the window. Garvey was getting into the sedan as his stubby sidekick loaded the stainless steel box into the trunk. After the car pulled away, Nick limped down the stairs, past several cops and out the front door.

Moments later, taking a quick detour, the Mustang rolled past a cop-infested house on Sunshine Ridge. Outside, an overweight man in a white t-shirt and boxers and a middle-aged woman in a pink robe and curlers were sprawled, spread-eagle, face down, in their front yard. They were being held at gunpoint by several uniformed policemen. Wearing his shades, Nick grinned and cranked up the radio as he sped away.

He drove to Wal-Mart and purchased a mini cassette player and batteries, then found the nearest Denny's. Carrying his laptop, on the way in, he stopped at the vending machine and bought a copy of the LA times. The title was intriguing but not too terribly interesting.

Police move in on Freak!

He knew it had to do with the headhunter case, but so did just about every other front-page story of the LA times lately. He tucked it underneath his arm and followed the young shapely waitress to a booth in the back. After ordering another black coffee and the daily breakfast special he loaded the batteries into the player, plugged in the headphones and pressed play. He listened intently as a man's voice came through the headset. It was clear that whoever it was knew Mercedes personally because he never identified himself. As Nick listened, he narrowed his eyes and cocked his head. On the tape the man stuttered through awkward attempts at being macho. Nick chuckled to himself and shook his head as the man's voice changed from low to high and back again. Overall, the tape offered very little for him to go on. The man spoke of a note and someone with mental problems. Although Nick felt that the tape had something to do with what happened at Mercedes', he wasn't sure what it was. He listened to the tape several times and then shut it off.

The waitress sat his plate on the table as he removed his headphones and said thank you. In between bites he logged on to the web address at the bottom of the business card he found at Mercedes'. A powerful and professionally designed web page popped up.

Mercedes Atwater Investigations. The page listed several suggestions for hiring a private eye, from finding out about a cheating spouse to obtaining entire background checks on perspective employees. The text loaded first followed by several graphics. Then, the head and shoulders of a beautiful and clever-looking young woman downloaded.

Her dark hair was soft and perfectly styled, yet full of life and natural looking. Her eyes were an emerald green, deep and intelligent. The look on her face was a perfect mixture of determination and genuine warmth. Except for some soft green eye shadow her face seemed to be void of makeup and as far as Nick could tell none was needed. She was beautiful. Nick's fork stopped and hovered at the mid point between his plate and mouth.

"Sir?" By the tone in her voice the waitress must have called to him more than once, but he had not heard her. He looked up, away from the laptop. She was holding a pot of coffee. "I'm sorry. I didn't mean to disturb you. I just thought you'd like a refill."

"Yeah…great!" Nick nudged his cup toward her. "Thanks!"

She smiled as black, hot, coffee poured out of the pot and bounced into his cup. As she left, he turned back to the screen. During the past eight years many women had expressed a romantic interest in Nick, however, he wasn't able to see anything more than friendship in any of them. He couldn't see women as women, only as other individuals. There had been room for only one *woman* in his heart, Allie. But now, as he gazed at the image on the screen, something tapped at the edge of his desire. Somehow, he saw the image, not as just another individual, but as a woman—a beautiful woman. A tinge of guilt crept into his soul and almost instantly the errant romantic feeling was gone.

He carefully looked through her website, but gathered little more information about her than he already knew. He copied several pages to his hard drive and wrote down the address to her office, then turned his attention to the newspaper.

Police Move in on Freak!

He was relatively certain that there would be no useful information in the story, but as it was, he had nothing else to go on. As he read the article, however, his enthusiasm grew. It said that some kids had spotted the headhunter entering and exiting an old house in El Monte. Nick wrote down the address and continued to read. The article went on to describe how the children managed to capture several photos of the man and later found the head of his latest victim. Nick looked at the photos. There were four in all. Three of them were of the back of the man's head. The fourth was of the back of the man's Lexus. Nick looked closely at the pictures of the man. Gauging from the background and the angle of his shadow, Nick determined him to be just under six feet tall. Outside of the fact that he wore nice clothes and drove a nice car, Nick wasn't able to tell much else. He looked at the photo of the Lexus and could clearly make out the last three digits of the license plate, *155*, but the other four were cloaked in shadow and all but impossible to read. He turned back to his computer, which still displayed *Mercedes Atwater Investigations*. After logging on to the LA times' website, he pulled up the online version of the same story and clicked on the photo of the Lexus. It was much clearer in color. He downloaded the photo and then opened it in Adobe Photo Shop. After cleaning up, enhancing and magnifying the image he was able to read two more digits. The license plate number was 3-?-?-1-1-5-5.

Next, he logged on to youroneprivateeye.com and requested a report on all Lexuses that were registered in California with the license plate number 3**1155. After typing in his VISA number and pressing return, a page popped up saying that the information he requested would be e-mailed to him within twenty-four hours. Nick finished his meal, shut off his computer, paid his bill and drove to El Monte.

CHAPTER SEVENETEEN

The sign at the top of the towering pole read *Heavenly Heart Motel*. The sound of the rushing freeway filled the air. Inside, Teddy happily accepted the key card for room 311 from the oriental man behind the counter and then asked, "Have you accepted the Lord Jesus Christ as your own personal savior yet?"

The face of the china-man looked like it was stuck in a perpetual state of bliss. His mouth was wide, his lips were thin and his slotted eyes were all but shut. He beamed with happiness. Instead of answering Teddy's question, he simply bobbed his head up and down and said. "Woom twee elebon."

Teddy shook his head and said, "No! Jesus. Have you accepted *Jesus* yet?"

The man kept smiling as he nodded and pointed toward the window in the direction of the hotel units. "Woom twee elebon."

Slowly, Teddy drug out the word "Jesus"

"Ah…yah, yah." At last, it appeared that he understood, but then he continued, "Twee elebon." Except for his widened eyes, his smile remained completely intact as he continued to point Teddy in the direction of the unit.

Teddy wished the Lord would give him the gift of tongues so he might communicate God's love to this poor unsaved soul. Finally, after giving the man a smile of confidence, Teddy left the office and drove the Lexus around to the back of the building. After backing up against a block wall, to hide his license plate, he carried two large suitcases up the stairs to the third floor and into his room.

He set the bags down, closed the door and flipped on the light. Home, sweet home. It wasn't the nicest room in the world but it would have to do. He was a soldier of the Lord and for some reason God had decided to keep the chamber of the gun empty and not bring Teddy home just yet. There was something God still needed Teddy to do. Teddy wasn't sure what it was, but he knew that it must be something very important, because God wouldn't have denied him everlasting peace if it weren't.

Teddy completely unpacked both suitcases and neatly stacked them in the closet. Among the things he unpacked was a copy of the LA Times newspaper. He cut out the front page and taped it to the wall beside his bed. *Police Move in on Freak!* He sat on the bed looking at the article and thought. Just a couple of hours earlier he had seen it as a sign that his time here on Earth had come to an end. Now however, he saw it for what it was, a declaration of war. The Devil was slick and he was trying to put a stop to Teddy's work, but he had underestimated the power of the Lord in Teddy's life. Sure, the LAPD would soon figure out who had been doing the good work, but God would no doubt keep Teddy safely hidden until all his work was through.

Teddy stood up, went into the bathroom, and looked into the mirror. As he stared into the eyes of his reflection he realized just how quiet it was. It was silent—ominously silent. He smiled at himself, trying to shake off the bad feeling that hovered just above the back of his neck, but it didn't go away. He relaxed his mouth, stopped smiling, and just studied his reflection. He turned his face, looked at his profile for a moment, then turned and looked at the other one. He was a very good-looking man, very good looking. And honest too, he was so honest. He never lied unless it was in the name of the Lord.

He turned on the faucet, which broke the ever-deafening silence, and cupped his hands under the running water. After smiling at himself one more time, he slowly lowered his face and splashed water on it. His reflection, however, did not copy his actions, but rather continued to stare at him. Startled, Teddy instantly looked up. Water was dripping from his face in the bathroom and in the reflection. Keeping his eye on the mirror, he turned his head to the left and then to the right. Had he imagined it? Yes, he must have. How could he possibly know if his refection was staring at him when he wasn't looking at it? He slowly turned his head, away from the mirror until he could barely see the reflection of his eyes looking back at him. He stood there for a half a minute or more and then slowly turned his head, just a bit, so that his eyes were just out his line of site.

Somehow, as he stood there, he knew that his reflection was still looking at him, watching him. An evil spirit passed through his body, making the hairs on his forearms stand up. He quickly looked back into the mirror, hoping to catch his reflection off guard. He stared into the eyes that were staring at him. There was something in them—something evil. He could feel it. He slowly brought his face up to the mirror. Satan was here, in the bathroom, with him, in the mirror. He turned the water off and left the restroom. He picked the key card up off the little round table by the door and continued on his way to his car.

He got in, started the engine and gave in to the overwhelming urge to look into the rearview mirror, but all he saw was himself. Satan had stayed in the motel room. Teddy was sure that the evil one would be gone by the time he returned. He pulled out of the motel parking lot heading for the old white house. The police may have taken the head of the young woman that Teddy had just sent to heaven, but he was fairly certain God would see to it that he was still monetarily rewarded.

Hopefully, God left the normal five thousand dollars in the freezer, probably not. Something had gone wrong and the police had found the woman's head. Maybe Teddy didn't pray hard enough or perhaps he should have been more cautious the last time he went into the house. Maybe it wasn't Teddy's fault at all. Maybe this was just all part of God's plan.

Teddy turned on the radio. An evangelist was preaching. "God wants you to know something, people..."

Teddy turned up the volume and leaned forward. He knew this preacher wasn't as in touch with the almighty as well as he was. Heck, he probably didn't even know the true meaning of salvation. Nevertheless, Teddy listened carefully. He had found that sometimes God used an out of touch preacher, like this one, to send him a message.

"He's been thinking about you!" The man wasn't yelling but he wasn't just talking either. He was zealously preaching and could, at any moment, break into a shout. "Yes, you!"

Teddy listened closely as he made a right turn. The three-story house was just ahead on the left. "He knows what you've been through. He understands your heart! He sees your hurt and he wants to heal you! He wants to reward you beyond your wildest dreams. Raise your hands, with me now, to heaven, and you at home, or driving in your cars, place your hands on the radio and lets pray together."

He did not park in front of the huge white house, but instead, pulled up behind a gray Ford Mustang across the street and at a distance away. He shifted into park and laid his hand on the radio. After praying, not with—but for the sinful preacher, he shut off the engine and headed across toward the house. The tall iron entry gate was covered in a spider web of yellow police tape. Teddy approached with caution. He knew the Lord would hide him from those searching for him, but it was not wise to test the Lord. The street seemed oddly quiet today, not at all like it had been on the last few occasions he had stopped in. He stopped and looked down the road from which he came. Not a soul was out. He looked across the street. Except for his Lexus and the Mustang, there were no other cars. The park, just beyond the Mustang, was void of people as well. The wind gently rocked a lonely swing. He continued his pan. The street, as far as his eyes could see, was empty and lifeless. He looked at the old white house. It too, looked strange, foreboding, dangerous. God would protect him.

He knew all the padlocks would be changed. The police would have made sure of it. But his key wasn't just any key. It had been given to him by an angel of the Lord and would be able to open any locks on the property. He reached into his coat pocket and withdrew it as he approached the gate. The police's lock, however had been cut and now dangled from the iron latch. Teddy stepped closer and carefully looked it over. This was odd. He looked up at the house and then at his God-given key puzzled. After stealing a quick glance over his shoulder, he carefully removed the broken lock and being careful not to snap the plastic tape, slowly pushed the gate open, which wasn't the *wisest* thing to do. The iron hinges creaked much longer than they would have if he had just opened the gate quickly. He stepped through the web and pushed the gate closed behind him, just as slowly as he had opened it. The creak was long and seemed even louder this time. Teddy winced. After replacing the broken lock, just as he had found it, he slowly made his way around to the back. Even from a distance he could tell that the new police issued, padlock on the back door had suffered the same fate as the one on the gate. Suddenly, Teddy realized what was happening.

Inside, even from the basement, Nick could hear the creaking of the gate. The flashlight beam swirled across the room and halted on an inconsequential plank of wood running across the far wall. He stopped his search and listened closer. There it was again. Damn! Cops! It had to be cops. No one else would be foolish enough to open and close the gate that slowly. Nick thought of the padlocks he had cut on his way in and his face soured. He carefully crept up the wooden steps and listened at the cellar door. He waited for a minute or two. There was no sound. After another minute or so he decided to sneak out and investigate. Just as he placed his hand on the doorknob and began to twist, a sound came from inside the house. He carefully relaxed his hand, letting the knob softly spin back into place and listened. Someone was at the back door, a cop no doubt.

He quickly turned around and sporadically illuminated various parts of the cellar, searching for a place to hide. If he were discovered, they would mistakenly take him to be the headhunter, who had fallibly returned to the scene of his crime. Like a bight spotlight on a very dark stage his beam lighted up one small section of the basement, hovered for a moment and then jumped to another. As he searched, he slowly moved down the stairs, away from the door.

Teddy walked up to the backdoor of the house, studied the broken lock and smiled. He knew what was happening. The last few days all became clearer now.

"'Caught you, demon!" He whispered as he quietly removed the lock and pushed open the door.

Those ghost-chasing brats who had spied on him yesterday, hadn't just been here by chance. This whole thing had been the work of the Devil and those kids were unquestionably his dedicated disciples. They probably weren't even kids. They were most likely demons masquerading as sweet innocent children who just happened to be *ghost chasing*. Didn't anyone else see the irony in that? How could the world be so blind to these obvious spiritual deceptions? The Devil had tried to expose Teddy and have him arrested, but failed. Today, Satan had sent yet another demon. This one was undoubtedly here to steel the money that God had left for Teddy. Now Teddy knew why the house had looked so foreboding from the street.

He walked inside and loudly slammed the door behind him. He wasn't afraid of a pathetic little demon. The Devil had made a big mistake by sending his henchman here today. Teddy felt the presence of a dozen angels behind him and thought about the deserted neighborhood. A spiritual war was about to go down and God, in his mighty and infinite wisdom, had cleared the street. Teddy grinned impishly as even more angels began to surround the house. He steadied himself and prepared for battle. He knew exactly where the demon was, and boldly walked directly to the cellar. The broken padlock was on the floor next to the door.

Teddy spoke for himself and all of the powerful angels with him. "We know you're in there! The place is surrounded! There's no way out!" He listened for the demon's response, but heard nothing. "Give yourself up and I'll make sure you're not tortured too badly!"

Teddy stepped back, withdrew his *ticket to paradise* and, in one smooth motion, kicked open the door. It slammed hard into the wall and bounced back again, almost closing in the process.

From the cramped quarters of his quickly acquired hiding place, Nick heard the police calling from just outside of the cellar door. They had the place surrounded; if he tried to escape they would open fire and cut him down in a shower of lead. He had a fairly good hiding place, but as soon as the canine units arrived he'd be discovered for sure. He wasn't LA's headhunter and shortly after he was arrested that truth would come out. Maybe he should just give up and take is chances with Detective Garvey.

The cops kicked in the door and light poured into the cellar. From the rafters, Nick watched as a single detective, gun in hand, crept down the stairs.

"Did you honestly think you were going to get away with this?" The detective said as he made his way to the cool concrete floor. "Huh? Did you?" Teddy chuckled. "You've finally met your match, demon."

Demon? Nick thought as he waited for the next officer to enter the room.

Something small scurried through the darkness, just out of sight. Teddy nervously pivoted in the direction of the sound and fired. The shot was loud and ricocheted several times off the block walls and concrete floor. Concern washed through Nick as he puzzled the situation. Either this guy was one angry cop with an itchy trigger finger, whose only desire was to bring in the headhunter's corpse, or he wasn't a cop at all. Either way things were a little more dangerous than they had first appeared. A few moments earlier Nick was only trying to sneak away without being caught. Now he would be just trying to stay alive.

Teddy walked over to the desk and looked at the oil lamp. He wanted to fire it up and use it to flush out the demon, but was unwilling to take the time and concentration. He looked toward the freezer, into the darkness and then back at the lamp. God would give him the vision he needed to see the demon. He looked back into the darkness and slowly moved in that direction.

Nick was balancing on two 2X4's almost directly above the cellar door. He listened for more cops, but heard none. If this guy wasn't a cop, then who was he? Teddy disappeared into the shadows at the far end of the basement. Nick shifted his weight, preparing to hang down and swing over to the stairs, but waited. If this guy were a cop, then his partner or someone else would be ready just outside the cellar door. Nick had one hand and one knee on each beam. He quietly lifted both knees off the beams, held himself in between them, and closed his eyes.

"One… two… three." He counted under his breath, then quietly lowered his body through the beams and silently hung from the rafters. His boots dangled just four feet from the floor. He quietly rocked his body back and forth, building momentum to swing over the railing and onto the stairs in front of him.

"You can't hide, demon. I *will* find you." After reaching into the freezer for his monetary reward and coming up empty-handed, Teddy released the lid and spun around angrily. "Where's my money?" A shadowy demonic silhouette floated down from the ceiling and hung, like a bat, swinging from the rafters.

Teddy smiled as he took aim and whispered, "Found you, demon," then squeezed the trigger.

Nick swung his feet back one last time and prepared to leap over the railing, and onto the steps, when a thunderous explosion went off behind him, followed by an immediate pain in his lower back. His body swung forward but instead of heaving himself up and over the rail, he let go prematurely and slammed into it, boots first. It cracked, but still kept Nick from making the stairs. He dropped, back first, and landed hard, on the concrete floor.

Teddy quickly rushed out of the shadows and loomed over him.

"Well, what do we have here?"

He extended his arms toward the demon and gripped the gun with both hands. "Thought you could get away with it, didn't you?" God had empowered Teddy's gun and all of its bullets to be just as dangerous to this under-worldly creature as it was to any normal person. Teddy knew that if he aimed at its head and squeezed the trigger, it wouldn't just be sent back to Hell. It would be totally and instantly removed from existence. That thought pleased Teddy—one less demon in universe. But he didn't tighten his grip just yet. No demon deserved to be let off the hook that easily, especially not this one.

Teddy thought back to the woman he had just sent home. God had instructed him to torture her and even gave him specific medicine and knowledge in order to achieve a torture session beyond normal comprehension. He hadn't quite understood why. He had assumed the girl had some unpaid sins she had yet to atone for. Perhaps that wasn't the case however. Perhaps, God was just training Teddy for what he needed to know now. An impish smile flashed across his face as he remembered the woman's screams of pain and her cries for mercy.

Nick, still reeling from the pain, looked up at his attacker. Illuminated only by the light pouring through the half opened cellar door above, the man's smiling face looked wickedly distorted. Nick slowly moved his legs to relieve some of the throbbing in his lower back. He winced, as pain shot down the back of his left thigh.

"Don't move, demon!" Teddy said as he studied the fiend. It sure didn't look like any demon Teddy could imagine. It looked just like a normal human man. He stood in wonder at how marvelously deceptive Satan could be. The creature moved again. Teddy fired a warning shot, into the overstuffed chair underneath the stairwell, missing the creature's right kneecap by just inches.

"I said don't move! Now where's my money?"

Money? Nick tried to make sense of what the man was asking, but couldn't. By now he was all but positive that this guy wasn't a cop, but if not, then who was he? In a weakened voice, Nick replied, "I don't know what you're talking about."

The demon's answer infuriated Teddy and helped the wrath of God find a way into his soul. Satan was the father of all lies. Nothing this deceitful demon said could be taken seriously. If it didn't want to tell him where it hid his money, perhaps it wanted pain. While uttering curses and damnations, Teddy used the toe of his shoe to force the wrath of God into the demon's skull.

Pain shot into Nick's head as the man stood behind him, kicking, once, twice, three times. Nick became lightheaded and woozy as the pain grew. Someone had mistaken his head for a giant walnut and was now trying to crack it open with the assistance of an enormous hammer. However, because it didn't instantly split apart and yield the delicious meat inside, the starved giant continued to hammer. Through water-filled eyes, Nick watched as the dark shadows in the rafters split apart and began to dance with one another and the room started to spin. Coming from the far end of a tunnel, Nick could faintly hear the man's/the giant's voice calling to him. "Where's my money demon?" Another kick—bam!—and then another.

The dark, dancing shadows grew larger and larger until they consumed every inch of the cellar, and then Nick found himself beneath a huge wooden chair in the giant's informal kitchen, carrying the golden goose in cradled arms and running for his life.

"Fee, fi, fo, fum, where's my money demon?"

Uncharacteristically frantic, Nick ran through the entryway, into the living room, where a well-groomed FBI giant stood, grinning. With distorted thoughts of fear and confusion, Nick picked up his pace and swiftly ran in between the giant's tall legs. The giant leaned forward, grabbing at the little man as he ran toward him, but fumbled and missed. Then, the giant was bent over and reaching through his legs, as Nick ran out the front door and into the courtyard.

Up ahead, Nick could see the top of the beanstalk poking through fog-covered ground. In the distance, over his shoulder, he heard the giant still calling to him. "Fee, fi, fo, fum, where's my money demon?"

The ground shook thunderously as the giant's footfalls landed closer and closer. Just as he approached the beanstalk the goose dissolved into thin air. "No!" His echoing cry continued as he turned his head and looked over his shoulder just in time to see the sole of the giant's shoe coming down fast on top of him like the lid of a giant trash compactor. He wanted to move, to get a way but for some strange reason he was frozen, unable to do anything but stand there and watch. Crunch! The giant's foot landed on top of his head, pushing him through the cloud-covered ground and into the muddied earth beneath.

"Where is it?" The ear-piercing yell was loud enough to snatch him out of his delusional state.

Still on his back, on the cold, hard concrete, Nick opened his eyes. He had returned to the cellar and was gazing up at the slowly moving shadows in the rafters. The unknown man was pacing anxiously back and forth and muttering something about Hell and damnation under his breath. The shadows were still moving and the room was still spinning, but not as badly as before. Nick listened as the man's shoes came within reaching distance, and then continued on past.

"God, Himself, intended for me to have that money, you know!" His ravings were getting louder. The spinning room slowed and the dancing shadows finally stopped. Still ranting, the man came to the end of his pace, turned around and proceeded back. "What am I going to do with you? Huh?

Huh? You're nothing more than a stupid little demon, just another henchman for the Devil. I'm really not sure what good it would do to torture you. Tell ya what, if you give back the money right now, I promise not to torture you too long! I might even be inclined to just shoot you and end your miserable existence without torturing you at all." He passed behind Nick again and kept walking. Nick listened but couldn't understand what the man was talking about. It didn't seem to make any sense. Perhaps he was still delirious or perhaps the man was just crazy.

Along with the ranting and raving, Nick began to hear the smack of the man's dress shoes fading as he paced away, then without pause, they would grow loud again as he returned.

"Serving the Prince of Darkness, answering his every whim, you make me sick! I bet you've been stalking me from the beginning! Haven't you?"

At last the room stopped spinning and Nick's head began to throb as the man made another pass, continuing to preach.

"Yeah! I bet you were there from the very first day, watching me, trying to foul things up, and hating me the whole time because you couldn't." He came to the end of his pace again, turned around and stopped. Then all at once his voice changed and took on a caring, sympathetic tone. "It must have been very, very hard for you, watching me send all those people to heaven and not being able to do a single thing about it." He resumed his walk. "Perhaps, that in itself has already been enough torture for your lost soul. Besides, we both know you'll never tell me where you hid my money, so I guess the only thing left to do is to get rid of you."

Nick's mind raced. Who was this wacko? Could he be LA's headhunter? No! Maybe? What if it was? That *would* explain the bizarre sermon he was giving. Nick's head ached as he thought.

Teddy walked up to the half-conscious demon, which was still staring at the rafters through half-glazed eyes. It wasn't going to experience the painful torture session Teddy had first envisioned, so he at least wanted it to know exactly what was about to happen to it. He wanted it to understand the terrible price one paid for falling astray and following the dark one. In a few short moments the demon's entire existence would come to a screeching halt.

Standing just beyond the demon's head, nearly out of sight, Teddy bent at the waste and leaned forward. He slowly waved his hand back and forth over the demon's unresponsive eyes and then said in a soft, judgmental tone. "You're about to die, demon." And he aimed his gun at its face and extended his arm so that the barrel was no less than two inches away. He kept his finger gripped tightly around the trigger and watched carefully, fully expecting the demon to lunge up at any moment and attack or at least try to dematerialize into the spirit world, in some lame attempt to get away. There would be no such luck however, because no quick movements would be quick enough, as Teddy was ready for anything. With the gun less than two inches from the demon's face, Teddy smiled, caught the demon's eye and caringly said; "Good-bye, demon."

Nick stared lifelessly at the rafters and watched the crazy man from the corner of his eye. The man stood over Nick with an evil grin and waved his hand back and forth across his face. Nick played catatonic and waited for the man to turn around. The room was no longer spinning and Nick was fairly certain he could stand up now, but he didn't know how badly he had been shot and how sluggish his defenses would be. After the man had determined that Nick was lost in a mental daze, he would most likely let down his guard and relax a little, giving Nick a chance to get the upper hand.

However, after waving his hand across Nick's line of sight several times, the man didn't turn around, but rather pointed his gun at Nick's face. Nick's heart raced as he puzzled the situation. Either this guy was testing Nick's commitment to catatonia or he was about to scatter his brains all over the basement floor. Maybe he *was* the headhunter after all. Nick thought about reaching up and slapping the gun away while simultaneously rolling over, but quickly dismissed the idea—too slow. It would be all but impossible to get a hand up to the gun before the man pulled the trigger. Out of choices, Nick decided to place his bet with the idea that the man was just bluffing, making sure Nick was truly in a daze and wasn't going to be a threat.

Then, at the last moment, Nick caught a glimpse into the stranger's demented eyes, saw a twisted dedication in them, and somehow knew he was about to pull the trigger. Not good! Nick's mind raced again as he searched for a way to save his life. The image of how jumpy the stranger became when a rodent had scurried through the shadows, flashed through Nick's mind. Keeping his body as still as possible, Nick turned the ankle of his right boot, knocking it into a piece of board that had fallen from the railing above. It wasn't very loud but it did distract the man for less than an instant, giving Nick just enough time to turn his head and dodge the bullet. Even while his head was turning, his hands were moving. One hand reached up and grabbed the man's wrist, pointing the gun away, while the other latched onto his ankle.

A moment earlier, just as Teddy was squeezing the trigger a faint knock came from the overstuffed chair just beneath the staircase at the foot of the demon. Startled and afraid that another demon might be materializing, Teddy raised his gaze and glanced into the darkness, but saw nothing. In that millisecond, Teddy's captured demon had miraculously dodged the bullet and grabbed Teddy's wrist. Teddy quickly looked back just in time to see it grab his ankle and pull his foot out from underneath him. He hit the ground hard. Metal connected with cement as the gun flew into the darkness and an instant later the demon was standing over him. Had God forsaken Teddy? Why had the demon been allowed to dodge the bullet and get away? Would Teddy be sucked into Hell now? His thoughts went rampant as he inched backward, like a fleeing crab, across the concrete floor. Perhaps he was supposed to have tortured it after all. God was punishing him for not listening well enough.

The demon took shallow breaths and hobbled through the darkness as if it were in pain. "Who are you?" It asked as it stopped and leaned up against a support beam in the middle of the basement. Small talk with a demon was dangerous. Everything a demon did was destructive. Everything a demon said was a lie. Teddy did not answer, but instead looked into the darkness where the gun had gone.

Nick turned to look as well. The gun was shiny and Nick was the first to see it. The stranger made a sudden movement in the darkness and Nick went for the gun. Halfway to it, he realized the man wasn't racing toward it with him, but instead, had gone in the opposite direction and was already at the top of the steps, exiting the cellar. Nick grabbed the handle of the gun just as the door squeaked shut. The darkness became even darker as Nick heard the stranger replacing the padlock on the other side of the door.

Nick wasn't sure, but had a fairly good idea that this guy was indeed LA's headhunter and if he was, then he was the best lead Nick had yet. He wasn't about to let him get away. With a throbbing head, aching back and sore left leg, he hurriedly shuffled toward the thin line of light squeezing beneath the cellar door. Once at the top of the stairs he tried the knob. As he had guessed, it was locked. Backing down a couple of steps, he pointed his gun at the doorjamb.

Outside, on the back patio, Teddy fumbled at the back door and dropped the lock for a second time when he heard the shot. He quickly picked it up and with trembling hands, finally managed to hang it on the latch, then anxiously ran around the house, for the front gate. As he rounded the corner and entered the front yard, the slick-soled surface of his left shoe slipped out from under him. He fell to the ground and smacked, face-first, onto one of the octagonal shaped stepping-stones. Losing momentum only briefly and ignoring the pain in his cheek, he scrambled to his feet and kept running. Another gunshot rang out as he reached the tall iron gate.

At the rear of the house, Nick used his gun-free hand to shadow his squinting eyes as he staggered out into the overly bright morning. His leg burned. It felt as if the veins running through the back of his left thigh had been filled with gasoline and then set on fire. As painful as that was it didn't even come close to the excruciating pain in his lower left side. And if all that wasn't already bad enough, his pounding migraine throbbed so hard that his vision oscillated between clear and blurred. He hobble-ran around the side of the house just in time to see the crazy man crossing the street. He ran up to the already open gate and let out a grunt of pain as he twisted his body to fit through the web of yellow tape. The crazy man got into a white Lexus parked directly behind the Mustang, and started the engine. Almost dragging his left leg behind him, Nick raced for his car. The Lexus backed up, and then shot forward, nearly clipping the Mustang as it headed straight for Nick. Nick leaped out of the way and tumbled over the asphalt to the curb. The Lexus raced by. Nick turned and read the license plate as it passed, 3BRI155. It *was* the headhunter!

By the time Nick got in the car, started the engine and shifted into drive, the Lexus had already made it to the end of the block and turned the corner. Nick's boot pressed down on the accelerator and the Mustang raced forward. He hit the corner just in time to see the tail of the Lexus disappearing around another turn. With a throbbing head, he followed the chase. He made the next turn and for a few short moments was directly behind the Lexus. He pressed down harder on the accelerator and the distance between the vehicles narrowed. As the nose of the Mustang closed in on the tail end of the Lexus, Nick remembered how he had all but totaled the last rental car he used. As a matter of fact, with all the money he had paid to the different rental companies over the last few years he was sure he should own one by now. Nevertheless, he gunned the engine, smacked hard into the back of the Lexus, and road its bumper.

"Got ya, you little bastard." He whispered as he briefly let off of the accelerator, allowing the Mustang to drop back just a little. The gap between the cars widened and just as Nick punched down on the gas pedal for a second ramming session, the Lexus unexpectedly turned left into a narrow alleyway. The Mustang continued forward, unable to make the sharp turn. The tires screamed as Nick slammed on the breaks and threw the car into reverse. By the time he had made it into the alley, the Lexus was already turning onto another residential street. Nick cut the corner close as a big blue ball on the next block left a yard full of happy children and bounced its way into the street. The Lexus turned again. The Mustang accelerated to catch up, as it followed. A young boy stepped off the curb and chased into the road after the bouncing blue ball. Nick pressed on the gas as he hit the corner. The ball struck the rear bumper of the passing Lexus and bounced high into the air. The kid stopped momentarily to avoid a collision with the Lexus and then resumed his chase. The Mustang flew around the corner just as the young boy made it to the middle of the street.

Nick saw something flying toward the windshield. Too late to turn the wheel, he winced and held his hand, palm out, in front of his face, as the rubbery ball hit and bounced back into the air. An instant later he saw the boy running blindly into the street, less than twenty feet ahead. He slammed on the break pedal and forced the wheel, hard to the right. A loud screech filled the air as smoke floated up from under the tires and black skid marks etched themselves into the asphalt. The skidding Mustang was still going way too fast. It had more than enough momentum to hit the boy and continued sliding another ten or twenty feet. The kid stopped and stared, wide-eyed as the screaming car approached. Realizing he wasn't going to stop in time, Nick took his foot off the break and gunned it. The Mustang still skidded sideways toward the kid, but then at the last moment shot forward, smacking hard as it went up, over the curb, and into a beautiful green lawn. Nick would have breathed a sigh of relief if it weren't for the fact that he was now heading straight for the side of the house. He couldn't believe how small the California yards were and by the time he had forced the wheel back to the left he was nearly on the front steps. The face of a middle-aged, pudgy woman wearing a shower cap and holding a mouthful of toothpaste, poked through puke-green curtains just in time to see mud splatter up onto the window as the back of the Mustang ripped out of her yard.

The car hit asphalt again and Nick pressed down on the accelerator, however the Lexus was nowhere in sight. He passed a street, quickly looked both ways, and seeing no sign of it, drove on. After searching long enough to ascertain that he had lost the chase, he pulled over to the side of the road and shifted into park. The pain in his head, though still severe, had lightened up just a little. He sat there a minute and calmed down. His seat was completely soaked in blood. Maybe he should go to the hospital now. He hit the steering wheel with the palm of his hand. Damn! The best lead he'd had in long time. Damn!

From inside the glove box, a muffled, musical tone came from the cellphone. He leaned over, winced in pain, and retrieved it. He looked at the caller ID and all his pains went away.

"Hello?" He smiled.

"Hello Daddy."

"Hey Peaches. How are you?"

"I'm okay, I miss you though."

"I miss you too, Sweetie."

"What are you doing?"

Nick looked down at the blood drenched seat, remembered being shot in the back, his head being used for kickoff practice, thought about the ball-chasing boy he had nearly ran over, the beautiful lawn he had just tore up and the crazy headhunter that he had been chasing, and then replied. "Nothing, you?"

"'Just thinking about you." There was a short pause as his smile widened and then she said, "Daddy?" The tone of her voice changed slightly and Nick could tell she had something important she wanted to say.

Looking out of the windshield and across the miles, picturing her tender little face, Nick said, "Yes Peaches?"

There was another short pause and then in a shaky, remorseful voice she said, "I'm sorry."

"Sorry?" Nick shook his head. "Sorry for what, Sweetie?"

"I wasn't very nice when you left and I didn't want you to think I didn't love you anymore." She began to cry.

"Oh sweetheart!" Nick's heart sank.

"It's just that every time we move I... I..." She paused again, "I don't know."

That familiar tinge of guilt crept into his heart and soon all of his recently acquired pains put together were no match for it. "I know you miss Mom," she continued to cry softly as she spoke. "I miss her too. I miss her a lot!"

Nick's vision began to blur again as his eyes filled with water and he remembered what Dottie had said about letting go of the past when holding onto it starts affecting the hearts of the ones we love in the present.

"I just wanted you to know...I love you, that's all, just I love you!"

"I love you too, Peaches." His voice crackled as a tear ran down his face. What in the world was he doing over twenty-six hundred miles away from his only daughter? He was chasing ghosts, that's what he was doing, chasing ghosts. After eight years he still didn't know what exactly it was that he was looking for. *Maybe* Dottie was right.

No!

Dottie *was* right. There was no *maybe* about it. He had always known she was. Perhaps he was finally getting to the place where he could accept it. God had blessed him with a beautiful little girl and no matter what he did or what he found out about what happened that tragic summer morning, nothing would bring Allie back. Nothing!

"I gotta go Daddy!" Her voice cheered up, "Dottie and I are going to a church picnic. I sure wish you were here."

"Me too, Sweetie, me too." Nick wiped his cheek.

"I love you Daddy!"

"I love you too, Peaches."

"Bye!"

"Bye."

Nick waited until she hung up before pressing the end button. He sat there, resting his phone-hand on his knee and staring out of the window for a few more moments. Then he replaced the phone in the glove box, switched on his computer and looked up the address to the nearest hospital.

Greater El Monte Community.

He memorized the directions, then turned his laptop off and pulled away from the curb. The Mustang found the main drive and passed the Heavenly Heart Motel on its way to the hospital.

CHAPTER EIGHTEEN

The numbers on the digital clock were out of focus and hard to read. Her eyes stretched open wide as she strained to clarify the image. 1:17 PM. She closed them for just a moment, let out a sigh of exhaustion and when she reopened them it read 5:03 PM. The image was clearer now and she didn't feel as tired.

"Alex?" Her voice was soft and sleepy.

There was no answer.

She repeated, louder, "Alex?"

There was still no answer. She sat up in the bed and looked around. Alex was slumped over, against the wall, next to the TV. Tilting her head to one side, she tried to recall the events of the last few hours. After arriving at the motel, afraid that her battered face would be seen by an attendant who might want to call the cops, she had Alex get the room. She remembered hobbling through the doorway and barely making it to the bed, but after that things became a little hazy. She fell in and out of consciousness as Alex reposition her legs on the bed and then fluffed the pillows beneath her head. The next thing she knew, Alex was standing, or was he floating, over her? A tiny red ball of light appeared out of nowhere and began to grow, until it consumed everything in sight. Somehow, she was in the operating room of a hospital and Alex was her doctor or was it the cell of a jailhouse with Alex as her jailer? The red light darkened and soon everything was cloaked in a dark crimson cloud that had a bizarre *liquidy* quality and carried the faint odor of blood.

Mercedes shook her head as she realized that she was confusing her sleeping world with reality. Her thoughts were all a jumble and it was hard to separate what really happened from her dreams. She decided to wait and let things come back to her at their own pace. Turning her attention to the lump of covers concealing her feet, she thought about her amputated toe and then looked around the room. After a quick scan revealed no sign of the toe-filled, cellophane bag, she glanced at Alex, and then slowly pulled the covers away from her feet. Her eyes narrowed and she sat in shock as all five of her toes were revealed. Quickly, she shifted her eyes to the other foot, which held the correct number of toes as well. It couldn't have been a dream; she remembered it all too clearly. She reached down, ran her fingers across the top of her toes, and stopped at her pinky, fully expecting it to fall off when she touched it. When it didn't, she squeezed it. Ouch! It felt like it was connected okay, but how? Her eyes once again rested on Alex, as she drew herself out of the bed.

On the way over to him, she was distracted by her reflection in the mirror, above the dresser. It wasn't the bloody face that shocked her, but rather, the absence of it. After a moment of hesitation, she slowly walked up to the mirror and studied it. As the tips of her fingers softly ran along the contour of her cheek bone, she remembered, with too much clarity, the excruciating pain that shot through her when Dirty Harry had rammed his foot into her face. At the very least, she was sure he had fractured her skull, but now, as she looked in the mirror, there was no sign that he had ever kicked her. As a matter of fact there wasn't a single part of her body that felt even the slightest bit sore. She looked at the bed and wondered if more time had passed than she thought, maybe three or four days, perhaps a week or longer? No, that wouldn't explain the sudden reconnection of her toe. With her hand slowly receding from her face, she looked back at Alex, whose head was now twitching and thought about her dreams.

She went over to him, squatted down and lifted his chin. His eyes were active under closed lids. They moved back and forth, rolling frantically as if he were watching an action movie on the back of his eyelids.

"Alex?"

He did not respond.

"Alex!" She held his chin for a moment more, wondering how long he would be out this time and then easily, lowered it back down, onto his chest.

She stood up, looked at the clock and thought about her meeting with Mrs. Jennings. After this morning's events she wasn't quite sure that she still wanted to go. Still looking at Alex, she felt bad, but couldn't keep herself from wondering whether she should even continue with the case at all. There was no contract between them and she wasn't under any obligation to go on. Anxiety grew within her and she began to pace as she wrestled with her thoughts. She wasn't a quitter, that was for sure, but then again she wasn't stupid either. No doubt, things were only going to get worse before they got better and when everything was all said and done, she wouldn't be receiving any pay for her efforts. Who works for free? In the back of her mind, she knew the right thing to do and it gnawed at her. She studied Alex. Who was this guy anyway? She didn't know him from Adam. For all she knew, he was just as dangerous as the people that were chasing him.

His rolling eyes and twitching body added an eerie ambiance to the room that sent images of zombies into Mercedes' head and made her feel like she could be the next victim in some cheap horror flick. Who are you Alex Kendallman and who are these people chasing you? Her thoughts drifted back to this morning when she was on the verge of becoming a human jigsaw puzzle. Alex was already out of the house and could have easily kept on running, but instead he fought his own fear and came back in to save her life. That had to carry some weight with it, didn't it? Sure it did. However, on the other hand, if it hadn't been for him, she wouldn't have been in a situation where her life was in need of saving, right?

"Look, damn it! Either you're going to help him or you're not!" She stopped pacing and spoke angrily to the woman in the mirror. "What's your problem? Huh? You just can't finish the things you start? What exactly is it that you're so afraid of anyway? A fake CIA man with a kitchen knife? C'mon, give me a break, you're tougher than that." She *was* tougher than that and she really didn't know what it was that had her so spooked. Slowly, she approached the mirror and stared sternly into her own green eyes. "All right, look you spoiled little rich girl, you're gunna see this one through! Got it? Just like you did with the FBI training, only this time you're not gunna bail out when the going gets tough; and when it's all said and done you'll look back and be able to say that you didn't quit. You're not a quitter; you're an Atwater, not just any Atwater either, you're Donald Atwater's daughter." She thought of her father's confident smile. "He wouldn't quit, not now, not after he gave his word, and neither will you. You said you'd help, and you will." After making up her mind to see things through, her thoughts once again returned to her meeting with Mrs. Jennings.

Not wanting to go unarmed, she thought about the spare gun she kept in the Corolla as she went into the bathroom to get ready.

Twenty minutes later, after leaving a note in case Alex snapped out of his daze and woke up, she was in the Corolla, checking her pistol. It was a small .38 Special with five rounds. She slipped it into the pocket of her oversized windbreaker and headed for Denney's. On her way, the driver of every car she passed seemed to be watching her, and every pedestrian was suspiciously on a cell-phone. As she pulled up to the light, a distrustful looking businessman stepped off the curb and approached the car. Her foot held the break pedal anxiously, waiting for the light to change as the man smiled and signaled for her to roll down the window. She reached into her jacket pocket and gripped the butt of the gun as a question formulated on his face. He tapped on the window and suspiciously reached under his coat just as the light changed.

Mercedes' tennis shoe released the break pedal and quickly pressed down on the gas.

The Corolla shot forward as the man jumped back, nearly stumbled over the curb and then flipped her off.

Mercedes looked in the mirror at herself. "Calm down, damn it! The whole world isn't after you. Nobody even knows where you are."

A few minutes later she pulled into the Denney's parking lot and parked next to a familiar looking black van. Refusing to let the paranoia get the best of her, she reassured herself, "It's just a van."

Inside, from a table near the back, Mrs. Jennings waved her over.

"Hi."

"Hi." Mercedes smiled as she took the booth across from hers and looked at her watch. "You're early."

Mrs. Jennings smiled back anxiously and then glanced around the restaurant.

Her anxiousness only added to Mercedes' paranoia, which Mercedes was determined to keep under wraps. "Thank you very much for meeting with me."

Mrs. Jennings nodded.

"You sounded pretty concerned over the phone. You said that the chemical I gave you was designed to work on the brain?"

"That's right."

The waitress approached the table, carrying a mug and a pot of coffee.

"What did you mean, exactly?"

Instead of answering, Mrs. Jennings asked a question of her own. "Where did you get it?"

"Hello ladies." The waitress refilled Mrs. Jennings' mug and then turned her attention to Mercedes. "Coffee?"

"Sure."

The girls waited as the waitress set the mug on the table, poured the coffee and then asked for their order.

"I think we'll wait." Mrs. Jennings looked at Mercedes, who nodded in agreement.

The waitress smiled and said, "Okay, just let me know when you're ready."

Mrs. Jennings waited for the waitress to leave and then repeated the question. "Where did you get the chemical?"

"I told you, it was given to me by a client of mine, on a case I'm working on."

Almost before Mercedes had finished her sentence, Mrs. Jennings began to speak. "Yeah, I remember. Who's the client?"

Mercedes hadn't expected Mrs. Jennings to be so brash and felt her paranoia giving way to agitation. "I'm sorry, that's confidential."

Mrs. Jennings sipped her coffee and then impatiently continued. "Look Ms. Atwater, I don't mean to be rude, but the drug you gave me is very dangerous and the people who designed it are even worse. If I would have had any idea that it was this drug you wanted me to look at for you I never would have agreed to do it."

"What are you talking about? Why is it so dangerous, and who are the people that designed it?" A chill ran through the back of her neck as Mercedes thought about Dirty Harry and his relatively friendly partner.

Mrs. Jennings nervously glanced around the restaurant for the second time. "All right." She shook her head and then tapped nervously on the side of her coffee cup as she spoke. "What you gave me last night is strikingly similar to another drug I worked on a few years ago, called HG7."

"HG7?"

"Yeah, it's a very dangerous drug that was originally designed by the CIA to make a person forget all of the events that had happened to them in the last day or so."

Mercedes listened and wondered whether or not Dirty Harry and his partner were really part of the CIA, like they said.

"About six years ago I got a call from a very close friend of mine who was working for one of Chryo-Plazz's competitors called Biotronics. He said that they had been contracted by the CIA to eliminate certain side effects in a new chemical of theirs, HG7. He was having major trouble solving a puzzle and asked if I could take a look. We were very close friends and even though I worked for a competing company, he knew he could trust me. The problem was pretty complex, but I'll try to make it as simple as possible. Okay, let's see." Mrs. Jennings paused for a minute as she struggled to find the words. "The drug worked on the hippocampus."

"The hippocampus?" The word sounded familiar and in order to make sense of it, Mercedes found her thoughts racing back to one of her least favorite subjects, biology.

"It's a part of the brain that's located just above the spinal cord." Mrs. Jennings pointed to the back of her head. "One of its main functions is to commit new thoughts or ideas into long-term memory."

"'Kay..." Mercedes squinted one eye, made a visual note and kept listening.

"Once a person was injected with HG7 they would forget everything that had happened to them during the last day or so. That's the part the CIA liked, however there was a fairly undesirable side effect."

"...And that was?"

"Three to four weeks after someone had been injected with HG7 their hippocampus would stop working altogether and they'd permanently lose the ability to formulate any new memories."

"Permanently?"

"Permanently!"

"And you call that *fairly* undesirable?"

Mrs. Jennings half-heartedly smiled and then continued, "CT scans showed that the hippocampus had shriveled up and all but vanished. The problem, as we discovered later was that HG7 worked by temporarily removing all of the nitric oxide from the hippocampus."

Mercedes frowned and wondered what nitric oxide was.

"Without nitric oxide the hippocampus is unable to do its job."

"Which is to turn new thoughts and ideas into long term memory?"

"Right. Along with stripping the brain of nitric oxide, HG7 also flooded the hippocampus with glutamate."

"Glutamate?" Her frown deepened.

"It's a chemical that nature designed to remove unwanted poisons from the brain, however too much glutamate and cells die. The amount of glutamate that HG7 introduced into the hippocampus was off the scale. Cells died by the millions and over the next few weeks 60 to 90% of all of the cells in the hippocampus died. Biotronics worked on the problem for years, but they were never able to fix it. Every time they'd reduce the amount of glutamate to nontoxic levels, there wouldn't be enough nitric oxide removed from the system for the drug to work. About three years ago the CIA found out that my friend was enlisting the help of an outsider, namely me. Fortunately, they never found out that I was the one helping. However, my friend had a fatal accident and the CIA pulled the plug. They confiscated all of Biotronics' research materials and I never heard anything more about it."

"So, the chemical I gave you last night is HG7?"

"Not exactly. The chemical you gave me is some enhanced form of HG7. I've named it HG7e"

"Enhanced form? So someone was able to fix the glutamate problem?"

"On the contrary, the amount of glutamate HG7e releases into the brain is 100 times greater than that of its predecessor. It releases so much glutamate into the system that any infected hippocampus would be ruined within hours instead of weeks.

The ladies sat in silence for a moment, as Mercedes took it all in. She tried to imagine what effect this chemical would have on Alex. Could it be the cause of his inability to remember the past? She thought about his gift for reading minds and her reconnected toe. "Is there any way this chemical could stimulate something in a person's brain that would give them the ability to do something out of the ordinary?"

"Something out of the ordinary? What do you mean?"

"Well…" Mercedes' face cringed and she felt foolish even while she asked it. "…Could this chemical somehow, give someone the ability to say… read minds?"

Mrs. Jennings looked oddly at Mercedes for a moment or two. "Do what?"

"Read minds. Could HG7 or HG7e somehow give a person the ability to read another person's thoughts?"

Mrs. Jennings sat wide-eyed as she spoke, "I don't know anything about *mind reading* Ms. Atwater, but I don't think that frying someone's brain is the way to achieve it."

"Right."

"Why do you ask?"

"No reason." Mercedes quickly changed the subject, "Is there anything else that you can tell me about the drug."

"Well, like HG7, it eliminates all of the nitric oxide and raises the glutamate levels in the brain, however it does a couple of extra things that HG7 didn't do."

"What's that?"

"Well, first, and I'm not sure how, it creates a chain reaction that sends an electrical impulse throughout the entire brain and wipes away any thoughts currently formulating, kind of like a jolt of electricity might do. Secondly, as a side effect of this jolt, any newly formed dendrites are destroyed."

"Dendrites?" A headache was beginning to form as Mercedes struggled to remember so many different definitions.

"They're an extension of the brain cell and are created whenever we learn something new."

"I see." Mercedes paused and then asked, "What do you think something like this would be used for?"

"That's a good question. I've asked myself that over and over and try as I may, I just can't imagine any purpose for it. Sure, it could turn a person into a vegetable, but there are dozens of other drugs out there that could do a better job at half the cost. Somebody invested a lot of money into this, and for what reason, I have no idea. It seams to be a completely wasted investment."

"And it would work on everyone the same way?"

"Yeah, and there's one more thing. I also found a common sedative in it."

Mercedes replied sarcastically, "So not only will it fry your brain, but it'll also help you sleep at night?"

"Right. Look Ms. Atwater, I've taken a big risk in coming here and meeting with you. The only reason I did is to let you know what kind of people you're up against. I don't know what sort of detective agency you run, but if I were you, I'd tell my client to go somewhere else. At Chryo-plazz, I've worked on other drugs for the CIA and I can tell you from personal experience that they don't play any games." Mrs. Jennings stood up, placed two dollars and a small vial of green liquid on the table, then firmly stated, "Please, don't call me again."

The restaurant grew big as Mercedes sat there alone, mulling the conversation over in her mind.

"More coffee?" The waitress approached the table and prepared to poor from the pot.

"No thank you. I'm getting ready to leave. May I please have the check?"

"Sure."

On the way back to the motel, Mercedes tried to make sense of everything, but had a hard time connecting the dots. She remembered Alex telling her that the men who were chasing him wanted to take him alive. Why would they want to take him alive only to turn him into a human vegetable?

"Okay, what do we have?" She spoke to herself as she drove. "A mind-reading toe surgeon with major memory problems, a couple of whacked-out CIA agents (or imposters pretending to be CIA agents), bent on human mutilation and let's don't forget the brain-frying drug that helps to cure insomnia." Her face scowled as she tried to figure out what her next move would be. "Think!" She needed to find out exactly whom it was that was searching for Alex and why. By now the police had cordoned off her house and probably her office as well; she wouldn't be able to use any of her normal resources. Thinking of Alex's note, she decided it would be best not to go to the police or any other law enforcement agency, at least not until she had a better idea of what was going on. The name *Biotronics* ran through her thoughts more than once and she wondered whether or not they were still involved in some way or another. Perhaps the two wallets Alex obtained this morning from the one-eyed corpse would be able to shed some light on things.

As she pulled into the parking lot of the motel, she caught herself half expecting to find a mysterious black van parked in some obscure place, just out of sight. The feeling was so strong that she drove completely around the motel twice before she finally accepted the fact that there wasn't one, and then parked. On her walk up to the room, as she continued to run the puzzle through her mind, she was absolutely sure that things were all ready weird enough and definitely didn't need them to get any worse. However, as she stepped across the threshold into the room, her tennis shoe squished onto a water-soaked carpet. A quick look around revealed that the entire front room was completely soaked and Alex was nowhere in sight.

"Alex?" Mercedes closed the door and tiptoed her way through the swampy carpeting, to the restroom. "Alex?" She rapped softly on the door and called again. "Alex, are you in there?" There was no sound, however through the small opening at the bottom of the door, a weird fog was slowly leaking into the room and then quickly evaporating. Mercedes put her hands to the door; it felt icy, like the cold steel of an industrial freezer. Suddenly, she was overcome with the feeling that death was in the next room. An overactive imagination quickly went to work and the vision of Alex's lifeless body flashed through her head.

As she pushed open the door, breaking the thin crust of ice that had formed around the edges, an icy gust of wind escaped the bathroom and sent a chill through her body. As the thick fog slowly dissipated, she saw Alex curled up in the fetal position, on the floor next to the bathtub. He lay trembling, staring, wide-eyed at the cabinet just beneath the sink and looked aimlessly toward Mercedes as she knelt down beside him.

"Oh my god! What happened?" His trembling lips only mouthed the words, as his terror-filled eyes connected with hers and beckoned for help. It was like handling one huge block of human ice, as she reached down, grabbed his nearly frozen shoulders, and then dragged him out of the bathroom. His cold, stiff clothes crackled off as she undressed him and then helped him get beneath the warm dry, covers of the bed. After turning on the heater and stretching his clothes out to dry, she returned and sat on the bed next to him. He seemed to be doing much better now and was improving fast. His lips had stopped trembling and his cheeks were regaining their color.

"Alex?" Mercedes asked softly.

He looked at her, but still said nothing.

"Are you okay?"

He nodded. "I think so." His voice was weak and shaky.

"What happened?"

"I'm not sure." With weary eyes he looked around the room and then rested them on the other bed, where Mercedes had woken up from earlier. "I had helped you into bed and then something inside me took over and began to heal you."

"Heal me?" Mercedes thought about the dream of red light and the reconnection of her toe.

"Yeah, in some way, I don't really understand how, I knew that I could help. It's like I could feel your pain as if it were my own and see your wounds—at the cellular level. I don't know how, but as I thought, your wounds began to mend themselves. It was weird. The next thing I knew, I was having another one of those freaky memories or whatever they are. Only this one was different."

"Different?"

"Yeah, the other ones I can still remember, but as soon as I came out of this one, it began to fade. Alex's eyes grew distant as he recalled as much of the memory as he could. "The sun was shining and we were laughing."

"We?"

He spoke slower as his mind went deeper into his thoughts. "Yeah, a friend of mine and I were playing outside, in some very cold water." He smiled a weak smile. "We were having a good time, but then something went wrong. My friend began to drown." His eyes narrowed and his smile faded into a frown. "I screamed for help, but no one came." His eyes shifted as he thought. "That's odd; I can't remember my friend's name. I knew it so clearly just a moment ago." He shook his head for a moment, but then his face brightened and he shot forward in bed. "But I do remember my name..." He looked at Mercedes excitedly and said, "It was Alex! It was Alex *S.* Kendallman!"

Mercedes' heart skipped a beat and she listened closer, pondering this new piece of information, as Alex continued, "The next thing I knew, I was drowning along with my friend. After that, there was this amazingly bright light. I can't remember too much more. When I snapped out of it, I was drenched in icy cold water, the carpet was soaked and the room felt like a freezer. I was afraid that if I went outside someone might see me, so I went into the bathroom, it seemed warmer in there. The next thing I knew, you opened the door."

Mercedes rose from the bed, found a piece of scrap paper and a pencil. "Here, quickly, I want you to write down everything you can remember about that memory, it may be our best lead yet." Then she asked, "Where are the two wallets that you removed from that guy in my apartment this morning?"

Alex pointed toward one of the drawers in the dresser. "I put them in there."

Mercedes opened the drawer, removed the wallets and took them to the little table next to the front door. They were nearly identical, with the only exception being that one was fatter than the other, indicating a larger inventory. The first one she opened, the thinner one, looked vaguely familiar, and proved to hold only the CIA identification that she had already seen. It carried the name Michael Joel Donaldson and displayed an address in the valley. She had run across other false IDs before, however this one looked fairly authentic and she wasn't at all certain whether it was a fake or not. The other one was nothing more than a normal wallet with several credit cards, a few family photos and a California driver's license. The photo on the license and the one on the CIA ID were the same, however the names and addresses were different. The name on the license was Michael James Haskell and his address was in the city of Irvine. One of the two IDs was a fake. Mercedes looked back at the CIA identification, examined it closely and decided that it had to be the phony. Why would someone, obviously old enough to drink, carry a bogus driver's license around with him?

While Mercedes examined the two different identifications, Alex sat on the bed with his back up against the headboard, holding the scrap paper in his right hand and the pencil in his left. The thin number two pencil dangled, point first, as he grasped it oddly by the eraser and tried to remember how to write. In his mind he could picture letters, numbers and even several foreign characters, as well as a vast supply of words, however he had no idea how to move the pencil in such a way as to transfer what he knew onto the paper. He looked up at Mercedes, who was completely submersed in her examination of the two wallets and thought about asking her for help, but just couldn't bring himself to do it. Why wasn't he able to do a simple task like write? Once again the world began to feel huge and he began to feel lost. His eyes left Mercedes and wandered back at the blank white paper, which already seemed to be an accurate record of his life. He lowered the paper to his lap as he dangled the pencil over it and thought about the last few days, which were all of the memories he had. The earliest ones that he could recollect were of him wandering the streets two nights ago and finally finding that place behind the super market where he could get some rest. He remembered lying there on a makeshift bed of old cardboard boxes, staring up into the cloud-coved night sky and pondering his situation. He thought about how he had felt that night and compared it with how he was feeling now.

Turning his head, he looked back at Mercedes with glistening eyes and wondered if she was truly capable of helping him. Would she be able to find out who stole his life and get it back for him? He remembered how detailed she had been yesterday when they were going over his situation. She made him tell her everything he could remember, down to the smallest detail. He remembered telling her about being chased out of the rain-filled parking lot? Wait a minute! What parking lot? His mind stopped in mid-thought as he tried, but couldn't remember a parking lot. His hand relaxed and released the pencil, nose first onto the paper as he questioned his memories. He remembered telling Mercedes about being chased through a parking lot, but he didn't remember it actually happening. He racked his brains, but the earliest events he could recall were of him wandering through the streets and then pondering his situation behind that grocery store. He thought about that for a moment and realized that the memories, which he had been pondering that night, were also of him being chased through a parking lot. He remembered remembering, but didn't remember the events themselves!

The world grew even larger now and an icy fear griped his heart as he realized that his memories were steadily funneling *through* his mind and then fading away. Tomorrow he wouldn't remember spending the night behind that super market and the day after that he wouldn't even remember meeting Mercedes. If this were how it was going to be then how would he ever get his life back? Although he couldn't remember them, he thought about the evil people that had done this to him. How could anyone be so cruel? The room closed in around him and a tear ran down his face as he sat in silence.

Still at the table, exploring the two wallets and for the moment completely unaware of Alex's deteriorating state of mind, Mercedes got an idea. She picked up the telephone, dialed information and requested the number to Biotronics. Perhaps, they were still involved in some way and this Michael Haskell guy worked for them. If she called and asked for Michael Haskell maybe, just maybe she'd get lucky and find someone who hadn't yet received the news of his death. If so, then she'd know that Biotronics was definitely involved and at least have a place to start looking for answers. After writing down the two numbers available, she hung up and then looked over at Alex, who almost looked catatonic. Damn! Not again!

She stood up from her chair and walked over to him, wondering where he was off to this time and for how long, but as she approached, she noticed the streams of tears rolling down his face.

"Alex?" As she guessed, he did not respond. "Alex?" To her surprise, his eyes slowly wandered over in her direction and gazed aimlessly at her face. "Alex, can you hear me?"

"A freak! A memory-less freak!" His words were full of anger and desperation.

"What? Alex, it's me, Mercedes. Are you okay? Can you hear me?"

His overflowing, water-filled eyes met with hers and she realized that he wasn't having another vision, but was rather contemplating his own situation. She drew closer and sat on the edge of the bed.

"What am I going to do?" He looked so lost.

She listened compassionately, not fully understanding the question and not really knowing what to say.

"What if we find out what happened, find out what they did to me, and what if, somehow were able to put an end to them chasing me? What then? Do I just go on living like a freak without a memory?" His jaws tighten and his fists clinched, as he glared, angrily, not into, but through her eyes at some unseen enemy out of reach.

"Oh Alex." She leaned forward and raised a hesitant hand to his shimmering cheek. "You're not a freak. You're a victim. And you'll build new memories."

He jerked away from her and snapped, "Will I?" His focus came back and he peered into her eyes as he continued, "My memory is fading!"

"What? What do you mean?"

"I can't remember being chased out of that parking lot the other day or hiding out in that apartment."

"What do you mean you can't remember it? If you can't remember it then how come we're talking about it?" Mercedes narrowed her eyes and shook her head.

"I remember telling you about it, but I can't actually remember it happening."

At a loss for words, Mercedes sat silently and began to feel the emptiness that saturated and surrounded Alex's world.

Alex looked down at the paper, which now had one lead mark from where the pencil struck it when it fell. "Not only that," he paused and then continued with a crackle in his voice, "but I have no idea how to write." He looked back at Mercedes. "I know what letters look like and I can even picture whole words in my head, but I have no idea how to make this pencil put them on that paper. How come I can talk, walk and do so many other things, but I can't drive or write? You say I'm not a freak, then what am I?" Even if, somehow the two of them could figure out what was going on and put an end to it, his life would still be meaninglessness.

They both sat in silence for a moment as Mercedes' eyes began to glisten with empathy and a feeling of helplessness. She wanted to tell him that he wasn't a freak and that everything would be okay, but she didn't want to lie. The truth of the matter was that she couldn't begin to understand how he felt. She thought about her friends, her family, her father. She had no idea what it could feel like to be so alone. Then suddenly, almost as a reflex, that old familiar feeling of determination welled up within her and she stood up and said, "Everything will be okay! I promise! I don't know how yet, but mark my words," she grabbed his chin and turned his face toward hers, "no matter what happens, I'll be here with you. You're *not* alone and we'll handle whatever comes, *together*!"

Mercedes was like an open book; there was never a reason to read her mind, because she spoke it. Everything she said, she meant. Even though Alex believed her, it didn't make him feel much better. She had no idea what they were up against, and in some way, even though he couldn't pull up a single memory to validate his feelings, he knew that it was bigger than both of them put together. Mercedes quickly wiped her eyes, moved back to the table, and picked up the phone. After dialing the first number and getting an after-hours automated voice mail system, she hung up and tried the next number. Like the last one, an automated operator came over the line, but instead of just giving her the option to leave a message, this one also gave her a menu. She pressed zero and was patched through to a live male voice.

"Hello, division seven."

Without missing a beat, Mercedes answered, "Hello, may I please speak to Michael Haskell. It's extremely important."

"Who was that again?"

"Michael Haskell."

"Just one moment please." After a brief pause, he came back on the line and continued, "Ma'am, Mr. Haskell doesn't work at this location, he works out of the Boris Lab."

"The Boris Lab, I see. Do you have that number?"

To her surprise, he gave her both a phone number and an address.

She hung up, looked at her watch and then turned to Alex. "I'm going to take a quick drive. Will you be okay for an hour or so?"

"I think so. I'm tired. I'm just going to rest a little."

"All right."

Mercedes grabbed her keys, checked her gun and walked out the front door. In her car, she got out her Thomas Guide and looked up her recently acquired address. After starting the engine and making her way to the exit, just as she was getting ready to turn onto the boulevard, she noticed the headlamps of an unidentified vehicle pull up behind her. Peering into her rearview mirror, she was gripped by a familiar sense of fear as she recognized it to be a suspicious looking black van.

CHAPTER NINETEEN

About the time Mercedes woke up and went to meet Mrs. Jennings, Nick was being released from the hospital. Well, he wasn't exactly being released, but he was leaving just the same. He had been treated for a bullet wound to the buttocks. The gun had been fired at such a weird angle, that the bullet went in the top of the butt and exited just above his thigh. It was as if whoever shot him had been standing directly behind him, placed the gun flat up against his back and pointed the muzzle straight down. The doctor's eyebrows had risen in skepticism when Nick told him that he had accidentally shot himself, while cleaning his gun.

While Nick was in the hospital he had extra time to think and because he had just got off the phone with Lisa before he checked in, most of his thoughts were of her. He had finally come to the conclusion that Dottie was right and he was only hurting his relationship with his daughter by not letting things go. He wished that he would have made this revelation sooner, but in any case he had finally made up his mind that no matter what he finds out here in California, this would be his last trip anywhere searching for stuff that had anything to do with Allie's death.

He decided that once he returned home he would clean up the cabin and get rid of the backlog of junk that he had been collecting over the last eight years, and then sell the place. Dottie was right about a lot of things and one of them was that the lifestyle in which Lisa and he had been living was not good. What kind of father had he turned into? As soon as he got back he would sell the cabin and then buy a house in Shady Springs, a very nice development on the other side of town. Lisa would still be able to attend the same school and keep the same friends. Nick was ashamed of himself for not being the kind of father that he knew he was capable of being, the kind of father that Lisa needed him to be. With the doctor working on his butt, his heart sank as he thought of how Lisa not only lost her mother that fateful summer morning, but her father as well.

With an extra padding of bandages on his rear end, Nick hobbled his way to his car and then drove back to the old white house in El Monte. As he passed it, getting ready to stop, he spotted a couple of black and whites poorly parked out in front and a handful of officers checking the lock at the gate. He had wanted to go back to the basement and finish his search, but because it wouldn't be wise to try sneaking by so many cops and because, as everybody knows, most cops are assholes, Nick drove past without stopping. He drove down to the end of the block, entered the parking lot of the playground, and pulled into a stall with a good view of the house. As he watched the cops stand around and pretend to work, he fired up his laptop and checked his email. To his surprise, youroneprivateeye.com had already replied. Hopefully they were able to match an address to the partial license plate number that he had sent them. After opening the file, while chewing on Gummy Bears, he found that there were thirty-two Lexuses that had the same license plate number combination as the one he requested information on. He quickly scanned through them and smiled as his eyes zeroed in on the number 3BRI155. It was the twenty-sixth one on the list and was registered to a Theodore E. Connelly. Among the additional information provided was a mug shot, which proved to be the photo of the man that Nick had had the altercation with in the basement of the house. Also, there was a ten-year work history, which showed a sporadic employment background, many different phone numbers and a current address in the city of San Dimas, California. In the usual way, he looked up the address and obtained driving directions.

Looking at the cops he whispered, "See ya boys," started the engine and wondered whether or not they had obtained this information yet and were able to narrow their search down to Theodore. He backed out of the stall and headed for Mr. Connelly's home in San Dimas. Sometimes the police utterly amazed Nick at how fast they could work through the clues and find the answers, but most often he found them to be more than just a little slow. On several occasions he wondered what it would be like to work on their side and help them make sense of the clues. However he never truly considered it to be a *real* possibility, because, as everybody knows most cops are assholes and he definitely never wanted to be an asshole.

The trip from El Monte to San Dimas took less than a half an hour and he passed the time by running things over in his head. This was the closest he had come to finding any kind of answers since that time, a year after Allie's death, in that warehouse in Atlanta. He had been following the trail of a local serial killer who had a thing for removing and allegedly eating the internal organs of his victims. Nick had managed to intercept a radio communication between two officers, giving him information on the whereabouts of the killer's latest hideout. The address was an abandoned warehouse just outside of town and as fortune would have it, Nick wasn't too far away. He'd never forget what happened that hot summer morning and how it reaffirmed his belief that there had been more to Allie's death than met the eye. As he drove across the dry, cracked earth and parked out front, he thought he had arrived before anyone else and hoped to find the killer still in the building. However, once inside he spied a baldheaded man in an expensive business suit talking to a deranged looking fellow who appeared to be on some kind of a drug. At first he had assumed that the man in the suit was FBI and the other guy was Atlanta's serial killer, but then he caught a tidbit of what the man was saying. It was something about being too sloppy and that his services were no longer needed. After pulling out his gun, Nick slowly crept up and crouched behind some boxes, trying to get a better ear on what the man was talking about.

"Now come on now Leonard, just put the gun to your head and then squeeze the trigger."

Looking through the tiny crack between two boxes, Nick could see that the deranged man was bent over, and softly crying. "But why? What if… What if I don't want to?" His slurred words were slow and his chin was covered with slobber.

The baldheaded man replied in a deep, rhythmic tone that seemed to have a hypnotic affect on his drooling partner. "You do want to. You do want to. You do want to."

The drugged man looked up at his hypnotist with a far a way look in his eyes and asked, "I do?"

"Yes, you do Leonard, you do."

"Oh, okay." For an instant the man's eyes were filled with light and he appeared to understand what he had to do and then he raised the gun to his temple, smiled and, just as the baldheaded man was backing away, pulled the trigger, splattering blood and brains everywhere.

Keeping the gun trained on the demented hypnotist, Nick slowly moved out from behind the boxes and loudly cleared his throat. "Not one of Atlanta's finest, now are we?"

What happened next completely shocked Nick and eventually became one of the main reasons why he was never able to let things go. The man wasn't in the least bit startled by Nick's sudden appearance and after casually turning toward him, he spoke in a clam relaxed voice, not in a voice of a man that had just been caught helping, or more precisely, making someone commit suicide. The short conversation that followed made Nick feel uneasy and nervous—something Nick almost never felt. "Awe, Mr. Chadwick. Searching for clues no doubt."

"How do you know my name?" As Nick steadily moved closer, he glimpsed an open briefcase on the floor next to the man's spit shined dress shoes, which contained a couple of already used hypodermic needles and more than one bag of clear liquid.

"Oh, I know a lot about you Nicholas. Tell me, how's little Lisa holding up after her mother's death?"

A lump of uneasiness found its way into Nick's throat as he stopped and curiously asked, "Who are you?" The man stood there for a minute without answering and then smiled as Nick heard the swoosh of the 2X4. He quickly spun around, just in time to see the large block of wood smack into his face and knock him into anther world. By the time he came to, the police had already arrived and the strange visitor was nowhere in sight. The police found a suicide note and after a brief investigation, although Nick stated otherwise, concluded that Atlanta's serial killer had acted alone in committing suicide.

Every investigation since proved to hold little more than token clues that never added up to much of anything. After that, he never got close enough to another killer to get any information out of them. Before he could get to them, they'd either disappear, be caught, be killed or commit suicide. Hopefully, this time things would be different. If he could just get to Theodore before anyone else did then maybe, just maybe he could get some of the answers he needed.

The Mustang turned the corner and approached the house at the top of the hill. It was a large cream-colored home and featured a perfect view of the city. The sun was beginning to set, casting an eerie radiance over the house as Nick parked the car and wondered if the headhunter was inside. As the afternoon was giving way to twilight, Nick quietly thanked the headhunter for letting him use his gun and then headed for the nearest window. The homes in the neighborhood were sparse and because of the angle of the house and the number of bushes in the front yard, Nick wasn't too terribly afraid of being seen. He made his way up to the window, cupped his hand over the glass and peered inside. He was looking into a vacant bedroom with nice furniture and several religious paintings.

After checking the widow, hoping he just might get lucky, but finding it securely locked, he moved on to the next one. It turned out to be a bathroom with an expensive ceramic tile floor, stainless steel sinks and several religious nick-knacks. This window, like the last, was tightly sealed and impenetrable. The sinking sun threw an ill-omened light, past the bushes and into the windows, which stretched long shadows off the sacred fixtures and sent a cool chill into the marrow of Nick's spine. The chill spread, as he moved to the front door and found it slightly ajar. He quickly glanced back to the street at his car and tried to envision how the door had appeared from there. He was almost, but not quite certain that it had been shut when he drove up. Stepping lightly, in his brown cowboy boots and holding the six-shooter in his right hand, he cautiously approached the door, expecting someone to walk through it at any moment.

Ever so quietly, he reached out with his left and gently pushed the door open. It pivoted swiftly on its hinges and swayed inward, coming right up to, but not touching the wall before stopping.

Like a shadow, Nick stepped through the threshold, onto the posh tile floor and his boots became socks as he silently made his way throughout the house. To an uneducated person, nothing about the place looked too terribly odd, but to someone who had been chasing serial killers for the past eight years as Nick had, everything about the place screamed freak. All of the rooms were neat and clean, without a trace of dirt, anywhere. Expensive spiritual works of art hung on each wall, with following eyes and strangely made the place look more evil than holy. Nick found four fully furnished bedrooms that looked as if they hadn't been occupied in years. The dresser drawers were all empty and the bedspreads were pulled so tight that if a coin would had been dropped on any of them, Nick was certain it would have bounced halfway back up. Moving from room to room, the only sounds Nick heard were those of his own movements and soon he began to believe that he was the only one in the home.

As night blended into twilight and he made his way through the ever darkening home, the deified figurines glared at him from every room and protested his blasphemous trespassing. Finally, he entered a room at the end of a long hall that appeared to be out of place with the rest of the house. At first, as he pushed the door inward he wasn't able to see much, for the sun had nearly set and room was all but black. Quietly, standing in the doorway, looking like a thug on a home invasion robbery, waiting for his eyes to adjust, he thought about the flashlight that he had left in the basement of the old white house, and was momentarily tempted to switch on the light. The blackness gradually lightened, and darker silhouettes began to take shape. As he walked into the room he could feel dozens of sacred eyes fall upon him as the many figurines steadily appeared out of the darkness. Before long his eyes adjusted to a point where he could make some sense out of the shadows. This room, unlike the others, was not as neat or well kept. Several articles of clothing hung over two half opened dresser drawers and more, some still on hangers, lay, spread out over the unmade bed. A small suitcase sat crumpled under the weight of a larger one next a disheveled bookshelf. On closer inspection, both proved to be empty. The bed was accompanied by two nightstands, one on each side. On the one closest to the door, just below the window, Nick found a pen laying on top of a piece of paper, which looked like a hand written note, however it was too dark to be sure. Pushing aside the thick heavy drapes, he lifted the paper from the nightstand and brought it up to the trickle of light leaking through the window, from a distant street lamp.

Dearest Mother,

Please don't be angry with me and don't believe their lies. The devil is strong, but God is stronger. You will be proud of me when you understand all the good work that I have done these last eighteen months. I have helped so many souls go home to be with the Lord.

Mother, I want to thank you, with all of my heart, for putting up with me as a child, when I was filled with all that sin for all of those years. I have never told you this before, but I am very grateful to have had a mother who loved me enough to do whatever it took to make me the God fearing man that I am. I don't know if I would be a good servant now, if you wouldn't have loved me enough to beat all of those demons out of me when I was younger.

Although I want to, I will not be claiming my heavenly reward any time soon. The Lord has seen fit to keep me here just a while longer, for what reason I am not yet sure, but whatever it is, I do believe it will be extremely important. I love you mother.

Love,

Your Teddy

If the house screamed freak, then this letter amplified that scream. Nick felt a tinge of compassion go through him as he thought about what Teddy's life must have been like as a child. Most people have no idea how much they shape the lives of their children. Some parents treat their children in ways that boggle the mind and then wonder why their kids have turned out the way they did. In the last eight years, Nick had learned that a mad man's behavior can almost always be traced back to a traumatic childhood brought about by a screwed-up parent.

Releasing the curtain, Nick replaced the paper on to the nightstand and thought about his own parents. Until their deaths, he had been one of the very fortunate people in life who had been blessed with very caring and loving parents. During the years that followed Allie's death, Nick often wondered what kind of person he would have turned into if he had been born to one of the parents of the lunatics he had been chasing. Most likely he would have became just like them.

Nick was all but certain now that the headhunter was not here. He probably read the newspaper article, saw the photo of the back of the Lexus and realized that it was only a matter of time before the authorities put two and two together and came calling. Psychos were crazy, but they weren't stupid. Fairly certain that Teddy would have been too smart to have left even a trace of evidence as to where he went, Nick decided to leave. He exited the bedroom, walked down the hall and into the entryway, but just before he walked out the front door, the phone rang. Startled at the broken silence, he stopped, turned around and followed the sound, through another hall, past a large kitchen and into the den. The phone sat on a small table next to an archway that led into an eloquent formal living room, which was illuminated by a light coming from a half opened doorway beyond.

Nick stared at the phone, watching it ring and resisted the urge to pick it up. Perhaps, if he answered it and pretended to be Teddy, he just might catch someone off guard and get a better insight into how Teddy thought and where he might have gone. He thought back to the fight he had with Teddy and tried to remember how his voice had sounded. As the phone rang again his temptation to answer it grew. Standing by the phone with the six-shooter in his right hand, pointing toward the ceiling, he finally reached over with his left hand and picked it up. Keeping himself silent, he brought the handset up to his ear, looked in the direction of the light and listened.

At first, he could only hear a faint breathing, letting him know that there was someone on the other end, but then, after a brief pause a male voice came over the line. "Teddy?" Nick stayed silent as the man repeated. "Teddy? It's the angel, Teddy."

Although the voice sounded familiar, Nick wasn't able to place it at first, but then his heart stopped as recognition ran through his mind. His thoughts raced back to that warehouse in Atlanta and a clear image of the baldheaded man entered his head. Nearly seven years had passed and the man's voice wasn't all that unique, nevertheless, Nick knew it was him. Nick held the phone to his ear, more tempted then ever to say something, but held his silence. After another short pause, the line went dead. Nick stood in the dark, breathing rhythmically and still holding the phone to his ear as he swallowed, trying to loosen the knot that had tightened in his throat.

The phone company's error-tones beeped loudly into his ear, followed by the automated female voice, "If you'd like to make a call, please hang up and try your call again or dial your operator to help you." Staring blindly at the light shining from beyond the living room, thinking about the incident in Atlanta, Nick slowly lowered the receiver and hung up. A few seconds later, after regaining his composure, he slowly crept through the dim living room, toward the light.

Just on the other side of the living room was a small utility room. The light was coming through an open door in the utility room that led down a flight of steps into a basement. Nick cautiously moved down the steps, listening carefully for any sounds that might be coming up from below. As he descended, his nose began to fill with a funny but familiar bleach-like odor that he couldn't quite place. At the bottom he closed his eyes and tried to discern the smell. If he had been blind and was only able to go on the scent, then he might have easily mistaken the basement for an abandoned hospital. The odor was strong and comprised of bleach, disinfectant and something else. Something he had smelled somewhere before. He took a deep breath, trying to focus on the strange odor, but the bleach was too strong.

Hoping it would come to him soon, he opened his eyes and looked around. The room was large and mostly empty, but the few items that were there were a bit peculiar. Nick shook his head in disgust as he had half expected this room to be here. They all had a place like this, a place different than the others in their lives, a place they transformed from the happy-go-lucky neighbor that you wave at while backing out of your driveway, to the twisted, perverted monster that you hear about on the six o'clock news. Nick called these places the Mr. Hyde zones (after the famous Dr. Jekyll and Mr. Hyde.)

He breathed slowly through his nose, trying to label the funny scent as he walked through the Mr. Hyde zone to a bizarre looking bed that turned out to be some sort of a homemade guillotine. It was fashioned for someone to lie on his or her back, and have to watch the blade as it made its deadly descent. Nick could almost hear the sound of metal on metal and almost feel the cold steel blade slicing through his neck as he imagined it running down the track, toward its victim. There were several items surrounding the bed. Among them was a rolling tray, topped with numerous surgical tools, an IV pole and a church podium. A bible lay opened on the podium with a scripture heavily underlined and circled in red ink.

For the wages of sin is death; but the gift of God is eternal life through Jesus Christ our Lord.

The handwritten scribble on the page next to the passage read: *Bring them to me oh Lord and I will send them home to you!* An eerie chill washed through Nick, as he thought about all of the people who must have suffered terribly in this room. With the cold chill creeping around the edge of his spine, he walked over to a tall, double-door cabinet and looked inside. It was full of gauze, surgical tape, painkillers, smelling salts and dozens of little metal dishes. The contents looked as if it had come from the supply closet of a local hospital.

Holding a gauze pad in his left hand, visualizing the torment that must have went on here and becoming more disgusted by the minute, the hairs on the back of his neck stood on end as he felt the presence of someone sinister standing directly behind him. Dropping the gauze to the floor, he spun around quickly with his finger ready to squeeze, but the basement was empty. Nick felt increasingly uneasy standing alone in the large death chamber as he carefully looked around the room. At the far end he saw a large metal door with a handle that reminded him of one of those commercial freezers used for storing meat and other foods. Still feeling the presence of an eerie unseen visitor, Nick guardedly made his way over to the door, deeper into the chambers of Hell.

A large padlock hung on the door, but hadn't been latched. When he pulled the door open, a quick burst of air escaped and sent a chilling whisper for help into the room. The whisper was filled with a concentrated amount of the mystery odor. Nick stopped, closed his eyes and breathed in deeply. He knew that odor, and it wasn't good—but what was it?

After a moment he opened his eyes and continued. Although it was cool, the room wasn't cold, as he had imagined it to be.

The only light came from the other end of the basement, and as he stood just inside the threshold, staring into the blackness, he instinctively called out, "Hello?"

Half expecting to get an answer he stepped forward and patiently waited for his eyes to adjust, and then once again he felt the presence of someone else standing behind him. He quickly spun around, but like before, no one was there. With his heart pounding and the darkness giving way to the light, he turned back around and began to see several eyes staring at him from dozens of little figurines which were scattered along the walls of the small room.

The figurines gradually morphed into something more hideous as Nick's eyes continued to adjust to the dim light. The room was about half the size of an average garage and the forward three walls, from top to bottom, had been turned into bookshelves. Instead of being filled with books, however the shelves were covered in faces, faces that were attached to heads! They looked like the manikins' heads found in the nearest salon, only these weren't Styrofoam, they were human. Eventually, enough light had filled the room so that he could see the full scope of the massacre. There were three to four heads per shelf and four shelves per wall.

The well-preserved heads had all been perfectly placed and were positioned to stare directly into the center of the room, which, unfortunately, was right where Nick was standing when his eyes finally adjusted. Dozens of eyes, still seemingly filled with life were peering at him and either begging for help or threatening to harm him. The sight was so surreal that Nick found himself wishing he were in a wax museum some place, staring at wax replicas, but knew the truth. Then suddenly he recognized the odor. It was formaldehyde. Wanting to puke, but keeping his composure, Nick slowly backed his way out of the room. The tiny bit of light played tricks on him and made it seem as if all of the eyes followed him out. The creepiness of the madman's home had finally worked its way beneath Nick's skin as he once again spun around to catch the phantom that wasn't there.

Nick decided that enough was enough and headed for the door. Twice more, once at the top of the stairs and then at the front door, Nick turned around expecting to find someone following him, watching him, but each time he saw no one. In his car, driving back to the old white house, he couldn't shake the eerie feeling that followed him from Teddy's death chamber. By now the cops had probably finished with the house and left. Nick was on his way to retrieve his flashlight and bolt cutters from the rafters in the basement, and finish his look around. Afterward, he would park across the street and stake the place out. There was a possibility that the freak would return and if he did then Nick would have a second chance at nabbing him.

A sinking sensation welled up inside of him as he imagined the baldheaded man getting to Teddy before he did. The more he thought about it the more he began to feel that maybe he was already too late.

Three blocks from the old white house, as he drove down the busy avenue he caught a glimpse of a two-toned white and gray Lexus exiting the driveway of The Heavenly Heart Hotel. As he slowed to get a closer look, he could see that the man driving was Theodore. Not wanting to begin another chase, Nick casually drove to the intersection, turned around, and staying three to four car lengths back, followed the Lexus.

CHAPTER TWENTY

Mercedes sat in the idling car, checking her gun, getting ready to obtain a closer look at the building, which sat across the street behind the tall barbwire fence. She had driven around the place three times and thought she had a pretty good idea of the layout. Besides the two men who manned the shack in the front where the gate could open and let cars through, the place was unguarded. The building wasn't too terribly big and she was sure that if it really was a laboratory of some sort, as the man on the phone had indicated, then it had to be the world's smallest. The nearly empty parking lot was too big for a building so small and she noticed two rotating cameras, one on each corner of the back gate. She shut off the engine and thought. All she really wanted to do was have a look around and then maybe come back tomorrow, in the daylight.

Just as she opened her door, put her foot on the blacktop, getting ready to exit, two men came, walking out of the of the double glass doors in the front of the building. She quickly sat back down, softly closed the door and watched them walk across the blacktop and get into a Toyota Camry. Fear and anticipation both ran through her as she recognized one of the men to be Haskell's fake CIA partner, Agent Young.

The men moved fast and appeared to have somewhere important to go. Light poured forward, in Mercedes' direction, as the Camry's headlamps came on and then the car abruptly pulled out of the stall and headed for a guarded entrance, which was already beginning to open electronically.

Inside the Camry, Patterson and Jackson carried on a conversation.

"So he's on his way there now?" Patterson asked, trying to contain his excitement.

"Yeah." Jackson looked forward and almost seemed perturbed.

"A church?" Patterson shook his head as an evil smile spanned from ear to ear. "You are a genius. How do you come up with these ideas?"

Wanting to roll his eyes in disgust and wondering why Mr. Davenport had insisted that he bring Patterson along, Jackson didn't reply. After Patterson's screw-up this morning, Jackson couldn't understand why he was still being allowed to do anything at all, especially something as important as help with Teddy.

"I can't wait to finally see Teddy in person. Do you think that maybe I can meet him, you know, before you have him blow his brains out?" Patterson's eyes grew large and a sadistic laugh escaped him.

"No." Jackson said sternly while keeping his eyes on the road ahead.

Disappointed in Jackson's abrupt response, Patterson sat quietly for the next few seconds, staring through the window at the passing city lights and then said, "You know, I don't understand why we even need these freaks anyway. All they do is fuck things up. We could do a much better job if we did it ourselves."

Jackson turned to look at the brainless buffoon and thought about pulling over and beating the shit out of him right there in the car, but somehow kept his composure. After a second of silence he shook his head at Patterson's stupidity and turned back to face the road.

As the Camry moved along the busy street, being secretly followed by the Corolla, Patterson could hardly keep his excitement down. Not only was he working with the legendary Raymond Jackson, something he was hardly ever permitted to do, but he was also going to be present while Jackson pulled Teddy's puppet strings.

Jackson usually worked alone and his work almost always surpassed even Mr. Davenport's highest expectations. On the rare occasions that Jackson did screw up, and they were rare, he'd have everything back in order quicker than anyone in the company. He was a true leader and an awesome asset to Biotronics. Whenever Patterson found himself working with this great man he would become a living sponge and soak up as much information about how he worked as possible.

"Did you bring the angel outfit?" Patterson admired Jackson for the extent that he would go to create a puppet. Teddy had been quite a bit smarter than the previous puppets that Jackson had created and from the very first encounter, he had done everything he could to ensure that Teddy would unquestionably believe that he was a true angel of the Lord. He used the usual drugs with Teddy, but just to be on the safe side, in case, somewhere, at some subconscious level, Teddy was still able to make a little sense out of things, Jackson totally played the part of God's ambassador.

The Camry pulled into the parking area of a huge Catholic church, as a Corolla drove past the entrance, to the end of the block and turned around.

"It's in the trunk along with a tranquilizer rifle." The Camry pulled into a stall and Jackson shut off the engine. "When we get inside, follow me to the platform. After I scope things out and get a good feel for the place you'll go up to the balcony and wait. I'll be on the platform, in costume, when Teddy arrives. Be ready when he walks in, but wait for my signal before you shoot." Jackson spoke in an authoritative tone.

"I know." Patterson replied sharply. If there was one thing that he didn't like about Jackson, it was the way Jackson treated him. He never seemed to be doing a good enough job and he always felt as if he were being treated like a child.

"Oh really?" Jackson spoke abruptly as he shifted in his seat and turned his body toward Patterson.

Patterson sat silently looking confused at the great man and didn't respond.

"Just like you and Haskell knew to wait for me this morning?"

Patterson felt ashamed and wanted to say something in his defense, but knew he deserved the rebuke that Jackson was giving him. Jackson was the master and Patterson had screwed up, screwed up big. Now he was getting what he deserved. He wanted to tell Jackson how he was only trying to prove that he could handle things without Jackson's help. When Jackson told him to wait until he arrived, Patterson felt as if Jackson didn't trust him. He had hoped that he would have been able to get Number Nine back and show Jackson just how reliable he could be.

"Do you have any idea just how badly you hurt the company today?" Jackson cocked his head and looked curiously at Patterson. "Just who is it that you think you are and what kind of a game do you think we're playing here?"

Patterson did not like to be lectured to, not at all, not even by the legendary Raymond Jackson, however he stayed silent and listened.

Jackson shook his head and closed his eyes for a brief moment, then continued, "The next time I tell you to wait, you better wait or the next person to be turned off just might be you." Jackson glared at Patterson, whose anger was building up like the pressure in a volcano, and then opened the door and stepped out onto the pavement.

Patterson stayed in the car for another minute trying to get a harness on his rage, but it only escalated. Blindly, he reached under his coat pocket and grabbed the butt of his gun. Nobody, nobody speaks to Gregory Patterson that way, not even the great Raymond Jackson. Was it his fault that things had went awry this morning? He didn't think so. If it was anyone's fault, it was Haskell's. Haskell wanted to be *all nice* to the bitch this morning. Patterson knew that approach wouldn't work, but went along with it anyway.

As he was removing his gun from his shoulder harness, with the volcano of anger getting ready to erupt, his car door, which he was somewhat leaning against, unexpectedly flew open causing him to momentary lose his balance and almost fall out of the car.

"What are you waiting on?" Jackson stood on the asphalt, holding a set of clothes in his left arm and the tranquilizer rifle in his right hand. "C'mon. Teddy will be here in a few minutes and we still have to set up." As Jackson offered him the rifle, Patterson released the gun, letting it slide back into the holster and felt the camaraderie between them. What in the world was he thinking? He knew that Jackson was only trying to teach him and he *did* screw up. Jackson was a great man, a great man indeed, and if he didn't like Patterson he wouldn't have said anything at all. Patterson thought ahead to the events that were about to take place and his anger gave way to the excitement that he felt earlier. Feeling like Will Smith from the movie *Men in Black,* Patterson got out of his car, grabbed the laser-rifle from the master, Tommy Lee Jones, and then with a kick-ass attitude, cracked his neck.

Mercedes sat in her car out on the road beneath a large oak tree and watched as two silhouettes left the Camry, strolled through the dark parking lot and then merged with the shadows on the side of the church. She waited for a moment, with gun in hand and once she was sure they had gone inside, she got out of the car and ran over to the Camry. After peeking through the windows and trying the doors, she continued her run into the shadows, where a side door waited.

Once inside she found herself in the middle of a dimly lighted corridor. To her right the narrow hall connected with several closed doors and then turned out of view. To the left, a stairway ran up to a landing where it too, turned and continued on out of sight. She softly latched the door behind her and listened carefully, trying to determine which way they went, but heard nothing. After a second more of contemplation, she turned and silently moved up the stairwell.

At the top, she found herself in a huge balcony area that overlooked the rest of the cathedral. A few hundred bucketed-seats covered the newly laid red carpet. Staying low, she made her way down the incline, past a dozen or more rows of seats and peeked over the four-foot high wall at the end. Although old, the well-kept church was still beautiful and majestic looking. Dozens of huge chandeliers hung overhead, filling the large house of worship with a soft mellow light and the beautiful stained glass windows, picturing saints, angels and other heavenly objects ran nearly from floor to ceiling.

The two men were down on the stage, standing next to the podium. The baldheaded man was putting on a weird looking robe and talking to the phony Agent Young, who was holding a huge rifle that looked as if it had come straight out of some science fiction movie. As the baldheaded man was placing a longhaired white wig on his head, the laser-toting lurch nodded, then walked through the cathedral and disappeared into an open hallway.

Outside, a Lexus casually drove around the corner and pulled into the parking lot, followed a few seconds later, by a unobserved Mustang which went on past the entrance and parked on the other side of the street almost directly across from a gray Toyota Corolla. Teddy smiled as he got out of the car. He knew that God had something important for him to do and he couldn't wait to find out what it was. The angel had just contacted him through his cell-phone and told him to come to this out of the way church immediately, as God had something important to tell him. Teddy thought it odd that every time the angel wanted to talk with him, he would either call his house or cell-phone, but he figured that God had a good reason for making the angel do it that way. Perhaps it was because Teddy was so holy and so righteous that he was constantly surrounded by demons that were trying to destroy him. So instead of having the angel risk getting into a holy battle, God just had him use the phone. It made sense to Teddy.

Through the windshield, Nick watched the oddity as the psychopath got out of his car and then danced his way, twirling every so many steps, to the front doors. Nick got out of his car, looked at the big church, which was quite a ways off from the main road and wondered what Teddy was doing here. Was there another basement here, with a head in it, like the one those kids found in the old white house? Pondering things over, he tucked his gun into the front waistband of his jeans and walked calmly across the street, past the Corolla, to the Lexus. After glancing through the tinted windows at the perfectly clean seats and empty floorboards, he pulled out his pocketknife and proceeded to drain all of the air out of the front passenger's side tier.

"You're not getting away this time," he whispered as the last of the air hissed away and the tire went flat. Then he stood up, refolded and pocketed his knife as he walked through the night air, to the front doors of the church.

As Teddy walked through the foyer and into the sanctuary, a spirit of peace washed over him and purged his soul. He saw the angel up in front and smiled to himself as he humbly moved past all of the empty seats and approached the altar. Teddy felt honored to be chosen for whatever task God had for him and he knew that whatever the task was, it was extremely important. He stepped up to the base of the platform and knelt down before the angel.

Crouching low, behind the side of an archway, Nick watched from the back, as the psychopath moved through the cathedral and then knelt down in front of a weird looking man with white hair, wearing a long white robe. The man in the robe was saying something, but Nick was too far away to be able to hear what it was. Wanting to find a closer place to spy from, he backed out of the archway and quickly moved down a hall, which ran parallel to the sanctuary, searching for a side door that might allow him to sneak back in, a little closer to the platform. At the end of the hall, a door waited, which led into an office and looked like it might belong to a bishop or someone important. Just on the other side of the small office, stood another door, half opened and Nick could hear voices coming through it.

Moving quietly, he made his way past the door and found himself in an area behind the platform. Peeking through a crack in the wall, Nick was able to hear the voice of the man in the robe. A lump developed in his throat and began to grow as he recognized it. It was the same as the one on the phone earlier, the same as the one that came out of the man in Atlanta—the baldheaded man.

The area that Nick found himself in had ceiling-less walls that stood just tall enough to conceal whoever stood behind them. Nick stood at the corner, where two of them met and found himself looking through the crack, in much the same way he had done in that warehouse, in Atlanta. Adding to the overgrown lump in his throat, a knot tied itself up in his stomach as he felt history begin to repeat itself. Looking through the crack, Nick could also see all of the empty seats in the church, including the ones in the front few rows of the balcony, where he noticed a dark haired woman peeking over the edge.

Mercedes watched as a well-dressed man calmly walked up to the platform and then knelt down in front of the costumed man on stage.

"What the Hell is going on?" She whispered as she struggled to hear what was being said.

Meanwhile, Patterson had finished climbing the stairs, walked into the balcony and was surprised to find another person already there, crouching down, next to the railing, spying on Jackson and Teddy. Not wanting to fuck anything else up and further disappoint Jackson, Patterson stood there, in the doorway and tried to figure out what the best move would be.

"…and the Lord is very pleased with all the work you have done." The white wigged, baldheaded man spoke in a deep, powerful voice as Nick waited and listened.

"God has sent me to tell you something very important, something about your future. He wants to let you know that he loves you. You are very dear to him." Nick listened as the man repeated the same thing over and over again, in different ways. It was as if he was stalling, but why was he stalling and what was it that he was planning to do?

Teddy knelt, with his face down, staring at the carpet, patiently waiting as the angel continued.

Nick looked back up at the balcony. Who's that girl and what's she doing up there? If Nick could see her from the crack in this wall, then he was sure that the phony ambassador of God could as well. Was she working with him, because, if she was spying, she sure wasn't doing a very good job.

Jackson stalled, waiting for Patterson to appear in the balcony, but the clocked ticked and Patterson didn't show. Jackson didn't want to tell Teddy that it was time for him to leave this world, without drugging him first, but he wasn't sure how much longer he could hold out. As he was telling Teddy all the things he knew Teddy wanted to hear, he noticed a brunette peeking over the balcony railing. Jackson had picked this church out very carefully and even came by earlier today to scope things out. He was sure that the place would be empty tonight. Who was that woman? Not the cleaning lady, she wasn't scheduled until tomorrow and everyone else was away.

Maybe she had bumped into Patterson and somehow put him out of commission. Not wanting to wait any longer and feeling like he already had enough mental control over Teddy, even without the aid of drugs, Jackson finally told Teddy the reason that God had summoned him here.

"Theodore Edward Connolly, the Lord has decided to give you your reward and call you home."

Teddy's eyes shifted in confusion. This wasn't right. Just this morning, when Teddy thought that God wanted him to come home, God had kept the chamber empty and didn't allow Teddy to cash in his ticket. Teddy would never argue with God nor question him, but even angels were fallible. Teddy listened and thought, not yet sure what it meant.

"The Lord has sent me to tell you that it is time to cash in your *ticket to paradise* and come home."

Cash in his ticket to paradise? What was going on here? Didn't the angel know that the demon had stolen it? Had God not told him? Teddy knelt, confused as the angel went on. "Listen carefully to me Theodore, the devil is strong and God has…"

Teddy was having a hard time focusing on the words the angel was saying because of all of the questions that were spinning through his head.

Behind the stage, as Nick was about to jump out and throw a great big monkey wrench into whatever it was that was going on, he spotted a man sneaking up behind the woman on the balcony. In the position she was in, it wouldn't be too difficult to latch onto her and just toss her over the edge, onto the floor far below. Impulsively, not knowing yet whether she was friend or foe, Nick shouted, "Behind you!" as he stepped out onto the platform, about ten feet to the right of the bogus angel. The next few events were governed by chaos and happened so fast that nobody had enough time to think, only react.

In slow motion, while Mercedes was turning to face the man behind her and Jackson was racing to make sense of what was happening, Teddy lifted his head and looked at Nick. The demon! In an instant, God gave him understanding and everything became clear. The angel of the Lord, Teddy's angel had been led astray by the Devil and now they were working together. This was just another fallen angel, trying to deceive Teddy, before he finished his work. With a fight ensuing on the balcony above and Jackson turning to face Nick, Teddy reached into his coat pocket and withdrew a stainless steel steak knife.

Just as Jackson pulled out his handgun, intending to put a bullet in the middle of Nick's face and just as Nick was lifting his gun, aiming for the man on the balcony, Teddy, in one smooth motion, sprang to his feet and lunged at the angel. A loud boom echoed through the cathedral and then another. Someone screamed in pain as more ear-piercing gunshots rang out.

Then, still firing warning shots at the man on the balcony, who was definitely winning the fight against the woman, Nick found himself squeezing repeatedly on the trigger of a gun that yielded no more bullets. Nick looked at the gun for an instant and then tossed it aside like a useless hunk of metal. He shifted his attention toward the wrestling match taking place between Theodore and the baldheaded man. Anxiety developed inside him and began to grow as he contemplated whether he should get involved in the wrestling match and demand answers from the baldheaded man or head for the balcony to save the damsel in distress. He looked up at the fight on the balcony and then back at the two men, rolling around on the carpet and decided that whoever she was, she would have to fend for herself. This was an opportunity that he just couldn't pass up. In the eight long years that he had been searching for answers, this had been the closest he had come to actually finding any. However, as he took a step toward the two wrestlers, only moments away from obtaining the answers that would squelch the demons in his nightmares, a bone-chilling scream pierced the air, causing him to look up once more at the fight above.

Only a second ago, the lady looked as if she just might get away. Now however, she was fighting just to keep from being lifted over the waist-high railing. Her attacker held her by one leg and one arm as she struggled and bucked violently. Nick looked back at the wrestlers for just an instant. *Damn*, he thought, as he left the platform and raced through the church in a mad dash for the stairwell. Moments later, his boot left the last step and he flew down the aisle toward the man, who had already heaved the woman up on top of the railing and was now struggling to push her off. From behind, Nick used his left hand to grab the man's right shoulder and spin him around. Even before the man had finished his spin, Nick's right hook was connecting with his face, knocking him back against the railing, right next to the woman, who Nick recognized instantly.

Mercedes was now all of the way over the rail, hanging on with one hand and slipping fast. Momentarily forgetting about everything else and thinking only of Mercedes' safety, Nick reached out his hand and, just as her grip failed her, Nick latched onto her wrist. His hand and her wrist were already sweaty and as she dangled helplessly, a good twenty feet above the chair-covered floor, she continued to slip. The sweat was more like oil than water and Mercedes felt her stomach drop as her life lay in the hands of a stranger. The floor looked even further than it did just a few moments earlier when she was solidly on the carpeting above.

As Nick leaned over the edge, reaching down with his free hand, Patterson came up from behind him and rammed a huge fist into his ribs. Because he was bending over and his lean side was stretched out, the pain was more than excruciating. Still holding on tight to a slipping hand and reeling from the pain of a bruised rib, Nick looked behind him and began to kick like a horse. The kicking took Patterson by surprise and Nick managed to land one right between the big man's legs.

Patterson momentarily broke off his attack and hobbled backward, clutching his lower abdomen, but before Nick could get a better hold and pull Mercedes up, Patterson withdrew his gun. He hadn't used it earlier with Mercedes, because she knew where Number Nine was hiding. He thought she would have preferred to tell him where Number Nine was rather than being thrown over the balcony.

Nick reached down with his left hand and latched onto her sweater, right above her right shoulder. As Nick dangled an anxious Mercedes around by her slowly peeling sweater, trying to latch back on to her hand, another gunshot echoed through the edifice. Mercedes' sweater continued to slip off her torso as Nick turned his head toward the sound.

Up until now Nick hadn't given the creep a second look; he hadn't even noticed what color the man's suit was. The only thing he had on his mind was keeping Mercedes from falling. However, as he stared down the barrel of the man's gun, he noticed just how ugly he was, and had to do a double take to convince himself that the man wasn't wearing a mask.

Obviously still in pain from the kick to his groin, Lurch smiled wide, knowing that he definitely had the upper hand now.

The scar-faced monster cautiously hobbled closer and spoke in a low slow rasp. "Where is Number Nine?"

With Mercedes still slipping out of her sweater below, Nick waited, thinking there was going to be more to the question, but there wasn't. Lurch tilted the barrel up, fired his gun again, missing Nick's head by just inches and yelled, "Where the fuck is Number Nine!"

Nick's eyes narrowed in confusion as he tried to figure out what this lunatic was asking him. *Number Nine*, what did he mean, *where's Number Nine?* Then, even though he knew he shouldn't, he just couldn't resist and replied in a helpful, understanding tone. "I don't know. Have you tried looking between eight and ten?"

Realizing this smartass had no idea what he was talking about, Patterson tried a different approach. "Tell that little bitch you're holding onto that if she doesn't tell me where Number Nine is right now, I'll shoot you in the fucking face and blow your fucking brains out."

Mercedes, now fully out of her sweater and using it like a rope, heard what the fake Agent Young said. Sacrificing her own life was one thing, but she had no right to sacrifice a stranger's, especially one who was working so hard to save hers. "Okay!" she yelled frantically, "but I'll have to take you there myself!"

"No deal!"

Another loud explosion went off above her head and she half expected the Good Samaritan to release her sweater, fall over the railing and land on top of her mangled body, at the bottom.

Above, Lurch had fired another warning shot and Nick decided that it would do no good to look at his ugly face any longer, so he turned his attention back to the damsel. Acting as if he was trying to pull her up, Nick took his free hand, reached into his coat pocket and withdrew his pocketknife.

After she realized that she wasn't crumpled up, dead on the floor, Mercedes started to climb up the rope-like sweater and repeated her offer. "I know where he is and I *promise* I'll take you to him if you let me up."

Still pointing his gun at the back of the smartass hero, Patterson leaned against the side of one of the chairs and considered her proposal. The company still had no idea where Number Nine was and if he played his cards right, this could be his chance to find out and regain Jackson's approval. Unfortunately, before Patterson had the chance to accept her offer the situation changed. With Mercedes climbing up, reaching Nick's hand and continuing on, Nick turned back around and swiftly threw the knife at the unsuspecting Lurch. It twirled end over end, like the tail blade on a helicopter and then sunk deep into the back of Lurch's gun hand. As Lurch dropped the gun and was screaming in pain, Nick turned back around and helped the sweater-less Mercedes finish her climb, back over the rail.

He awkwardly looked into her soft green eyes as she stood before him, in her nearly see-through brazier. Then once he was certain that she was standing firmly on the carpet, his strong hands released her petite waist and handed over her sweater. After exchanging an awkward smile, he turned to face Lurch who was already coming at him, full throttle. He looked like a crazed linebacker on his way to make the winning tackle. Not being one to stand in a man's way, Nick quickly stepped a side and coaxed the charging bull into the solid wooden railing. Lurch hit the half wall headfirst, and so hard he bounced. Nick used the opportunity to repay the big man for hitting him in the ribs earlier by ramming his boot hard into the man's side, causing him to spit up blood.

Keeping Mercedes safely behind him, Nick backed away, into a better position and waited for Lurch to attack again.

Patterson struggled to his feet and then quickly glanced over the balcony at the platform below. Teddy was gone and Jackson's lifeless body was hanging, head first, over the edge of the platform, soaked in blood. Patterson turned in rage and yelled, "No! This is all your fault, bitch!" And then raced at Nick one more time. Like before, Nick stepped to one side, shielding Mercedes as he went, and let Lurch race on past, however this time Lurch anticipated the move and managed to grab Nick's jacket and yank him to the floor. Nick's head, which was already bruised and sore from this morning's fight with the headhunter, smacked hard into a blunt piece of metal protruding from one of the auditorium seats and knocked Nick unconscious.

Patterson straddled the stranger, who was flat on his back and out cold, then pulled back and proceeded to pound on his defenseless face.

Mercedes, who had just finished putting on her sweater, frantically looked around, spotted and ran over to her gun. It had fallen beneath one of the seats when the CIA imposter had kicked it out of her hand earlier. With the phony Agent Young using his fists, trying to put holes through the Good Samaritan's cranium, Mercedes raised the gun above her head and fired.

Patterson stopped swinging, looked up at the wall, then slowly turned his head, halfway around and glared at the bitch behind him.

"Now, Ms. Atwater, be careful with that. You don't want anyone to get hurt, do you?"

Mercedes' eyes were solid and her face held just a touch of anger as she steadily stretched the gun out with both hands, toward the imposter. After considering his question and imagining a slug exploding in the middle of his face, she sternly said, "Get off him! Now!" and fired a warning shot just to the left of the man's head.

Damn bitch! Patterson slowly rose to his feet and turned to face her, then cracked his neck. The railing wasn't too far behind the bitch and Patterson was fairly sure he could tackle her and pull her over it with him before she got off enough bullets to stop him. He looked at the rail, smiled, and then carried the demented smile back to her. Although he liked the idea of the bitch dead, he didn't favor dying with her in order to make it happen. The entrance to the balcony wasn't far behind him, and with that evil-eyed smile, he slowly backed up.

Mercedes fired another warning shot and for an instant the lunatic stopped, but then Nick moaned and Mercedes glanced down, giving the creep a chance to bolt through the doorway and disappear down the stairs. Mercedes wasn't sure who this good-natured stranger was, but didn't believe he was her enemy.

Keeping the gun ready, in case the lunatic came back upstairs, she slowly moved over to the man on the floor and knelt down beside his beaten up face.

Maybe it was the eloquent church surroundings, or perhaps it was the fact that he had received two head traumas in one day, but whatever the reason, Nick opened his eyes, looked up into the face of an angel and weakly asked, "Am I dead?"

Mercedes smiled and almost chuckled at the handsome, bloodied hero and softly replied, "No."

Nick's eyes widened as the angel gradually morphed into the beautiful woman from the Internet photo. "Mercedes." He said while straining to sit up. For a moment he just sat there looking around, dazed and then remembered were he was and what was happening. With another splitting headache he sprang to his feet looking for Lurch.

"It's okay, he's gone." Mercedes stepped in front of him, reached up, gently put her hand on an area of his chin that didn't look as sore as the rest of his face and tilted his battered head down to get his attention. "We need to get you to a hospital."

Both of Nick's cheekbones were bright red and puffy, his nose was crooked and the area around his left eye had swelled up like a small water balloon. A flood of blood was pouring down from an unseen cut, somewhere on the top of his head. He made Rocky look good. "No, I'm fine." He backed away, staggered over to the balcony and looked at the stage. "Damn!" he said as he hurriedly shuffled past her toward the stairs. Skipping two and three steps at a time, Nick unsteadily flew down the stairs and entered the sanctuary with Mercedes close behind. He raced up to the stage and knelt down beside the lifeless, wide-eyed baldheaded man who was lying in a pool of blood. He had been stabbed repeatedly in the face, neck and chest. The handle of a common kitchen knife still stuck out from one of the wounds.

Nick stared at the body, blank-faced for a moment as Mercedes walked up behind and asked, "What's going on?"

Without hearing the question, Nick quickly lifted his head and anxiously whispered, "Teddy."

"Excuse me?"

He hastily stood up and ran past Mercedes on his way to the Lexus. As he exited the front doors of the building he could hear her yelling something behind him, but because he was only thinking about catching Teddy before the psycho could get away, he couldn't tell what she was saying. Nick's heart sank as he ran into the parking lot and then over to the empty blacktop where the Lexus had been parked.

"Shit!" He said as he stomped a boot hard into the pavement and spun around angrily. The little dance step shot a load of pain into his already throbbing head, causing him to wince and double over.

Mercedes, still on the font walk of the church by the huge double doors, stood like a statue and stared in Nick's direction.

Nick slowly walked over to her and found that she was staring, not at him, but at a Toyota Camry parked just on the other side of where the Lexus had been. "He's still here," she whispered, without lifting her eyes.

"Who's still here?" Nick asked, but this time it was she who didn't hear him. He carefully put his hands on her shoulders and repeated the question.

Her eyes slowly shifted away from the car and met his. "The phony CIA agent."

"Who?" Even with his busted up face, she could still see the confusion in his eyes.

"Agent Young, the guy who almost threw me off of the balcony in there." Mercedes pointed.

Nick's heart lit back up as he turned and looked at the doors of the church for a second then back at the Camry. "That's his car?"

Not sure just who this guy was and needing answers of her own, Mercedes asked. "Who are you?"

Not wanting to waste time on small talk, Nick anxiously repeated the question. "Is that the lunatic's car?"

Mercedes felt out of the loop and was beginning to get angry. "Look, I know you saved my life in there, so I guess you can't be all that bad, but would it be so hard for you to just tell me who you are and what the Hell is going on?"

Nick looked at Mercedes, who looked lost and needed to be told something, but not knowing exactly what to say, he replied, "Nicholas Chadwick," tried to smile, but it hurt too much and then continued, "As far as what's going on, I was hoping you could tell me."

"What?"

"Look, how 'bout we discuss this later, okay?" Nick said anxiously.

Mercedes looked around into the night and then replied, "Fine."

With that Nick tried smiling for a second time, but once again his swollen face wouldn't permit it, so he turned and cautiously walked back into the foyer, with Mercedes reluctantly following. The baldheaded man might be dead, but the lunatic wasn't, and he was still here, somewhere. Nick wasn't sure whose side the lunatic was on, but figured that he tied into things somehow. Nick had dozens of questions for Mercedes too, but reasoned that she'd be around later and figured that he should find the lunatic before he got away.

As Nick and Mercedes walked back into the sanctuary, they both looked up at the empty platform and froze. Then Nick ran up to the stage, stared at the spot where the body had just been and did a slow 360. After seeing nothing out of the ordinary, he looked back at the carpet. There weren't any dragging or crawling marks—not that Nick thought the guy had somehow came back to life and crawled away. The man had been dead, right? No one could have lost that much blood and still been alive, could they? Nick thought back and pictured the man's blank stare. It looked pretty real to him. Once again, looking around the room, Nick wished he would have reached over and felt the man's neck for a pulse, just to have been sure.

"Where'd he go?" Mercedes stood behind Nick, staring at the blood-soaked spot where the body had been.

"I don't know," Nick replied as he left the stage and wandered over to an archway in the side of the sanctuary. Through his non-swollen eye, he looked at it carefully. A tiny smudge of blood near the foot of the archway, tattled that the man, or at least his body, had gone this way. Quietly, Nick continued to follow the trail, with Mercedes right behind, until he came to a small corridor, which Mercedes recognized.

A whisper broke the silence. "That door," she pointed, "leads to the parking lot. I followed the men through it earlier when I arrived."

Still not sure how Mercedes fit into everything, Nick looked at her oddly and wondered what she was doing following them in the first place, then looked back at the door. He opened it and just like she said, it led to the parking lot, however to Nick's dismay, the Camry was gone. "Damn it! Damn it!" Nick began to kick at the small shrubbery near the building.

Mercedes stood and watched for a minute, until his tantrum was over and then asked, "Okay, *now* tell me, what is going on here."

Nick looked up with his swollen face, shook his head and said, "I have no idea."

Mercedes rolled her eyes and raised her voice. "Bullshit! If you have no idea then what in the world are you doing here and why are we sneaking around looking for that lunatic?"

Her anger only made her look more attractive and realizing that whoever they were, they were probably gone, Nick said, "Why don't we talk about it over some food? I'm starved."

Mercedes looked at him strangely and said, "You're in no condition to eat."

"I'll be all right, just wait until the swelling goes down."

"We really should get you to a hospital."

"No. Honestly, I'm fine. I just need something to eat and a little rest." Realizing he wasn't going to give in, she considered food. So far, there had been very little to go on and she decided that it wouldn't be smart to pass up an opportunity to find out what this guy could tell her, but at the same time, she didn't want to leave Alex in the motel alone for too long—especially after what had happened last time. She paused and looked at the man, who just risked his life to save hers and then said, "Okay, but I have to check on a friend first. Do you want to meet me somewhere?"

"A friend?" Nick asked.

"Yeah. Well actually a client, a friend, a client."

Nick looked oddly at her and then asked, "All right. How 'bout I just follow you?"

Follow her? She thought. Should she trust him? He did save her life and if this was some elaborate trap to find out where Alex was, well then...no, she didn't believe that. "Okay." She looked around. "Where are you parked?"

Nick pointed in the direction of her Corolla. "Out on the street."

"Me too." She frowned as she walked past him on the way to her car. Nick turned around, looked at the side door one more time, wondered if anyone was still in there and then followed after Mercedes.

On occasion, when it was necessary, like during his drive to Beverly Hills this morning, Nick would break the speed limit, but for the most part he drove along at a very acceptable pace. Following behind Mercedes, however, seemed to be more like a chase than a drive across town. She flew through lingering yellow lights, forcing Nick to run the red ones. She made quick, unexpected turns, nearly running over pedestrians in the process. Nick couldn't imagine why she was in such a hurry. Perhaps, she had received an urgent cell-phone call from someone in trouble. Whatever the reason, Nick was convinced that she drove like a maniac.

Meanwhile, in the Corolla, not wanting to get separated, Mercedes made sure to drive extra slowly. This Nicholas guy had just been beaten to a bloody pulp and couldn't even see out of his right eye. Even though she drove slowly, several times she felt that she nearly lost him, and almost turned around to go back, but just before she did, his headlights would pop around the last corner and she'd keep going.

As she turned into the parking lot of the motel, she noticed that the door to her room was slightly open. *That's odd*, she thought as she parked. Less than a second later, Nick's Mustang pulled up beside her car. Like shadows in the night, they both got out of separate cars and stood together, facing the motel.

"What is it?"

"The door to my room is open." Her voice was monotone and Nick could hear a hint of fear in it.

"Are you staying here alone?"

"Not exactly." Mercedes kept her eyes fixed on the unit across the parking lot.

"Not exactly?"

A cold chill ran through her spine as a shadow momentarily broke the flow of light pouring through the open door. She took a couple of steps forward and then froze solid as she heard a crash escape the room.

Beside her, Nick paused. "Who's in there?"

Seemingly unable to hear anything except the noises coming from the room, Mercedes stayed silent and then quickly jumped, as not one, but two silhouettes slid across the curtain. A moment later, she withdrew her gun and ran toward the unit, with Nick right behind. She was quick for her size, but Nick got to the door before she did. He leaned his back, flat up against the stucco wall, with the partially opened door to his left and listened carefully, but didn't hear anything. Mercedes stood to the right of Nick, holding her gun up, ready to fire. Nick looked at the gun and thought. If he was going to go in first then he should have it, but as he glanced up, he could see that there was no way she was going to let go of it. Well then, maybe she should go in first. No, something inside him just couldn't see that happening. *Damn*, Nick thought, this can't be good.

For a second it was as if they knew what each other was thinking. Nick looked at Mercedes and with his beaten up face, gave her a look that said *get ready to cover me, I'm going in*. Mercedes met his eyes with a confident affirmation and tightened her grip. Nick held up three fingers and then slowly counted under his breath as he folded his ring finger, and then his index. He turned back, looked at the opening, folded down his last finger and quickly moved through the door.

A man in a black suit. A broken lamp. Another man holding a gun. Someone on the bed. A blunt object coming fast. Everything went black.

CHAPTER TWENTY-ONE

"Where am I?" Nick blinked his eyes open and looked around at a blurry room.

"It's okay." A soft familiar voice floated into his ears.

It felt as if he'd been asleep for days. He tried to sit up, but then felt pressure on his chest as Mercedes said, "Relax," and then asked, "Are you thirsty?"

Until she said something, he hadn't noticed just how thirsty he was. His lips were parched and his throat felt as if he had been breathing desert air. She grabbed a plastic cup of water next to the bed and held it up to his lips. With her other hand helping to steady the back of his head, Nick drank half the cup, paused for just a second and then finished it. She placed it back onto the stand beside him and said, "I was beginning to wonder if you were ever going to wake up."

"Where am I?" he asked again.

"You're in my motel room."

"What happened?" Nick was beginning to feel the telltale signs of another bad headache coming on.

"They knocked you out cold and managed to take my gun before I could do any real damage. The next thing I knew, I was listening to the birds as I woke up. You were still out."

"How long?"

"Well, it's 1:30 now." Mercedes thought. "You've been out since last night."

"Damn!" Nick completed his task of sitting up this time before Mercedes could interfere. "I gotta get to the Heavenly Heart Hotel."

"Where?"

"The Heavenly Heart Hotel."

"Why?"

"That's where I saw him last."

"Who?"

"Theodore Connolly." Nick spoke as he quickly threw the covers off him and got out of bed, wearing only his boxer shorts. "LA's Headhunter." Moving around the room, gathering his things, he became acutely aware of the lack of clothing on his body and then realized that she must have undressed him while he was a sleep. The thought of her peeling his clothes off him, while he was unconscious, sent a queasy feeling into the pit of his stomach.

"LA's headhunter?"

"Yeah." Nick zipped up the front of his jeans and then pulled his shirt over the top of his head.

"I still have no idea what's going on," Mercedes said with aggravation creeping into her words.

"Well that makes two of us."

"How does the headhunter fit into all this?" She waited for an answer as she handed him his boots and then gathered up her keys.

"I have no idea. Where's my Gummy Bears?"

"Your what?" Mercedes was becoming more frustrated by the moment. This Nicholas guy obviously knew more than what he was saying, and for some reason he wasn't sharing it with her.

"My Gummy Bears. They're little chewy candies in an assortment of colors. I just bought a new pack the other night." Nick's words trailed off as he spotted and scooped the bag up off the floor. "I'm guessing, they took your gun, right?" he asked on his way to the door.

"Right," she answered as she followed him out into the parking lot.

Halfway across the parking lot, with Mercedes right behind him, Nick stopped and turned around. "Where're you going?"

Mercedes hadn't expected him to stop, much less spin around, and it caught her off guard. She bounced off him, stepped back, embarrassed and then firmly said, "I'm going to the Heavenly Heart Hotel, with you."

Nick wasn't sure why, maybe it was because he had saved her life and he didn't want it to have been for nothing or maybe it was because he was starting to develop some unwanted feelings for her, but whatever it was, he didn't want her to get hurt. He knew he had no right telling her what to do, but before he could stop himself, it just came out. "No you're not."

Mercedes looked at this fool who thought he could tell her what to do and then replied, "Oh, yes I am."

"Not with me, you're not."

"Fine." With that she raised her eyebrows and coldly walked over to her Corolla.

Nick stood alone with his back to Mercedes and his hands on his hips, in the middle of the parking lot, feeling a little embarrassed. After a moment he turned around and headed over to the Corolla with an apology on his lips. He was going to tell her that he was sorry and it would be safer if she rode with him, but before he had the chance, she pulled on past him and exited the parking lot, in the wrong direction.

Nick's face, although not a hundred percent, had healed considerably. He watched the back of the Corolla pull out and then whispered to himself, "She doesn't even know where she's going."

He smiled and just stood there for a moment wondering whether she was going to turn around and come back or not. After a couple of minutes, Nick got in his Mustang and headed for the hotel. He figured, with all that determination, she'd probably find it and with the way she drove she might even get there before he did.

On the way to the hotel he reached into the glove box and checked his phone messages. He had received nine of them and all but one had been from Lisa. The other one was from Dottie. She was just a little panicked when Nick hadn't returned any of Lisa's calls.

"Hello? Dottie?"

"Nick! We've been so worried. Are you okay?"

Nick's cell-phone beeped, indicating that the battery was low.

"Yeah I'm fine. Is Lisa there?"

"Hold on."

Nick thought about the car charger he kept in his computer bag, which was in the trunk. Before the battery died, a young sweet voice got on the phone. "Daddy?"

"Hello, Peaches." Nick smiled. "How have you been?"

"Okay, what about you? I must have called a thousand times!"

"I know sweetie. I wasn't able to get to the phone, but I'm okay."

"Daddy," she hesitated, "you weren't in jail again were you?"

Nick thought back to all the times that Lisa had tried to get a hold of him and he had been put in jail for interfering with police business, and then smiled. "No sweetie, I promise, but listen, my battery is about to go dead and I don't have my charger with me, so I'll have to call you back, later tonight, okay?"

"Well, I guess. When are you coming home?"

"Soon Sweetie. And I've decided something."

Lisa listened silently to hear what he had to say.

After a moment of silence, he said, "This is it, this is my last trip anywhere, looking for answers."

A lump developed in Lisa's throat. "You mean, you found something?"

"Well, maybe, but that's not why I've-" Before he could finish his statement, the phone died and he didn't even get the chance to say the most important thing of all, I love you.

He turned into the drive of the Heavenly Heart Hotel and pulled up behind a gray Toyota Corolla.

Through the glass walls, Nick could see Mercedes standing in the lobby, talking with an oriental gentleman and even from inside his car he could tell that she was becoming more than a little aggravated.

The little brass bell above the door chimed as Nick walked into the room. Mercedes continued with the man, pretending to be unaware.

"The-o-dore," She drug out the name and spoke louder, as if she were talking to a deaf man.

The china man continued to smile and said, "No thank you." She turned away, acknowledged Nick, and shook her head in frustration. Nick simply stepped past her to the counter and laid down a copy of the LA times. After letting the oriental man have a good look at the front page, Nick flipped to the story, which featured a picture of the back of the Lexus. Nick removed his shades and pointed at the car, then slid his finger down to the license plate. After leaving his hand there for just a moment more, he grabbed the pen off the counter and wrote out 3BRI155. The never-ending smile on the china man died, and his slotted eyes became as wide as silver dollars, as he appeared to understand what Nick was asking.

A nervous hand quickly reached underneath the counter and pulled out a record book containing the names and license plate numbers of recent guests. After opening it and finding the correct page, he ran a skinny finger down the column and stopped at the handwritten name of Theodore E. Connolly. The accompanying license plate number read *3BRI155*.

The china man's fear-filled face looked at Nick and he nodded his head quickly as he asked, "He's headhunner, huh?"

Nick just smiled and nodded back, then looked back down and read. According to the ledger, Theodore had checked into room 311 yesterday and checked out this morning. Nick said, "Thank you," and turned around. Mercedes was behind him, trying to read the ledger when he softly bumped into her. "Sorry," he said as he slid his shades back over his eyes and moved aside. Mercedes stepped up, read the ledger, smiled respectfully at the petrified china man and then ran to catch up with Nick.

Nick waited out in front of the office as Mercedes flew out the door and hastily approached him. She had a question on her lips as she walked up, but right before she asked it, Nick spoke. "Weren't we supposed to get something to eat?"

Mercedes stopped, and with her mouth still opened and an authoritative finger raised, just looked at him for a second, but said nothing, then slowly closed her mouth as he continued, "Where's a good restaurant, where we can sit and talk?"

Mercedes was still brewing with frustration and anger, but didn't want to say something that would jeopardize a chance to sit down and get some answers, so she only said two words, "Follow me." With that she spun around and headed for her car. What is it about her, Nick wondered as he watched her get into the Corolla. When he heard the engine crank over, he remembered just how crazy she drove and made a mad dash for his car. By the time he got in and turned the key, the Corolla had already pulled forward, went around the little island and was exiting the parking lot.

Fifteen minutes and several frightened pedestrians later both cars pulled into Applebee's. Inside, Nick ordered the biggest burger on the menu, extra fries and a large chocolate shake, while Mercedes had the half order of shrimp Caesar salad and a glass of iced tea. The waitress took their order, smiled and turned away.

"So, are you going to tell me what's going on?" Mercedes asked with an eyebrow raised and more than a hint of frustration in her voice.

Knowing that she didn't want to hear *I don't know* again and hoping that she knew some piece of the puzzle that would help him, Nick decided to start at the beginning. He began by telling her about what happened to Allie eight years ago. The waitress delivered their food as Mercedes listened to some of the investigations he had been on, including the one seven years ago in Atlanta. He told her about meeting the headhunter in the basement of the old white house and how he followed and lost him in that small residential neighborhood. He conveniently avoided telling her that he had almost ran over a small boy and nearly tore up someone's yard. The waitress refilled her tea and he ordered another shake as he told her how he saw the Lexus pull out of the Heavenly Heart Hotel.

"I followed it to the church, snuck in, and the rest you know."

Mercedes carefully pulled the fork out of her mouth, pondered and slowly chewed her food as she soaked it all in.

"It's your turn now. How do you fit into all this?" Nick took another huge bite of his burger and waited for her to answer.

Mercedes continued to chew slowly and thought about the question. His story hadn't been anything like she hoped it would be. What did all of that have to do with Alex and the men chasing him? Nick hadn't mentioned anything about mind reading or someone experiencing another person's memories. She swallowed her food, sipped her tea and thought, as Nick patiently waited, munching on his burger and glancing through the dessert menu.

Finally, she asked, "Have you ever heard of a chemical called HG7?"

Nick brought his glass up to his mouth and shook his head as he sucked chocolate shake though on oversized straw. Mercedes lowered her fork, wondering how much she should tell him. She thought back and remembered how unbelievable it sounded when Alex barged into her office and told her that he could read minds. She never would have believed it, if it hadn't been for him knowing about that run in her stockings. She remembered how hard it was for him to convince her, and *he* could actually do it. Damn, poor Alex. She had been way too rude with him. Now she was in his shoes, but with one small exception, she couldn't read minds. She had no way of proving what she knew.

She swallowed hard and then asked, "Do you believe in mind reading?"

Holding the french fry in front of his mouth, Nick paused and wondered where the question came from. "What do you mean?"

"You know," Mercedes was beginning to feel uncomfortable, "Mind reading. Do you believe that a person could read another person's thoughts?"

Nick lowered the french fry to his plate without eating it and thought about the question. "I'm not sure; I don't think I do. I've never really given it much thought, why?"

Mercedes bit her bottom lip, looked out the window and contemplated before continuing. She was about to look like a total idiot and that was something she really didn't like to do. She looked back at Nick and said, "I didn't believe in it either." She paused for a half a second and then went on, "but then I met Alex."

"Alex?" Nicked stopped eating entirely and just listened to her.

Mercedes took a quick deep breath, exhaled and focused her attention out the window as she spoke. "A few days ago a man ran into my office and claimed that he could hear the thoughts of those around him. He said that he had lost his memory and that there were these people chasing him." She looked back at Nick, who was now giving her his full attention. "I didn't believe him at first. I thought that it was some kind of joke or something, but it wasn't."

Nick sat silently and tried to make sense of what she was saying. Maybe they, whoever they were, had somehow gotten to her and for whatever reason, screwed with her brain, somehow and messed with her thoughts like they did Leonard's and Theodore's and God knows who else. Nick thought about the drugs he'd seen in the briefcase on the floor, next to Leonard's feet as she spoke.

"He knew things that he would have had no way of knowing."

"Like what?"

"Well for starters, I was sitting behind a desk when he ran in the door. He couldn't see anything below my waist. The stockings I was wearing that day had developed a run." She looked intently at Nick. "I didn't even know it was there until *just before* he mentioned it. It was as if he heard me thinking of it and then said something."

Nick had never been one to believe in the supernatural, but at the same time he would be the first to admit that he didn't know everything. She sure seemed to believe in what she was saying. Nick narrowed his eyes and offered, "Maybe he just got lucky."

Mercedes turned her head and looked sideways at him. "He got lucky, at the exact time that I noticed it?"

"Maybe." Nick shrugged his shoulders.

Mercedes scrunched her eyelids together and shook her head in amazement. "How can you say that?"

Nick looked back innocently, shook his head and shrugged his shoulders again, then spoke before he thought. "I don't know. I don't think that a run in my stockings would be enough to convince me that somebody could read minds."

"A run in *your* stockings?" The image of this he-man sporting tights brought a chuckle to her lips as she looked queerly at him, then calmed down and remembered how hard it was to believe it herself. Wiping her mouth to stifle her laughter, she nodded in agreement. "Well, right after that, I cleared my head, thought of something else, and had him guess what it was."

Having a hard time believing or discounting what she was saying and still feeling a little embarrassment over his poor choice of words, Nick picked up his french fry and resumed eating. If for no other reason than the food, this meeting was going to be a success.

She spoke as he ate. "I was thinking of an oil portrait of my father and without even trying, he guessed it."

Not knowing how to react and with a mouthful of food, he looked at her, nodded his head in agreement and then politely reached for the dessert menu again.

Mercedes quit speaking for a moment and just looked at him. He was going through different expressions as he turned the pages.

It was obvious he didn't believe her, and no matter what she said, he wasn't going to either. She couldn't blame him. She wouldn't believe her if she were him.

"Look, I'm not crazy and I'm not lying to you either. Even after he guessed that I was thinking about the oil portrait, I still wasn't totally convinced, so I tried him again."

Nick had decided on the vanilla blondie as he listened. He could tell that she was speaking from the heart and he still didn't know how to take it.

"I thought of my social security number and just like before, he guessed it without skipping a beat."

Nick pushed his empty plate to the edge of the table, leaned back and sat quietly for a few seconds, then asked, "Where is this Alex guy now?"

With shame, she looked away from his eyes, down at the table, and her expression saddened. "I don't know, when I came to this morning, he was gone. I'm guessing they took him."

"They? Who's they?"

"I'm not sure exactly, but I think a company named Biotronics is involved."

"Okay," Nick pondered and shifted his eyes as he thought.

Feeling the fresh ink of the word *moron* drying across her forehead, Mercedes stopped talking completely and for the next few minutes they just sat across from one another in the awkward silence. Nick still didn't know what to make of what she was saying, but he definitely hadn't ruled anything out. She believed it, that was for sure and Nick didn't think that she was nuts, nor did she seem like the type of person who was easily fooled. He tilted his head, raised a boot up onto the seat beside her, folded his arms and breathed in deep. She had the most amazing green eyes and he couldn't remember the last time he had seen hair as radiant.

From the corner of his eye, Nick glimpsed the waitress walking past and said, "Excuse me," to Mercedes and then got the lady's attention. He quickly ordered the vanilla blondie, handed her the plates from the table and then turned his attention back to Mercedes, who was now placing a notebook on the table, in front of her.

"Anyway, mind reading aside..." Suddenly, her demeanor had made a dramatic change, from amazement to *strictly business*. "...Alex wanted me to find out who was chasing him and why. The day before he ran into my office he had discovered a note in his pocket. It said that the people who were chasing him were using him in some kind of *human experiment*, where they were screwing with his mind."

Nick's ears perked up as the pitiful image of Leonard crying in that warehouse in Atlanta, once again popped into his head. He thought about the weird way in which the man had responded to the baldheaded man's voice.

"Can I see the note?"

"I don't have it. I took it to a friend of mine who's a professional handwriting analyst. He's still looking it over."

While Nick was thinking about Leonard and several other cases that he had been involved with where either mind control or brain experimentation might fit the bill, Mercedes set a large syringe filled with bright green liquid on the table.

"This was in his pocket as well. I had someone I know at Chryo-plazz take a look at it for me. She recognized it and said that it was a chemical that the CIA had been working on. She said they were trying to create a drug that would erase a person's memory of the last few days, but were never able to make it work."

Nick picked up the syringe, held it up to the bright light shining through the window and looked closely at it as she spoke. "She said that no matter what they tried, all it ever did was fry the subjects' brains."

While he was twisting the vial, watching the phosphorus green liquid roll around inside, she opened up the folder and handed him an 8X10 snapshot of a man's face. It had been taken from above, at an angle, and Nick could see the traces of a car door around the edges, indicating that the man had been behind the wheel of a car. "I got a visit from these two baboons around 6 AM yesterday."

Nick recognized the man to be the one-eyed corpse from her apartment.

The waitress set a saucer with a steaming hot vanilla brownie, topped with a scoop of vanilla ice cream and covered with caramel syrup, on the table as Mercedes withdrew a second photo. "You probably don't know that guy, but I'm sure you know this one. It's the jerk-off who was trying to throw me off the balcony at the church."

Nick pushed his vanilla blondie aside, then reached up and grabbed the second picture, which was of Lurch.

"I snapped them while they were out on the street, just before they barged into my house and tried to turn me into a human jigsaw puzzle. They said they were CIA, but I didn't believe 'em. That one claimed to be Agent Donaldson, but his driver's license says otherwise." She placed a California driver's license on the table and slid it over to Nick. Nick looked down at the name, Michael Haskell.

"Unfortunately, I wasn't able to get jerk-off's real ID," Mercedes pointed to the photo of Lurch, "but he claimed to be Agent Young."

With a photo of Michael Haskell in one hand and the phony Agent Young in the other, Nick's heart stopped as Mercedes slid a third print across the table, next to the driver's license.

"And, I believe they both work for this man."

CHAPTER TWENTY-TWO

A brand new number two pencil scribbled on a sheet of paper on the clipboard and then the man took two steps on the sanitized tile floor and stopped. After looking up and scribbling a few more notes, he walked across the room, flipped off the lights and went out the door. The dim room was lighted only by many different colored pin sized lights that either shown steadily or blinked on and off from various electronic devices. Two tall clear cylinders stood vertically against the wall. Inside each one, a lifeless, naked body stood, leaning back slightly, while dozens of tiny electrodes recorded brain waves. The invisible gas inside each container ensured that neither subject would awaken, and the padded belts around their waist, arms and legs along with the slight backward incline kept them from crumpling over and falling to the bottom of the cylinder.

The subject inside one container was male and the other was female. A number on the front of the glass at the top of each cylinder identified each one. The number on the female's cylinder was 12 and the one on the male's was 9. Both subjects appeared to be sleeping. However, they did not dream. The indicator needle on the EKG unit barely moved, indicating only the simplest brain activity.

Dr. Boris, an elderly and distant-looking man, stayed awake around the clock monitoring Number Nine. There were other people that could do this job, but because of the recent events with Number Nine and the fact that it had been gone for so long and even thought that it was a *real* human with amnesia, he decided that he'd feel more comfortable monitoring it personally.

When the team finally caught it and brought it back in, Dr. Boris demanded to run the diagnostic tests himself, to find out what went wrong. The unit was nearly beyond repair. Miraculously, its *brain* had retained nearly seventy-two hours of memory in the frontal lobes, which was easily recorded and transferred to hard disk. At first Dr. Boris was afraid that it had somehow grown new dendrites, but fortunately, test revealed that it hadn't.

After running several different tests, the results of which he had not puzzled through yet, he *clear-washed* its *brain* and totally eradicated its memory. His small, 8X8 work area, which featured a state-of-the-art computer on top of a long desk, two filing cabinets and three wall mounted monitors was cluttered with papers. The monitors were linked wirelessly to several cameras located throughout the lab. The image currently being displayed on monitor one was of the dimly lighted room where the two units, nine and twelve where located. Monitor two was a close-up of Number Nine's face and monitor three, which was usually focused on Number Twelve's face, was now displaying an image of Number Nine's body from the neck down to just below the knees.

Dr. Boris was slightly overweight, but not fat and wore the traditional white lab coat. He was clean-shaven and his thinning gray-white hair made his round face look pudgier than it really was. A smile would no doubt make him look jolly, however at present and for the last few days a scowl dominated his countenance. The door was standing open, and Stan, one of the few people Dr. Boris didn't mind working with, rapped on it and stepped across the threshold. He handed the doctor a clipboard and then noticed the heavy dark bags under his eyes.

"You should seriously consider getting some sleep."

"I'm fine, thank you." Dr. Boris took the clipboard and stepped toward Stan, causing him to move back into the hall. Once the doctor was close enough to grab the door, he quickly swung it closed and turned back to his work, at the same moment and unknown to the doctor, Number Nine's eyes twitched, but the EKG needle didn't move.

CHAPTER TWENTY-THREE

With his heart pounding hard and fast, Nick lowered his boot from the bench, beside Mercedes, sat up and placed the two photos he was currently holding onto the table then picked up the third one. It wasn't a photo, like the other two. This one was a black and white computer printout of an eloquent-looking, mature man, in his mid-fifties or early sixties. The smile on the man's face reminded Nick of the kind found on politicians. Even in this black and white picture, Nick could see that his clothes weren't cheap. Nick stared at the photo intently, unable to swallow and for the moment, unable to breath.

He had recognized it the second he laid his eyes on it and almost instantly he could hear her scream echoing through his mind. He was back at the riverbank running through the bushes and jumping over brush. He could see everything with heart-wrenching clarity. For just a moment, his focus rested on the capsized kayak thrust up against the poplar tree. Then, in slow motion, he turned and looked up the path into the woods and saw him—the man in the photo. He stood there, next to his pudgy little companion, with his hand on his chin, pondering, or was he waiting?

From the other end of a long distant tunnel Nick could hear Mercedes speaking. "This is Mr. Jonathon Davenport, the owner of Biotronics, and half a dozen other businesses."

She only said it once, but the name, Jonathon Davenport, echoed through his mind like a resounding explosion as he stared at the picture remembering how the man just stood by and watched as his Allie drowned. Mercedes went on speaking, but Nick couldn't hear her. The roar of the rapids were too loud and his vision too intense. After an unknown amount of time with him stuck in the past, Nick felt his body sway and then realized that something in the present had pushed on his shoulder.

"Are you okay?" Mercedes' hand was on its way back to her side of the table.

Nick looked up from the printout and quietly stared at her for a second, then gasped, apparently his first breath since he saw the picture.

His mind slowly stumbled back into the present as Mercedes spoke again, "What's the matter?"

Nick looked back down at the image. "I know this man." He paused and swallowed, forcing the lump in his throat to subside, then continued. "I only saw him once and only for just a short time. But his image was burned into my mind and I'll never forget it. He was one of the two men that stood by and watched Allie die that day. You said his name is Jonathon Davenport?"

Mercedes nodded. "Yeah."

"Where'd you get this printout?"

Mercedes had already answered that question before he asked it while he was staring at the print, but apparently, he hadn't heard what she said, so she began again. "This morning, while you were sleeping, I did some research on Biotronics. I got that photo off one of their web pages. Biotronics was founded in 1967 by Jonathon Davenport and Henry Boris." Mercedes handed Nick another computer printout.

"This is the other guy?" Nick asked as the anxiety inside him grew and he studied the two photos, listening to what Mercedes had to say.

"The odd thing is, the company seems to have just popped up out of nowhere."

"What do you mean?" Nick set the printouts on the table and looked up at Mercedes.

"Well, Jonathon Davenport worked most of his life as a commodities broker and in 1966 filed bankruptcy. His financial records show that he didn't have two cents to rub together. Likewise, a couple months before Biotronics opened its doors, Henry Boris had been fired from his previous job with the state and didn't have any money either. However, somehow, in between the time that Henry Boris lost his job and the two men founded Biotronics, Jonathon Davenport received a very large sum of money from a man named Robert H. Dennard, who later went on to invent the world's first microchip."

"What does Biotronics do?"

"That's a good question. Mostly, they manufacture computer parts, but they have their hand in a little bit of everything, all the way from secret government contracts to tennis shoes."

"Secrete government contracts?"

"Yeah. Apparently, they have several high dollar contracts with the military."

"Doing what?"

"I don't know. That's why they call it *secret*."

As Nick scooted out of the booth he asked, "Do you have the address to Biotroncis?"

Realizing they were leaving, Mercedes hurriedly snatched up the photos, license and syringe while she spoke. "Yeah, why?"

"Because I'm going to drop by and pay this Mr. Davenport a visit." Nick looked down at his uneaten dessert for a second then offered his hand to Mercedes, who didn't use it to get out of the booth.

"Why?"

They walked to the front register and asked for their bill as he spoke. "I don't know yet."

Mercedes looked confused.

"Look, all I know is that this guy has something to do with what happened to Allie and might even be responsible for her death. I got to see him." Nick turned and looked fixedly into Mercedes' eyes. "In one way or another, I've been looking for *this* man for eight years now."

Nick paid the bill with a trembling hand then walked out into the parking lot.

"What are you going to do when you see him?"

"I don't know." Nick marched straight for his car, stopped at the door and turned around. "Can I have the address, please?"

Mercedes walked around to the passenger's side as she spoke. "Sure, I'll give it to you…in the car."

Nick didn't really need to get it from her, he could have looked it up in seconds on his computer, but he decided to try and make up for his previous poor behavior. He nodded, slid on his shades and hit the automatic door locks. They got in and Nick started the engine as Mercedes pulled out a slip of paper.

"According to their website, Mr. Davenport runs Biotronics from the company's headquarters, which is in the Trend Star building, downtown."

"Do you know where that's at?"

"Yeah."

Mercedes gave Nick directions along the way as they spoke. "You're not going to do anything crazy are you?"

"That depends on your definition of *crazy*." Nick kept his eyes on the road as he answered.

"Well, what exactly *are* you going to do?"

"I don't know…maybe I'll invite him out to a day at the river."

"Turn at the next light." Mercedes pointed toward the left.

The Mustang pulled through the lingering yellow light and accelerated as it turned onto the four-lane blacktop. Mercedes had always had a knack for being able to tell the bad guys from the good guys and from the very beginning she could tell that Nick was one of the good guys. She was fairly sure, but not completely positive that he wasn't going to do anything stupid. Nick weaved in and out of traffic and ironically, Mercedes found herself holding the passenger's side hand brace, to keep steady.

"The place is bound to have a ton of security, you know."

"I know."

"Maybe we should wait, scope things out and come back later."

"No, I got to see him now."

"That's it up there, I think." Mercedes pointed to a set of four high-rises on the next street. Nick quickly navigated his way around the block and found a metered parking space just down the avenue from a dark reflective high-rise with giant gold lettering above the entrance that read *The Trend Star building*.

Nick turned the ignition off and stared at the wheel as he took several slow steady breaths, then put his hand on the door handle, looked at Mercedes and said, "You better stay here."

"The Hell with that!" Mercedes opened her door and was out of the car before he could respond. Not in any type of mood to argue, Nick got out, dropped a few coins into the slot and then headed across the street with Mercedes right beside him. Cars stopped and waited as Nick, seemingly unaware, single-mindedly headed for the lobby doors. Nick could feel the iceman resurfacing.

Inside, they didn't bother with the information desk, but rather went straight to the wall directory, where they found the name Jonathan Davenport. Moments later they were in the posh, mirrored elevator on their way to the sixty-eighth floor. The mild elevator music only magnified the tension and now Mercedes was the one who found it difficult to swallow. She wanted to say something to lighten the air, but wasn't sure what. She fidgeted slightly, bit her bottom lip and shifted her eyes around the small chamber as Nick stood, seemingly calm, still wearing his shades and staring at the doors. Mercedes looked up at the digital floor counter which indicated that they were flying past floors and rapidly approaching their destination: 55, 56, 57. A moment later the elevator swayed, Mercedes' stomach dropped and the bell chimed. Floor 68.

The doors opened and Nick calmly stepped out onto the lavish floor. Just ahead and to his right was a waiting area with a black leather sofa and matching chair. There were magazines placed on top of a glass coffee table with gold trim. To the left, a young, sweet-looking blond sat behind a counter-desk and looked up as Nick approached. Just to the right of the blond between her and the waiting area, stood a set of huge, dark double doors that lead into Mr. Davenport's personal office. The lady smiled mechanically at first, but then became confused as Nick walked past her, without stopping.

"Excuse me sir! You can't go in there!" Nick heard the lady's voice behind him, as he exploded through the doors and entered the room, like a hurricane hitting the shoreline of a small island.

Mr. Davenport sat across the room on the phone and looked up when Nick entered the office. Nick didn't bother going around the sitting area. He flew right through the middle of it, knocking the chair backward to his left and pushing the loveseat at least three feet to the right. Before Mr. Davenport could hang up the phone and call security, Nick had made it across the room and was already around the large desk. For just an instant Mr. Davenport's eyes held a hint of recognition in them, followed by fear, but then, almost instantly he pretended to be confused.

"May I help you?"

Nick grabbed his chair with both hands and swiveled it, so that Mr. Davenport faced him, then reached up and removed his shades, dropping them onto the desk. With one hand on each arm of the chair and his eyes only inches from the old man's, Nick asked, "Remember me?"

After a second of silence, where Mr. Davenport acted like he was trying to recall whom this madman was, he replied, "I'm sorry, I don't."

"Bullshit!" Nick's face contorted with anger as he heaved the chair across the floor, toward the glass wall.

Mr. Davenport's chair, with him in it, flew backward and slammed into the glass. Mercedes stood in the middle of the office where the leather sitting area used to be and thought that the wall would shatter for sure, but it held. Mr. Davenport sat, dazed as Nick closed the gap, and then grabbed him by his suit coat and yanked him out of the chair. He brought the old man's face up close and gave him another chance. "Are you sure?"

Still holding the dress coat with his right hand, Nick reached around the old man, with his left and pulled the chair away. Mr. Davenport swallowed hard and thought for another moment as Nick waited, getting ready to throw the old man against the wall again, this time without the high-back chair.

"I'm sorry." Mr. Davenport shook his head. "I don't remember you."

"No?" Nick slammed the old man, hard into the glass and then brought his face even nearer. "Take a closer look!" Nick turned his head, offering the man his profile and in the process spotted the man's personal bathroom. After a second of silence and thinking of the river, he said, "Maybe water will jog your memory." With that and as the old man continued to reaffirm that he didn't know whom Nick was, Nick dragged him across the room, toward the restroom. Meanwhile in the outer office, Mr. Davenport's secretary hung up the phone with security and stepped back across the threshold, just in time to see Mr. Davenport and Nick disappear into the lavatory.

Nick pushed the old man over, backward and pinned him, face up, to the counter, just to the left of the basin as he turned on the water. The position was so awkward that Mr. Davenport had a hard time keeping his balance, much less fighting back. The edge of the counter pressed hard into Mr. Davenport's back like a blunt knife and he stumbled, losing his balance as Nick slid him to the right and shoved his head into the sink. Water rushed directly onto his face as he closed his eyes and held his breath. After a few seconds without air, he tried to breathe, coughed, spit and turned his head, but it did little good.

Finally, Nick shouted, "You sure you don't remember me?"

Gasping for air and believing he was going to drown, Mr. Davenport conceded, "I remember you! I do!"

Nick, now full of rage grabbed the man's chin and forced his face to look straight up at the oncoming water. This wasn't even a fraction of the torment that Allie had gone through.

With his eyes tightly shut and his face turning purple, he spit out water as he did his best to scream, "I do know you. I do!"

"Who am I then?" Nick asked as he pulled the old man's head up just a bit and then shoved it back down, knocking the back of it against the stainless steel drain stopper.

"You're the guy from the river!" The man shouted.

Nick turned off the water and pulled the man up, so they were face to face again, haphazardly scraping his head on the side of the faucet in the process.

With a trickle of bright red blood running down the side of the man's water-soaked head, Nick asked, "What's my name?"

Shaking, now obviously full of fear, the old man replied, "I don't know your name."

Astonished and aggravated at the man's resolve and willingness to continue the charade after all of this, Nick said again, "Bullshit!" and pushed his head back down as he turned the water back on.

"Okay! Okay!"

Nick hesitated, holding the man's head just inches from the menacing water.

"It's Chadwick." The man gasped in exhaustion.

Nick turned off the water and heaved Mr. Davenport onto floor, just outside of the restroom, then leaned up against the door jam, breathing heavy. "What happened that day at the river?"

Mr. Davenport looked up, through bloodshot eyes, panting and said, "Your wife died."

"No shit Sherlock!" Nick kicked the old man in the side, right below his ribs, with just enough force to grab his attention. "What happened after that?"

The man looked up and acted bewildered for a moment as Nick pulled his foot back and threatened another kick.

"Okay, okay!" The old man held his hand up in a surrendering motion and then blinked slowly. He looked down at the carpet and into the past as he lowered his hand and Nick waited.

"You must understand something." The old man looked back up at Nick. "Your wife was already dead and..."

Just then, a deep voice came from the other side of the room where the tall double doors were. "Don't move!"

Nick looked up at the rent-a-cop, who was pointing a 9 mm glock in his direction. Even worse than a cop, was a wannabe cop. If all cops were assholes, then every one of these guys were double assholes.

"Step away from Mr. Davenport." Most of these guys were losers who couldn't make it as real cops, so they got jobs in the private sector. Working here, in the eloquent offices of the Trend Star building, Nick knew that this guy probably didn't get many opportunities to shoot someone and was no doubt, trigger-happy.

The man's eyes were intense and hinted at the desire to squeeze the trigger. He held the gun in his right hand and used his left, gripping his right wrist, to steady his aim. Reluctantly, Nick conceded. He held his hands up and slowly moved back, toward the glass wall. Mr. Davenport scuttled to his feet and made his way around, behind the guard as a team of security personnel, all with guns drawn, stampeded into the office. Nick looked at all of the firepower in the room and thought about the thick glass walls—a bad combination.

The guards circled Nick and moments later, he and Mercedes were cuffed and standing in front of Mr. Davenport's desk. Everyone waited as Mr. Davenport sat in his high-back chair, wiping his face and trying to compose himself. After a moment the head of security said, "We called the police, they're on their way."

Mr. Davenport thought about that for a moment and then said, "Call them back, Rupert. Tell them it was a false alarm and that everything is okay."

"Excuse me?"

"You heard me."

"But, sir this man just tried to kill you."

"No, no he didn't." Davenport chuckled. He's just a little confused. Many years ago his wife drowned in a tragic accident and I happened to be there, that's all. I'm sure Mr. Chadwick didn't mean to hurt anyone, right Mr. Chadwick?" Mr. Davenport looked back up at Rupert. "Now, call the police back and let them know that everything is all right and we don't need them."

Rupert stood, befuddled for a moment and then walked into the outer office to call the police. Mr. Davenport never ceased to amaze everyone with his generosity and kindness. Some thought he was too nice for his own good. "Uncuff them." Mr. Davenport gestured to one of the guards, who couldn't help but smile and shake his head at Mr. Davenport's overwhelming compassion for this thug, as he undid Mercedes' cuffs. Nick thought about leaping over the desk and strangling the old man as the pressure on his wrists subsided. Once freed he stepped forward, toward Mr. Davenport, and once again everyone pulled their guns. As he reached his hand out toward the now confident and dignified looking old man several guards got ready to cut him down in a shower of lead. Instead of wrapping his hand around the old man's neck, like he wanted to do, Nick simply lowered his hand to the desk and latched onto his shades, then said in a calm cool voice, "See ya soon."

Nick turned, glanced around the room and slid his glasses over his eyes, then calmly headed for the door, passing a confused Rupert along the way. Mercedes coyly approached Mr. Davenport's desk, grabbed a business card, smiled graciously and then ran to catch up with Nick, who was just stepping into the elevator. Neither of them spoke all the way to the car and halfway back to Applebee's.

Mercedes finally broke the silence. "For a minute there, I thought you were going to kill him."

"It'll take a lot more than a little water to kill a piece of crap like Davenport."

It was silent for a little while longer as they both thought about that. Then Mercedes said, "I don't get it, why did he let us go? Why didn't he press charges?"

The Mustang pulled up, next to the Corolla and Nick shut off the engine as he replied, "He can't kill us in jail. If he would have pressed charges, he wouldn't be able to get rid of us, and he's probably afraid that we might be able to say something that would make the authorities take a closer look at his business. If I were in his shoes I wouldn't want the extra heat."

"So what do we do now?"

"Well for starters we gotta find you another place to bunk. They obviously know where you're staying."

Mercedes thought about Alex and remembered the promises she made to him just hours before he was taken. "You're right. Do you think they're watching us right now?" Mercedes looked around the parking lot.

"Not likely. Davenport was surprised to see us coming, so he couldn't have had us tailed while we were on our way to his office and I didn't see anyone following us since we left. I doubt anyone knows we're here. Is there anything you need at your motel?"

"Well I just bought a couple changes of clothes. They're there."

"Anything else?"

Mercedes thought. She hadn't taken much from her townhouse and everything about Alex was either with her or in the Corolla. "No, why?"

"Good, we'll just leave your motel the way it is. You can come and stay with me."

"Now just slow down there, speedy."

"What? I was planning on getting us separate rooms."

Mercedes thought for a second and said, "Yeah, I guess you're right. Where do you think we should stay?"

"Not sure. It would be smart to get a room in an up class hotel, one that has security. Hold on." Nick reached behind her seat and retrieved his computer bag. Mercedes watched as he navigated his way around the net and located a high quality hotel nearby. Within minutes he made a reservation and paid for a room.

"Do you think that's wise?"

"What?"

"Using a credit card number to reserve our room? I mean, don't you think they'd be able to find us that way?"

"Sure they would, if that's where we were staying." Nick grinned.

"We're not staying there?"

"No—too far from the action. I'd rather be closer to that lab you mentioned. I think that would be a good place to start looking for some answers. What did you call it, The Boris Lab?"

"Yeah."

"Do you have the address?"

Mercedes shuffled around and located her handwritten note. "Here it is."

Moments later Nick located a decent motel just a couple of blocks from the lab and downloaded the driving directions. Mercedes sat, pretty impressed, as she watched Nick work.

"We'll be staying here."

She shook her head and smiled. "Ever thought about becoming a private eye?"

Nick chuckled. "No, not really."

"Well, I bet you'd make a good one."

Following him to the motel, Mercedes thought about the ferocity in which he dealt with Mr. Davenport. There had been so much passion and vengeance in his actions. The love he had for his wife must have been immense. Mercedes thought back, but couldn't recall a single old boyfriend who loved her half as much. She wondered what it would be like to be in love with someone who had that much fire inside of him for her. He was like a powerful knight who had been so smitten by the one he loved that even after she had been gone for eight years he was still willing to kill for her. The mere thought of the power of that kind of romance was overwhelming. She fancied the idea of him ever being able to love another with as much intensity, but quickly dismissed it. A love like that only came around once in a thousand years—If that.

CHAPTER TWENTY-FOUR

Mr. Davenport sat in his high back chair, tapping the erasing end of a pencil on the edge of the desk and intently staring at the empty glass, which had just been full of vodka. The burning sensation of the drink was still evaporating from his lips and off his tongue as he thought. One of the qualities that he prided himself on and one that enabled him to be so successful with Biotronics was his ability to stay calm under pressure. However, the last few days had tested that ability and pushed it to the very brink of its limits. Currently he was using all his willpower not to scream.

Everything that could have gone wrong had gone wrong. Outsiders had found out about Number Nine, the extent of which wasn't clear yet. Raymond Jackson, who had been with the company for the past seven and a half years, was now dead. Wow, Raymond Jackson was dead. At that thought Davenport shook his head, stopped tapping, and turned in his chair. His eyes opened wide and he looked across the vacant room, not focusing on any one thing in particular. His thoughts continued. Theodore was still out there, somewhere, lurking like the madman he was. And to top everything off, Nicholas Chadwick had finally put two and two together and somehow found his way to Biotronics and then up to Davenport's office.

Mr. Davenport picked up his shot glass, took it to the wet bar and poured from the already open bottle of vodka. After downing it in a single drink, he twisted the lid onto the bottle, set the bottle on the shelf, and then headed back to his desk. He had to get himself together. Soon Gregory Patterson would be here, a company man that Raymond had stumbled across a couple of years ago. Davenport had telephoned him right after Chadwick left. Patterson wasn't Jackson, that's for sure, but what he lacked in some areas he more than made up for in others. Jackson had been intelligent and methodical. He had always planned things out and thought of every contingency. Patterson however, ran more on instinct and gut feelings, but Davenport was convinced that Patterson's instinct was uniquely honed and would serve well for the task that lay ahead.

Mr. Davenport had combed his hair and freshened up after the altercation with Chadwick, however he still didn't look his usual best. He sat in his chair for a moment, tapping his shoe on the carpet and then stood back up and headed for the bathroom. He looked in the mirror for a few seconds, and then reached for his comb, all the while, thinking and planning.

"Mr. Davenport, Mr. Patterson is here to see you." The intercom, on his desk sounded with Julie's voice. Mr. Davenport walked over to his desk, calmly sat down and put on an air of confidence, then pressed the talk button on his phone.

"Thanks Julie, send him in." As he spoke, he reached into the top drawer of the desk, pulled out a computer disk and laid it in front of him.

Davenport was silent as Patterson opened the tall oak door at the far end of the office and quietly traversed the large room. Without speaking, Mr. Davenport gestured for Patterson to sit down. Patterson took the seat and waited in silence. The two men sat quietly, across the desk from one another as Mr. Davenport stared inquisitively at Patterson's menacing face. He was about to entrust this henchman with a very important task, one that might just hold the very fate of the company. Although, it was a simple task, it wouldn't be easy.

After a few more seconds of silence, Patterson, obviously nervous, asked, in his usually raspy voice, "Am I in some kind of trouble sir?"

Mr. Davenport stared back for a second, pushed his chin up and thought, but didn't answer. He swiveled his chair a little to the left and then a little to the right. He strummed his fingers on the arm of the chair, took in a deep breath and then leaned forward, with his elbows on the desk. "Gregory." He had never called him that before, it had always been Patterson, but now he needed to be a little more personal. He needed the outcast to feel closer to the company, more like he belonged. "I don't believe I've told you just how pleased the company is with you lately."

Noticeably relieved, Patterson sat and listened. "You've done well. We've had a few setbacks here recently, this is true, but nothing the company can't handle." Mr. Davenport paused, squinted his eyes and then continued. "As you know Greg, Jackson is no longer with us."

For the first time since he sat down, Patterson looked away from Mr. Davenport. His stark eyes sunk in even deeper in their sockets as they floated down to the desk and then onto his lap. Mr. Davenport continued, "I know you thought a lot of him, and he thought a lot of you as well." Mr. Davenport knew that wasn't true, but was fairly certain that Jackson wouldn't be contesting it anytime soon.

Patterson's eyes shot up quickly.

"That's right…"

Patterson looked curiously at Davenport.

"He did, and because of that, I am going to entrust you with a very important assignment, one that you must not fail at."

Patterson's ears perked up as he waited to hear what the company needed of him.

"Through the years, the company has acquired a mortal enemy, one who wants nothing more than to do major harm to Biotronics, a man who doesn't have all the facts and who doesn't want them, either. Up until recently, we've been able to keep this lunatic at bay, but things have changed."

Mr. Davenport rose to his feet, walked over to the glass wall, clasped his hands behind his back and stared out at the city. "If we don't do something fast, he might just bring the whole company down. Now, normally, I'd be discussing this type of matter with Jackson, but, unfortunately he's no longer here."

Once again, Patterson looked away in sadness, but almost instantly his eyes found their way back to Davenport. He knew what was about to be asked of him and he sat poised, like a trained Doberman, just waiting to hear the word *kill*.

"His name is Nicholas Chadwick. You've already met him. He was the guy with Mercedes at the church, the other night.

"The bitch." Patterson snarled, just under his breath, as he focused at the back of Mr. Davenport's dress coat.

Still looking out the window, Davenport unclasped his hands and pointed a finger aimlessly into the air. "There on the desk in front of you is a complete file on this man. Take it."

Patterson looked down at the desk and saw a CD case, labeled Chadwick. He picked it up and put it in the inside pocket of his coat.

"It would be nice if it looked like an accident, although, at this point, it doesn't have to."

"What about Mercedes?" Patterson asked in anticipation.

"Awe Mercedes, yes. Well, it is unfortunate, but I do believe she knows a bit too much for her own good now, but take care of Chadwick first."

Mr. Davenport paused, letting Patterson soak it all in and then said, "You'll be working with Travis Thorndale."

Patterson abruptly stood up. "I'd rather work alone."

Mr. Davenport turned around and nodded his head. "I know Greg, but Thorndale has some technical expertise that may come in handy."

"Yeah, but I'm running the show, right?"

"Of course you are." Davenport's voice was calm and distant as he turned back to the window. "I wouldn't have it any other way. He's waiting for you now, down in the garage. I'm giving you the Camry, in memory of Jackson." Patterson's eyes grew large as Davenport turned back around and walked over to his desk. "I trust you'll drive it well."

Patterson nodded, thinking of Jackson and still looking at the glass, where Davenport was just standing.

"As soon as you leave here, I want you to go over to the lab. The good doctor has extracted Number Nine's memory of the last few days. Look it over, you might find something useful." Mr. Davenport paused, peered deep into Patterson's deranged looking eyes, and emphasized, "This is your chance, Gregory, don't blow it."

Patterson grinned impishly. "Anything else sir?"

"I do believe, that's enough, don't you?" Davenport sat down and smiled warmly at Patterson.

"Yes sir. Don't worry about anything. I'll take care of it."

"I'm sure you will."

With that Davenport picked up a pencil, opened a notebook and began to look busy. Patterson sat there for a few seconds, listening to the led as it scribbled on the page then got up and left the room.

Patterson hated the elevators at the Trend Star building because every wall inside every one of them was a floor-to-ceiling mirror. And mirrors, along with every other reflective surface reminded him of that which he did not care to be reminded of. It was bad enough that he had to use one before work, in order to stay groomed properly. He didn't need some mindless piece of glass in the elevator to remind him of just how ugly he was. He had known how hideous he looked for as long as he could remember.

Although he couldn't recall a single fact about the worthless woman who bore him, he was certain of one thing. The reason she gave him up was because of his repugnant looks. Every single one of the nine different foster families he lived with as a child, had been sure to tell him, repeatedly, just how ugly he was.

Several times he had been thrown into the basement and locked conveniently out of sight, while one of his foster mothers (if one could even call her that) entertained her guests. She didn't want to be embarrassed by his repulsiveness. Once, he was left there for so long that he had to be taken to the hospital and treated for dehydration.

On another occasion, in another place of torment, and at the very tender age of six, his foster *father* (another deceptive title) nearly caned him to death. He claimed that the boy's *scarred* face had scared all of his *pretty* lady friends away. Riding in the elevator and unavoidably glancing at the many demons in the mirrors, he could feel the cane, once again, slapping painfully into his bare back and legs.

Whap! In a dark dreary place, a thick red mark appeared over the top of tender pink flesh.

"I'm sorry, I'm sorry." A young boy cried with tears of hurt and confusion pouring from deep dark sockets.

Whap! Another mark.

"You ugly pathetic beast! It's all, your fault. What are you?"

Whap!

"What are you?"

"Ugly." A whimper escaped remorseful, trembling lips.

"I can't hear you, boy!" A strong arm pulled the solid oak cane back into the air.

Whap! A bone shattered.

"What are you?"

Whap!

"Say it louder!"

Whap!

Barely conscious, filled with fear and pain, the little boy spoke as loud as he could. "Ugly! I'm ugly!"

Whap!

In the elevator, Patterson gritted his teeth and clinched his fists, as the memory forced its way into his mind. He shut his eyes, exhaled and suppressed it, pushing it back into the deep, dark hole, where he kept it. After a few minutes, the memory faded. He knew he was ugly and he didn't need the wall on the inside of the Trend Star elevator to remind him.

Ignoring the many images of himself and focusing on the digital floor counter overhead, he forced himself to think about his good fortune. The company had finally recognized his unique talents and was allowing him to demonstrate them by having him get rid of the bitch and her Ken doll boyfriend. Patterson remembered Nicholas' pretty face and couldn't help but glance back at the demon in the mirror. Images of the man's handsome face being smashed to bits with a sledgehammer brought a warm feeling into Patterson's soul. Killing the *pretty boy* would be nothing but pleasure. Patterson grinned at himself.

Down in the garage, Patterson found the Camry. Thorndale, a weasel-faced man with light brown hair, dark brown eyes and a poorly groomed goatee, sat behind the wheel. He was in his late twenties, early thirties and just like everyone else in the company, wore a dress suit. Patterson knew, however that just because he wore one, didn't mean he knew how to dress properly. More often than not, his coat was wrinkled and his tie didn't quiet reach the top of his slacks, and on occasion, one or more of the shirt buttons that his tie failed to cover, hung undone. Patterson was convinced that he was better dressed to work as a used car salesman or perhaps a cheap hit man for the mob instead of an up class executive for an outstanding company like Biotronics.

Patterson coolly walked up to the door and softly rapped a knuckle on the glass. Thorndale looked up and grinned, then gestured for Patterson to go around to the passenger's side. Patterson stood for a second, honestly confused and then reached for the door handle, but before he could latch onto it and pull it open, Thorndale hit the power locks and locked the door.

Thorndale grinned again, as Patterson's blood began to boil and then shouted through the glass. "Go around, *I'm* driving."

Patterson didn't like this at all and instinctively drew his gun. He pointed it through the glass at the little weasel's head, and sternly commanded, "Get out."

Continuing his folly, Thorndale rolled his eyes, shook his head and started the engine. The rage inside Patterson grew and he almost pulled the trigger. The only thing that stopped him was the fact that this was Jackson's car and he owed Jackson more respect than that. Patterson took another moment, breathed in deep and then re-holstered his gun.

"Come on... now get in." Feeling like he had won, Thorndale smiled and tilted his head toward the passenger's side.

Patterson slowly walked around the car, cracking his neck as he passed the trunk and then opened the passenger's side door. Instead of taking his seat and buckling up, Patterson instantly reached his left hand behind the weasel's head and latched onto a fistful of hair. Before Thorndale knew what was happening, Patterson had his right hand fastened around his windpipe. Thorndale bucked, let go of the wheel and fought back. He placed both his hands onto Patterson's right wrist trying to loosen his ironclad grip. Patterson responded by leaning over, almost standing up, inside the car and straddling the little man. He pulled back harder on his hair and forced his right hand to tighten its hold.

Deprived of oxygen and still violently struggling to get free, Thorndale's vision began to fade. Finally, just before he blacked out completely, right as he stopped resisting, Patterson let go of his neck. With Thorndale gasping, trying to reopen his crushed windpipe, Patterson reached over, pulled the door latch and pushed him out. Patterson calmly walked around the car, stepped over the little man and took the seat behind the wheel.

He closed the door, calmly buckled up, lowered the window and rasped, "You've got thirty seconds to get your ass in the car or I'm leaving you here." With that he shifted into reverse and noted the dashboard clock. Still holding his neck, Thorndale got to his feet and hurriedly stumbled around to the passenger's side. Even as Thorndale was pulling the door shut, Patterson released the brake and the car shot backward, skidded to a stop and then raced through the parking garage, in search of the exit.

A good fifteen minutes later, on their way to the Boris Lab, Thorndale, still gathering himself together spoke up. "Fuckin' freak! You didn't have to be an ass. What were you trying to do, kill me?"

"Shut the fuck up, before I do." Patterson rasped.

Thorndale looked at Patterson, who now wore sunglasses and kept his eyes on the road. He had heard about him, his antics, his unorthodox way of doing things, but until now he never experienced any of them. A few miles down the road, Thorndale took a chance and spoke again. "So, what does the old man want us to do?"

"He doesn't want *us* to do anything." Patterson paused to let that sink in and then continued. "The company requires *special* services from me."

"Fine hot shot, what is it that the company wants *you* to do?"

"Oh nothing, just kill a couple people."

"Kill a couple people? Wow!" Thorndale raised his eyebrows and looked out the window. "Who?"

"Nicholas Chadwick and Mercedes Atwater."

Thorndale thought about that and remembered rummaging through Mercedes' office a few days ago with the late Raymond Jackson. "I see. And if this is *your* assignment, then what the Hell am I doing with you?"

"You're going to help me find them."

Still looking out of the window, Thorndale nodded. "'Kay, but I ain't killin' nobody."

"Pussy!" Patterson, still focusing on the road, grinned.

"What?" The weasel looked shocked. "Because I would rather not kill another human being—that makes me a pussy?"

"Yup."

"Whatever!" Thorndale shook his head and then looked directly at Patterson. "You are one twisted cookie, you know that?"

"Yup." With that Patterson turned his head, met the weasel's eyes and gave him a malevolent grin.

CHAPTER TWENTY-FIVE

After checking into the Lamp Light Motel, Nick sat, across from Mercedes, at the small wooden table, perusing different Internet sites, looking for any information available on the Boris Lab.

He chewed on Gummy Bears as he tapped, clicked and typed, then suddenly he shook his head and widened his eyes. "Oh wow, look at this! Biotronics has had laboratories all across the country, and get this, most of them, like the one here, were named after our friend, Henry Boris." He looked up at Mercedes, and found that instead of paying attention, she was distantly gazing into the parking lot, through the gap in the heavy cream-colored curtains.

"Hey, you okay?" When she didn't answer, Nick snapped his fingers and waved an opened hand in front of her face. "Earth to Mercedes, hello…come in Mercedes."

"Huh?" Her daze broke and her worry filled eyes met his.

"You okay?"

She glanced back to the window for a moment, and then returned her gaze to Nick as she shakily replied, "Yeah, I'm fine."

With several programs loaded into his computer and even more hard-to-find websites filling up the screen, Nick reached up, grabbed the top of the display and closed the laptop. "No you're not." He raised his eyebrows, giving her that *you can't fool me* look and asked, "What's wrong?"

She looked back confidently and tried to reaffirm her statement, but was unable to get past his all-knowing glare. Finally, she simply repeated, with even less confidence than before, "I'm fine!"

Instead of debating the issue, Nick silently tilted his head to one side and lowered his eyebrows from their all-knowing raised position to a *get-real* scrunched one. After a few intense moments, Mercedes emphasized, "Really!" then, with a burst of exasperation, shot up and escaped into the bathroom. Nick sat alone in the quiet room for a couple of minutes, wondering what had brought about the sudden change in Mercedes' emotional state, and whether or not he should chase after her.

His muscles flexed as he almost got up, but then paused. Nick was naturally a caring person, but he wondered—was he beginning to care just a bit too much for this girl? Would he be jumping up so quickly if she were someone else, say Dottie, for example? He knew the answer even before he finished asking himself the question. There was definitely something about Mercedes that made her different from everyone else, something that attracted him to her. That something however, was the very reason why he had to keep his distance. He had room in his heart for only one woman, and that woman, albeit, no longer here, wasn't Mercedes. On the other hand, Nick wasn't the type of person to hesitate. If he felt a friend needed someone to talk to, he'd be the first to start the conversation. Finally, not knowing what was wrong, and perceiving that what she probably needed most right now was a little space, Nick pushed her to the back of his mind, reopened his laptop and continued his search.

Meanwhile, in the bathroom Mercedes stood in front of the mirror and thought about the last few days. They had been absolutely overwhelming and she couldn't believe half of what had happened. Slowly, during the last day or so, she had begun to question her own memory. Did Alex really read her mind? How is that possible? Could he have just had a lucky guess, as Nick had suggested? There was no way. Right? She looked down at her tennis shoe and thought about her toe. How did he do that, or did he? Maybe her toe hadn't been cut off in the first place. Maybe she just thought it had. Her head had been aching for days as the questions just kept creeping in. Things like this just don't happen. Holding back a river of tears, she raised a trembling hand to her forehead, stepped backward, to the tub and sat on the edge.

Bringing in business hadn't been easy to do, and she could count, on one hand the number of cases that she had handled since the beginning. For the last year or so, she had continued to tell herself that all she needed was *the big one,* the one case that would give her recognition and put her name on the map. This one was definitely big enough; however, a case in which one half-expected Rod Sterling to step out of the shadows wasn't exactly what she had had in mind. So, what if she *was* able to solve it? Would it bring the kind of attention she wanted? Doubtful! This case was probably better suited for someone like a parapsychologist, definitely not a fact-finding, hardnosed PI, like herself.

And what about her client, Alex? She had made him a promise that no matter what happened he wouldn't be alone anymore. She had told him that no matter what came along, they would get to the bottom of things together. Less than two hours later he was gone, taken off to God knows where, by God knows whom. Like so many times before, she had begun with a truckload of zeal and determination only to end in muddied defeat. She raised her head and peered at her reflection as droplets of water fought their way into the corner of her eyes.

In the next room, Nick's screen currently burned with the city blueprints of the Boris Lab. It was a small, single story, 2200 square foot, rectangular shaped building, and it appeared to have way too much parking space.

Nick clicked on a page in the background, brought it to the front and began to read. Biotronics first purchased the plot of land last year from a company called Westec Housing that specialized in rental property. After demolishing the abandoned apartment complex, Biotronics erected the current building.

As Nick read on he discovered that Westec had themselves obtained the piece of property form an old underground railroad company and the earth directly beneath the Boris Lab had long ago been tunneled away. Now filled with gut wrenching anticipation, Nick looked up from his computer and peered aimlessly out the window.

Biotronics had purposely picked out that specific spot in order to make use of the underground area. Nick was willing to bet that the aboveground laboratory held nothing of significances and that all the interesting stuff was kept deep below, under tight lock and key. He was also willing to bet that getting down there wouldn't be as easily done as getting into Mr. Davenport's office had been.

The wheels inside his head began to turn as he looked back to the screen and continued to read. He was sure that at least some of the answers he sought were waiting to be found down there, deep below the earth's surface, but how to get there? He needed more information than what was currently displayed, and after a few seconds he found and pulled up the old railway tunnel blue prints.

Surprisingly, many years ago this piece of real estate had been a major subway station, with overlapping tracks descending six levels deep. A small city could be down there and nobody would be the wiser. Nick studied the blue prints and committed to memory the basic overall structure of the tunnels, which he was sure would still be essentially the same. He also memorized the maze of ventilation ducts that lay hidden in the walls of the old subway, and just to be safe he downloaded all the images to his laptop.

After making a fairly extensive study, he shut off his computer and began to formulate a plan. A moment later he lightly rapped on the bathroom door. "Hey, I'm going for a ride, wanna tag?"

Mercedes abruptly pulled open the door. "Where're you going?"

"I need to see a friend about some tools."

"Tools?"

"Yeah." Nick smiled wide, quickly raised and lowered his eyebrows, then turned toward the door.

A half an hour later, after a quick reconnaissance drive around the Boris Lab, Mercedes found herself sitting with Nick at a dimly lit bar in Uncle Bob's tavern, speaking with a tall brawny looking man who could have easily passed for Mr. Clean's twin. As Roger and Nick spoke their hellos, Mercedes couldn't help but notice an overly intoxicated, elderly gentleman sitting alone at the other end of the bar, who mysteriously defied the laws of gravity.

At first he was sitting perfectly straight, but then, ever so slightly, he began to lean as if he were a little off balance. Instead of correcting his posture however, he somehow stabilized himself and maintained his awkward position. Surprisingly, after a few more moments, his lean continued until he once again found a way to steady himself and sustain an even steeper incline. Unconsciously, Mercedes' head began to tilt in the direction of the old man's lean.

Her trance was broken however, by a change in Nick's tone and the mentioning of her name. "Roger, I'd like you to meet Mercedes."

A smile dominated the big man's face as he tossed a white dishcloth over his shoulder, politely tilted his head up to release a large inhalation of smoke, and then amorously said, "The pleasure's *all* mine." Across the bar he offered her a large hand. She grabbed back, but instead of shaking it, Mr. Clean bent over and gently kissed the back of it. Mercedes blushed and smiled awkwardly as she pulled her hand out of the giant's clutches and back to her side.

Without asking, Roger took out a tall glass mug and filled it full with MGD, sat it in front of Nick, and then looked at Mercedes. "What're you drinking, Sweetie?"

With just a touch of piousness, Mercedes batted her eyes and corrected the overgrown Romeo. "It's Mercedes…and I'll have a rum and coke, thank you."

The wide smile on Mr. Clean blended into an impish grin as he nodded and went to work on her order. While pouring an overly long shot of Bacardi into her glass (perhaps to loosen her up), Roger spoke to Nick. "So, catch the headhunter yet?"

Mercedes looked curiously at Nick.

Nick smiled at her confusion while answering Roger, "I never said I was after him."

Roger set Mercedes' drink in front of her and let out a little chuckle, "Yeah, I remember," then took a quick puff on his cancer stick, made a slight grimace and asked, "What happened to your face?"

Nick's smile continued as he raised a hand to a cut just above his left eye. "Is it that bad?"

"Well, let's just say, I wouldn't go out with you."

After laughing just to be polite, Nick took a rather large gulp of his beer, sat the mug on the counter and then in a more serious tone said, "Roger I need a favor."

The big man exhaled, flicked his ashes into the tray and replied, "This sounds serious."

Nick nodded. "It is."

"What do you need?"

Nick looked over at Ned, who was now sitting—if one could still call it that—at what had to be close to a forty-five degree angle, and said, "Guns." Keeping his gaze on Ned, he continued, "...I need a couple of guns."

"A couple of guns?"

"Yeah, nothing too fancy, a couple .22s will do."

"A couple of .22s, huh?"

"Yeah." Nick took his gaze off the leaning tower of Pisa and appeared to give Roger his full attention. "I was thinking you might know someone who might know someone that I could talk to or at least point me in the right direction."

Nick's experiences in life had etched into him the unique ability to stay consciously aware of his surroundings at all times, and even now, while it appeared that Roger had his full attention, he was completely conscious of small nuances coming from Mercedes. Perhaps this was just how she was—distant, superficial, and insecure, but Nick didn't think so. As a matter of fact, her mood had been rather peculiar ever since she jumped up and hid in the bathroom, at the motel. If this Alex guy really did read her mind and somehow reattach her toe, or even if she just *thought* that he did, then the odds were pretty strong that she was feeling more than a bit overwhelmed.

Roger nodded, pushed up his chin and all-knowingly hummed, "Ah huh," and then asked, "And what do you need these guns for?"

Nick scrunched his face sheepishly and replied, "That...I can't tell you."

Roger nodded and hummed again. "Ah huh." Then after a few moments of clock-ticking silence, said rather assuredly, "Well, then I can't help you."

Nick looked at Roger puzzled. He was sure that after the incident the other night, Roger would be more than willing to help. Then after a moment's reflection he realized that he barely knew this man and that he was under no obligation to help at all. Upon even deeper thought, he began to feel a little cheap for even asking in the first place. The puzzlement on his face turned into a warm smile as he kindly said, "Well, thanks anyway," and then gulped down the last swallow of his beer.

Roger spoke blatantly. "For what? I didn't do anything."

"Yeah, but I probably shouldn't have asked in the first place."

The lumberjack shook his head and laughed, "I didn't say I *wouldn't* help ya."

Nick looked up even more puzzled than before.

"I said I *couldn't* help ya...not if you can't tell me what you've gotten yourself into." He took a long drag of his cigarette and then continued. "Look, you saved my livelihood the other night, not to mention my life, and in my book that makes you a friend, and you don't turn your back on your friends, at least I don't." The three of them sat in silence for a half a second longer, then he went on. "Now, if I'm gonna help, I'm *gonna help*." He then gave Nick a blasé stare and asked, "So, what're we into?"

Nick glanced, blank-faced at Mercedes, who returned a look of confusion and uncertainty. The blasé look in Roger's eyes reminded Nick of some forgotten scene from the Godfather that he couldn't quite place. Finally, he caved, and with a whisper of a voice, began to fill Roger in on some of the highlights, conveniently omitting certain information that would no doubt make—if not him, then Mercedes—out to be a good candidate for the funny farm.

Roger topped off their drinks and listened to the story, politely stopping Nick every so often to replenish Ned's beer or wait on a straggling client who stepped up to the bar. When Nick had begun his story, the place was relatively empty, but as happy hour quickly approached more and more people were entering the bar. Finally, when Nick brought up the Boris Lab and indicated that it was the reason he needed the firepower, Roger held up a hand, stopping him in mid-sentence, and then said, "My relief comes in at six o'clock."

Mercedes looked at her watch. "That's just over an hour from now."

Mr. Clean nodded and then asked, "Where are you two staying?"

"Room seventeen, the Lamp Light Motel, over on Rulings Avenue." Nick said.

As Roger scribbled down the information, Mercedes was sure to interject, "We *are* in separate rooms."

The lumberjack looked up and grinned, "Sure ya are," and then glanced at the clock on the wall and spoke to Nick. "'Kay, it's 4:43 now. I can get what you need and be at the motel by nine. How's that?"

"Perfect. Thanks Roger."

"Don't thank me yet."

Nick smiled and then pulled out his wallet, "What's the damage?"

The bartender gave Nick another one of his blasé looks, slowly closed his eyes and shook his head. "Put that away."

"No." Nick chuckled and affirmatively said, "I'm going to pay for our drinks."

"No you're not, they're already paid for. Now, get outa here. I'll see you at nine."

With that, Nick pushed his wallet back into the seat of his jeans and left the bar.

CHAPTER TWENTY-SIX

With dark-shaded glasses like Will Smith and his rookie sidekick on their way to kick some alien-scum ass, Lurch and the weasel marched into the luxurious lobby and approached the desk. Although the large room was filled with people, mainly businessmen and women, it was relatively quiet and the loud tapping on the marble floor from the quick-paced alien hunters, sounded as if the secret service had just entered the hotel. The weasel, who had to walk a bit faster to keep up with his taller partner carried a black briefcase.

After visiting the Boris Lab where a quick scan of Number Nine's memory yielded no trace of Nicholas Chadwick, Travis Thorndale discovered that the man had reserved and paid for a room here at the Ramada. On their way over, Patterson had reluctantly let Thorndale drive so he could go over the company file on Chadwick. Viewing the contents of the CD on his laptop, Patterson learned a great deal about this Nicholas Chadwick and was extremely fond of his iceman days. As he studied the file he became more and more convinced that a man like Chadwick wouldn't make a mistake like using a credit card, that could be easily tracked, to check himself into the hotel. Nevertheless, this was their only lead.

Almost in unison, the tapping stopped as the two men stood in front of the counter.

"May I help you?" A kind looking clerk dressed in a white shirt, dark brown dress coat and matching bow tie stood behind the counter and smiled at the odd-looking pair.

"We'd like a room, please." Patterson tried to look friendly.

"Do you have a reservation?" The clerk tried not to, but couldn't keep from staring at the scarred face before him.

"No." Patterson rasped.

"Just a moment."

The clerk looked down and began to type, but before he got very far, in a slightly higher pitched voice than his towering partner, the weasel-faced man interrupted. "We need something on the eighteenth floor."

Without raising his head, the clerk asked thoughtfully, "Oh, have family or friends up there?"

"No." Thorndale replied quickly and without thinking.

The clerk lifted his eyes and looked at the weasel, whose peculiar grin only added to the bizarre request. He sensed something strange about the two men, but wasn't quite able to put a finger on it. Perhaps it was just little bits of everything: the corny way in which they had marched into the lobby, the spooky features of the big man's face, the fact that neither one of them removed their sunglasses. Nevertheless, he smiled again and resumed his typing, but as before was quickly halted, this time by the taller man. With a deep rasp and a fake smile, he said, "We want the room next to 1824."

Thorndale turned, looked over the top of his sunglasses at Patterson, and imagined thumping the big man's head, with his finger for being so obviously stupid. He turned back just in time to see the clerk looking up curiously. The clerk asked, "Any particular reason?"

Beneath their shades, the Blues Brothers stared back in silence as the clock ticked. Patterson realized—a bit too late—that he had phrased his request poorly and didn't quite know how to recover. Thorndale's mind raced, wondering how his big friend was going to answer, then after what felt like an exceptionally long period of time, Lurch finally rasped with a simple, "No."

Sensing something was wrong, but not knowing what, the clerk looked down, hit a few more keys and then stated, "I'm sorry gentlemen, but were are completely full." He looked up hesitantly. His attempt at smiling was poor and came across half-heartedly. Neither of the two men smiled back and after another second of silence, Lurch insisted, "Look again."

The clerk swallowed hard and tilted his head down once more. After strumming the keyboard again, he shook his head and reaffirmed his previous statement. The look in the man's eyes suggested that he expected to be grabbed by the neck, pulled over the counter and then beaten to a bloody pulp. In fact this was exactly what Lurch wanted to do, but somehow he kept himself restrained. Doing his best to stay calm, Lurch gave the clerk a transparently fake smile and turned away.

After leaving the lobby, the dynamic duo found the elevator, made their way up to the eighteenth floor and then straight on to room 1824. Although the room had already been paid for, there was no evidence that Nicholas had actually checked in yet. As a matter of fact the evidence suggested the contrary. The original plan, if one could even call it a plan, was to get a room on the same floor, perhaps, the room next door and then wait until Nick and hopefully the bitch showed up. Unfortunately, that was no longer an option. So, now it was on to plan *B*, but just as with plan *A*, there really wasn't a plan B.

Holding his Glock in his right hand, Lurch pressed an ear up to the solid oak door while the briefcase toting weasel stood behind him, grasping his own gun, and nervously glancing up and down the quiet hall. After a few seconds of hearing nothing but silence, Patterson rapped on the door. There was no answer. A moment later he knocked again and rasped, "Room service." Still there was no response.

The big man stepped back from the door and looked at the Weasel who shrugged his shoulders in return. Next, Patterson moved to the neighboring door, 1822 and knocked on it. Just before his second knock, a young female voice floated though the doorjamb, around the door. "Who is it?"

Like a young child about to do something very naughty, Patterson grinned mischievously and once again, rasped, "Room service."

"I didn't request anything from room service," the unseen woman replied. As the door handle turned, Patterson moved his gun behind his back and with his evil face, tried to smile warmly.

The door opened inward and a young soft-looking brunette peeked through the crack. "What do you got?" She grimaced at the evil-looking bellhop.

She couldn't have been any older than twenty-four or twenty-five and wore a short pink, silk bathrobe. The length of her hair was hard to tell, as it had been pulled up off her shoulders and fastened behind her head. Patterson's smile uncontrollably morphed into an evil grin as he reared back and slammed hard into the door, knocking the young woman back onto the blue carpet.

Still charging, Patterson dexterously twirled his gun around and pounded the butt of it hard into the young woman's skull. Her head spun violently and her eyes closed as a small trickle of blood oozed from her temple. Now inside the room, the weasel stuck his head out into the empty hall, looked left and right, then closed and locked the door. He moved from the door to the girl, set the briefcase down, knelt over her petite body, and placed two fingers on her delicate neck. Relieved after finding a pulse, he looked up at Patterson and accused, "You almost killed her."

"Awe." Patterson looked mockingly depressed.

Thorndale gave Patterson a curious look, shook his head and then grunted as he said, "Here, help me get her to a chair so we can tie her up."

Patterson watched in amusement as the weasel strained to lift her. Finally, Patterson holstered his gun, moved Thorndale aside, bent over and easily removed her from the floor. Once they had her securely tied to a chair and gagged, Thorndale filled a small plastic cup full of tap water and splashed it in her face. She coughed, spat and came to. For a minute she seemed a bit dazed, as if she didn't know where she was, but then her eyes found Patterson's evil face and she began to tremble with fear.

"Who else is here with you?" the demon rasped.

"She can't answer you Sherlock. She has gag in her mouth." Thorndale shook his head and rolled his eyes.

Lurch shot an evil glare over to the weasel and was half tempted to blow the little man's head off, but kept his composure. Looking back at the girl, he repeated his question. With tears streaming down her face, she shook her head.

Her trembling increased and she began to sob as Patterson softly pressed the muzzle of his gun against her temple. "We're going to remove your gag now," he whispered, "and if you would like to live and see tomorrow you'll be as quiet as a little tiny mouse. Understand?"

Fearfully, she nodded.

Patterson gestured at the weasel, who reached behind her head and loosened the gag which fell, first onto her chin, and then down around her neck. Quiet whimpers escaped her as she did her best to remain silent. Holding his gun, Patterson cracked his neck, moved backward a couple of steps and sat on the edge of the bed. He smiled wickedly, put his gun away and said, "We don't want to hurt you. We just need to use your room for a while. Now I have to know…who are you staying with here?"

Sniveling, the young woman hesitated and then said, "My husband."

The lie was obvious and it infuriated Patterson. For some time he just stared at her then finally he pushed up a contemplating chin and leaned to the right, looking over the back of her chair. After getting a good look at her hands, he stood up, leaned in close and whispered, "Don't you know, it's not nice to lie."

With his mouth next to her ear and her panic-stricken eyes nervously shifting over his shoulder, Patterson reached down, softly took hold of her naked wedding band finger and asked, "Where's your ring?" With that, he slowly bent it back, shooting a small jolt of pain into her arm. The pain intensified and just before she screamed, he let go, then moved back to the edge of the bed.

"Now, I ask you again, who are you here with?"

Terrified of being caught in another lie, and believing the man had meant what he said about not wanting to hurt her, she confessed, "No one."

"No one?" Patterson raised his eyebrows, turned his head a little to the right and appeared to be checking her face for lies.

"No one. I'm here on business." She insisted.

Nodding his head, convinced of her sincerity, Patterson looked at Thorndale and smiled. "Put the gag back on her."

As Thorndale refastened her gag, Patterson stood up and removed a pillow from beneath the bedspread.

"Here." He offered.

Puzzled, the weasel accepted it and then asked, "What's this for."

Patterson's grin went from wicked to pure evil as he said, "I'm going to help you get over your little problem."

"My problem?"

"Yeah… Killing is *not* as hard as you think."

Suddenly, Thorndale understood. His eyes opened wide and he dropped the pillow. With the patience of a good coach, Patterson removed his gun and pointed it at Thorndale's head. "Now I would hate to have to shoot you like this. No doubt, it would disturb the other guests, but I guarantee you that one of us *is* going to fire a gun here in the next minute. Either you are going to pick up that pillow, wrap it around your gun, place it to the young lady's head and pull the trigger or…"

Gripped in fear, Thorndale repeated, "Or?"

"Or, I'm going to paint the walls with your brains." Patterson looked around and nodded as if he were trying to imagine the new look on the room.

All of a sudden the young woman realized her own fate and her muffled screams escalated as she struggled frantically to get loose.

Patterson didn't know why he was going through so much trouble for a weasel like Thorndale. He sure didn't deserve it. Perhaps, Patterson just felt sorry for the little man. In any case, Thorndale would be a better man because of it and he would no doubt be very thankful one day.

Uneasily keeping his eyes fixed on the gargoyle, Thorndale gradually reached into his coat and withdrew his gun, then slowly squatted to the floor and reclaimed the pillow. As if in some kind of depressed trance, he shifted his gaze from the madman and looked at the young woman. Her terror-stricken eyes met his and through horror-struck tears, she dismally pleaded for her life.

With beads of sweat appearing around his brow, he swallowed hard and reluctantly placed the pillow against the side of her face. Inevitably, she tried to pull away, but he simply pressed it in harder until finally he had her head firmly pinned to her shoulder. Patterson's smile widened as Thorndale's anxiety grew. Little by little, Thorndale lifted the gun, inching it ever closer to the damsel's pillow-covered head.

Thorndale was moving painstakingly slow and even though Patterson found the woman's whimpers exhilarating, this was no time to be a pussy. "Hurry up, I'm not going to wait forever," Patterson commanded.

Finally the muzzle of Thorndale's gun lightly touched the pillowcase and still he hesitated.

After what seemed like forever, with Thorndale holding the gun next to the pillow, instead of pressing it in harder and pulling the trigger, he relaxed his arm, lowered it to his side and admitted, "I can't."

Obviously aggravated at the exceedingly slow-moving pace of events, Patterson offered his young apprentice motivation. "I'm going to count to ten Thorndale and if you haven't killed her by then, I'll blow your head off."

Patterson smiled lovingly and after a brief pause, began to count. "One…"

Thorndale looked as if he just might cry, and with a trembling hand he raised the gun back up to the pillow.

"Two…"

Thorndale took a deep breath and shut his eyes tight.

"Three…"

He had always known that Biotronics wasn't completely innocent of murder, but up until now he had never thought that he would be the one to have to pull the trigger. Thorndale was a lot of things, but a killer wasn't one of them and as he pondered his position, he was sure that he wouldn't be able to go through with it.

"Four…"

He imagined himself turning the gun on Patterson, but couldn't get past the image of his own head exploding as Patterson pumped a lead round into it. He thought about throwing the gun down and trying to make a run for it, but was certain that Patterson would pick him off before he got out of the room.

"Five…"

Thorndale's breathing deepened as he tried to concentrate on the task at hand.

"Six…" Patterson shook his head in exasperation, and then rattled off in quick succession, "Seven, eight."

Urgently, Thorndale opened his eyes and peered at the woman who now had her own eyes tightly shut, and instead of trying to scream, appeared to be praying. Thorndale imagined what Hell would be like as he soured his face, reluctantly pressed the gun hard into the pillow and filled his lungs all the way up.

"Nine." The tone in Patterson's voice was filled with expectancy. With a sweaty palm, Thorndale tightened his grip on the gun.

Several trickles of liquid fret rolled down Thorndale's face as Patterson firmly and disappointedly announced, "Ten," but just before Patterson splattered the little man's brains across the room, Thorndale surprised himself and fired his gun. Feathers shot into the air and floated softly downward. The shot was louder than the grinning Patterson would have liked, but he believed it was manageable. Thorndale stood wide-eyed and shaking, still pressing the muzzle hard into the limp pillow. The praying woman was now silent as bright red splatter marks covered the wall. For a second, the room was dead silent, but the silence was soon interrupted by the eerie sound of blood droplets, dripping onto the carpet. The blood flowed from her blown apart skull, onto her lifeless body and accumulated into a puddle on the light blue carpet below.

Patterson breathed in deep, nodded proudly and then holstered his gun. Smiling like a proud father, he walked over to the statue-like weasel, patted him on the back and relieved him of his weapon. After placing the man's gun on the bed, he went over to the kitchenette, and opened the half-sized fridge. Still trembling, Thorndale continued to hold the pillow against the corpse's face as Patterson remarked on how hungry he was. Slowly, Thorndale released the pillow and in a trancelike state moved to the bed.

"What do you think about ordering pizza?" Patterson asked as the refrigerator door swung closed.

The weasel didn't answer, but instead stared lifelessly at an inconsequential spot on the bed.

Patterson went to the phone, opened the phonebook and looked up the number to Pizza Hut. After ordering a large pizza and a couple of two liters of Coca-cola, Patterson walked over to his catatonic partner and snapped his fingers twice.

"Come on, snap out of it. You've got work to do." After Thorndale offered no response, Patterson gave him a little nudge and then repeated, "C'mon."

Thorndale looked up and his glazed eyes met the madman's. Patterson grinned, "That's it," then he raised his eyebrows innocently and continued, "It's just not that bad. Now come on; let's get to work." With that Patterson walked past the corpse to the door, grabbed the briefcase and turned around. Unfortunately for Thorndale his eyes, once again, were focused back on the same spot on the bed.

"This just won't do," Patterson muttered as he brought the briefcase over and set it down at the edge of the bed. Slightly aggravated, he moved past Thorndale, reached beneath the bedspread and pulled out another pillow. "What we need here is a little motivation." Thorndale's eyes followed Patterson's hand as it reached through his line of sight and snagged his gun, still lying on the bed. Next, Patterson brought the pillow up next to the weasel's face.

Startled, the weasel jerked away and looked up curiously at Patterson. "What are you doing?"

Patterson grinned and raised his eyebrows. "Hey, there you are. Now, we've got work to do."

"What are you doing with the pillow?"

Patterson tossed the pillow back up to the top of the bed and in a rather serious tone said, "See, the thing is if you're not going to do what you're supposed to, then you're of no use to me, and to be totally honest, I didn't really want to work with you in the first place."

The weasel blinked, swallowed and nodded in quick succession, then said, "Yeah, okay, right," as he got up and moved to the briefcase. He picked it up and doing his best to keep his eyes off the corpse, carried it across the room and placed it onto the table. After quickly thumbing through the combination, he pulled it open, reached inside and pulled out a slim black box. It was about as long and thin as a CD jewel case but only half has wide. Along with a place to plug in a phone cord, it featured a thin blue wire, which came out of the bottom and connected to something somewhere inside the briefcase. Thorndale did a bit of fiddling with the device and then reached for the telephone.

Patterson watched as the weasel disconnected the phone cord from the base of the phone and then plugged it into the little black box. Next, Thorndale removed a miniature laptop, which was what the other end of the blue wire was connected to. As Thorndale worked, his energy and spirits rose. He pulled the screen of the laptop up and hit the power button. The display lit up and the software loaded almost immediately. Thorndale hit a couple of keys and then waited as a dial tone, followed by a succession of beeps indicated that the computer was dialing a four-digit number. The screen displayed an image of a telephone with the number 1824 blinking beside it. Just after the last beep-tone ended, the screen went blue and the word *negotiating* in large yellow type began to blink in the center. After a moment or two the word *negotiating* was replaced by the word *connected* and then, in a flash, the screen changed again. Another image of a telephone with an interactive console and the non-blinking word, *listening* dominated a pale blue screen. The weasel ran his finger over the track pad and navigated the little arrow to a volume control on the console. He set the volume at maximum and then looked up at Patterson, who reassuringly patted him on the back and then moved to the window. The machine had dialed into the next room and was now acting as a listening device. The moment anyone entered the room, Patterson and Thorndale who hear it.

Forty-five minutes later, after the weasel had used the Internet to find out, among other things, the make, model, and license number to the car that Chadwick had rented, the dynamic duo sat on the bed finishing their pizza. Thorndale was fine as long as his eyes stayed off the dead woman's body. However, when they didn't and he inadvertently caught a glimpse of her corpse, he had to fight to keep from regurgitating his food, and oddly, it took all the energy he had to keep from looking. Patterson, on the other hand had no problem looking at the young woman and in between bites of pizza, covered in bright red tomato sauce he even commented on what a fine job the weasel had done, taking into consideration of course, this was his first kill and all.

After swallowing the last bite of his pizza, Patterson pulled out his cell-phone and dialed the security team at the Boris Lab. Before he left, he had informed them to keep an extra sharp eye out tonight, for he suspected that *Nicholas soon would be there*, a pun that no one laughed at.

John Botelli, head of security answered the call. He was a tall man with a large build and neatly groomed, dark black hair. "Hello?"

"John it's Greg. How is everything?"

"It's quiet."

Moving the drapes aside and looking through the window at the setting sun, Patterson nodded. "It's early."

"Yeah well, it's still quiet."

Patterson turned around and looked at the weasel, who was on his own cell-phone. "Keep me posted."

"We can handle whatever happens here," John replied.

"Right." Shaking his head Patterson pressed end, slipped the phone back into his pocket and whispered, "Iceman," then waited for the weasel to end his call.

Thorndale sprang up and ran to the desk. After fumbling around for a pencil and a piece of paper, he began to scribble. "Yeah. Got it, thanks."

"Who was that?"

The weasel looked up, smiled at his frowning partner and replied, "We've been sent on a wild goose chase."

Patterson narrowed his eyes and cocked his head. "What are you talking about?"

"Someone logged onto the company website earlier this afternoon and downloaded all of the building plans for the lab. The boys were able to do a reverse trace and pinpoint the server and determine that whoever did it did it wirelessly."

"Chadwick!" Patterson snarled.

"There's more. They were able to continue the search and locate the wireless tower that Chadwick was using. A couple of the boys were sent out to canvas the area and..." Thorndale's smile widened as he did a short drum roll pause. "Chadwick's Mustang was just spotted at the Lamp Light Motel, just two blocks from the Lab." The weasel's smile changed as if to say we got him.

"I knew it!" Seeing no other way to release his frustration, Patterson kicked the corpse. Thorndale watched as the woman's stiffened body fell over and crumpled onto the carpet. Her death had been completely in vein. Chadwick had never planned to come here. While Thorndale stood in a half daze, unconsciously shaking his head, Patterson quickly cleaned up the electronics and repacked the briefcase. After eliminating any traces of them being there, Patterson tugged Thorndale out into the hall and locked the door.

Thorndale quickly snapped out of his daze as Patterson shoved the briefcase into his gut, then the two of them made a brisk walk toward the elevator.

CHAPTER TWENTY-SEVEN

"I love you too, Peaches and I'll be home soon. I promise."

After a long overdue heart to heart with Lisa, Nick hung up the phone, leaned back in his chair and interlaced his fingers behind his head. He gazed across the room at the white plastered wall and thought about the night to come and the answers, as well as the dangers that might be found beneath the Boris Lab. From the very first moment he had discovered that the Boris Lab was built over the top of an abandoned subway station, the wheels in his head had been turning. The biggest question on his mind was how to get down there without being caught. Jumping the twelve-foot high, barbed wire fence and waltzing across the parking lot without being seen, just wasn't going to happen. And even if somehow he were able to get over (or maybe through) the fence and onto the lot without being seen, how would he manage getting into the building? Once inside, there were bound to be security cameras and the odds were pretty good that a hidden elevator wouldn't be too clearly marked.

He unclasped his hands and leaned forward as he thought. According to the information he obtained from the Internet, the old subway station had been very large. Perhaps Biotronics didn't use all the space available. Nick turned to the desk, fired up his computer and pulled up the blueprints of the old subway station from his hard drive. Just as he remembered, the area was huge. Nick began to envision how one might use it to build an underground hideaway. They would probably start with the structure above ground and work their way downward, then spread out a little. Nick tilted his head and squinted his eyes. He ran his finger just above the surface of the screen along the tracks coming and going, then pulled up an image of the current city blueprints for the surrounding area. After layering the images, one on top of the other, he was able to see that several of the old tracks ran directly beneath some of the newer roads. One road in particular, ran just outside of the imaginary underground hideaway. After hitting a few more keys, he found out that an underground sewage system ran parallel with and directly below the road. With any luck there may be a way to get from the sewage canal into the old underground train tunnel and then into the lab.

Nick sat for a few more minutes thinking, then shut off his computer and went to Mercedes' room. After knocking and hearing her yell that it was open, Nick turned the handle and stepped inside. To his surprise, Mercedes was dressed in sweats, on the carpet, doing the splits. Somehow, her forehead was touching her knee and both of her hands were firmly gripping the toes of her right foot. The sight of her sent pain into his thighs and sparked sexual attraction in his soul.

"You okay?" Nick said with a look of confusion.

"Yeah, why?" Mercedes' soft brown hair fell across her face as she tilted her head and looked up at him.

Nick just pointed as his head bobbed back and forth and then shook left to right. He finally lowered his hand and said, "Never mind."

Mercedes tossed an angelic smile at him and said, "I'm just getting ready for tonight."

"Yeah…" Nick bobbed his head again and sucked air through his teeth. "Well…" He cautiously moved to the desk, purposely standing directly behind her, out of her line of sight. "I wanted to talk to you about that."

To his amazement, while still on the floor, doing the splits, Mercedes turned the upper half of her body around and gave Nick a curious look.

As Nick opened his mouth getting ready to speak, Mercedes glared and he said nothing. He looked at the carpet, cleared his throat and then looked up sheepishly. After an awkward silence, he finally blurted out, "Do you have to go tonight?"

In a flash Mercedes was on her feet. "What do you mean, do I have to go?" Nick stood silently as she peered at him with icy eyes of fire, the rage inside growing. "Are you crazy? What are you—some kind of male dominating chauvinist pig who thinks that women can't hold up under pressure?"

Looking like the frightened puppy in the window, Nick cautiously shook his head.

"Of course I have to go!" In an elevated voice, Mercedes finally answered the question and then turned it around on him. "What would you say if I asked you the same thing?"

Nick quickly shifted his eyes searching for a response. He wasn't a male chauvinist pig, was he? No! He just knew how dangerous it was going to be tonight and how hard it would be for one person to get down there and back alive, much less two. Finally he spoke. "I was just thinking that…"

"Well don't!" Mercedes snarled angrily and spun away. The tone in her voice suggested tears. This took Nick by surprise, but instinctively he stepped forward and gently placed a comforting hand on her shoulder. She breathed in deep and held back her tears.

Curiously, Nick asked, "Wanna talk about it?"

Mercedes didn't respond and after a few moments she could no longer keep her eyes dry. Nick reached up with his free hand and grabbed her other arm, getting ready to turn her toward him, and then said softly, "It's okay."

"Is it?" She spun around with tears streaming down her cheeks and backed away. "Is it really okay?"

Before Nick could answer she spoke again. "Tell me Nick, what part of this crazy twisted freak show do you think is okay…huh?"

Nick could see that she didn't really want the answers; she just needed to vent the questions.

In her excitement the tears stopped and she began to use hand gestures as she spoke. "Is it okay for people without memories to go around reading other peoples minds? What about almost being chopped up alive by Frankenstein's brother? Huh? Is that okay? And tell me, Nick," she slowed down and began to tear up again, "is it okay to meet the man of your dreams only to find out that his heart belongs to some woman who died God knows how many years ago?"

The room was silent for a moment and then Nick spoke. "Eight." He swallowed hard and nodded his head. "She died eight years ago."

Mercedes raised a trembling hand to her forehead and began to calm down. "I'm sorry." She shook her head and wiped her tears. After letting out a *how stupid am I* laugh, she moved back and leaned against the dresser.

"It's just so crazy. To be honest, I don't even want to be involved in this, this, whatever this is." She looked toward the window and continued. "Nothing would make me happier than to wake up in my bed tomorrow and find out that this whole thing was a dream."

Nick was confused. If Mercedes truly felt this way, then why did she insist on going tonight? Then as if she was the one who could read minds she opened her mouth and with two words answered his question. "My dad." She chuckled and shook her head. "Man! What would he think of me if he could see me like this?"

Nick pulled out the chair and sat down, unknowingly giving her what she'd needed all her life, but had never had—someone who'd listen. He found out just how great her father was and how insignificant she was. Before long he began to understand. All of her life she had lived in the shadow of what she believed was the greatest man who ever lived. Unfortunately, he never offered her one kind word. He never told her the words *good job* or that he was proud of her or even that he loved her. As the floodgates of her emotions opened, Nick couldn't help but think about the relationship with his own daughter and wondered what kind of father she thought he was.

Mercedes' biggest decisions in life had been based on what she felt would please her father. In her eyes, everything she had ever done had fallen short of his minimum expectations. With new tears flooding her face and running onto her neck, she moved to the edge of the bed and sat down.

"After I failed at the academy," she swallowed hard and with empty eyes, looked at Nick, "I opened Atwater Investigations, hoping that somehow I could make up for it. But I could never get the damn thing off the ground. My dad keeps sending me money, but," she shook her head, grinned and looked at the carpet. "See, every time things get a little too difficult, I bail out." Suddenly a look of determination filled her eyes and she glared at Nick. "And I'm not going to do that this time!"

Nick wanted to tell her that she didn't need her father's approval, that she was a wonderful person with or without it. The odds were pretty good that no matter what she did, she would never get his approval. Nick's heart went out to her and he moved closer, but stayed silent and continued to listen.

"When Alex first ran into my office and I decided to help him, I thought that this might just be the break I was looking for. I knew he couldn't pay me, but I thought that I could make a name for myself if I solved it. But then I began to realize what a stupid idea that was. Even if I can solve it, who would believe it?"

"The worst part about it is, with all my zeal and determination I promised that I won't turn my back on him; that I won't give up. Damn it, I have to go down there tonight. Alex is out there somewhere and he's only got one friend in the world, me! He's counting on me."

Mercedes looked up, licked the salt off her lips and forced a smile. Surprisingly, Nick was squatting in front of her, and his beautiful brown eyes were just inches from hers. With his right hand he softly reached up, wiped a single tear from her left eye, and smiled. "It'll be okay...I promise." The back of his fingers softly caressed downward, along the side of her cheek, and then stopped next to her chin. His strong fingers gently took hold of it as he looked sternly into her eyes. "We will find Alex." She couldn't remember ever hearing someone speak with as much confidence before and for a moment the universe melted away as she gazed, lost in the strength of his unwavering stare. Then, as if being pulled by gravity they both slowly leaned toward each other.

With their lips only centimeters apart several loud gunshots echoed from outside and prevented the would-be kiss. Instantly, Nick pulled Mercedes to the floor and hovered over her, covering his head.

The rat-a-tat-tat continued and sounded as if it was coming from just outside the door. Nick stayed low realizing that sooner or later a bullet and probably more would find them. However, as the firing continued, he noticed that nothing in the room was shattering. Cautiously, he slowly raised his head and looked up at the un-shattered window, the unbroken door and the perfectly intact room. The firing stopped. His mind raced for a moment and then it clicked, the shooting had taken place two doors down, in his room. Staying low, he hurried across the carpet to the base of the window and peeked over the edge just in time to see Mr. Ugly from the church and another man disappear into his room. In the parking lot the Mustang looked more like a ton of Swiss cheese than an automobile. The windows were shattered and all four tires were flattened. Nick thought about the rental company.

"Damn!" He whispered as he looked back into the room at Mercedes, who was now crouching next to the bathroom door and waiting. The look in his eyes told her that they weren't going out through the front door and since neither one of them had guns they weren't going to hold up inside the room either.

As Nick was squatting his way back across the room, a light bulb went on inside Mercedes' head and she disappeared into the bathroom. Nick followed behind and entered the restroom just as Mercedes was opening the little window over the top of the commode. After helping her, Nick squeezed his way through and tumbled onto the concrete drainage area behind the motel.

Meanwhile, Patterson and Thorndale had completed a quick walk-through of Nick's room and were briskly on their way back to the front desk. Angrily, Patterson flung the door open, walked around the desk, stepped over the corpse and took another look at the register. After whispering, "separate rooms," he hurriedly ran out of the office toward the second unit.

Now peeking around the corner of the motel into the parking lot, Nick and Mercedes spotted the Corolla. Except for a couple of ricochet-created dents, it appeared to be okay. Just as Nick was inching forward, trying to ascertain where Mr. Ugly was, another set of gunshots went off. Instinctively, he covered his head and ducked, but quickly fought the urge and looked around the corner. Mr. Ugly and his shorter sidekick partner were now firing into Mercedes' room. Nick pulled his head back around the corner, grabbed her hand and whispered, "Get ready! Were going to run to the Corolla," then waited for the gunshots to stop. Mercedes returned a look of apprehension, shook her head and opened her mouth to speak, but it was too late. The gunshots had ceased and Nick leaned forward just as Mr. Ugly was kicking in the door. The moment the two men went into the room, he tugged on Mercedes and they ran across the lot, toward the Corolla. Crouching low, Nick pulled open the driver's side door and ushered Mercedes in, then followed behind.

The Corolla was directly across from Mercedes' motel room and parked nose first, up against a cinder block wall.

Keeping his head below the headrest, Nick whispered to his slouching partner, "Give me the keys."

Mercedes looked back awkwardly and replied, "I tried to tell you, but you pulled me across the parking lot before I had a chance. I don't have them."

"You don't have them?" Nick looked confused and slightly concerned.

With a worried look, Mercedes widened her eyes and rattled her head. "I don't have them. They're back in the room."

Nick shifted his eyes in thought and confidently whispered, "Shit," then bent his head beneath the steering wheel and began to study the wiring.

Nervously waiting while Nick worked, Mercedes watched her room through the passenger's side mirror. Before long the phony Agent Young, gun in hand, stepped across the threshold and anxiously looked over the parking lot. At that very moment, Nick tugged on a handful of wires and shook the Corolla. The lump in Mercedes' throat grew and she found it impossible to swallow the build up of saliva resting at the far back of her mouth.

The car shook again and a loud thud came out from out from under the steering column. The phony Agent young quickly turned his head and looked directly at the Toyota. Mercedes wanted to tell Nick to stop, but found herself unable to speak. Agent Young took a step toward the car and paused, then looked around the lot one more time before running to the corner of the building out of Mercedes' view. Not knowing was unbearable, so being as careful as possible, she shifted her body and peered between the seats, through the back window just in time to see him disappear beyond the stucco wall. Just then the car started and, at the same time the second man stepped out of the room. At first he just looked curiously at the Corolla, but then acknowledgment found his eyes and he raised his gun.

Nick flew out from beneath the steering wheel and told Mercedes to please return her tray to its upright position and observe the fasten your seat belt sign as he shifted into reverse and burned rubber, straight toward the little man.

Thorndale hesitated as the backend of the car raced toward him like a charging bull, but at the very last minute he dove out of the way, landing belly first on the walkway and let the Toyota to crash into the stucco wall. For a second, while Nick was shifting gears, the trunk of the car was inside of Mercedes' room. Then another dark cloud of burnt rubber filled the air as the car pealed away and headed for the street.

Even while the tires were still gaining traction, Patterson emerged from the far end of the building, steadied himself and took careful aim at the fleeing Toyota. He squeezed off a round and hit the back window, causing it to explode into a million pieces. Less than an instant later the same bullet made its way through the windshield and the couple squeezed their eyes shut as fragments of glass shot in every direction. As Nick was turning the wheel and rounding the corner onto the avenue, Patterson took aim again and this time hit the back passenger's side tire.

"Gotcha!" He snarled under his breath as the car disappeared around the corner. The soles of his dress shoes smacked against the blacktop and the tail of his black coat flapped behind him as he ran toward the Camry, already parked out on the street. While he shifted into drive, narrow-mindedly focusing on the Corolla, Thorndale pulled open the passenger's door and jumped inside. Just ahead of them the crippled Corolla had made it to the end of the block, turned left and was driving out of view, beyond the brick wall of the Quickie Mart.

Patterson pinned the gas pedal to the floor. His tires spun in place for a half a second and sent their own bit of smog into the air. Then the Camry shot out into to the street, cutting off a Camaro and forcing it to swerve into oncoming traffic. Through the back window, Thorndale watched as the Camaro slammed, nose first into an oncoming Chevy.

With an evil grin on his face, Patterson turned the corner, expecting to see the Corolla just ahead, but to his surprise the road was empty. His grin faded into angry confusion as he carefully looked from side to side.

Just as Thorndale was in the middle of asking, "Where did he go?" Patterson spotted the tail end of the Corolla peeking out from the narrow area directly behind the Quickie Mart. Instinctively he immediately turned the wheel, causing the left front tire to just miss the driveway. With a thud, the car bounced up onto the six-inch high curb and all but slammed into the rear of the Corolla before coming to a stop. Patterson was out of the Camry before Thorndale even opened his door. Holding his gun with both hands and whispering the words, *Iceman*, Patterson cautiously but quickly approached the back of the car.

Keeping his eyes peeled for any movement from inside, he made his way around the backend and then along the driver's side of the car. At first it appeared that the car was abandoned, but then, just as he was passing the driver's side back door, Patterson was overcome with the eerie feeling that the Iceman was crouching low, getting ready to shoot. Impulsively, Patterson unloaded his gun into the car, shattering the rear and then the driver's window and all but destroying, both the driver's and passenger's seats from behind. Just as he cleared the shattered back window and got a good view of the empty front seats, he ran out of bullets.

While Patterson stood at the rear of the building reloading his gun and the nervous Quickie Mart owner dialed 911 from the counter near the front, Nick and Mercedes were tiptoeing their way through the recently stocked warehouse portion of the store. Holding the phone to his ear with his shoulder, the Indian owner reached into the cabinet below the register and withdrew his already loaded shotgun, then squatted below the counter. With a fresh supply of ammo, Patterson and Thorndale cautiously entered the back of the building. Less than fifteen feet away, Nick and Mercedes froze behind a couple of cardboard boxes labeled *Huggies* as the door squeaked open and light poured into the room.

Patterson took a brief look around the dark, box-filled room and then headed straight for the double doors that lead into the front of the store. The weasel followed behind as Patterson exited the tiny warehouse and entered the seemingly empty storefront. The two men watchfully walked past the canned and bottled beer, candy bars and chewing gum on their way to the front door.

The Indian, now with his eyes tightly shut, feet flat on the floor, and knees in his chest, sat with his back up against the wall, hugging his gun and listening to dress shoes stepping across the tile floor. This would make the fourth violent crime here this month, two robberies, a drive-by and now this. He had purchased the gun just yesterday and hadn't yet had a chance to take it out and practice. Trembling, not knowing exactly what was happening, he began to whisper silent prayers.

The bell chimed as Patterson walked past the register and out through the front of the building. After seeing no sign of Nick or Mercedes, he turned around and looked back into the store at Thorndale, who was standing beside the counter, listening to the faint whispers coming from the other side. Patterson slowly walked back in, chiming the bell once more as Thorndale quietly pointed toward the register. Patterson looked at the vacant counter, heard the whispers and then glanced back at Thorndale.

Following a moment's contemplation, Patterson fired several shots into the length of the counter, hoping to hit whomever hid behind it. After the counter was full of lead, he noticed the spiral phone cord coming out of the wall unit and disappearing below. The tension on the cord changed and Patterson stepped up to the counter, peeked over the edge and marveled at his luck.

A man from India sat an the floor, hugging a shot gun, and right smack dab in the center of his head, where an Indian woman might have a red dot, was a hole made by one of his bullets. While he was admiring his handiwork, the sound of a boiling teapot filtered into the store from outside. Still leaning over the counter, he cocked his head and listened carefully, then stood up straight and took two steps toward the door. The whistling grew louder and then faded, louder and then faded, until finally he was able to make out what it was; the police were on their way.

With the snarl of a wild animal being chased away from its food, Patterson turned from the door, glanced at the phone cord one more time and then quickly retraced his steps through the store, to the Camry.

Three black and whites skidded around the corner, past the Camry, which appeared to be just driving by and stopped in front of the store. As Patterson and Thorndale drove by another set of police cars at the motel, Nick and Mercedes were catching their breath, less than a block away from the Quickie Mart.

"Looks like they found us." Mercedes said in between pants.

"Yeah, they're fast, like that. What time is it?"

"Five-forty five, why?"

"Roger."

Bent over, with her hands on her knees, Mercedes turned her head and looked curiously at Nick.

"He's planning on meeting us at the motel at nine, we need to get to a phone and call Uncle Bob's Tavern before he leaves."

"Right."

With that and still not quite having caught their breath, they both stood up straight and resumed their trek.

CHAPTER TWENTY-EIGHT

"Uncle Bob's."

"Yeah, is Roger there?"

"Speaking."

"Roger, it's Nick."

"Hey, what's up buddy?"

"Listen, we aren't going to be able to meet at the motel, tonight."

"Why, what happened?"

"It's a long story."

"Yeah, I bet. What'd you do?"

"What do you mean, what did I do." Nick looked blank-faced at Mercedes as he spoke.

"Well, you didn't tell a stupid redneck joke and try to make someone laugh and then shoot them in the throat, did you?"

"No." Nick looked away from Mercedes, narrowed his eyebrows and chuckled. "Wish I would have though, but I don't think Mr. Ugly laughs."

"Mr. Ugly?"

"It's a long story."

Roger drew out the word, "Okay," and after a short pause asked, "So, where're we going to meet?"

"Might as well meet right there where you're at."

Roger nodded as he doused his cigarette. "Same time?"

"Yeah."

"Cool, see ya then."

Nick returned the handset to the pay telephone and spoke to Mercedes. "He's going to meet us at the bar."

"'Kay. Same time?"

"Yeah."

Mercedes looked around at the busy avenue and bobbed her head. "So what do we do 'til then?"

Nick raised his eyebrows, slowly shook his head and nonchalantly replied, "I'm free."

Mercedes threw a fake smile his way.

Then, with a boyish charm that she hadn't seen from him, Nick asked, "How 'bout I buy you a drink?"

After a brief pause, Mercedes nodded and replied, "Yeah, good idea. I think I could use one right about now."

Nick smiled, turned back to the phone and thumbed through the yellow pages for the number to the local cab company. Less than an hour later, they were sitting in a quiet booth, at Uncle Bob's Tavern, sipping on mixed drinks.

Meanwhile, at the Boris Lab, Patterson sat across from Thorndale fixatedly looking through the Iceman file. His coat lay draped over the back of a neighboring chair weighted down by his gun-filled shoulder holster. The sleeves of his dress shirt were rolled up and his hair was uncharacteristically messy, making him look even more monster-like than usual. Thorndale could see the rage inside him growing with every click of the mouse and was sure that sooner or later the madman was going to explode. Thorndale had tried to slip off to the water cooler or the bathroom several times, but Patterson demanded that he stay put. Thorndale twiddled his thumbs as Patterson read, then suddenly, Patterson's face brightened and his demeanor changed as he whispered to himself, "A daughter?"

He leaned forward and began to read with anticipation as an evil smile slowly formed across his face. After a few more minutes of reading he pulled out his cell-phone and dialed Nick's home number in West Virginia.

On the third ring, Nick answered. "Hey, we're not in right now, but I can be reached by cell and if you need Lisa, she's staying with her aunt at 555-2003, thanks." *Beep.*

Patterson quickly scribbled down the number, hung up and redialed.

He sat silently as a middle-aged woman's voice came over the line. "Hello?"

Patterson's eyes grew wide as he listened for a minute and thought.

"Hello, who is this?"

Patterson pressed end and smiled, then grabbed his coat and commanded, "C'mon."

An hour later, while Patterson and Thorndale sat aboard the company jet, flying over Arizona on their way to West Virginia, and the company was doing a reverse trace on the number 555-2003, Nick and Mercedes were slow dancing across the wood planked floor of Uncle Bob's.

With her arms wrapped around his neck and his hands gently fastened to her hips, Mercedes whispered, "You're quite a dancer."

"Thanks, you're not too bad yourself."

Mercedes smiled as Nick softly but quickly turned them both around and then dipped her toward the floor. Gravity pulled her away from him and she looked up into those beautiful brown eyes just as the music stopped. A small group of admirers had gathered around them and began to clap as Nick, still leaning over her, carefully reeled her in and softly kissed her lips. The kiss was brief, but sent chills into both of them. Felling that old familiar tinge of guilt, Nick pulled her up, made sure she had her balance and then led her across the floor, back to their table.

"Something wrong?"

"No, I'm okay. You?"

"No."

For a minute or two they just sat there saying nothing and then Nick broke the silence. "So, do you have any kids?"

"No, do you?"

"Yeah, one. Her name's Lisa. She'll be turning fourteen this year."

Surmising that Allie was already on his mind, Mercedes offered, "I take it, she's Allie's daughter."

"Right."

Wanting to stay clear-headed for tonight, they had only had one mix drink and now Mercedes drank water while Nick nursed a beer. Mercedes looked down at her glass. "'Must be hard on her, losing her mother, like that."

Nick nodded and gazed up at the people on the dance floor "Yeah, but I think it's harder on her losing her father." his sipped his drink.

"Losing her father, what do you mean?" Mercedes looked confused.

"Well," Nick's eyes met hers, "I really haven't been there for her since her mother died. I've been too busy trying to figure out what really happened."

Sensing the sensitivity of the current conversation, Mercedes smiled warmly and softly changed the subject. "What's she like?"

Instantly, Nick's demeanor brightened, "She's amazing! She's brilliant. She's funny."

"Do you have a picture?"

"Yeah." Nick leaned forward and pulled out his wallet just as Roger walked in the door.

Nick handed her the photo as Roger approached the table. "Hey guys."

"Nick looked at his watch and commented, "You're early."

"Yeah, I know, ahead of schedule." The big man grinned with just a hint of conceit in his voice as he grabbed the top of a chair, twirled it around and straddled the seat resting his forearms on the back. "So what do ya got, pictures of the bad guy?"

Mercedes looked up and snarled, "Bite your tongue."

Roger raised his hands in defense as Nick said, "It's a picture of my daughter."

"Oh." Mr. Clean's eyes opened wide as he held out an oversized hand.

"She is cute. How old did you say she was?"

"Thirteen. She's my everything."

After admiring it for a few more seconds, Mercedes passed the photo to Roger, who also gazed at it for a second or two and then handed it back to Nick. "'Just about the same age as my daughter."

"Oh really what's her name?" Nick asked as he re-pocketed the photo.

"Ashley. She's almost fifteen. She lives in Santa Barbara with her mother." His naturally cheery face momentarily lost its warmth as he added, "I don't get to see her very often—once a month if I'm lucky. Her mother can be a real bitch sometimes." He tried to chuckle, but it came out fake.

Nick thought about Lisa and how fortunate he was to be able to see her whenever he wanted and then felt guilty for not spending as much time with her as he should have.

Mr. Clean lowered his voice and changed the subject. "The six o'clock news told me why we couldn't meet at the motel."

"Oh really?" Nick asked as he sipped his water.

"Yep. And so did the six-thirty news, and the seven o'clock news and the seven-thirty news, and I would be willing to bet that the eight o'clock news is running your piece right now."

"Wow, I didn't know the news ran every half hour out here."

"Normally, it doesn't." Mr. Clean laughed. "What in the world happened to that place?"

Nick put on his best innocent face. "I didn't do anything."

"Nothing?" Roger cocked his head and widened his eyes.

"All I did was check into the place," Nick shrugged his shoulders, "and do a little research on my computer."

"Well then who destroyed half the motel and shot up the parking lot?"

"Awe." Nick raised his eyebrows, lifted a finger and slowly nodded. "That would be Mr. Ugly."

"Mr. Ugly?"

Nick took in a deep breath and then affirmatively replied, "Yeah."

Roger looked confused as he slowly asked. "And…who is…Mr. Ugly?"

"Lurch's twin." Mercedes quickly interjected. Nick glanced her way with an affirmative face and held up his glass of water.

Roger looked as if he was becoming more confused by the second as he unrolled an unopened box of Marlboro's from his sleeve.

"Mr. Ugly. You remember—the guy I told you about from the church." Nick added.

Suddenly, a light bulb went on inside Roger's head. "Oh!" He stuck a stick between his lips as he asked, "Is he really that bad?"

Nick and Mercedes looked at each other for a moment, then turned back to Roger and simultaneously agreed, "Oh yeah!"

"Okay, so what's the plan, Stan?" Roger asked while lifting his eyebrows and lighting his cigarette.

"Did you bring what we need?"

"Yep, got it in the minivan." Roger tilted his head and grinned impishly.

"Great, let's go take a look."

The three of them stood up, made their way across the dimly lit tavern to the back door, and then out to the minivan parked in the far dark corner of the lot, behind the building.

They stood like shadowy hoodlums in the night, barely visible up against the black backdrop of the van as Roger inserted the key into the lock and opened the door. Two cardboard boxes with the words 26" stereo color television printed across each, sat on the carpeted floorboard of the mini van. Nick glanced at Roger who told him to go ahead and open one.

Nick stepped forward, pulled up on the cardboard flap and reached into the nearest box. He grabbed the fist gun he laid his hand on. It was a submachine gun. With eyes open wide, he shifted the gun to his left hand, reached back in the box and withdrew another. This one was a double barrel shotgun. With a gun filling up both hands, he bent forward and looked over the contents of the open box. Along with guns of every type, there were sticks of dynamite, grenades and even plastic explosives.

"Damn! All I asked for was a couple of handguns."

Roger scooted in, opened the second box, pulled out a .9mm Glock, and offered it to Nick, who had to put the shotgun back to accept it "I know." Roger grinned as Nick took the gun. "Look, I don't think it's a real good idea to be out here with all these guns in my van, so why don't we head on over to my place and get a game plan going?"

"Good idea." Nick nodded as he replaced the submachine gun into the box and then pulled the clip out of the handle of the Glock. After checking the rounds and with Roger's permission he slipped the gun into the inside pocked of his leather jacket and stood back while Roger pulled the door shut.

Roger lived twenty-five miles east of LA, in the relatively quiet suburb of Azusa, a city chiefly comprised of minorities, and on hot summer days while working in his front lawn, the huge, light-skinned Roger stood out like a sore thumb. He shared the small cream-colored home with his petite, live-in girlfriend, Margarita, who, as Roger put it spoke just enough English to support a perfect relationship. She was part Puerto Rican, part Hispanic and part unknown. Roger was convinced that it was this unknown part of her that drove him wild. On their way there Nick took advantage of the travel time to fill Roger in on what had happened at the motel and then at the Quickie Mart.

The headlamps of the van rounded the corner and came three quarters of the way down the block before turning up onto the concrete drive. With the engine still running, a black-silhouetted Roger got out, removed the padlock from the garage door and opened it, then returned to the van and drove up, inside. Following Roger's instructions, Nick got out of the van and found the long wooden hoe that was used to lock the garage door down from within. By the time Nick had finished securing the door, Roger and Mercedes had made it into the house where Roger was introducing the two ladies.

"And this," Roger gestured as Nick stepped across the threshold, from the garage into the kitchen, "This is the man I told you about, from the bar." Margarita, a sliver of woman with long dark hair, dark eyes and a beautiful cream-colored, olive complexion stood between Mercedes and Roger, wearing a white braided top and a long muddied-colored pleated skirt. As Nick put on his best *nice to meet you* face and began to wipe the bottom of his shoes onto the mat, Margarita began to tremble. Everyone stood silently and Nick froze as she placed her hands over her mouth below her watering eyes and slowly approached him. With the tears in her eyes growing, she removed her hands from her face and cupped them around Nick's cheeks. Not quite sure what was happening, but somehow able to feel the pain and fear inside her, Nick just stood there, warmly looking into the young woman's eyes, and wondered what was going to happen next.

After studying his face for what seemed like forever, she spoke. "You save me Roger life, dank you." Repeating the words, *thank you*, she bowed her head, grabbed his hands and kissed them over and over.

With Margarita's tear-filled face in his chest, an uncertain Nick softly stroked the back of her hair as he looked at Roger and wondered what kind of a tale she had been told. Roger smiled back awkwardly then turned to the fridge and tried to break the mood by asking if anyone wanted a beer.

Without turning away from Nick and Margarita, Mercedes held out her hand and Roger placed a cold can of Budweiser in it. After a few more awkward moments, Margarita finally let go and stepped back. She turned to Roger and Mercedes, smiled gracefully as she wiped her face, then disappeared down the hall. No one spoke, as Roger quietly handed a Budweiser to Nick and then cracked the top on his own.

Not sure he wanted to know, Nick asked, "What just happened?"

Roger leaned up against the counter, looked aimlessly across the room and replied, "Margarita's father drank a lot, and when she was twelve years old, he went out one night and never came home. The next day, she found out that he had gotten into a bar fight and was killed. She hates the bar and is paranoid that the same thing is going to happen to me one day."

Nick took a swig of his beer as he listened.

"I guess I shouldn't have told her what happened the other night, I don't know." The big man shrugged his shoulders and took a seat at the kitchen table. Nick and Mercedes joined him as he repeated the question he had asked earlier, in the bar, "So, what's the plan?"

Nick shook his head. "I'm not sure, all I know is that somehow I'm going to get into the Boris Lab and find out what's there."

Mercedes sat at the table to Nick's right and raised her eyebrows as she cleared her throat. Nick shook his head and rephrased his statement. "Mercedes and I are going to get into the Boris Lab and find out what's there."

"Excuse me?" Roger leaned forward and peered across the table at Nick. "And just how do you plan on doing that without any guns?"

"Roger?" Nick struggled.

"Yes Nick?" Roger raised his eyebrows and gave Nick the same nonchalant stare he had given him in the bar earlier.

"I can't have you go with me."

"Last time I checked, your weren't my father and I'm telling you, I'm going."

"Roger, you can't go! I can't take the chance. It's too dangerous. These guys play for keeps, and I have no idea what's down there."

"And it's not too dangerous for her?" Still leaning forward, staring at Nick, Roger lifted a curled finger from his beer and pointed at Mercedes.

"Hey, this is my case, I have to go." Mercedes chimed in. Nick glanced at Mercedes, looked back at Roger and shook his head in frustrating disbelief.

For a second all was quiet as the two men stared at each other, then a grin found its way to Roger's face as he leaned back in his chair, took a swallow of his beer and stated, "I really don't see where you have a choice in the matter, unless you want to go unarmed. Because as of right now those are my guns and wherever they go, I go."

Nick lifted his eyes and stared blank-faced at the wall cupboard behind Roger and said, "Fine," then shook his head and repeated, "Fine."

"Good, glad that's settled. Now, what's the plan?" Roger asked for the third time.

Nick sat silently for a minute trying to figure out who was more stubborn, Mercedes or Roger, then finally decided to forget it and go on. "Okay, *We* need to get into the Boris Lab, but I'm not sure how to do it. When I was looking over some city blueprints this afternoon, I found out that there are several sewage canals that parallel the old subway system. There might be a way to get from the sewage system into one of the old tunnels and then into the lab."

Roger scrunched his face and looked at Nick as if that was the stupidest thing he had ever heard.

Mercedes' eyes opened wide as she asked, "That's your plan?"

Nick quietly shrugged his shoulders and nodded as Mercedes continued, using hand gestures as she spoke. "We're supposed to crawl into the crap tank," She paused for a second, shifting her eyes, struggling to find the right word before continuing. "Blast...drill...or dig our way through *solid* concrete, into an old subway tunnel that *may or may not* be there, and then, if we're lucky, we might stumble across a secret underground laboratory that *may or may not exist*? And we're supposed to do all of this in the middle of the city without getting caught?" Mercedes paused, lowered her hands to the table and expectantly asked, "Is that your plan?"

Nick was amused by Mercedes' over-dramatized speech, but kept from chuckling and instead calmly asked, "You have a better idea?"

Being put on the spot wasn't easy and Mercedes didn't have another idea, much less a better one, but that didn't stop her from responding, "It sure isn't jumping into the local crap hole and searching for secrete passageways. That's for sure!"

Roger scrunched his eyebrows tightly together and looked down at the tabletop as he recalled the story Nick told in the van on their way over. "Wait a minute." Still looking down, he held a pointed finger into the air. "Nick, didn't you say that you were looking up this information while you were in the motel?"

"Yeah, why?"

Roger looked up, "Well you left your laptop there, didn't you?"

"Yeah." Nick answered curiously.

"Well, are you sure that Biotronics didn't get it? Because if they did-"

Nick interrupted, "If they did, then they'll be expecting me."

Mercedes cleared her throat.

Nick looked at her and corrected his mistake. "They'll be expecting us."

Roger looked at Nick with regret.

"Damn!" Nick said. Then still looking at Mercedes, he added, "Don't worry, it doesn't look like we're going to use the crap tank idea after all."

Mercedes just smiled softly and lowered her hands to her lap.

As the three of them sat in silence pondering the situation, a cheerful Margarita reentered the kitchen and asked if anyone was hungry.

"Starved!" Roger replied then looked back at Mercedes and Nick. "How 'bout you two?"

"Sure."

"Need some help?" Mercedes asked as she stood up from the table and approached Margarita. Margarita smiled graciously and declined the offer, but Mercedes insisted and before long the two ladies were preparing a late night dinner.

After grabbing a couple more beers from the fridge, Roger and Nick stepped into the garage to look over the guns and think up another idea. Margarita handed a block of cheese to Mercedes and began to cut up pieces of chicken.

"He es coot." Margarita smiled and quickly raised and lowered her eyebrows.

Mercedes smiled bashfully, "Yeah, he is."

"You es wife?"

As she began to grate the cheese a giggle escaped her, and she replied, "No. We're just friends."

Meanwhile out in the garage Nick picked up a Colt .45 automatic, looked at it for a moment and then placed it beside six other guns now piled together on the floorboard of the van. He shook his head and reached back into the box as he asked, "Where in the world did you get so many guns?"

As Nick pulled out an old Tommy gun from the 1920's Roger replied, "Well, nearly half of these are mine. I'm an avid collector. And most of the others come by way of old friends who *owe me*, but the really cool ones, like this one here," he paused long enough to reach into the box and pull out the last gun. It was an SIG-Petter, an awesome piece of metal and Roger was proud to hold it as he continued, "like this one here came from various people I've met while working in Uncle Bob's. I guess you could say it's just one of the many fringe benefits you get from owning a bar." The smile on Roger's face grew as he handed the gun to Nick and then unrolled the pack of Marlboros from his sleeve.

Nick looked at the gun for a moment, unimpressed, added it to the pile, then walked across the garage and took a seat in one of the two folding chairs facing the opened side door of the van. As the lumberjack was lighting up, Nick took a swig of his beer, stared at the semi-polished concrete floor, rested his elbows on his knees and firmly stated, "There's got to be a way to get down there!"

"There is." Roger replied confidently, while dangling a cigarette between his lips and waving a match through the air to extinguish it.

Nick's ears perked up and he raised his head in anticipation.

"We just haven't thought of it yet, that's all." Roger finished his thought.

Nick's eyes shifted up, over and then down before they ended up fixed on the same spot of the floor. Mentally picturing the images from his computer, Nick pulled out his Glock and despondently shook his head as Roger moseyed his way over and took the remaining seat. The two men thought in silence for the next fifteen minutes, as Roger puffed on his cancer sticks and Nick fiddled with his gun. Finally, Roger's voice broke the silence as he began to offer an idea. "Why don't we…" He paused, gazed back at the floor with wide eyes, took the last swallow of his beer and a long puff on his cigarette before he continued. "Why don't we make an anonymous phone call to the LAPD?" He turned and looked at Nick as he went on. "We can claim that we're terrorists or something and that we've just planted a bomb in the bottom floor of the Boris Lab." Nick slowly raised his elbows from his knees and met Roger's eyes as the big man continued with this harebrained idea. "Once the place is swarming with cops and all the security has been shut down we can sneak into the building and find the secret elevator." Roger's proud smile spanned from ear to ear as he waited to hear Nick say what a great idea it was.

Instead of saying *good idea*, Nick scrunched his face and looked at Roger as if to say that that was the stupidest thing he had ever heard. After a moment or two Roger blank-facedly asked, "What?"

Nick just shook his head, slowly lowered his elbows back onto his knees and said, "And you thought my idea was bad."

Roger sat there, dumbfounded for a second longer and then replied, "I'm serious."

Nick sat back up, quietly stared at Roger for a moment and then asked, "Are you feeling okay?"

Roger shifted puzzling eyes around the garage as Nick stood up and began to cross his path on his way to fetch another Budweiser.

"Wait." Roger held a nearly finished cigarette in front of him and somewhat unconfidently affirmed, "It could work."

Nick squinted his eyes, shook his half smiling face and thought, and then smiled wide as he offered, "Okay, why don't we run it past Mercedes then?"

"Fine." Roger agreed as he rose from his chair and followed Nick back into the house.

In the kitchen Margarita handed Nick plates and silverware while Roger explained his idea to Mercedes. Mercedes' bean-stirring hand began to slow and finally stopped as Roger asked, "So, what do you think?"

Mercedes completely let go of the wooden spoon, tilted her head to one side and then quickly snatched the freshly opened beer from Roger's hand. "I don't think you need any more to drink. It's obvious that the alcohol is seriously affecting the processing power of your brain," Mercedes said as she scrunched up her eyes curiously and then placed the can on the shelf above the stove. Roger stood speechless for a moment, and then looked over at Nick who was now politely sitting in one of the seats at the kitchen table. Nick offered Roger an innocent look of surprise and shrugged his shoulders, as if to say *who would have thought?* Roger regrettable shook his head, reached over the top of Mercedes, reclaimed his beer and made his way to the table across from Nick.

After a Mexican style dinner, the four of them found themselves in Roger's den thinking of different ways that they might get into the Boris Lab. Spanish speaking Margarita didn't participate in the conversation, but rather sat in an overstuffed rocker, knitting and trying to understand what everyone else was saying. She could understand English fairly well when it was spoken to her slowly, but she had a very difficult time when she was with many people who were talking fast. Although she couldn't understand everything being said, she was able to pick out a word or phrase here and there that troubled her. Whenever that happened, she would curiously glance over at Roger, who would look back reassuringly and smile. His smile was fake and she did not return it but instead glared, leaving Roger to wonder just how much she was really understanding.

Mercedes had decided to wear away a path in the dark brown carpet as she continually paced through the room, from the fireplace to the hall and back again. Roger sat in anticipation on the edge of his seat, smoking one cigarette after another and holding different expressions on his face, most of which were tight and full of puzzlement. Nick however, had removed his cowboy boots, placed them neatly beside the coffee table beneath his leather jacket and was comfortably stretched out on the couch. He stared up at the stuccoed ceiling with his fingers interlaced behind his head and listened to Mercedes shoot holes in all Roger's ideas and vice versa.

The team went on in this fashion for more than an hour and a half until Mercedes' face lit up and everything changed. She stopped pacing the floor and stood in the middle of the room, then slowly turned toward Nick and asked what at first sounded like a stupid question. "The Boris Lab has got to be state-of-the-art, don't you think?"

"No doubt."

"And that means the best security system with closed-circuit cameras, motion detectors, door accessibility with high level clearance only—things like that, right?"

Nick looked over at the now gesticulating Mercedes and curiously affirmed, "This has been the problem the whole night."

Mercedes' face brightened as she calmly lowered her hands to her side and smiled, then announced, "Well it's not a problem anymore gentlemen."

Nick cocked his head and sat up as Mercedes asked Roger if he minded her using the phone. Even before Roger was finished shaking his head and replying no, Mercedes had picked up the handset and began to punch buttons. The two men exchanged a curious look and then simultaneously glanced at the clock on the wall.

It was five minutes past eleven when a night-capped Ernie Baxter in a full bedtime gown rolled over and answered the menacing ring. "This better be good!" He snapped with all the tenacity that might scare away a small mouse.

"Hello Ernie." A soft beautiful voice floated through the phone and into his ear.

Ernie swallowed hard and asked, "Mercedes?"

With Nick sitting on the edge of the couch and Roger leaning forward, listing with curious anticipation, Mercedes replied, "Yes, it's me Ernie."

Nick and Roger once again exchanged odd glances as Nick rose off the couch and made his way across the room, to stand behind Mercedes.

On the other end of the phone line, Ernie's eyes opened wide as he sprang forward in his bed and was unable to speak.

After a few seconds of silence, Mercedes asked, "Are you there, Ernie?"

Ernie swallowed hard once more and forced a crackling, "Yes." through his lips.

"This isn't too late to call you, is it?" Mercedes asked innocently.

"No! No, not at all!" Ernie replied sharply. "I was just um…" His eyes scanned the room as he reached for something to say and quickly rested upon the magazines lying on the desk next to the computer. Without thinking, he replied, "I was just catching up on some Play Boy." His eyes grew even wider as he realized what a stupid thing he had just said. "What I mean is…" His mind raced as he tried to correct himself and once again the words came out wrong. "What I mean is, I was thinking of you." He winced, thinking about the playboy comment and connected the palm of his hand to his forehead as he sat in silence. Deciding it would be safer to sit quietly, until he was more awake, he kept his mouth shut and just listened.

Mercedes raised an eyebrow and thought about what he said for a second before she continued, "Ernie, the reason I'm calling is because I have another job for you."

Enthralled with the thought of seeing her again soon, Ernie turned, dangled his legs over the edge of the bed and quickly bobbed his head up and down. "Yeah, okay, sure. I can do that!"

Mercedes almost laughed as she reminded him that he didn't even know what the job was yet. "How do you know if you can do it, Ernie, if you don't know what it is?"

MEMORIES

Ernie looked confused for a moment then filled his eyes full of determination and confidently stated, "If you need it, Mercedes, then I can do it!" He tightened his chin and nodded affirmatively.

Mercedes stood, puzzled, as she shook her head and then hesitantly replied, "Okay. I'll need to come by in the morning with a couple of friends and I'll need your help all night tomorrow. How early can we come by?"

Ernie swallowed hard as he imagined what Mercedes' friends looked like and then enthusiastically said, "As early as you want. Heck I don't care, you can come now if you want."

"No, I think now is a little too late, I need to rest first. We'll be there in the morning."

"Okay, yeah. That's fine. That'll work. I'll see you then."

Mercedes let out a small giggle as she said, "Good night, Ernie," and then hung up the phone.

Ernie dropped the phone to his lap, looked over at his Star Wars night-light and thought about tomorrow.

"What was that all about?" Nick asked curiously.

For the next twenty minutes or so, Mercedes filled Nick and Roger in on her friend Ernie Baxter. As she spoke, Nick couldn't help but to envision some kind of a cuddly little puppy genius, sitting fearlessly at a keyboard, hacking his way into impenetrable computer systems, just hoping to receive a pat on the head from the beautiful Mercedes. At the same time however his anticipation continued to rise as he began to realize that they just might have found the way in.

"So, you really think this Ernie guy can help us get past the security system?"

"Absolutely! Ernie is a genius."

With his anticipation still growing, Nick shifted his eyes away from Mercedes and began to ponder as he slowly made his way back to the couch and sat down. Could this really be it? For eight years he had searched for phantom answers that he wasn't even sure existed, and now he was only a day away from finding them. What was down there, waiting to be found? Will it be another goose chase or will the puzzle pieces he sought actually be there?

He rested his elbows on his knees and took in a deep breath as he thought. So many times before he had been close, but each time the puzzle pieces would snap away, as if attached to a giant rubber band and disappear, far out of his reach. He couldn't keep form thinking that someone was down there beneath the lab at this very instant dismantling it and by tomorrow there would be nothing left to find.

"You okay?" Mercedes' voice busted through his anxiety.

With his face filled with concern, Nick looked up and answered her question with a slow nod.

"What's wrong man?" Roger looked puzzled.

Shaking off his concern, at least on the outside, Nick replied, "I'm fine... really," and then looked at the clock. "Well, it looks like nothing is going to happen tonight, so why don't we all try and get some rest. Something tells me we're going to need it."

Nodding his head, and not fully buying into Nick's lie about being fine, Roger replied, "Good idea, I'm tired," and then shifted his grin from Nick to Mercedes and back again as he said, "I'm sorry guys, but I don't have a spare room. The best I can do is offer you the hide-a-bed and the recliner. It folds all the way back." He paused for a second as his smile widened and then said, "The hide-a-bed's large enough to sleep two." He raised his eyebrows and then continued, "In either case, I'll go get some extra covers and let ya'll figure it out."

Roger made his way down the hall, followed by an agitated Margarita as Nick removed the cushions from the couch and handed them one at a time to Mercedes, who in turn lined them up along the wall.

"You can have the bed. I'll take the recliner," Mercedes offered as she leaned the last cushion against the wall.

"Nah, I can't sleep on these things. I hate the bar that cuts right across the center of your back. I'd much rather take the recliner." Nick unfolded the bed as he spoke.

"You're not just saying that to get me to take the bed, are you?" Mercedes asked as Roger reentered the room, carrying several blankets, a couple of pillows and one of Margarita's nightshirts.

Meeting him halfway Nick took the linens and said, "Thanks," then placed the majority of them on the folded out couch and tossed a single blanket and pillow onto the chair.

"Need anything else?" Roger asked.

Nick look around the room and then at Mercedes, who looked back and shook her head. "No, I think that'll do it."

"Cool. Now, what time do ya'll want to leave in the morning?"

"Early." Nick replied.

"Seven?"

Nick turned and asked Mercedes. "How early does this Ernie guy get up?"

Mercedes thought about it for a second and then smiled, "Whenever I knock on his door."

Nick turned back to Roger and said, "Seven sounds good."

Roger nodded. "'Kay then, I'll wake ya up at six."

"That'll work," Nick replied as he made his way to the recliner and unfolded his blanket. After showing Nick and Mercedes where the light switches were, Roger once again disappeared down the hall.

Fully dressed, except for his boots and leather jacket, Nick sat in the recliner, stretched the covers over his body and leaned back. Mercedes hesitated, then grabbed the nightshirt and headed for the bathroom. A few moments later a barelegged Mercedes reemerged and entered the room. Belonging to the shorter Margarita, the nightshirt wasn't quiet long enough for Mercedes and barely covered her bottom. Cuddled up on his side with the covers up around his neck, Nick watched as Mercedes bent down, placed her clothes next to the couch and then began to make up the bed.

"You know, you never did answer me," she said as she threw a heavy quilt over the top of the already sheeted mattress.

"Answer you? About what?"

Mercedes finished fluffing up the pillow and folded back the blanket as she replied, "About whether you were telling the truth when you said that you didn't like these pull-out beds because of the bar that cuts through your back."

Nick shifted in the chair and was almost unable to hold back his laughter as he asked, "Do you *want* me to take the bed?"

"No, I'm fine." Mercedes rolled her eyes and slid beneath the blankets.

Nick waited for a moment, until she was comfortably situated and then asked, "Are you going to turn off the light, or do you want me to?"

Beneath the covers of her warm bed, Mercedes thought about it. Damn! After a moment and just as she was sliding out of bed, the light switch clicked off and the room went black.

"I was going to get it," she said.

"Yeah," Nick's voice came back through the darkness.

CHAPTER TWENTY-NINE

The helicopter touched down at precisely one-thirty-seven in the morning, and with blades still slicing through the cold night air, a devilishly grinning Patterson stepped out onto the West Virginia blacktop, followed by his wannabe sidekick, Thorndale. They had traveled in Lear from the company's private hanger in California to the Charleston airport and then continued on by chopper to the small airstrip just outside of Beckley, where a company car awaited. Like demons in the darkness the two men made their way to the sedan, accepted the keys from the man beside the car, tossed a small case into the backseat and pulled away.

The shadowy car glided through the night like a phantom on its way to a kill. The thirty-minute trip was made in less than twenty and Patterson turned off the headlamps as the ominous car silently pulled up the long dirt drive to the sleepy, neighbor-less house. It was an older, white two-story home that stood out strongly against the dark mountainous backdrop.

Patterson shut off the engine and stared at the house as he tightened his leather gloves, withdrew his gun and checked the magazine. Thorndale sat quietly and watched as Patterson reached into the case in the backseat, grabbed the silencer, a cloth, and a small sealed vial of chloroform. After attaching the silencer to the end of the gun and slipping the cloth and vial into his coat pocket, he turned to Thorndale and with an evil grin asked, "Ready?"

Determined not to look weak and get himself into another mess, Thorndale nodded silently and pulled on the door handle. The two men stepped out of the car and slowly made their way across patches of stringy grass, to the steps leading up to the wraparound porch. To the weasel, walking half a pace behind Patterson, the night seemed to be alive. It echoed with a strange harmonious sound, and brought images of millions of tiny samurai soldiers lurking in the shadows, sharpening their swords against one another. As Patterson stepped onto the sagging wooden planks, a meow came from the swing hanging from the porch, and a fleeting shadow leaped through the air, lightly touched the top of the railing and continued off into the darkness.

The swing still rocked as the two men stepped up from the last plank onto the porch. With the wood creaking beneath the soles of his shoes, Patterson made his way to the front door, pulled open the spring loaded, wooden screen and checked the lock. Smiling, he looked over his shoulder at Thorndale, turned the knob and pushed open the door. It pivoted quietly on its hinges as he turned back around, faced the blackness and stepped across the threshold.

Four dress shoes stepped lightly onto the hardwood floor as Patterson reached into his pocket and withdrew a tiny, pen-sized flashlight. He twisted the end and a bright, white beam of light shot through the dark room and revealed a light blue shawl draped across the back of an old wooden rocker. The beam moved to the left through the blackness, across dark brown paneling to a white-plastered archway. Beyond the opening, in the next room a wooden dining table and matching chairs sat on timeworn linoleum. The beam kept going, passing the sink and stove, before making its way back into the current room. Along the white wall, it passed the clock and finally found the staircase, just a couple of feet to the left of the two men.

Patterson led his shadowy partner to the stairs and slowly crept up the steps, passing sickening photos of happy strangers as he went. Halfway up and with his head barely peeking over the top of the second floor, he paused and focused the light onto a familiar looking face, disgustingly smiling out of an old 8X10. Securing the penlight between his teeth, he reached up and removed the photo from the wall. It was a picture of Nicholas Chadwick. He was standing in front of a lake, next to an innocent looking young girl. Lisa! Patterson grinned as he quietly ran the muzzle of the silencer along the surface of the glass and thought about how thrilling it was going to be when he was finally able to put a bullet into the pretty-boy's head.

Just as he was reconnecting the picture to the wall a loud bang echoed from kitchen below and startled him. He twitched, and the picture missed the nail. It dropped five feet, slammed loudly onto the step and quickly bounced, passed Thorndale, down the stairs. Patterson swiftly snatched the light form his teeth and followed the shattering picture as it tumbled its way to the bottom. An instant later, he hastily shifted the light toward the kitchen. After seeing no sign of life, he decided to shut off the light and stand motionless in the dark.

Before long, something or someone began to stir from one of the rooms on the second floor. "Who's down there?" A middle-aged female voice floated through the air. Patterson readied his gun as he waited. From where he stood he could see over the top of the wall, onto the landing and down the hall.

"Fu-fu? Fu-fu, is that you?"

Fu-fu? Patterson thought about it and remembered the black shadowy figure that leaped off the swing. Fu-fu was the cat's name. Down the hall, the floor creaked as the woman called out again. "Fu-fu?" An instant later a meow came form the bottom of the steps. Something clicked, and light poked through the cracks around the edge of a door near the end of the hall. Patterson ducked his head below the landing and listened carefully.

Everything was quiet for a few minutes and then someone opened a bedroom door. "Fu-fu?" The voice was louder. Patterson was almost overcome with the urge to leap up and fire around in the direction of the voice, however he managed to hold himself back. He was still hoping to find the little girl asleep, and didn't want to create any more unnecessary noises.

The cat trotted its way up the steps, passed Thorndale's and Patterson's dress shoes to the landing above.

The floor sagged and gave out a little pop as Martha Rodman, dressed in a thick pink robe stepped across the threshold of her room and welcomed the cat inside. "You silly cat, you. What did you knock over down there, huh?" she asked in a babyish voice as she closed the door and then clicked off the light. With indiscernible baby tones still coming from her closed room, Patterson turned on the flashlight and the two men quietly continued their ascent.

Like professional burglars, they made their way to her door. Patterson handed the light to the weasel then reached down with his left hand and gripped the doorknob. He turned it quickly, and rapidly pushed open the door. Thorndale shown the light into the room and quickly found a puzzled Martha Rodman.

"Who's that?" she asked while holding her hands in front of her face, trying to see past the blinding light. Without answering her, Patterson squeezed the trigger and pumped a silent round between her eyes. She immediately slumped over, nearly landing on the fleeing cat.

"Meow."

With Thorndale still holding the light, Patterson quietly pulled the door closed and continued on to the next room. Once again he grabbed the knob and abruptly opened the door. To his surprise and delight, at the other end of the flashlight beam, he found an innocent looking little girl snuggled up beneath her covers, fast asleep. He smiled as he handed his gun to Thorndale and withdrew the chloroform and cloth. He twisted open the top of the vial and doused the cloth as he approached the bed.

Lisa was happily dreaming of her father when something shook the bed. She opened her sleepy eyes just in time to see a dark shadowy figure hulking over her. Before she even had time to think, something covered her mouth and everything went black.

CHAPTER THIRTY

Nick sat in the garage tossing copper pennies across the room into an old tin coffee can. He was making one out of every four or so. He tossed again. Okay, maybe one out of every five. He tossed another, one out of six? He was getting ready to toss the next coin when the kitchen door opened and a sleepy-eyed Mercedes peeked her head into the room.

"You all right?" she whispered.

"Sure. Am I being too loud?" Nick responded while holding a penny between his fingers.

"No." Mercedes paused and yawned before she rephrased the question, "What's wrong?"

"Nothing." Nick answered confidently as he turned back toward the coffee can. "I just can't sleep," he said as Mercedes stepped barefooted onto the cold concrete floor and he tossed another coin, one out of every seven?

"Can't sleep, huh?" Mercedes nodded suspiciously as she stood by the door, holding it an inch from closing.

"Nah." Toss. The penny hit the edge of the can and clanked inside. Bingo! Nick smiled.

"Thinking about tomorrow?"

Nick paused in mid-toss, just before the penny left his hand and clutched it tightly. "Yeah." He swallowed hard as a chilly Mercedes let the door latch softly and slowly made her way over. His eyes lifted from the can and he gazed aimlessly across the room as he spoke. "It seems like forever and yet only yesterday, at the same time." He shook his head as Allie's face flooded his thoughts and Mercedes rubbed warmth into her shoulders. "For eight years, I've been searching for some kind of an answer. Something that would put some reason into the madness that took place that day." He blinked, tightened his eyes and turned his head away from a caring Mercedes. Maybe he was afraid he was on the verge of shedding a tear that he didn't want her to see, or perhaps he was just looking deeper into the past.

Mercedes' hand left her shoulder and found its way to his as he forced down another swallow. "Eight years!" This time his voice crackled with an empty anger and for the next few moments the room was silent. Finally, Nick expelled a large breath through puckered lips as he turned to Mercedes and said, "You should be sleeping."

She nodded and raised an eyebrow. "So should you."

"I don't get much sleep these days."

"These days? You mean every day for the last eight years?"

"Yeah, something like that." Nick's focus swam back into the present as he noticed just how cold Mercedes was. Immediately, he rose to his feet. "C'mon." he said as he respectfully directed her back toward the door. While she kept the warmth from escaping through her shoulders, Nick politely opened the door and gestured. She stepped up, and Nick, still holding the door above her head with his left hand, turned around tossed the last coin, and even though he was twice as far now as when he was sitting, the penny found the can. Yep. One out of every four. Nick smiled to himself as he turned off the light and followed Mercedes into the kitchen.

"Want some coffee?" Mercedes asked in her *don't wake everybody up* voice.

"No, I'm still hoping I'll find some sleep tonight," Nick said softly

"Wanna talk?" Mercedes offered.

Nick thought about it for a moment. Maybe she needed to talk. Maybe she needed to listen. "Sure."

She led him back into the living room, sat on the edge of the bed and said, "Okay, talk."

Nick felt awkward, as he stood in front of her with nothing to say. He looked over at the empty recliner and hesitated before sitting down beside her on the pullout.

"I don't have anything to say."

"Well, what do you want to talk about?"

"What do you mean, what do I want to talk about? What do you want to talk about?" he asked.

"What do you want to talk about?" she returned the question.

At a loss for words and feeling a bit awkward, Nick stood up and bobbed his head. "Well, I um…" He looked around. "I uh don't really have anything else to say."

Mercedes raised another skeptical eyebrow, patted the space beside her and lovingly commanded, "Sit down."

He almost hesitated, but thought better of it and sat back down.

"I know you're nervous about tomorrow."

Nick turned to her empty-faced and after a short pause, asked, "What if they're not down there?"

Mercedes sat confused. "Not down there?" She squinted. "What are you talking about? What if *who's* not down there?"

Nick's eyes searched as he spoke and for the first time since they met, she saw flickers of uncertainty in them. "The answers. What if I *never* figure out what happened that day?"

Mercedes listened with warmth and empathy.

"So many times I've been so close." He shook his head and gazed down at the blankets with eyes that almost glistened. "And somehow, every time, everything just, just seems to dissolve into thin air. And now…" He swallowed hard as he thought. "I just can't keep myself from thinking that someone is down there, beneath the Boris Lab right now, tearing everything apart, and by tomorrow there won't be anything left." He looked up confidently, peered into her eyes, and asked, "Tell me, is that what's going to happen? Are we going to go in there tomorrow and find nothing?"

Mercedes' eyes filled with water, but didn't overflow as the answer he needed eluded her. After a few silent moments of staring into his unwavering eyes she reached over with a petite hand, grabbed his and with a crackle in her voice, said, "She was one lucky woman."

Nick's expression shifted as his face filled with puzzlement. How dare she say that? Since when was it considered *lucky* to be dead?

Mercedes shook her head and looked past his eyes into some imaginary land, far away and continued, "To have been loved so much by someone so special." The water finally overflowed and ran down her cheek as she brought her attention back to Nick's lost look. "Some people spend their whole lives just dreaming of half of what she had." She raised her tender hand to his strong face. "Even if it *was* only a short time." She paused and somehow her conviction filled eyes grabbed his heart. "It had to have been worth everything to her. I know it would have been to me."

Nick's look of confusion morphed into admiration and for an instant he saw past the here and now and felt an incredible connection with her, but almost as fast as the feeling came it was snatched away, replaced with an overwhelming feeling of guilt. He nodded his head and quickly looked away from her beautiful eyes as he grabbed the covers and gently wrapped them around her.

She sat quietly, angry at the guilt she saw in his eyes and confused at her feelings for him as he bundled her up, turned off the light and returned to her in the dark. Staying on top of the covers, Nick sat down next to her and leaned up against the back of the couch. He held her silently in the dark, wondering about tomorrow and waited for the sun to rise.

"Hey lover boy, wake up." Nick heard Roger's voice as his eyebrows rose, but his lids remained shut.

"I knew you'd end up there."

"Huh?" Nick finally pulled his eyelids apart and Roger's smirking face came into focus. The next thing Nick noticed was the aroma of the coffee that Roger was offering him. Nick organized his thoughts. He must have dropped off sometime before dawn, but why was Roger smirking? Nick stretched as he tried to squeeze the sleep out of his eyes and then noticed that he was no longer leaning against the back of the couch, but was rather stretched out on the mattress and cuddled up next to Mercedes. He wasn't even above the blankets. He was facing her back and his left arm was draped over the top of her waist. He stretched again. Oh my God. His legs were tangled up with hers.

"It's not what it looks like," he mumbled as he untangled himself from a just-now-waking-up Mercedes.

"Sure buddy." Roger winked as he handed Nick the coffee.

Nick moved to the edge of the bed, sipped the coffee and noticed how sore his back was. Stupid bar.

"What did I miss?" Mercedes murmured as she rolled over and moved clinging hair away from her face.

"Apparently, nothing." Roger smiled and raised his eyebrows.

"Huh?"

"Don't listen to him," Nick said as he stood up and scanned the room for his boots.

Just then, a joyful Margarita entered the room carrying a fresh cup of coffee for Mercedes.

Mercedes kept the blankets wrapped around her as she sat up and accepted the coffee.

"Hey Nick, come out to the van and help me figure out what guns we'll need tonight."

"Be right there," Nick said while slipping on his boots.

Roger walked out to the garage as Margarita asked if anyone wanted breakfast.

"I'll help," Mercedes offered as she stepped out of the bed and pulled the bunched up nightshirt down to cover her panties. As she went into the bathroom, Nick made his way into the garage.

Before long the *Three Musketeers* were in the van and on their way to Ernie's.

"So, you sure this guy will help us?" Roger asked.

"Oh yeah." Mercedes smiled while touching up her face in the overhead mirror.

Chewing on Gummy Bears, Nick puzzled, "You have a thing for this guy or what?"

While applying a little bit more lipstick, Mercedes shifted her gaze toward him and raised her eyebrows in a sort of *who knows* fashion.

Twenty minutes later the van pulled up to an older beige home in a not-so-brand-new neighborhood. Roger parked across the street and for the next few moments, beneath their dark shades, he and Nick just watched the house.

"It's okay guys," Mercedes said feeling a bit like a sardine, sandwiched in between the two brawns. "He's on our side."

"What if the guys from Biotronics got a hold of him?" Nick asked.

"Yeah, good point." Roger turned his head away from the house and looked at Nick and Mercedes. "And what if they're still in there, right now waiting for us to come in?"

"I didn't think of that," Mercedes said as Roger turned back to look at the house.

"They could also be outside, watching the house as well." The Three Musketeers scanned the street looking for anything out of the ordinary.

After a few seconds of growing intensity the feeling overwhelmed him and Nick announced, "This is crazy," as he opened the door and reached under his coat for his gun. Roger got out, wearing a long brown trench coat that completely concealed the shotgun beneath, and met Nick as he made his way around the van. Mercedes closed the door and ran across the street to catch up with the two cowboys.

On the porch, with a gun-toting guy on both sides of her, Mercedes rapped on the old wooden door. In no time at all—almost as if he had been standing there just waiting for her to knock—Ernie excitedly opened the door.

"Hi Mercedes," He said while pushing on the bridge of his glasses. "I thought you were going to bring a couple of friends."

"I did," she replied. Just then, Nick and Roger stepped into view and ushered her and Ernie inside.

"What's going on?" Ernie nervously demanded as Nick peeked through the heavy drapes for any sign of Biotronics.

"Ernie, these are my friends, Nick and Roger." Mercedes offered introductions.

"These are your friends?" Ernie asked with wide eyes.

"Good to meet you, man," Nick said as he passed Ernie on his way to another widow.

"What's going on?" Ernie asked again.

"Why don't we go downstairs?" Mercedes offered as Nick turned away from the window.

"Downstairs?" Nick asked.

"I thought we were downstairs," Roger added.

"Yeah, it's where Ernie does all his work," Mercedes answered Nick's question while smiling proudly at Ernie.

"All my work?" Ernie repeated while still trying to make sense of this tragic turn of events. Where were the girls that Mercedes spoke of last night, and who were these brainless, Neanderthalic thugs?

"Your work, Ernie. Your office. Where all your computers are, remember?" Mercedes' smile stiffened.

Finally, Ernie's gears kicked in and in a nervously macho tone he straightened his back and replied, "Yeah, that's right, *my* office." Mercedes wrapped her arm in his and nonchalantly walked him toward the basement door. Nick pocketed his gun and he and Roger followed, through a clutter-filled house and down into the basement. Somehow, Ernie felt more secure here as he confidently strolled across the tile floor and took a seat in front of the largest of three computer monitors, which was currently displaying the floating word *Mercedes*.

Looking past Ernie's love struck stare, at the monitor, Mercedes smiled, cocked her angelic head and softly said, "Awe."

Ernie replied with a dreamy eyed, "Huh?" and turned away from her, toward the screen. Beyond embarrassed, he immediately nudged the mouse and imploded the screensaver, revealing a crimson letter etched on yellow paper.

"Did that just say Mercedes?" Nick scrunched his eyebrows together as his tennis shoe left the last step.

Ernie shifted his eyes from person to person, not really sure what to say.

"Did what just say Mercedes?" Roger descended the stairwell, behind Nick.

"Never mind," Nick replied as he walked up, grabbed an armless rolling office chair and straddled the back of it.

Roger stepped up to the group, holding his shotgun, barrel pointed at the ceiling, while Ernie demanded for the third time, "What in God's name is going on? And could someone please tell Mr. Macho over there to put away that—that gun! It's making me nervous."

With a smirk hiding just beneath his calm attitude, Nick looked at Roger and nodded. Roger lowered the gun and concealed it beneath his trench coat.

"Ernie, Nick and Roger are friends of mine and they're helping me with the case I'm working on."

"Oh, you mean the one with the crazy guy?"

"He's not crazy, he's just involved in something out of his control, but yes, that's the one."

"I don't know, Mercedes." Ernie scrunched his eyes in a geeky, macho type way and said, "I've just spent the last few days going over the note you left me and I really don't think this guy's all there."

"I know Ernie, and he's definitely going to need some help when this thing is all over, but he isn't crazy. I think that the people who are holding him have really screwed up his brain."

"People who are holding him?" Ernie asked.

Mercedes took a deep breath and wondered where to start. "The note I gave you came from a man who lost his memory. He asked me to find out about his past."

Ernie listened for the next twenty minutes as Mercedes brought him up to speed on everything.

"A couple days ago, somehow, they found out where we were staying and took him."

"Took him?" Ernie pushed on the bridge of his glasses.

"Yeah."

"Took him where?"

"We believe, they took him to a hidden underground laboratory, beneath a building called the Boris Lab." Nick answered his question.

"Boris Lab?" Ernie's palms began to sweat as his interest grew. One of the things that made Mercedes so irresistible was the fact that she was a private investigator and always involved in secret espionage type stuff, like this.

"The Boris Lab is a laboratory owned by Biotronics. Anyway, we need to get into it and get Alex back and we need you to help us," Mercedes said.

"Me? But what can I do?" Ernie asked excitedly, waiting to find out how he fit into everything.

"Biotronics is state-of-the-art and we believe that the lab is completely automated or at least controlled through a central computer system."

With that, Ernie spun around in his chair, began to type and within seconds the group was looking at the company's website. "Ahuh! It says here that the company manufactures pharmaceuticals," Ernie said in a macho tone.

"I'm sure they do," Nick replied while remembering Lenny splattering his brains all over the warehouse in Atlanta.

After a bit more typing and snooping, Ernie turned to Mercedes and said, "I don't think I can help."

"What do you mean you don't think you can help?"

"Well," Ernie turned back to the screen, "Biotronics looks like a pretty sophisticated company." He shook his head.

"Yeah, but you're a pretty sophisticated guy." Mercedes was becoming concerned.

"You don't understand. Even if I could break their codes and hack into their system, these guys are too smart to have their security system accessible to dial up."

"What does that mean, accessible to dial up?" Roger asked.

"Well, see there are two different types of networks: those online—or that can be accessible through the telephone—and those that are not connected to a phone line at all. Now, I could get into the first one from here, but the second...there's just no way to hack in."

"All right, but what if their system is accessible through the phone line?" Nick asked.

"Well, if it was, then I could hack into it."

"And do you think you could navigate your way around pretty easily, unlocking doors, shutting off cameras, things like that?"

Ernie turned back to the screen. "Sure, but I'm telling ya, their security system isn't accessible through the phone line."

"How would we check for that?" Mercedes asked.

"There's no way, really. I'd have to have a Biotronics computer number to call into and poke around with."

The Three Musketeers looked around at each other, knowing that neither of the other two had a number for Ernie.

Finally, after a few moments Nick said, "He's right. These guys wouldn't have their security system accessible to an outside line."

For the next few minutes the group just sat there, silently looking at one another and then Mercedes said, "Sorry Ernie, didn't mean to waste your time."

"It's okay, Mercedes you didn't waste my time. You never waste my time!" Ernie replied, promptly.

Mercedes nodded and pushed away from the table that she had come to lean on. For the next few moments the room felt a bit hopeless and then Nick confidently asked, "What if you could connect directly to the system?"

"What do you mean?"

"What if there was a way to physically wire your computer directly to their security system?"

"Then..." Ernie pondered. "Then, I'd be in, I guess."

"And you're sure you could get past all of their security codes without being detected?"

Ernie thought about it for a second, looked at Mercedes' angelic face and then replied with an absolute, "Yes!"

"What's on your mind, Nick?" Mercedes asked.

"Well, what if we load Ernie's computer system into the van and park it just outside of the Boris Lab?" Nick shifted his eyes from Mercedes to Roger and back. "If we can get him close enough, I think I might be able to splice him into the system."

"How?" Mercedes asked.

Nick shook his head. "I don't know yet."

"You don't know?"

"Wait!" Ernie broke into the conversation. "What if we used a wireless Ethernet?"

"Good idea!" Nick replied. "Do you have a wireless connecter here?"

Ernie placed his hands flat on the table in front of him and began to smirk. "Do I have a wireless connecter here? Do I have a wireless connecter here? Do microprocessors crunch incalculables?" His eyes grew wide as he stood up and said, "Follow me, oh curser seeker of knowledge."

Curser seeker of knowledge? Nick raised an eyebrow of confusion as he followed behind Ernie.

A frown developed on Mercedes' face as Nick shadowed Ernie through the room. What in the world was happening? What on Earth was an Ethernet? And how come Nick spoke so much *geek* lingo? Ernie was Mercedes' friend. She understood him. Nick and Ernie needed her to translate, didn't they?

"The only problem with this is that we'd have to get awfully close, because the signal is only good up to about five-hundred feet." Ernie's voice floated across the room as he and Nick stood looking over a shelf filled with various electronic devices.

"Five-hundred feet, huh?" Nick thought back to the schematics of the Boris Lab that he had downloaded. "There's a guard shack out by the street. Ya think we could splice in from there?"

"Absolutely!" With the prospect of being part of Mercedes' investigative team, Ernie was becoming more excited by the second. "A guard shack's gotta be wired to the security system, don't you think? I mean the security shack not on the security system? I don't think so." Ernie nearly snorted with excitement.

Nick nodded and grabbed a couple of items off the shelf as Mercedes finally asked, "What exactly is an Ethernet?"

"It's a means of informational transportation that supports a local-area network protocol, using a bus topology with a transfer rate of up to a hundred megabytes per second." Ernie proudly defined the word *Ethernet* as Nick carried several items across the room and laid them on the table next to Mercedes.

"What?" Mercedes struggled to understand what she just heard.

"It's a way for one computer to talk to another." Nick simplified Ernie's explanation, while looking at a blue and black box, about the size of a portable CD player.

"Oh." Mercedes nodded her head as Ernie added a few more items to the pile on the table.

"We might need this," Ernie said while holding up a small silver apparatus.

"Yeah," Nick replied as he looked up, narrowed his eyebrows and took the device. Ernie, now empty-handed, immediately reached back into the pile, excitedly grabbed another small mechanism and said, "'Might need this too.'"

"Right." Nick nodded as he accepted the second piece of equipment.

"And this?" Ernie quickly reached back into the pile and grabbed again.

"What is all this?" Roger asked.

"Well, this here is the network transceiver." Nick emptied his hands and held up the small blue and black box. "It's what we'll use to connect Ernie's computer to the ones in the Boris Lab." He extended a retractable antenna as he spoke.

"And this?" Roger picked up and studied one of the thing-a-majigs that Nick had just lain down. "It looks kind of like a phone jack splitter, or something." He frowned.

"It's an Ethernet adapter," Nick replied. "Depending on how their system is connected, we'll need something like this to splice in."

"Or, something like this." Ernie grinned as he held up another small gadget, which reminded Roger of a cable TV adapter.

"In any case, it looks like we've got everything we need, right here. And you're sure you're going to be able to get into the system, right Ernie?" Nick asked again as he laid the box on the table and continued to eyeball the rest of the equipment.

"Positive," Ernie replied, while pushing on the bridge of his glasses. "This is too exciting. I'm going to be a sleuth!"

"Yeah." Mercedes nodded. "You know, we're going to have the computers connected, but what about us?"

"What do you mean?" Roger asked.

"Well, if we're going to be in the building and Ernie is going to be in the van, don't you think we'll need some way to communicate with him?"

"Good point." Nick looked up at Ernie, who was already proudly marching his way over to a short cabinet, next to one of the smaller monitors. "What about it, Ernie, do you have any radios here?"

"Do I have any radios here? Do I have any radios here?"

Here we go again, Mercedes thought as she shook her head.

"You mean like, these?" Ernie quickly spun around and grinned as he revealed two small handheld walkie-talkies.

"Yeah, just like those." Mercedes narrowed her eyebrows as she walked up and accepted one of the radios.

"And look, they got neat little headsets too." Unable to contain himself, Ernie uncontrollably snorted with excitement as he plugged a wire into the top of his radio and fastened the headset to his head. "Ernie to Mercedes." Ernie's excitement grew. "Come in Mercedes, can you hear me, Mercedes?"

"Ernie." Mercedes raised her eyebrows and flattened her face. "You're only five feet away from me, of course I can hear you."

"Oh, right." Ernie held up a pointed finger and then turned his back and whispered, "Ernie to Mercedes. Come in Mercedes. Can you hear me, Mercedes?"

Nick and Roger watched as Mercedes filled up with embarrassment and then reluctantly spoke into her radio, "Yes, I can hear you, Ernie."

For the next second or two the basement was completely silent as everyone watched Ernie and then, all of the sudden a loud snort came through Mercedes' handset. Ernie's snort grew louder as he turned around, with a thumbs-up and grinned at the three serious faces in front of him.

After a few more seconds Ernie's snorts stopped and the team began to plan their journey into the Boris Lab. Twenty minutes into it however, something gut wrenching got Nick's attention. He, Roger and Ernie were in front of the computer monitor, discussing the best layout for the inside of the van, when Ernie nudged the mouse and revealed Alex's letter for the second time this morning. Two words immediately leaped off the screen and into Nick's soul, they were, *Alex Kendallman.* Nick's vision narrowed and for the next few moments he was looking at the monitor through a long tunnel of warped reality. Instantly, his mouth went dry and his eyes began to water as he leaned forward and all but forced Ernie out of his chair. He grabbed the mouse and reduced the image so that the entire note could be read. For the first time in a long time, perhaps the first time in his life he began to tremble.

Your name is Alex Kendallman.

Nick read the first five words of the note and then just the fourth and fifth ones. He read them over and over again and seemed to be in some kind of mental loop. His eyes became fixed on them and for the next few seconds he was paralyzed and could not look away. He recognized the handwriting and couldn't believe what he was seeing.

"Allie." His whispered word finally broke the silence. Unable to swallow, he tore his eyes form the screen, turned to Ernie and aggressively asked. "Where did you get this?"

Ernie shrugged his shoulders and shook his head, afraid of the burning intensity in Nick's eyes. "That's the note she brought me." He hesitantly pointed at Mercedes, but for the moment Nick was oblivious to his gestures and couldn't see anything but the computer man's face.

Nick stood up and grabbed Ernie by the collar. "You saw her? How? That's impossible, she's dead! Who are you?" Tightly clutching Ernie's collar and with his eyes full of fire, Nick glared at Mercedes and Roger. "Who are you people?" A moment later he pushed Ernie away, causing him to lose his balance and hit the floor.

Not knowing what to expect and having no idea what might happen next, Mercedes and Roger took a couple steps back.

"Nick, it's okay." Mercedes held up an innocent hand.

"What's going on?" Nick demanded.

"It's all right, man." Roger added his assurance.

"No, it's not. Why is my dead wife's handwriting on Ernie's computer screen?" Nick pointed to the screen, behind him.

"What are you talking about? That's the note Alex gave me." Mercedes said.

Nick felt himself perspiring and his knees weakening as he tried to make sense of things.

After a few intense moments Roger asked, "I thought your wife's name was Allie."

"No, that's just what I called her. Her name was Alexis."

"Alexis? Alexis Kendallman?"

"Kendallman was her maiden name."

Mercedes looked at the screen and offered, "Maybe it just looks like her writing."

"And the names being identical is just a coincidence? No, that's her writing and that's her name." Nick aggressively tapped the screen.

From the tile floor, Ernie frowned. "Um…" He pointed a shaky finger at the monitor. "That can't be your wife's writing, not unless she was mentally ill or something." He turned his finger around and pushed his slipping glasses back onto his face.

"What are you talking about?" Nick glared, curiously.

"Well, that may look like your wife's writing, but, I've been analyzing it for the last few days. There are little nuances in it that can only be attributed to someone who has got some real mental issues." Ernie answered, apprehensively as he slowly inched backward across the floor.

Nick turned to the screen. "Issues? Like what?"

"Well, for starters that person's got some identity problems." Ernie stood up and dusted himself off.

"Identity problems?"

"Yeah."

"What do you mean?"

"It's hard to explain. I'm not even sure I understand, myself."

"What, like she doesn't know who she is, or something?" Nick asked.

Realizing he was back far enough to feel safe, Ernie let out a sigh of disgust and replied, "Something like that."

"I'm telling you," Nick looked at Mercedes, shook his head and pointed at the screen one more time, "That's her writing."

Mercedes wanted to tell Nick that Ernie was a retired graphologist and knew exactly what he was talking about, but then she suddenly remembered what Alex had told her during their last conversation together, and her face went blank. "Wait a minute." She looked at the computer monitor. "He said he remembered his middle initial."

"What?" Nick sat confused.

"The last time we were together, Alex said that he remembered what his middle initial was. He said it was S." Then, for a moment she was talking more to herself that anyone else. "Alex S. Kendallman." She repeated it louder and faster. "Alex S. Kendallman. Oh my God…Alexis Kendallman." Her face went pale as she wondered what it might mean. Was Alex Allie? She looked at Nick as her mind raced.

Embarrassed by his outburst, Nick looked at everyone in the room, shamefacedly and then leaned forward, with his elbows on his knees and his face in his hands.

For a moment, the room was completely silent, and then instinctively Mercedes moved to Nick. "It's all right," she reassured him as she rested a shaky hand on his shoulder.

"What in the world did they do to her?" A muffled question came out of Nick's hands. No one really knew how to answer that, and for the next few seconds the room remained soundless.

Finally, Ernie broke the silence. Being carefully positioned behind Roger, he said, "I don't know if I want to work with him, Mercedes. I think he's dangerous."

"He's not dangerous, Ernie. He's just confused," Mercedes said.

Nick unburied his face and looked up sheepishly at Ernie. "I'm sorry man. I'm not like that, I just seen Allie's writing and," he paused for a moment and when he continued his words were distant and lost, "got spooked."

Ernie shifted his eyes around the room snobbishly, as he thought. "It's all right, I guess."

Nick nodded and smiled weakly, then turned back to the screen and asked, "What was this Alex guy like?"

"I don't know." Mercedes shrugged. "He was kind, a little shy. We didn't really have much time to get to know each other."

"What did he look like?"

"Um…" She gazed into the passed. "He stood about six foot, blond, rather on the frail side."

After a few more seconds, Nick shook his head and asked, "What does this mean? Is Allie still alive somehow in Alex's body?"

"I don't know, but we're going to find out." Mercedes reassured him as her grip on his shoulder tightened and her determination began to resurface.

"Where's the original letter?" Nick asked, still staring at the screen.

"It's over here," Ernie reluctantly replied and then cautiously moved to a cabinet across the room. Nick stood up immediately and went to Ernie, who held out the letter and fearfully backed away. Still feeling the shame of his earlier actions upon Ernie, Nick politely accepted the letter and began to read.

"Why is it written twice?" He asked.

"He wanted to find out if he was the one who wrote it," Mercedes replied.

"What do you mean?"

"Well, he found the note in his pocket, and at first he thought someone else wrote it, but then he found a red pen in another pocket, so he copied it to see if he was the one who had written it in the first place."

Nick swallowed hard as he gazed at his wife's handwriting.

"You okay?" Mercedes asked, barely able to speak herself.

"Yeah." Nick kept staring at the note.

"This is way too weird," Roger finally admitted as he rubbed a huge hand across his confused, bald, head and then unrolled the pack of smokes from his arm.

After a few more moments, Nick's attitude shifted and his eyes refocused, holding more resolve in them than they had since the day Allie died. He refolded and pocketed the note then with vengeance saturated word said, "Let's get back to work."

The group spent the rest of the morning planning their incursion and loading up the van. After lunch, they took Ernie's older model, compact white Mazda and drove around the lab a few times. Mercedes took pictures and Nick made mental notes. The bathroom-sized guard shack sat out on a quiet street across the road and kitty-cornered to an old, rundown apartment complex. A crow's nest camera spied on the shack from the top of a pole coming out of the roof of the main building.

The crew parked in front of the apartments as Nick studied the guard shack and began imagining different ways of getting in without being spotted by the camera. The only way he might get into the small building without being seen would be for him to start out directly across the street and keep the guard shack between him and the camera as he approached.

Fortunately, the door into the little room faced the street and was unobservable by the camera. Somehow, someone would have to lure the guard out of the building and keep him occupied while someone else snuck up in plain sight, went into the building and hooked up the transceiver. *Right!*

Nick shook his head as he thought. Maybe they could just shoot the guard, hook up the transceiver and hope no one came to the guard shack. No. Nick frowned. That wasn't his style. He couldn't shoot an innocent person, unless, maybe with a tranquilizer dart.

"Let's get back to your place, Ernie." Nick squinted his eyes from the backseat. "I need to think."

The Mazda sped back to Ernie's and for the rest of the afternoon and into the evening the team worked and reworked their plan. About eight it seemed as if the planning was as good as it was going to get. Nick looked up, noticed the clock and thought about Lisa. It would be 11 PM in West Virginia and the girls would most likely be asleep. Nick thought about it. He hadn't spoken to Lisa in a while and with the promise of danger on the horizon he felt an overwhelming desire to hear her voice and let her know he loved her. He went to the phone and dialed Dottie's number.

After about six rings and no answer, he hung up and tried again. This time he waited for about ten rings before hanging up. Where were they? Nick sat on the edge of the couch as a funny feeling crept into his chest. They were probably just out somewhere, but why so late?

"You all right?" Mercedes walked in holding a cup of hot tea.

"Yeah, I think so."

"What's wrong?" Mercedes could see the concern on Nick's face. "Thinking about tonight?"

"No," Nick said while still, half in thought. "I just called Lisa."

"Something wrong?"

"I don't know. There was no answer."

"She's probably just out and about."

"Yeah, I guess you're right. It's just that it's so late back there. There's a three-hour time difference."

"Oh yeah. I forgot about that. Don't worry Nick, I'm sure they'll be home any time now. Why don't you come into the kitchen and I'll make you a cup of hot tea."

Nick looked up and smiled. "Make it coffee, and you're on."

In the kitchen, Nick had to settle for some herbal tea, as Ernie didn't drink coffee.

"What kind of computer hacker doesn't drink coffee?" Nick asked as he pulled the tea bag out of the cup.

"I don't know." Mercedes smiled. "Ernie's one of a kind."

"You think he's still mad at me for grabbing him?"

"I don't know. I don't think so. I think he's mad at you because I like you."

Nick smiled.

"You worried about tonight?" Mercedes changed the subject.

"Yeah, a little, you?"

Mercedes let out a small laugh to relieve the anxiety and nodded over her tea.

Nick shook his head as he was once again overtaken with her beauty. "Ya know, sometimes you seem so tough and then-"

"And then?" Mercedes demanded with eyebrows raised.

"And then, at other times you seem…"

"Yes?"

"You seem so soft." Nick pause, shook his head, and then continued, "I don't get you," he admitted, as he took a drink of the unlike-coffee liquid.

Mercedes smiled, enjoying being mysterious.

CHAPTER THIRTY-ONE

Joe Gleason, who being no relation to Jackie Gleason, was said to have looked just like him, had just poured himself a cup of coffee from the thermos and was looking over the day's funnies when a crippled Mazda limped passed and tire-flopped to a stop. Tonight, like every night this week, had been rather dull, and Joe curiously welcomed a little change of pace. Not wanting to give the company a second more of his time than he had to, he clocked in at exactly 5:00 PM and had less than two hours left on his shift. Having already been warned to be extra careful this evening, he raised his handset to his lips and reported the car. From inside the shack he observed, as an extremely sexy woman, wearing a skintight skirt short enough to be taken to jail over, got out and cussed the tire. His heart skipped a beat and he was unable to swallow his mouthful of éclair as he watcher her bend over and reveal more than he had ever remembered seeing in a public place.

With his eyes fixated on the tragedy-struck young lady, helplessly rummaging through her trunk, Joe's good-natured heart welled up within him and he reasoned that he just wouldn't be a decent human being if he didn't offer to assist her. While forcing the clumpy donut through his dry gullet and quickly running his fingers through his thick dark hair, he pilfered through the clutter around him and located his peppermint chewing gum. After a rapid chew, only long enough to freshen up his eager mouth, he spit the gum into the wastebasket, wiggled his jaw and confidently stepped out of the building.

With his plump, round hands purposely fastened to his thick leather belt and his eyes focused where they probably shouldn't have been, Joe walked up and in a deep macho man's voice, asked, "Everything all right, there, little miss?"

Pretending to be startled, Mercedes spun around and painted her face with fear.

Innocently, holding his hands out, Joe reassured her with a warm and fuzzy chuckle. "It's okay, I work here."

Mercedes looked around fearfully and then, with a hint of suggestiveness, asked. "What do you want with me?"

Her sheer white blouse was nearly half undone and Joe found himself once again looking where he probably shouldn't have been as her question played gymnastics with his brain. "I noticed you were having trouble, I just thought you could use a hand," he said, while trying to tear his eyes away from her nearly exposed breasts.

Mercedes looked around innocently as an unobserved shadow secretly floated behind the security guard on its way to the guard shack. "Do you know anything about *stupid* flat tires?" She airheadedly accepted Joe's help.

Joe smiled as he stepped up to rear of the car, almost touching the beautiful young woman and looked through the trunk. Trying not to break a sweat, the overweight security officer unbolted the tire and removed it from the trunk.

The door to the shack silently latched shut, and a phantom vanished below the window just as Joe turned around and bounced the spare onto the asphalt.

"We'll have this fixed up in no time for ya." Joe smiled as Mercedes seductively rubbed her hand over her bare neck.

Inside the tiny building, on his knees, Nick hunted around for the Ethernet hub and found it hiding far back, on a deep, low shelf behind a stack of old newspapers. As luck would have it, it was almost the same shade of blue as his little box. After plugging in the transceiver he placed it behind the hub and extended the antenna.

While Joe, who had messed up his hair with greasy hands and finally began to sweat, was securing the spare onto the Mazda, Nick radioed to Ernie.

In an empty looking van in front of the apartments, Ernie sat, surrounded with the latest in computer technology. "Hold on," he whispered into his headset as he punched a few keys on his keyboard.

"Hurry up, Ernie!" Nick urged anxiously as the guard tightened the last lug nut.

"I'm going as fast as I can," Ernie replied while Nick watched Joe lift his smudged smile toward Mercedes and brush the hair out of his twinkling eyes.

Nick turned around, placed his back against the wall and slid down onto his butt as he waited for Ernie's okay.

Just as Joe was fastening the flat into the trunk, Ernie whispered back into the headset, "Okay we're connected."

It's about time, Nick thought as he turned around and peeked over the windowsill. The guard was done with the tire, but was happy enough to linger with Mercedes, who was harmlessly tracing the edge of a button on her blouse as she spoke.

"Thanks again, I can't believe you were here... um...?" She reached for his name as Nick quietly snuck out of the building and made his way back across the street, into the shadows.

Taking hold of his gold nametag, Joe smiled proudly and said, "Joe, Joe Gleason."

After being sure Nick was out of harms way, Mercedes changed her tone, thanked the man one more time for his help and pointedly made her way around to the driver's door.

"What's the matter? Did I say something wrong? Is there something wrong with my name?" The puzzled guard followed behind the sexy woman as she got back into the Mazda.

"There's nothing wrong with your name, Joe. I think it's kind a cute." Mercedes smiled as she started the car and popped it into drive.

"Cute, huh?" At her window, the puzzled guard smiled as she stepped on the gas and raced out of his life forever.

Meanwhile, Nick had made it back to the van where Roger and Ernie waited. "How's it going?" He asked, while pulling the door closed.

"Okay, but it's going to take me a while to crack their codes," Ernie replied.

"Crack their codes? I thought we were in," Roger said.

"No, we're just connected. Ernie still has to get past their security and into the system."

"How long is that going to take?" Roger asked.

"Not too long." Ernie spoke as he typed. "An hour, maybe two."

"Hum, an hour?" Roger turned to Nick. "So, what do we do for an hour?"

Just then Mercedes' voice came over the radio, and remembering her attire, Nick grinned at Roger and said, "I can think of a few things."

"Hey guys, how did it go?"

Nick spoke into his radio. "Good. Ernie is working on the codes now."

"How long?"

"About an hour."

"Good, I'm going to find a bathroom and change. I'll radio you guys when I'm back in the area."

"So much for that idea," Roger said as Nick brought the radio back up to his lips.

"All right, we'll see ya in a few."

At 1:15 AM Mercedes, Roger and Nick stepped out of the Mazda, adjusted their headsets and checked their guns.

"All right Ernie, we're in place." Nick spoke into the night as he retrieved a small black duffle bag from the trunk.

"Okay guys…" Ernie leaned back, his face illuminated by the light of the screen, and rubbed his hands together. "There are two cameras on the west side of the building."

Nick reached into the bag and raised a tiny pair of binoculars to his eyes. "I see one," he said. "It's attached to the corner of the building."

"Right, and there is another, out at the southwest edge of the lot."

Nick panned his binoculars across the property and after a focus adjustment, located the second camera, which was attached to the top of a thirty-foot pole and had a great bird's-eye view of the entire west side of the building. "Tell us when," Nick said as he lowered the camera and gazed across the street at the twelve-foot high barbed wire fence.

One of the three monitors in front of Ernie displayed a complete floor plan of the lab, including everything that wouldn't be found on any city blueprints. On another monitor, Ernie was able to see the exact same split-screen camera images being watched inside the lab, by lab security. The last monitor displayed Ernie's commands and hacks as he typed. Ernie typed away at his keyboard and isolated the images on the two west side cameras. Since they were both outside and captured very little change in scenery, Ernie decided to freeze the images just long enough to let the team pass and enter the outer offices.

"All right, the coast is clear." Ernie's voice entered their ears.

"Let's go," Nick said as he bagged the binoculars and stepped off the curb. The Three Musketeers crossed the street and walked up to the fence as Nick pulled a small set of bolt cutters from his pouch. Mercedes and Roger withdrew their guns and kept their eyes pealed as Nick went to work on the chain link. Instead of cutting a huge hole that would easily be seen by the camera once Ernie reactivated it, Nick snipped the very bottom of one of the links, and like a corkscrew, twirled it upward and unstitched the fence. In no time, he had created an opening large enough, and the team quickly slipped inside. After everyone was through, Roger helped hold the fence together as Nick weaved the link back into place and sewed up the hole. As the team ran across the blacktop and then hugged the wall of the building, Nick wondered why they hadn't thought to dress better. Roger wore jeans, a white t-shirt and still had on that bulky, not to mention ugly, brown trench coat. He, himself sported tight fitting jeans, his thick leather jacket and those clod-hopping boots he loved. Mercedes was the only member of the team who appeared to show any sense. She had pulled her hair into a ponytail, dressed in all black cotton from her neck to her ankles and glided across the ground like a ghost in her Nike running shoes.

The team made their way along the wall to the corner of the building and stopped. "Ernie, we're at the northwest corner," Nick said with his gun in his hand and his back to the wall.

"Hold on." Ernie's voice entered everyone's headset. After typing in a few more commands, Ernie grinned and then said, "All right, I've frozen the entrance cameras and taken the magnetic seal off the front doors, but..." He paused and his face went somber. "It's a manual lock and I can't help you with it."

"Don't worry about it, Ernie." Nick said as he rounded the corner and eyeballed the door. "I got it covered." Nick reached into his bag of tricks and withdrew a flat leather pouch. He unfolded it on the concrete, revealing several long metallic utensils. After handing his gun to Roger and carefully assessing the lock, he selected two tools from the pouch and in less than a minute unbolted the door. Nick picked up his gear, grabbed his gun and retrieved a small flashlight. With his tools neatly tucked away and the door standing open, Nick shown the light into the darkness and asked, "Ernie, the door's open. Any motion detectors or invisible infrareds we should know about?"

"Not in that room." Ernie smiled and the team stepped onto the tile.

"Which way, Ernie?"

"There's a set of double doors on the other side of the room," Ernie said while looking at the monitor and bringing a potato chip up to his mouth.

"I see 'em," Nick said as he made his way around a counter, heading for the doors.

"On the other side, there's a corridor. Halfway down the hall, third door on the left," Ernie crunched, "there's a room. Inside the room, there's a door that opens to a stairwell. The stairwell leads to the basement." As Nick slowly opened the door to the corridor and shown the flashlight down the hall, Ernie turned to another monitor and enlarged one of the camera images, which revealed a normal looking basement, made of cinder block walls and a concrete floor. However, at the far end sat a uniformed security guard.

Roger and Mercedes followed as Nick made his way to the third door on the left. "There's a guard in the basement," Ernie said as Nick quietly opened the door.

"A guard in the basement?" Mercedes puzzled her face.

"I'm sure it's not really a basement," Roger said.

"Shhh!" Nick gestured as he poked his head into the next room. The team crossed the room as Nick asked Ernie whether the guard would be able to see the door opening from where he sat.

"Which door?" Ernie asked.

"The door to the stairwell." Nick shook his head.

Ernie studied the camera image and the floor plan carefully. "I don't think so." Ernie raised his eyebrows.

"You don't think so?" Nick's tone changed as he turned off the flashlight and stared dumbfounded into the darkness, waiting for Ernie's response.

"Well." Ernie moved his face closer to the monitor and shook his head. "I can't really tell."

Nick shook his head again as he thought. "Which way is the guard facing?"

"He facing the stairwell, but he's at least fifty feet away and I don't think he can see the top of the stairs, but I'm not sure."

Hoping to be able to sneak past and avoid a confrontation so early into the incursion, Nick pressed on the earpiece as he asked, "Where do we go once we are in the basement?"

"Well, directly behind the guard there's a door." Nick cringed as Ernie continued. "The city blueprints has the room listed as a storage area for hazardous chemicals, but according to the schematic that I'm looking at there's an elevator in there which leads to rooms that are not on the city's blueprints."

"So you're saying that, somehow we have to get past that security guard?"

"It looks that way."

"And I bet he's just sitting there, looking at the stairwell with a radio in his hand, isn't he?"

Taking Nick's irony seriously, Ernie looked at the monitor carefully and said, "No, no, he's just sitting there, reading the paper."

Looking into the darkness, Nick thought for a second and then replied, "He's reading a paper?" If he was distracted by a paper, then maybe someone could get down the stairs and cross the room before he noticed, but then what? Nick rubbed his temples.

"We have another problem, guys." Ernie said with an urgent tone as he hit a few keys on the keyboard and enlarged an image on one of the outside cameras. "A car just pulled up to the security gate, outside."

Nick turned the flashlight back on and quickly looked around the room for a place to hide.

"It's entering the lot now," Ernie said as Nick continued to look around the room. Except for a few small under-the-counter cabinets, which wouldn't even hold Mercedes, the room offered no promise for hiding.

"Two men are getting out of the car." Ernie enlarged the image. "It looks like that Davenport guy."

Nick thought. Why would Davenport be here so late? "C'mon guys," Nick said as he crossed the room and went back into the hall.

MEMORIES 311

"They're approaching the front doors," Ernie said nervously.

"Ernie, we're back in the hall. I need you to direct us to a safe room to hide in."

"The next door down is marked as a janitor's closet."

"Right," Nick said as the team moved down the hall and then slipped into the room. Inside, in the dark, they listened as shoe tapping indicated the presence of the men. A door opened and shut, and the tapping ceased.

"Ernie, tell me when they get to the basement," Nick whispered.

"Will do." After a second, Ernie spoke again. "Okay they're there."

"C'mon," Nick said as he exited the broom closet and made his way back to the top of the stairwell.

"Have they made it past the security officer yet?" Nick asked.

"Not yet," Ernie said curiously. "They seem to be having a conversation with him."

Nick puzzled through the dim light at Roger, who met his gaze with a shrug.

"Wait! Okay, the guard is getting up. He's unlocking the door. All right, the two men are entering the room now."

Nick nodded, as his mind shifted and he once again began to think of ways of getting past the guard without being noticed.

"Wait a minute," Ernie said abruptly, while scrunching his eyes at the monitor. "The guard just laid his keys on the desk and is now walking across the room."

The team listened as Ernie continued. "He's opening the bathroom door. He went inside."

"Something doesn't feel right," Nick said as he hesitated in the dark.

"C'mon man," Roger whispered, as he grabbed the handle and opened the door. "We gotta hurry while he's in the bathroom."

"Wait." Nick grabbed Roger by the arm.

Roger turned and looked at Nick for a moment and said, "This is too good to pass up, man. It's perfect," then turned back around and hurried down the stairs.

"He's right," Mercedes said as she passed Nick and followed Roger into the basement.

"That's the part that bothers me," Nick said as he closed the door and moved down the stairs.

Halfway down, Nick whispered loudly, "Wait—the camera."

At the bottom of the stairs, Roger and Mercedes froze as Nick whispered, "Ernie?"

"I'm working on it," Ernie said while hitting a few keys. "Okay, there." He looked up at the monitor. "You're good to go." With that the Three Musketeers quickly crossed the room and Roger snatched the keys off the desk.

"It's my turn to get the door," he whispered gallantly, as he inserted the key into the lock.

"Wait a second, Roger," Nick whispered back, and then spoke into his headset. "Ernie, have the two men entered the elevator yet?"

"That's a big ten-four," Ernie replied while reaching into the bag of chips.

Nick nodded at Roger who turned back, unlocked the door, and then tossed Nick the keys. After laying them back on the desk, Nick followed Mercedes and Roger into the hazardous chemicals' room.

"All right Ernie, we're out of the basement. You can reactivate the camera, now."

"Got it," Ernie said as he typed out a command on the keyboard.

"We also need an elevator," Nick said while reading the words, *insert card here*.

"Coming up!" Ernie said as he hacked away.

A few seconds later an amber light came on above the door and a bell softly chimed. The metal door pulled open as Ernie snorted proudly, "Your car, my good people." As the three stepped inside, Ernie asked, "Floor please?"

"Which floor did Davenport get off at?" Nick asked.

"The bottom," Ernie replied.

"Take us to the bottom, then," Nick said as Roger nodded in agreement. Mercedes gripped her gun as the door closed and the elevator lowered. "Ernie, what about cameras on the bottom floor?"

"Hold on," Ernie said as he downloaded the camera information for the bottom floor. "Oh, my God," he said under his breath as he stared at the monitor.

"What?" Nick asked uneasily. "What is it?"

"Well there are six cameras on the bottom floor. One of them is of the outside of the elevator. It's empty at the moment and," Ernie hit a few more keys, "is currently experiencing a brain freeze. There's another one in the corner of an office designated for Dr. Boris, and I guess that's Dr. Boris moving around in there." The elevator came to a stop as Ernie continued, "Then I've got an image of some kind of control room."

"Control room?" Nick asked as the team cautiously stepped out of the elevator.

"Yeah, I guess it's a control room for the lab."

"The lab?" Nick asked while slowly moving down the hall."

"Yeah." Ernie swallowed hard. "That's where the really weird stuff's at."

"Like what?" Nick stopped and pressed on his earpiece.

"Well, I'm looking at three images." Ernie shook his head and soured his face at the monitor. "One is of the whole room. It's about the size of a large living room. There are dozens of computer devices in there and they all seem to have something to do with two naked people who are standing up in a couple of round glass tubes."

"Naked people?" Nick asked while looking at his comrades.

"Yeah, and the other two images are close-ups of the," Ernie paused and raised his eyebrows as he unconfidently offered, "naked couple?"

"Naked couple?"

"Yeah. A guy and a girl, both in weird glass tubes, one labeled twelve and the other labeled nine."

"Nine?" Mercedes spoke louder than she should have and her voice echoed down the hall. "That's Alex," she whispered.

Thinking of Allie, Nick spoke into the headset, "How do we get there?"

The team followed Ernie's directions as he disabled security systems and unlocked doors. The path took them down a deserted hall, past Dr. Boris' office.

"Wait," Nick whispered as they passed.

"What?" Roger asked, under his breath, overly anxious to press on.

Nick readied his gun as he held a finger up to his lips and then softly asked Ernie to deactivate the camera to the good 'ole doctor's office.

"Hold on," Ernie replied as he typed in a few more commands. The image blinked and instantly Dr. Boris was standing in a different location. Ernie had programmed the computer to replay the last ten minutes of Dr. Boris' camera. "Done."

"I don't think this is such a good idea," Roger whispered nervously as Nick grabbed the door handle and wondered why his friend was in such a hurry to press on.

"Ready?" Nick asked.

Mercedes held up her gun and Roger reluctantly nodded as Nick mouthed the words, "Three, two, one," and then rushed in, pointing his gun at Dr. Boris.

"What is the meaning of this?" The doctor insisted.

"Shut up and sit down!" Nick commanded as Roger softly latched the door.

The good doctor nervously stumbled over to his desk and took his seat.

"I don't know what you're trying to prove, Mr. Chadwick, but you're not going to get it done with guns."

A foolish statement, obviously the doctor didn't know just how much Nick wanted to use his gun and pump a hole into the fat man's head; something he would undoubtedly do before the evening was over, and then he will have accomplished at least part of what he wanted to do, and he will have indeed, done it with a gun. The lump in Nick's throat grew as he stared at the man's pudgy little face, remembering how he stood on the riverbank that day and did nothing as his Allie drowned.

"So, you remember me then?" Nick asked, through gritted teeth.

"Of course, I remember you. There isn't a day that goes by that I don't think about what happened." Dr. Boris reached into his coat, pulled out a white handkerchief and blotted his forehead.

Nick's eyes began to fixate and his face tightened as he forced the next question. "And what exactly was it that happened that day, doctor?" Nick tightened his grip on the trigger and struggled to hold off, at least long enough to hear the answer.

The doctor breathed in deep, took a shaky drink from the glass of water beside the monitor, then removed his glasses and rubbed on the bridge of his nose. "You must understand," he shook his already shaky head, replaced his glasses and looked up, past the barrel at Nick, "that, what we did that day we did for the good of all mankind."

Nick waited as his jaw locked and he lost the ability to swallow.

After a short pause Dr. Boris said, "And it's not like we were the ones who killed her, you know."

Unable to contain his rage and desperately wanting to pull the trigger, Nick pulled back and kicked the chair out from beneath the doctor.

Almost before the doctor hit the floor, Nick was on top of him. Still holding his gun, Nick reached down, grabbed the doctor by the collar, and jerked him up off the floor. Pulling him close, Nick aggressively whispered in his ear, "Fuck you!" and then threw him across the room, landing him a few inches away from Roger's feet.

"Um… guys…" Ernie's voice sounded nervous.

Nick took a step toward the pathetic doctor who was now frightfully feeling the tile floor for his missing glasses.

As Nick latched on to the doctor for the second time, Ernie spoke again. "Guys?"

"What is it Ernie?" Mercedes answered as Nick pulled the doctor close again.

"Someone just activated Dr. Boris' camera."

"Oh shit." Mercedes looked up at the camera, in the corner of the room. "They can see us?"

Nick made no attempt to step over the glasses and avoid shattering them as he aggressively led Dr. Boris back to his over-turned seat.

"No, not yet. I'm still playing Dr. Boris reruns, but they keep calling to him over the computer intercom."

"Intercom? Then why don't we hear them?"

"When I reset the camera, I shut off the intercom as well, as a precaution."

After situating the evil scientist back in his chair, Nick leaned in close, put the barrel of the gun up to the man's head and said, "Now, I'm only going to ask you one more time. What the fuck happened that day?"

"It's a long story."

"Well, I have nowhere to go."

"They want an answer, Mercedes." Ernie's voice was urgent.

"Can't you answer them?"

"Me?"

"Sure. Can't you just pretend to be Dr. Boris?"

"I don't even know what he sounds like, and besides they're watching him right now, well his image anyway and it's not even anywhere near the microphone. Wait a minute." Ernie watched in amazement as the replay of Dr. Boris walked across the room and leaned over the desk, blocking the camera's view to the microphone. Ernie thought, *it's now or never* and then hit a few keys and quickly blurted into his own computer microphone. "Stop bothering me."

A group of uniformed security officers scratched and then shook their heads as they began to disperse from around the monitor.

Meanwhile, Dr. Boris had begun to recant the events of yesteryear. "...I had taken the experiments as far as they could go."

Nick pulled his gun back, relieving the pressure from Dr. Boris' face as he listened.

"We were experimenting on the human brain."

Mercedes scrunched her face and took a step closer as she too, began to listen.

Dr. Boris dove further into the past. "It all started back in January of 1966. A doctor by the name of George Ungar and I were working in a state-funded laboratory, studying the brain and how it organized memories. We had been working off of the findings made a half a decade earlier, by James McConnell. In 1960 he had successfully transferred the memory of one worm to another." Doctor Boris took another drink of water. "We were working with rats then and had made an amazing amount of progress in just six short years, and then, without warning, they shut us down."

"Who?" Mercedes asked.

Boris looked up dumbfounded. "Why the government, of course. Ungar found a way to continue his work with the rats. I was devastated. I remember going to the Red Eye, a local bar. John and I would often meet there and have drinks."

"John?" Mercedes spoke again.

"Jonathon Davenport. Anyway he happened to be there that night. I'll never forget it. I told him what had happened. I don't remember too much else about that night." He thought for a moment and then continued, "He kept buying me drinks. That, I do remember. I also remember talking all night, well I think I belly-ached while he listened. I think I said more than I should have. A week later he approached me with the idea. He had filed for bankruptcy a few months earlier and was running a little TV repair shop. He offered to let me use the basement of his shop to continue my experiments. He wanted me to try and mimic memory, synthetically."

"Mimic memory syn-what-ically?" Mercedes felt herself getting lost.

"He wanted me to develop a new memory system for computers, based on what I had learned from the rats."

"And?" Nick kicked his chair.

"Six months later I created the world's first microchip. I'll admit it doesn't work at all like the brain and the very first one was extremely crude, but the inspiration for it came straight from what I had learned form the rats."

"That's a lie." Nick kicked the chair again. "Intel created the first microchip."

Back in the van, Ernie listened and nodded as he crunched on another chip.

"Actually, if you'll do a little research, you'll find that the history books credit a man by the name of Robert Dennard for creating the world's first microchip."

Ernie made an *oh yeah, that's right* face as he bobbed his head up and down and continued to listen to the story.

Dennard. That name sounded familiar and then suddenly Nick remembered the conversation he had had with Mercedes at Applebee's and it clicked. "You sold him the technology."

"No, not me." Boris shook his head. "I'm not much of a salesperson. John does all of that."

"Get to what happened with Allie."

Boris nodded. "Yes, well I am. We took the money from the sale and founded Biotronics. I was able to resume my experiments, but John had stepped things up a bit." A nervous hand reached for another glass of water. "Quite a bit, actually, and he gave me human subjects to work with, instead of rats."

Mercedes scrunched her face in discussed.

"It's not like we were doing anything unethical. We had their complete consent." Boris looked up and focused his attention innocently at the evil woman. "I think you'd be more than surprised to find out just how many people are willing to line up and be test subjects if you offer them the right monetary reward. And besides, my work with them," Boris lifted his voice to a slightly superior tone, "led to the world's first 256-K static ram chip, which in fact we were able to sell to the Fairchild Corporation for even more money than what we had received for the original microchip. And," his condescending tone escalated, "almost every major computer advancement the world saw during the seventies and eighties came from Biotronics, in one way or another. However," Boris lowered his eyes, "in 1980 our experiments had came to a halt." He shook his head. "Up to that point it had truly been amazing. We had successfully begun to transfer bits and pieces of memory from the brain of one person to the brain of another." He paused to take another drink. "But each time we did, the subject receiving the memory would suffer some type of seizure. It was puzzling for a while, but then I figured out what was happening. The seizures were a result of what I now call *conditional overload*. It has to do with the way the brain grows and locks in memory. See, once the brain starts to form its own memories, it will not easily accept others. What we needed was a brain that hadn't developed any memories at all." At this point, Dr. Boris seemed to have forgotten the severity of the current situation and began to ramble with excitement. "I'll never forget working with the first group. We had no way of knowing just exactly what we were in for. The memory transfers that were done over the next two years were incredible, but then the babies began to die."

"Babies? You were working with babies?" Mercedes' stomach turned as she shook her head and just about decided that she had heard enough.

"They were test tube babies. The ladies that bore them weren't even their real mothers. They had no mothers actually." Boris chuckled. "I guess you could say that we were their mothers."

"Oh my god." Mercedes covered her mouth as she had a painful revelation and then said, "Alex was one of the babies."

"No, not exactly. Number Nine, or Alex as you call it, was part of the second batch."

"Excuse me!" It was Mercedes who kicked the chair this time and even without Nick's cowboy boots she was still able to jar the doctor good and get his attention. "Alex is not an *it*. He's a person, with feelings and emotions, and babies don't come in batches."

Instead of arguing with her, Dr. Boris just shyly ducked his head for a moment and then continued. "We found out that the brains of," he paused, looked at Mercedes and chose his words carefully, "newly created babies, even though they are unaffected by conditional overload, they aren't developed enough to process full blown memories. After some more research I concluded that what we needed was an empty brain, but one that was about 11 or 12 years old. That's when we decided to processes the second group of test tubes. Number Nine was the ninth of twelve in that group. All but two died before age 11."

"From?" Mercedes asked.

"We're not really sure, but the general consensus is that they died from a lack of human contact. We had to keep their brains on a delicate balance between learning enough to keep them growing, and staying empty enough to have them be useful. All unnecessary human contact was strictly prohibited."

"Love." Mercedes' eyes began to water. "They died from a lack of love," she whispered, angrily.

Again Dr. Boris looked away and said nothing.

"Get on with it," Nick insisted, with his stomach souring, not sure he really wanted to hear how all of this tied in to what happened with Allie, but knowing he had to.

"Well, Number Nine and Number Twelve both survived past their eleventh year and Number Twelve was the first to start receiving memory injections. Back then we used memories from living people. We would extract the memory of the person by inserting a thin probe into the base of their scull and on into the hippocampus. This proved to be useless however, because the memories that we got were scattered and choppy. That's because we really weren't able to truly get at the hippocampus like we needed to. Back then Biotronics was located in West Virginia. After a very botched up memory transfer, John and I decided to take a short break and get some air to kick around some ideas. I'll never forget that day." Dr. Boris' voice dropped. "We took a drive and ended up at New River. Ironically it was a beautifully clear day."

Nick's mouth fell open slightly as he stood in silence and began to fill with revelation. "You fucking bastard. You let her die so you could get at her memories."

Once again ashamed at the truth, Boris just nodded and sadly looked away.

"You fucking bastard!" Nick repeated as he uncontrollably pulled back and struck the doctor with his gun-filled hand.

As blood poured from his left temple and with Nick raising the barrel of the gun to the side of his head, Dr. Boris blurted out, "It didn't start that way. We were sitting there in the car with the windows down, discussing what we were going to do when we heard a scream. Right away we both got out of the car and ran down to the riverbank and that's when we saw her. She was fighting the waves, trying to get out of that menacing kayak when it flipped."

"Without thinking, I started toward her, intending to help, but then John gabbed my arm. At first I didn't understand, but then he looked at me and-" He paused as his eyes filled with water and when he continued there was a crackle in his voice. "And I knew what he was thinking. What we needed was right before us. All we had to do was wait. I stopped and turned back toward the river and, and did nothing. Inside, my stomach was turning, but I did...I did nothing." Dr. Boris began to tremble with remorse and, for an instant he almost seemed to welcome the bullet in Nick's gun, but then strangely, as he resumed talking, his tears dried and he became cold and condescending once more. "Her memory transfer was incredible, incredible. We were able to..."

"That's enough, Dr. Boris." Roger's voice sounded out of place as he stood by the door holding a cell-phone to his ear.

Nick turned to Roger, puzzled.

"All right Nick, you need to step away from the doctor, now." Roger spoke softly and gestured sadly with his gun.

Still confused, Nick cocked his head and asked, "What?"

Roger reached down and turned the door handle. The door slowly swung open and Mr. Davenport appeared in the doorway, shadowed by two armed guards.

"Roger? What are you doing?"

"I'm sorry, Nick. I really am, it's just that, well I really needed the money."

"You really needed the what?"

"Money, Nicholas, money. It's what makes the world spin," Mr. Davenport answered.

"I don't understand."

"Let me see if I can clear things up a bit." Mr. Davenport spoke, pompously. "After finding out that you had made an appearance at Uncle Bob's Tavern, I decided to pay Roger here a visit. As it turns out he was having some major financial challenges and owed some of the locals a considerable amount of money. I really had no idea if you were going to contact him again, but I'm glad you did. It worked out nicely for everyone. I told Roger to call me right away if he heard from you and I'm glad to say... he did."

With the confusion and hurt inside him thickening into rage, Nick raised his gun toward Mr. Davenport and uncontrollably squeezed the trigger. *Click.* He pulled again. *Click.* He puzzled at the gun as Mercedes raised hers and fired. *Click.*

"Did you really believe that your guns were going to work?" Mr. Davenport spoke. "Where do you think they came from? For a smart man, you really are stupid, you know that? You really think that Roger was able to come across an arsenal of that magnitude so quickly?"

Nick peered at Roger and honestly asked. "How could you?"

"Hey look man, it's not like you and I were best buds or anything and like I said, I *really* needed the money."

"Bastard." Mercedes glared.

"All right, enough of this, now come, I have a nice little surprise for you, Nicholas."

Even though he was blinded by rage, Nick was still instinctively aware of his surroundings and, with lightning speed, he reached past the doctor and grabbed, then shattered the mouth of the water glass on the edge of the desk. As Davenport hesitated, not willing to pull the trigger and accidentally hit the doctor, Nick grabbed the doctor and brought the jagged edge of the glass up to his throat. With tiny droplets of bright red blood poking out from beneath the glass Nick confidently said, "We're not going anywhere. I'm not done yet."

"Now Nicholas, put the glass down."

"Does it look like I have the word moron tattooed across my fucking forehead to you? Now, put your guns on the floor, or I'm going to send your precious Dr. Frankenstein here to memory Hell."

"I'm afraid we can't do that Nicholas. If you'll just turn and look into that monitor beside you you'll understand why."

As Nick was turning his head toward the screen, Ernie back in the van was having a few problems of his own. His fingers were moving across the keyboard with lightning speed while Jackie Gleason and a group of uniformed wannabes stood outside the van, demanding to be let in. Finally, with a loud crack, the passenger's side window shattered and a hand reached inside and pulled up on the door handle. Back in the lab, Nick had finished turning his head and was looking at the monitor. On the screen was an image of Mr. Ugly and Lisa! Grinning, Lurch held the sleeping beauty with his left arm and was pressing the barrel of his gun hard into the back of her skull.

Outside, the guards pulled open the door and entered the van just as Ernie lifted his finger above the enter key.

"Freeze!"

Ernie looked up, tapped the enter key and then raised his hands above his head. "Is there a problem?"

With Nick's heart in his throat and his grip on the doctor weakening, the lights went out.

CHAPTER THIRTY-TWO

The blackness was sprinkled with bright red and white explosions of gunfire as glass shattered and shadows scuffled in the darkness. Someone cried out in pain. It was Roger.

"You idiots, stop firing." Davenport's voice busted through the chaos. Immediately the gunshots ceased and a small beam of light sliced though the pitch and landed on the cowering Dr. Boris. Holding the tiny flashlight, Mr. Davenport watched as the doctor slowly turned his head toward the light and then, trying to rise, bumped the back of it on the bottom of the desk. Mr. Davenport quickly flashed the light around the room, but somehow Nicholas and Mercedes had already managed to slip out. The light came to rest on Roger, who stood weaponless and doubled over, apparently suffering from a kick to the groin.

"What in the Hell is going on?" Davenport demanded as one of the guards raised a radio to his lips.

"I have no idea sir," he said and then pressed and held the speak button. "Lester, what's going on? We have no lights."

"I don't know. I think someone just cut the power to the building," a voice came back.

"Well can you get backup lighting?"

"I'm not sure. I really don't know what happened yet. I can't access anything."

"We need lights ASAP."

Even before he released the talk button this time, Mr. Davenport grabbed the radio and began to speak. "There's a manual override lever in the electrical room. One of you idiots better get your ass down there and get me some lights, and I mean now!" Mr. Davenport shook his head at the pathetic doctor, shoved the radio into the chest of its owner and then walked out of the office, turned to his right and shined the light down the hall.

As he began to walk, one of the guards asked him whether or not he wanted someone to head in the opposite direction, just to be safe.

"No! Everyone stay with me."

"But sir, what if he went the other way?"

"He didn't go the other way," Davenport said confidently.

For a moment voices were silenced as shoes tapped on the tile floor, and then almost as if he couldn't resist asking, the guard spoke again. "Excuse me sir, but how can you be so sure he didn't go the other way?"

"Because, you idiot, his daughter isn't the other way." The team walked and Roger hobbled through the dark toward the lab.

Meanwhile, with the power off, the invisible gas inside of Number Nine's glass chamber began to dissipate, and under the blanket of darkness, eyelids began to move, indicating rolling eyeballs beneath.

Nick and Mercedes reached the door of the lab, and remembering what happened the last time Nick gallantly rushed into a room unarmed, Mercedes offered him her newly acquired gun. "Take this. I borrowed it from Roger."

"Thanks," he whispered as he anxiously pushed open the door and crossed the threshold in the dark.

Oddly, the answers that Nick had needed so desperately for that last eight years, didn't matter to him anymore. Everything that had motivated him to press on all this time had suddenly been pushed out of his mind. There was only one thought running through his head. Lisa! He held onto the gun with sweaty palms and felt his way through the darkness like a ghost. He had to move slowly because it was so dark. He tried to remember the layout from the monitor, but more often than not he found himself bumping into things.

"We'll have lights for you in just a second, sir." Nick heard a radioed voice float through the darkness from across the room and crouched down behind a large piece of equipment.

"Nicholas?" Mr. Davenport called out. "Oh, Nicholas?"

Nick's heart stayed in his throat and a drop of sweat began to trickle down the side of his face.

"We know you're here Nicholas. Why don't you make this easier on everybody and come out of hiding?"

Nick was nearly overcome with the urge to fire a bullet in the direction of the voice, but held back for fear of hitting Lisa.

"Let her go, you bastard!" Nick shouted, taking the chance of revealing his location.

"Now, I'm not too sure that's a good idea and to be perfectly honest with you, I'm not quite sure where she is at the moment. Tell ya what, why don't you come out of hiding and we'll discuss it. I'll be fair. I promise." Davenport's voice grew louder as he spoke and Nick could hear scuffling coming his direction. Holding onto Mercedes' hand, Nick felt his way along the wall and moved quietly from one computer console to another.

Just as Nick was getting ready to move again, the backup lights came on. Countering his momentum wasn't easy and he almost stumbled as he swayed to a stop, barely staying out of sight, sandwiched between the back of a computer console and the lab wall. Mr. Davenport and his henchmen stood in the middle of the lab holding guns and carefully studying the room. Although the area was relatively small, several devices kept them from locating Nick and Mercedes. Hiding places included the three computer terminals directly ahead, the two large monitoring devices which kept track of Number Nine's and Number Twelve's vital signs, located on each side of the glass tubes, and the glass tubes themselves. Lisa and Patterson were not in the room.

Even though the backup lights were on, none of the equipment was working, and in the gasless chamber, unseen by everyone, Number Nine's left pinky finger began to twitch.

Mr. Davenport motioned for one of the guards and Roger to go to the left wall, while he and the other moved to the right. They left the center of the room and moved slowly to opposite walls. As Roger and his newly acquired lowlife partner cautiously crept up to the two glass tubes, Roger found himself more than slightly distracted by the bizarre bodies inside. Their skins seemed to be almost grey and their eyes were slightly open. Roger shook off the feeling of death as he thought about Nick. He could not see past the tubes, as only the front of them was glass. Suddenly, as he was getting ready to peek around one of them, Roger was filled with the images of Nick's icy demeanor and quick thinking at Uncle Bob's. He hesitated, tightened his grip on his gun and then quickly poked an anxious head around the tube. To his relief, the area was empty.

Not sure if his new gun would work, Nick steadied himself, keeping watch in all directions and prepared to pull the trigger. From the corner of his eye Nick spied something black moving along one of the walls. He turned just in time to see a black coat sleeve and blond hair snapping back behind one of the large computer terminals, less than twenty feet away. Nick raised his gun, but didn't fire. Just then, Mercedes pulled on his shirt and called his attention to movement in the other direction, where he just glimpsed the tail of Roger's brown trench coat receding back behind another large piece of equipment at an equally menacing distance. Again Nick pointed his gun, but didn't fire.

Forcing the lump in his throat down and focusing on the moment at hand, Nick positioned his back up against the wall and fixed his eyes straight ahead centering his attention on his peripheral vision. Before long, Nick spotted another movement and, with lightning speed he spun in that direction. A man was crouching low and peeking around the corner, pointing his gun in Nick's direction. Having already made up his mind to shoot the first thing that moved, Nick squeezed the trigger twice, hitting the man once in the shoulder and then in the face. The shots were loud and in less than a moment the man's body laid face down and lifeless.

Realizing that whoever else was with him was probably in no big hurry to poke another head around the corner and get it blown off, Nick spun around in the opposite direction. Spying a dress shoe and a crouching knee, Nick took aim and squeezed once more. The knee exploded, sprinkling bright red blood onto the wall as a man cried out in pain. Unfortunately, it wasn't Davenport.

"Daddy!" The scream was piercing and Nick's eyes opened wide as he recognized Lisa's voice. Once again, his heart was in his throat and the air around him began to thicken. For a moment, he crouched, paralyzed and listened, but the scream wasn't repeated, instead Mr. Davenport's voice broke the silence.

"Nicholas, I don't want to hurt her."

Nick's palms began to sweat as his mind dove into uncertainty.

"Believe what you will, but I'm not a murderer. However, if you don't put an end to this silly game right now, you'll leave me no choice."

With the moisture in his hands working away at his grip, Nick started to shake, and tiny droplets of sweat began to pool at the edge of his crown. "Bastard! Fucking bastard!" His cries were directed more at death than at Davenport. Nick's thoughts raced. The last time he beat death, it had taken the one he loved in his place. He wouldn't let that happen again. Somehow, Lisa was going to live through this, even if he had to die for it.

"Nicholas?" Davenport spoke again.

Nick squeezed his eyes tight as he thought.

"Nicholas?" Davenport's voice was slowly moving closer.

Damn it! Nick's eyes burst open, revealing an intensity and focus that hadn't been there since his Iceman days. "All right!" He paused as the muscles around his eyes tightened "But first, let her go."

"Now you know I can't do that, Nicholas," Davenport said and then thought for a moment. "But, she doesn't know anything, so I give you my word that she won't be harmed."

Nick shook his head. "I can't trust you-fucking piece of shit!"

"You're right, you can't, not for certain, but if you take a moment and think back, there were a few times I could have killed you, but didn't. Remember the warehouse in Atlanta?"

Nick listened carefully to Davenport's voice as it drew nearer, getting a good fix on its location.

"After you were hit with that two by four, when you were out cold, I could have easily taken your life, as a matter of fact, Jackson thought it was a good idea and all but begged me to let him, but I wouldn't allow it. I didn't need to kill you then and I don't need to kill your daughter now."

"If you want to see tomorrow, you'll let her go now," Nick warned as he readied himself to stand up and open fire at the spot where Davenport's voice was coming from.

Davenport thought for a moment, and understanding the type of man Nick was, spoke to Patterson, making sure to be loud enough for Nick to hear. "Gregory, if anything happens to me, you are to put two bullets into that little girl's head, understand?"

"Yes sir," Patterson answered enthusiastically.

Nick hesitated, thought for a moment and then jerked in frustration.

"Now you were saying, Nicholas?"

Nick knew the same threat wouldn't work on Lurch, who probably welcomed death and couldn't wait to meet Satan and find out just who was the uglier.

Davenport listened for a moment, and hearing no reply, spoke again. "Nicholas, I'm getting tired of this. Tell ya what, I am going to start counting, and if you haven't tossed your gun out and stood up by the time I reach five, I'll have one of your daughter's fingers cut off and tossed over, how does that sound?"

Nick's eyes searched aimlessly as he thought.

"One." Davenport began to count.

A droplet of sweat broke free and ran down the side of Nick's face.

"Two."

Nick began to think of Lisa, being held by that monster and loosened his grip on the gun.

"Three. There won't be a six Nicholas. Four." Davenport's voice was just as cool and collected as it had been when he had first started counting. "Five!"

"All right!" Nick shouted as his gun slid across the tile floor into the middle of the room, and he and Mercedes slowly stood up, with their hands out, where they could be seen.

"Martin, get his gun," Davenport commanded as he stared at Nick, holding a pistol at his waist. "Martin?" Davenport spoke again, but there was no answer.

Mr. Clean poked his head up from behind one of the terminals on the other side of the room and said, "Um, if Martin was the guy with me, then he can't hear you."

Davenport glared at Nick for a moment and then said to Roger, "Very well then. You get the gun."

Roger walked over to the middle of the room, grabbed the gun and headed toward Davenport. Mr. Davenport gestured for Mercedes and Nick to move out from behind the terminal. Before long they were all standing in the middle of the lab as Roger and Davenport kept a close gun on Mercedes and Nick.

"You know in many ways I admire you Nicholas," Davenport spoke. "Your tenacity, your dedication. Your-"

"We had a deal!" Nick interrupted.

Davenport nodded and as he radioed for Patterson to bring Lisa, Mercedes had begun to look around the room. She spotted Alex and her heart sank. Even though she had seen the image of him in the glass tube on the monitor in Dr. Boris' office, somehow, he hadn't looked as helpless as he did here. "Oh my God, Alex," she whispered as she unconsciously took a step toward him. The tube that held him was a good three feet off the floor, supported by various pieces of stainless steal rods and electronic devices.

As she aimlessly wandered over to the tube, Mr. Davenport slowly lowered the radio from his mouth and softly spoke. "Yes, but his name isn't really Alex, you know."

Mercedes walked up and placed her hand on the glass tube. As Mr. Davenport followed behind her, Roger looked at Nick, gave a single nod and motioned for him to move toward the glass tube as well.

"Honestly my dear, what you're looking at isn't really a person at all. It doesn't have a past. It has no memory. It really doesn't even have a soul. It's nothing more than a memory processor—an advanced computer."

Mercedes thought back to the other day, in the motel room, when she had promised Alex that no matter what happened he would never be alone again. She remembered him calling himself a freak. Looking up at Alex's face, torn between anger and despair, Mercedes said, "His name... is... Alex!"

Mr. Davenport took in a breath and thought for a moment, then nodded. "That was the only memory we couldn't erase. It was the first, truly successful, transfer that we did. See, we did it before we removed the hippocampus and amygdala."

Mercedes turned around and stared, half glossy-eyed at Davenport as he pointed to the back of his head and continued. "They're two organs, located deep in the center of the brain, and I'm sure I'm not telling this exactly right, but they're responsible for turning our short-term memories into long-term ones. Dr. Boris said it wasn't a good idea to do the transfer without removing them first, but we really didn't have a choice. We couldn't wait." Davenport stopped and then calmly looked over at Nick. "See, the brain cells in your pretty wife's head were quickly deteriorating, and back then we didn't know how to preserve the brain like we do today."

Nick's eyes began to gloss over, and the only thing keeping him from tearing the evil man to shreds was the thought of his daughter.

Mercedes turned back around, looked at Alex for a moment and then let her eyes wander over to the person in the other tube. "Number Twelve," she whispered angrily as she shook her head.

"Yes, Number Twelve." Davenport cocked his head in disappointment as he spoke. "We originally had high hopes for that one, but for some reason it would never transfer memory correctly. These two units were the only ones out of the batch that survived beyond their eleventh birthday. We have them together here in hopes of figuring out why the one works and the other one doesn't."

Mercedes' face flattened even more and a couple of tears rolled down her cheeks as she listened to the cold-blooded words of a lunatic. What was it that allowed some people to be so cold and so evil? What enabled a man like Davenport to refer to flesh and blood people as nothing more than parts to a computer? Mercedes turned around, glared at Roger and shook her head in shame. Just then, Dr. Boris and Lurch entered the room. Lurch was holding onto a silently terrified little girl.

"Daddy!" Seeing Nick, Lisa came to life and began to squirm.

"It's okay peaches," Nick reassured, holding his hands out in a calming fashion and fighting the expression of fear that hid just at the edge of his face. With Lisa's terror-filled eyes begging for her daddy's help, and with his hands still out in front of him, Nick slowly shifted his eyes and glared at Davenport. "Now, let her go."

Davenport nodded obediently. "A deal's a deal." He paused. "But she does know an awful lot." He turned to Dr. Boris, who was tending to the missing kneecap man. "Henry, would you be kind enough to take this darling little girl here into your office and help her forget the last few days?"

Horrified and confused, Dr. Boris very slowly stood up, adjusted his glasses and then meekly said, "But you know what that'll do to her."

"Yes. It will erase her memory of the last few days." Davenport smiled and then looked at Nick. "It's the only way."

Instantly, Mercedes' thought went back to her conversation with Dr. Jennings. "Oh my god! Not HG7?" Her wide eyes shifted from the jolly Davenport to the nearly petrified doctor, whose returned expression all but confirmed her fear. She looked back at Davenport and pleaded. "But that'll kill her."

Davenport smiled reassuringly and warmly said, "My dear, first of all it won't *kill* her, and secondly, it's not HG7."

"It's HG7e!" she said and then turned to Nick. "It'll kill her!"

"What is she talking about?" Nick asked. "What are you planning to do to her?" Nick's eyes shifted back and forth between Davenport and Boris.

"It's a simple procedure, really." Unable to swallow, Nick turned to Davenport and listened. "It's just an injection that will erase any memory she has of the last few days."

"I won't do it." Dr. Boris uncharacteristically crackled.

Davenport's smile faded as he looked at the suddenly reformed doctor.

"And you can't make me." Dr. Boris stood strong with a paper-thin wall of courage.

Mr. Davenport nodded, understandingly. "Very well then, I'll do it."

"What the Hell is HG7e?" Nick demanded.

"I told you Nicholas. It's nothing to be concerned about. It's a simple drug that will help her forget what she doesn't need to know." Then Davenport paused again and thought of another idea. "Or would you rather I let her share in your fate?"

"He's lying." Boris found the courage to speak again. "That chemical will fry her brain."

"We don't know that," Davenport snapped.

"Oh yes we do, and we have countless records to prove it."

"Shut up!" For the first time tonight, Davenport raised his voice in anger. "Gregory, get her ready!" He demanded. Patterson smiled impishly and began to take Lisa out of the room.

"Wait!" Nick cried, desperately. Patterson stopped at the door and turned around as Davenport listened to the plea of a father trying to buy time. "She won't remember anything, right?" He asked.

"No, nothing about the last few days anyway." Davenport answered.

"Well, then can I at least say goodbye."

Davenport looked curiously at Nick, who finally seemed to be getting the drift of things. After what seemed like forever, Davenport's eyes shifted to the nearly traitorous doctor. Davenport could not afford to lose the doctor's intellect, not just yet, so, in an attempt to redeem himself and appear less like a monster and more like a human being, he said warmly, "What the Hell," and then turned to Patterson, "Let her go."

"Excuse me?" Patterson rasped.

"Let them say goodbye."

Confused but forever obedient, Patterson slowly released her, and quicker than a flash of lightning, she was in her father's arms. "Oh, daddy," she cried as tears streamed down her cheeks.

"It's okay baby," Nick reassured as he held her close and secretly reached into his coat pocket. Confusion filled the room as Nick nodded at Roger, withdrew another pistol, and quickly took Lisa back, toward one of the computer terminals. In an instant, Mr. Clean had a huge hand on Davenport, spun him around and shoved the barrel of his gun up to his neck.

"Drop it, rich dick!"

Davenport's hand loosened its grip, and his gun slipped out and fell to the floor as he asked, "What's going on? Roger, what are you doing?"

"What's it look like, your royal dickness? Did you really think that you had bought me?" As Mercedes stood, befuddled, trying to figure out just what was happening, Patterson reached over, grabbed a handful of her hair and nearly chipped her teeth as he forced the barrel of his gun into her mouth.

Roger turned toward Patterson. "Let her go or God here gets a head full of lead!"

"Do as he says Gregory!" Davenport added his commandment.

"Don't worry sir, he won't shoot you, because if he does, I'll kill the bitch." Patterson grinned at Roger.

Davenport's eyes grew wide as he filled with fear. He couldn't believe that Patterson would risk his life on such a gamble.

Patterson, consciously careful not to make the fatal mistake of turning his back to Nick's location, inched closer to Roger and Mr. Davenport. In a moment he would squeeze the trigger, scattering the bitch's brains throughout the lab, and while the big bald showoff was reeling from the shock, Patterson would blow his head off. The two men locked eyes. Roger's expression of anger was clearly masking the fear underneath, but the demon had no fear. He just stood there grinning, almost daring Roger to pull the trigger.

After reassuring Lisa, Nick peeked out from behind the terminal. Last night in the garage when Roger had told him about Davenport's phone call, Nick wanted to call the whole thing off, but Roger insisted that as long as Davenport thought that Roger was on his side, they'd have the upper hand. Nick shook his head as he watched Lurch and Mr. Clean stare one another down, and then to his horror he watched as the back of Mercedes' head exploded. Nick took aim at Lurch, but before he could get a round off, Lurch had withdrew his gun from Mercedes' mouth and fired on Roger. He shot only once, but the hit was fatal. The bullet entered Roger's head right between the eyes and the big man went limp. Enraged, Nick squeezed the trigger repeatedly, hitting Lurch several times in the upper body.

While Patterson was being pumped full of lead, Mr. Davenport quickly joined Dr. Boris safely on the floor, behind a large piece of equipment.

Patterson got the wind knocked out of him, stumbled back, and lost his balance, but somehow managed to squeeze a few rounds off before he hit the floor. Nick's right shoulder exploded in pain, and he was knocked backward. His head hit the floor hard and for a moment he lay on his back, unconscious. When he came to the fist thing he saw was the sinister twinkle of Lurch's dark sunken eyes. Nick's ankles had already been bound and now Lurch was leaning over him tying his wrists together, behind his back. Immediately, Nick began to squirm, but it was too late. The evil man had finished and was pulling away. By his slower than normal movements, Nick could tell that Lurch had been wounded pretty badly, but the evil man's grin was as strong as ever.

Blood-soaked Patterson slowly stood up and stepped back, revealing Davenport, who although disheveled, had a firm grip on Lisa. "You really are a shit, you know that?" Davenport said and then gestured for Patterson to take hold of Lisa. "And a terrible father, might I add. We had a deal, Nicholas. I was going to let her go, but not now."

"You asshole!" Nick said.

"Now, now is that any way to speak in front of your daughter?"

"Go to Hell."

Angered and clearly tired of the night's long, drawn out sequence of events, Davenport turned and reached for Patterson's gun. "Let me see that for a second."

Patterson handed him the gun and Davenport pointed it at Nick's good shoulder and pulled the trigger, knocking him backward and shooting another jolt of pain into his body.

"Stop it!" Lisa screamed as tears streamed down her face.

"Oh shut up!" Davenport commanded and then turned to her and fired again. Nick's eyes opened wide and all the pain in his body suddenly vanished as he watched Lisa get knocked to the floor.

"No!" He screamed as his face turned red and his wounded shoulders flexed incessantly in an unsuccessful attempt to break free of the ties. "No! I'll kill you. You son of a bitch, I'll kill you!" He screamed and bucked so hard that he managed to turn himself over, from his back to his stomach and back again.

Watching the pretty boy's body thrash violently on the tile floor exhilarated Patterson. His grin widened and he began to chuckle as the helpless, pathetic fool squirmed before him. His laugh was momentarily interrupted, however as he coughed up bright red blood, but as soon as he brought a hand to his mouth and realized what he had coughed up his chuckle resumed.

Unable to think clearly, Nick continued to squirm and fight against the cords that bound him until eventually all his energy was gone. Completely out of breath and with his anger fading into a sense of loss and futility, Nick stopped trying to tear free, turned to face Lisa and rested his cheek on the tile. His water-filled eyes fell on his daughter, and although her hair covered most of her face, he could still see the cold stare of her unblinking eyes. "No," he whispered softly as his eyes began to gloss over. "No."

She was lying face down and still wore her nightshirt. The bastard must have taken her from her bed. As the pain and aches slowly crept back into his body, Nick watched as a pool of blood slowly accumulated beneath her tender stomach and wondered if she had been awake or sleeping when the evil man came. Then suddenly, Dottie's words resounded through his brain, "There's a time to move on, and when our effort in trying to work out the mysteries of the past, no matter how bizarre or painful, start seriously affecting those we love, it's time to let go." Why hadn't he been able to just let things go? He finally knew just what had happened to his precious wife, but at what cost?

Davenport and Patterson were talking, at least he thought they were, but by now he had just about tuned everything out and could only focus on Lisa.

"Peaches," he whispered as tears poured from his blank stare.

Suddenly, someone or something took hold of his hair. It was Davenport. He lifted Nick's head and looked into his eyes. "Did you hear that Nicholas?"

While his cheek was on the tile, Nick had begun to drool and now, as Davenport spoke, there was a thin string of saliva connecting his mouth to the floor. "We're going to use you and your daughter for the next memory transfer." Davenport was happier than he had been all night. "Aren't you excited? Do you know what that means? We are going to record your memories. You'll live forever, well your memories will at least."

Davenport let go of Nick's hair and Nick's face hit the floor hard, but he felt no pain.

"Gregory, this is going to be the best memory transfer yet. You know what makes for good memory transfers, don't you?"

"Yes sir, a traumatic death experience."

"Very good Gregory, very good. So, what do you think's going to happen next?"

Patterson's grin widened and his deep eyes brightened as he spoke. "We're going to torture them?"

"No." Davenport stressed, "*We* are not going to do anything. *You* however, are going to do the torturing. *I* am going to go have a quick chat with the good doctor and get the equipment ready.

For a moment Patterson stood there, speechless and looking a bit like the kid who had just walked into the chocolate factory.

As the two men planned, Nick's thoughts drifted back to the last day he had seen his Allie alive. It began as one of the happiest days of his life. She looked so beautiful as she got into the kayak. The golden rays of the sun weren't quite complete until they bounced off her radiant hair. Nick shut his eyes and merged into the past as Patterson leaned over and gabbed him by the hair. Patterson pulled Nick up and with a six-inch knife, slowly, ever so slowly cut off Nick's ear, but Nick didn't feel a thing. He was back at the river, happily chasing after Allie, in the kayak.

The lack of response angered Patterson and he shoved the blade into Nick's cheek, slicing through his gums and gouging out a couple of teeth in the process. Back at the river, Nick smiled as he caught up with Allie and returned her splash. Patterson became enraged and dropped Nick's bleeding face back onto the floor. "You think that's funny, do ya? Well, what about this?" Patterson asked, as he moved to Lisa and grabbed her hair, intending to do the same to her. When he lifted her head, however and seen her open, lifeless eyes he realized that she was already gone and let go of her head as well.

"Damn you!" Patterson rasped as he kicked Nick in the ribs. "Mr. Davenport wants a good memory transfer! And that's what I intend to give him." Patterson was in worse shape than he had thought and the kick was so violent that it took the wind out of him. His chest began to ache. He had been shot at least four times, but none of them were fatal. A couple of them were in the upper chest, closer to his shoulder than his heart. One of them hit the left side of his gut, and another must have shattered a couple of ribs as it entered the right, lower area of his chest.

He became a bit dizzy, coughed up more blood, and began to double over. He smiled as he noticed he was wheezing and within moments found himself sitting on the floor tying to catch his breath.

Meanwhile, Nick had lost the will to live and his vision had turned sour. As his life slowly faded, he found himself standing in the rushing water trying to dislodge his drowning wife.

"No!" He screamed.

Now, in his dream and unlike the events that actually took place eight years ago, things were different. Instead of staying fixed in one spot as he tugged on her body, she sank deeper. The harder he pulled the deeper she went. He pulled with all his strength and for a moment it seemed as if he was making progress, but then suddenly, everything around him changed. He was on his stomach lying in a small pool of water, just outside of the river's mainstream.

Back in the lab, Patterson had caught his breath and was just about to resume his torture session when he noticed a pool of crystal clear water seeping into the laboratory, just beneath the pretty boy's head. Holding his chest, Patterson curiously leaned over to have a better look. The pool was growing fairly quickly, but where was it coming from? Before long the water reached his shoes, and Patterson lifted Nick's shoulder and rolled him over. Nick's eyes were open and motionless. Patterson took his eyes off the dead man and carefully studied the floor, but still couldn't tell where all the water was coming from.

At the river, Nick was overtaken by a sense of profound peace, as he lay face down in the pool of water, but as some strange force rolled him over, he remembered that Allie was still stuck in the kayak, drowning.

"No!" He screamed and reached up with both hands. "Allie, no!"

Patterson jumped back in shock, as the corpse broke free of its restraints, shot two hands up into the air and screamed for Allie.

Two separate realities were unfolding simultaneously. In one of them Patterson was standing in a small puddle of water, watching an animated corpse reach for the ceiling, and in the other, Nick was lying face up, in his own pool of water, outside, by the river.

Nick tried to get up and run back to the river to help Allie, but for some reason couldn't.

"Allie!" he screamed again.

Davenport and Dr. Boris entered the room just as Nick's lifeless body was shouting for the second time.

"What in God's name is happening?" Davenport asked as his dress shoes tapped on the surface of the ever-increasing water.

Patterson looked blank-faced at Davenport for a moment and then returned his eyes to Nick and asked, "Is he dead?"

"Of course he's not dead," Dr. Boris replied.

"Then why are his eyes so empty and why don't they blink?"

Dr. Boris didn't answer him, but rather gazed around the room at all of the dead bodies and said, "Jonathan, I'll have no part of this," and then reached for the door. He grabbed a hold of the handle and pulled, but nothing happened. The door wouldn't budge. Just then, Nick shouted again. "Allie!" and as he did the seeping water developed a spring and began to bubble in even faster.

Back at the river, Nick was still calling for Allie and trying to get up. After his last shout, however something strange had happened. The main flow of the river shifted and as a consequence a considerable amount of water was being diverted into the pool he was in. The water was growing deeper and deeper, and Nick still couldn't move. Soon it was up to his ears, and in no time at all it would be covering his face. Nick's thoughts however, stayed focused on Allie, and again he screamed.

Dr. Boris grabbed the door handle with both hands, placed his foot against the wall and pulled back with of all his might, but the door just would not open. Then suddenly, Nick screamed again. This time his cry was louder and longer, and the acoustics in the room played havoc with everyone's ears, making it sound inherently deranged and as if it was coming from everywhere at once.

Davenport looked down at his shoes. The water was nearly covering the top of them. Soon it would be up to his ankles. At first he looked puzzled, but then the puzzlement changed to concern as he looked over at the doctor, who was making yet another unsuccessful attempt to open the door. As Davenport swished his way over to the door to give the doctor a hand, Nick screamed again. "Allie!" This time there was no mistaking it. The sound did come from everywhere at once, and then Patterson rasped.

At first they didn't hear him, but then he shouted it. "Its eyes are open!"

Dr. Boris and Davenport turned around and naturally looked at Nick, but then instantly noticed that Patterson wasn't looking at Nick. His eyes were fixated in the direction of the two glass tubes. Both men, Boris and Davenport raised their eyes at the same time and saw that Number Nine was staring aimlessly into the lab. As soon as they saw it, Nick's voice filled the air again and this time vibrated the walls. The shout grabbed Number Nine's attention, and it turned its head to look in Nick's direction.

Meanwhile, at the river, Nick found himself completely submerged beneath the water, but even now while he was deprived of air, the only image that he could see was his drowning Allie. He screamed from below the surface, "Allie!" He had to get up. He had to find a way to get back to the rushing water, back to his Allie. He had to save her.

Davenport stood for a moment, bewildered, and then Nick's scream vibrated the walls again. This time it was gurgled and unclear, but there was no mistaking it. He yelled for his Allie! As Nick's scream echoed through the room, Number Nine's glass tube shattered, and Biotronic's prize experiment floated up into the air.

The three men stood motionless and watched Number Nine's naked and stiff body drift weightlessly into the center of the lab. Then suddenly, without warning, it removed its gaze from Nick and glared in their direction. Its emotionless countenance appeared to be hiding a ton of pent up vengeance and sent an eerie chill through both Davenport and Dr. Boris. Davenport swallowed hard, took an unconscious step backward and noticed that the water was nearly up to his knees.

The three men watched as Number Nine began to tilt forward, in their direction. Soon it hung, diagonally leaning toward them, and with its hands rigidly at its sides, it started to move. As it slowly began drifting toward them, Davenport and Boris quickly reached for the doorknob. Together, they gave it all they had, but it still wouldn't move. As the two men scrambled to get away, Patterson, although awestruck, felt no fear. He slowly raised his gun, took careful aim and, with a somber face, calmly wheezed, "Goodbye."

He pulled the trigger, but oddly the gun didn't fire. *Click!* He squeezed again. *Click!* With Number Nine inching ever closer, he quickly examined the gun, made sure there were bullets in the clip and then fired again. *Click*! His confidence slowly gave way to apprehension as he swished backward through water that was now above his knees and continued pulling the trigger. *Click, click, click.* Number Nine came within inches of Patterson's failing gun and stopped. Patterson finally began to feel the immensity of the situation when Number Nine's already intense eyes now began to glow.

With his wheezing worsening, Patterson dropped the gun and turned to help the other two men open the door. As before, however the door showed no sign of giving. It might just as well have been welded shut.

The glowing in Number Nine's eyes was somehow connected with the water level in the room. The brighter they shined the quicker the room filled. Soon the glow shown so brightly that it obscured any sign of Number Nine's eyeballs, and water began to pour from the top four corners of the lab. It started in trickles, but before long was gushing in. Water began seeping across the ceiling causing the overhead lights to pop. One at a time they exploded until finally the only light in the lab was the eerie blue light shining through Number Nine's eyes.

As the water level raced toward Davenport's waist, he hurriedly reached into his coat, retrieved his cell-phone and quickly dialed a number, but the moment he pressed the *send* key the phone sparked, popped and burned his hand. He yelled in pain, dropped the phone and grabbed his wounded paw.

Dr. Boris finally gave up on the door and turned to face the demon. He adjusted his glasses, forced down a swallow, and then with a crackle in his voice pleaded, "I don't want to die." His words only made matters worse. Number Nine turned its head, and with empty sockets of light, peered at the doctor. Then suddenly, a woman's voice screamed out of its somber face, "Help me!" and an unnatural chill shot through Boris' spine, as he instantly knew to whom it belonged.

The bloodcurdling feeling of inevitable retribution welled up inside him, and he knew what it meant. It was time to pay up. He shook his head and fearfully whispered, "But I didn't do anything. I didn't do anything." And the very instant he said it he knew that that had been his sin. *He didn't do anything.*

Just then Number Nine's jaw dropped open and a blinding amount of the same blue light shot forth. It shown like a spotlight on Dr. Boris and all at once the water stopped filling the room. For a moment the laboratory was completely silent, and everyone stood absolutely still. Number Nine, still in the air, just above the water peered at Dr. Boris from less than five feet away. Soon, the fear overwhelmed him and the doctor began to tremble. He tried to speak, but for fear or some other reason he couldn't get his mouth to open. Then suddenly, something latched onto his ankle and yanked him violently below the surface.

While Davenport and Patterson stood, preparing to be the next victim to be yanked into the water, Nick had just about run out of air, and with the very last breath that he had, he screamed, "Allie!"

Being the last that Nick had to give, this scream was more intense than all of the previous screams put together, and everything in the lab shook. Number Nine's mouth shut as it turned its head and looked at the water just above Nick. Patterson decided to take advantage of the distraction, and with one smooth motion he pulled out his knife and lunged at the experiment gone wrong. Still gazing in Nick's direction, Number Nine quickly raised its hand up in front of Patterson, causing him to freeze in mid leap. Patterson stood, muscles locked, perfectly balanced on the toe of his dress shoe. He could think, and he could breath, but except for his eyes he could not move. Then Number Nine's other hand rose toward Nick, and the water just above him began to sway. Davenport silently snuck backward and watched as Lisa and Nick's bodies bubbled up out of the water. They both appeared to be lifeless and floated facing each other in a semi-fetal position.

Gradually, the image in Nick's mind began to change until he found himself back in the lab, and once again looking into the blank stare of his motionless daughter. Somehow, all of this time he had managed to hold on, but for what? Now as he gazed into her unblinking eyes, he decided that it was time to let go. A calming sensation overtook him as the blue light around her beautiful face began, first to blur and then to fade, until all he could see were her precious eyes. Just as he was letting go of the very last strand of life within him, Lisa gasped. She was alive. Nick tried to fight, but he was already too far gone. His vision continued to narrow as he struggled to suck in air, but couldn't.

Sneaking along the wall, trying to put as much distance between himself and Number Nine as possible, Davenport was startled by Lisa's unexpected gasp and nearly slipped in the water. Then, Number Nine's fingers slowly began to move, and as they did, Nick's head starting glowing blue and the slice in his cheek stitched itself back together. Teeth floated to the top of the water and reattached themselves to his gum line as his ear somehow melted itself back on, to the side of his head. Number Nine's fingers continued to wiggle, working the blue glow downward, into Nick's chest, and before long, the two bullets lodged there worked their way out and hung in the air just above his body. As the skin sewed itself back together, the bullets began twirling around one another. They continued to pick up momentum until they appeared to be a single piece of metal, flickering in the blue light. Then, without warning, as if they were released from an invisible slingshot, they rocketed toward Patterson. He watched with horror as they entered his skull one after the other, and then without warning, the mysterious force that held him, loosened its grip and he plunged below the surface of the water.

By now Nick's vision had gone completely dark and the strange calmness that permeated him had all but chased away his desire to live, but still, he held on. If he could only take a breath. Then, the blue glow moved into his diaphragm, causing it to flex. His lungs expanded and much-needed oxygen entered his bloodstream. A moment later he regained his vision, and Lisa came into view. She was wheezing and didn't look well at all.

Then Number Nine's fingers shifted toward Lisa, allowing gravity to regain its hold on Nick. As her stomach began to glow, Nick moved to Lisa, took her in his arms, and tried to ascertain just exactly what it was that was happening to her.

From the corner of the lab, sandwiched between one of the electronic apparatuses and the two walls, Davenport watched with dread as the bullet worked its way out of Lisa's gut and began to spin in the air just above her body. He stood with his back to the corner trying to squeeze or perhaps wish his body through, when suddenly the bullet left its location and raced toward him. He shook his head and screamed, "No!" as it approached. Then miraculously, instead of entering his skull like the bullets that shot at Patterson, this one only grazed his cheek.

At first, Davenport wasn't quite sure whether he was dead or alive, but then he slowly raised a hand to his face and began to laugh with joy. The bullet had missed. Unable to resist the urge, he briefly gave in to the feeling of relief and sighed. As he did however, he shifted his weight and slipped. Worry, once again, filled his countenance as he disappeared below the surface. Under the water he worked frantically to regain his footing, but oddly enough as he did, he managed to get his head caught between the terminal and one of the walls.

His fear only added to his plight, and the more he struggled to raise his head, the worse things got. Soon his head was wedged so tightly that he couldn't move it up or down, and to make matters worse he could feel the surface of the water lightly swaying up against the backside of his head, letting him know that oxygen was only inches away. He struggled in vain for a few more seconds and then reached up out of the water and desperately began banging on the side of the terminal.

Across the lab, Nick had just about got a good grasp on what was happening. It had taken him a few minutes to sort through the bizarre surroundings. He had woken up in a dimly lighted room filled with water, and although he had remembered being shot twice, he felt no pain. The oddity of the situation was so profound that for a moment he wondered if he had died, and whether this strange place was somehow connected with Hell, but then he saw Lisa and instantly dismissed the idea. He may have belonged in Hell, sure, but there was no way that Lisa did. She looked to be half dead, floating on top of the water, just in front of him. Instantly, he went to her and watched in amazement as a bullet squeezed itself out of her gut and then flung itself across the lab at Davenport. Miraculously, Lisa was being healed.

The only light in the lab was coming from the eyes of an eerie looking zombie-like person floating above the water. The image almost made Nick rethink his Hell explanation, but on second thought, after taking a closer look, he surmised that it was more likely to be Alex than some under-worldly creature. After gazing up at the strange sight for a few moments, he wondered whether or not Allie's memories were really inside there somewhere. A lump formed in his throat as he thought about what that might mean.

Now, as Nick stood there staring at Alex and wondering about Allie, Davenport began banging for help. Nick's first reaction was to let the bastard drown, but as Davenport continued to slam his open palm against the metal, Nick couldn't help himself. After telling Lisa to stay put and glancing up one more time at Alex, he began to wade his way through the water. As he did however, a strange thing happened. The closer he drew to Davenport, the thicker the water became. Somehow, with every step, the water directly in front of him seemed to be solidifying just a bit, into some sort of jell, until he could no longer move forward. It was as if some strange force didn't want him to continue, didn't want him to save Davenport.

Nick turned, looked over his shoulder at Alex, and found that Alex was looking directly at him. Then Nick noticed that there was a faint glow coming from the water around his legs. Alex was the one who didn't want Davenport saved.

"But you can't just kill him," Nick said, but Alex did not respond, nor did the water loosen its grip. As Nick turned back toward Davenport, he remembered just how much he had wanted this evil man to die, but now with Davenport helplessly under the water, drowning, a sour feeling crept into Nick's gut.

This was the pinnacle of what he had wanted for eight years. To find out what had happened and ultimately make someone pay for taking his Allie, but as he stood there in the dim blue light listening to the frantic poundings of a drowning old man, he realized that nothing, not even this, was going to bring his Allie back.

As Davenport's pounding began to fade, Nick tried with all his might to lift a leg, but couldn't, and then suddenly all was quiet. Davenport had stopped banging. An instant later the water relaxed its hold, and Nick raced through the water toward the old man.

Reaching him, Nick latched onto the man's shoulders and pulled with all of his strength, but Davenport wouldn't budge. Finally, Nick decided to try it the other way and began pushing down on the back of his head. A few seconds later the hold on it loosened and it slipped out of the wedge. Immediately, Nick reached below the water and pulled the man up. As he did so, the water level in the room began to drop off.

Nick pulled the old man's face out of the water and saw that his eyes were open and staring aimlessly out of a face that was locked in an expression of utter horror. The water level continued to diminish and soon the old man's corpse was sitting on the tile and leaning against the wall.

As Nick ran his fingers over Davenport's face, shutting his eyes, he thought about his Allie and pondered the irony of Davenport's death. How could Davenport have known that by standing on the bank that day and deliberately doing nothing as one of God's most precious and beautiful creatures drowned, eight years later he himself would suffer the same fate?

Nick tried to determine, but couldn't quite figure out whether he felt better or worse. On the one hand, the mystery of what had happened to his wife had finally been solved, and the man responsible had paid for his crime, but on the other hand, because the mystery had indeed been solved, Nick's quest was over, and in some strange sense that seemed to make life a little emptier.

What had Nick been hoping for all these years? He had never been one to commit cold-blooded murder, but on the deepest level, he couldn't help but to take joy in Davenport's death, but still it wasn't enough. Something was missing, but he couldn't put his finger on exactly what it was. His heart started to ache and tears welled up in his eyes as he thought about Allie. A brief smile flashed over his countenance as the tears began to run down his cheeks.

Why did she go away? As quick as he asked the question, he was given answer. Her death had been his fault. Deep down inside he had known it all along. He was the one that talked her into kayaking. He was the one that dragged her out of bed that day, and it was he that helped her get into her kayak. It wasn't Davenport; it wasn't Dr. Boris; it wasn't some strange mysterious force; it was he. Sure, Davenport was an evil man, and maybe the world was better off without him in it, but he didn't drown Allie, Nick did.

As Nick squatted beside davenport's corpse, feeling sorry for himself, the blue glow around the lab began to fade, and before long he found himself straining to see. He thought about Lisa and raised his eyes, but by now it was far too dark to see across the lab. After, standing up and taking a step, he noticed that the water had all but gone and Alex was no longer floating in the center of the lab, but was rather across the room and either sitting or kneeling on the floor.

Nick called for Peaches.

"I'm okay Daddy! I'm over here!" Her enthusiastic voice sounded strangely out of place and came from Alex's location. As Nick approached and the dark images began to take form, he spotted three shadows sitting on the floor with their backs to him. He figured that the one glowing was probably Alex, and he was fairly certain that the little one beside him was Lisa, but he had no idea who the other person was. Alex's glow had dwindled considerably, but Nick could tell that he was leaning over yet a fourth individual. Nick walked around the silhouettes and recognized Mercedes as the one whom Alex was tending to. Instantly, his heart leaped into his throat as he realized what was happening. Alex was trying to bring her back from the dead.

Nick was instantly filled with anticipation. If Alex was healing Mercedes then that must mean that the unknown silhouette sitting beside Lisa was Roger. Nick lifted his eyes, and just as he had guessed, Mr. Clean was alive! With growing anticipation he returned his gaze to Mercedes, and noticed a faint glow coming from her head. He moved closer, knelt down beside her face and looked across at Alex. He sure didn't look the same as he had earlier. His eyes were still glowing, but not nearly as brightly as before, and his face looked sunken and drained. Nick shifted his eyes back to Mercedes and watched as dozens of tiny white fragment around her head began to move together. They looked almost fluidic as they began fusing themselves to each other, making larger and larger pieces. Then somehow, the larger pieces kind of melted or merged themselves to the back of her head. Nick sat in awe as he watched her skull put itself back together.

The glow in Mercedes' head brightened as a weird sucking noise came out of it. Nick grabbed her cold hand and narrowed his eyes as he watched her lifeless mouth open. The sucking grew louder, and then with a wet pop, the bullet floated up out of her mouth. As Nick's eyes followed the bullet into the air he could not help but to notice Alex. He appeared to be even worse now than he had been just a few seconds ago. His glow was nearly gone and his eyes were beginning to droop. Then Nick noticed something else. As the glow in Mercedes' head brightened, the glow in Alex's eyes diminished. It was taking all the energy he had to heal Mercedes.

Worry crept into Nick's gut as he wondered whether or not Alex had enough energy left to save her, and still remain alive. If Alex died, then any lingering memories of Allie would die along with him. Nick became riddled with guilt as he struggled with his thoughts. If one of them had to die, shamefully, he wasn't sure whether he'd rather it to be Mercedes or Alex. It wasn't that he wanted Mercedes to die. It was just that some part of Allie was locked deep inside Alex, and he couldn't bare the idea of the last of her being taken away—not again, not at least without a chance to say goodbye. As the glow began to fade from Alex's eyes, the last of Mercedes' skull melded into place, and just as the glow gave way to a pitch-black room, Mercedes gasped. She was alive!

"Hey there," Nick crackled in the dark.

"Where am I?" Mercedes tried to sit up.

"It's okay. You're alive." Nick replied as he supported her back and helped her rise.

"What happened? And why is it so dark?"

"You were shot," Nick replied, "but now you're okay. Now you're okay."

"I can't see anything!" Mercedes said anxiously.

"Don't worry, nobody can. All the lights went out."

"All the lights went out?"

"Yeah, it's a long story."

Nick helped as Mercedes stood up. "The last thing I remember is being grabbed by that freak and," she paused a minute as she thought, "having a gun shoved down my throat."

"You're okay now."

Just then the previously sealed door unlocked itself and slowly swung open allowing light from the hall to enter the lab.

Everyone looked around the dimly lighted room at the shadows of the dead men. Davenport's corpse was right where Nick had left it. Dr. Boris' body had been twisted up like a pretzel and might have passed for one of his very own experiments that didn't quite make it. Lurch lay on his back, by the now half-open door, staring up at the ceiling with two holes in his head.

"What happened?" Lisa voiced the question that was on everyone's mind.

"Don't know," Nick replied as his eyes finished their stroll around the room and returned to Alex. He looked lifeless and Nick's heart sank, but then he looked at Mercedes and was sure that the right choice had been made. For a second Nick watched Alex's chest, hoping to see it expand as it filled up with air, but it did not.

Finally, he bent over to get a pulse, but just before his fingers found Alex's neck, Alex opened his eyes. It was startling and a little eerie, as if someone just flipped a switch and turned Alex on. Nick wasn't quite sure, but he thought that he could still see a faint glow shining through his eyes.

Then, like some weird cyborg out of a science fiction movie, Alex got to his feet, turned toward the tube holding Number Twelve and began to tremble. For a moment, Lisa thought she could see sadness in his eyes, but wasn't sure. Just then things took a turn for the worse.

After a night of such outlandish experiences, one would think that none of them would have been the least bit surprised to see what happened next, but the Three Musketeers and Lisa stood wide-eyed and became mildly concerned as the tile floor directly beneath Alex's feet began to tremble right along with him. Like shockwaves, the trembling spread out in all directions. As it met with the walls and began to climb, Roger and Lisa decided that now was a pretty good time to leave and quickly made their way to the door. Mercedes and Nick, however both lingered behind, wanting to grab Alex and bring him along, but not quite certain if it were safe enough to do so.

As the quaking grew worse, the room quickly began to fill with urgency. If things kept going the way they were, before too long the group would find themselves standing at the epicenter of a full-scale earthquake.

"Come on! We gotta get out of here!" Roger yelled from just outside the door.

"Daddy!" Lisa urged.

Barely able to remain standing, Nick and Mercedes looked at each other with an expression of *it's now or never,* and then as if their actions had been choreographed, they simultaneously reached out and took a hold of Alex. The instant he was grabbed they both half expected to be electrocuted or perhaps something worse, but to their relief nothing happened. At first they tried to walk him out, but his legs would not cooperate. Finally, they each threw an arm around their necks, heaved him up and carried him across the ever-worsening, vibrating floor. Halfway to the door, Roger impatiently shook his head, and against his better judgment came to help.

Just as he was relieving Mercedes the, second glass tube shattered with a loud bang. They all turned quickly and noticed that the woman who had only been referred to as Number Twelve, had fallen to the floor. The shaking was growing worse, and Nick knew that if he didn't go back and get her right then that it would be too late. Without time to think, he had Roger take Alex's arm and then started back across the floor. As he did, however Alex's hand suddenly came to life and like the head of a striking snake, latched onto his arm and held tight with an ironclad grip. Struggling to free himself, Nick watched as a huge metal ceiling beam came crashing down on Number Twelve, killing her instantly. If Alex had not grabbed him when he did, Nick would have been right there next to Number Twelve when the ceiling dropped.

"C'mon!" Mercedes yelled, afraid that if they waited much longer they would all suffer the same fate. As the team hurried down the hall, on their way to the elevator, the place began to shake itself apart. Panels were coming loose from the walls; parts of the ceiling kept dropping from above, and as before, the overhead lights began to blow out. The quaking became so violent that walking was nearly impossible.

"We have to leave him here!" Roger yelled, raising his voice to be heard over the commotion.

"We're not leaving him!" Mercedes snapped as she held onto the wall for balance.

"But he's the one causing all of this shit!"

"Maybe so, but we're not leaving him!"

Roger looked to Nick for help, but instead got a stern look that let him know that if Alex wasn't leaving the building, then nobody was. Roger shook his head and reluctantly stumbled on.

Soon the team reached the elevator, and as Mercedes reached up and held her finger over the button, she began to rethink their exit strategy and her stomach soured. "What if it's already broke?" she screamed, "or worse, what if the damn thing breaks down while we're in it?"

The next thing she knew, Nick was pressing her hesitant finger into the button. "We don't have a choice, and we don't have time!" Moments later, the oval indicator lighted up, and the thick metal doors parted.

The inside of the elevator didn't look the slightest bit appealing. It seemed to wobble in a whole different direction than the rest of the building and there didn't appear to be any working lights inside. Mercedes and Lisa watched as Nick and Roger stumbled in with Alex, and then with their hearts in their throats they followed behind. The quaking caused the elevator to sway back and forth so badly that it felt like a small ship in a violent sea, and Mercedes just knew that they would never get to the ground floor. She struggled to regain her breath as she watched Nick reach over, press the button and seal their fate.

The ride to the top felt like an eternity, and every few seconds Mercedes' stomach would drop a little more as the elevator slammed hard into the outside shaft.

"What is going on? Why is he doing this?" Roger asked.

"I don't know, why don't you ask him?" Nick replied.

"Maybe he doesn't like the place," Lisa offered her wisdom.

Just then, the swaying elevator slammed into the shaft so hard that it dented clear through to the inside. Everyone was knocked to the floor, and Mercedes thought that she heard one of the outside cables snap.

"Did you guys hear that?" she yelled.

"Hear what?" Lisa asked, not really sure she wanted to know.

"It sounded like one of the elevator cables just broke."

Everyone's eyes strolled around the darkness, and Nick got to his feet as they all listened carefully, but the sound was not repeated.

"We're not going to make it!" Mercedes shouted.

"Yes we will!" screamed Lisa confidently. Then, at the tail end of her confidence, another cable snapped. This one was loud enough for everyone to hear. For an instant, the elevator stopped its shaking and hovered silently like a battered ship that had just entered the eye of the storm, and then with another loud pop, it began to plummet. Less than an instant later it stopped with a jolt.

Screams filled the darkness as Nick's mind raced. They had to be somewhere near the top by now. Nick reached out, felt his way around the elevator and found the seam where the double doors met.

"Roger, gimmee a hand!" He grunted, as a tiny ray of light made its way through the crack and glowed at the center of the doors.

At first Roger didn't understand what Nick was asking, but then as he saw the glow between the doors brighten just a bit, he leaped to his feet and found the opposite side of the doors. The two men worked with all their strength and before long, pulled the doors apart.

Unlike some fairytale or a fictional novel, the elevator wasn't caught at the edge of a floor or halfway between floors, with some mysterious rung-ladder just outside. No, just like life, the elevator had found the strangest possible place to stop. The men pulled open the doors to find the landing just in front of them. The elevator couldn't have been better positioned if it was in perfect working order and someone had pressed the button for this particular floor.

Wide-eyed and amazed, the group quickly shuffled out into the quaking building. Roger and Nick with Alex in tow were the last to exit. The instant they stepped clear of the doors, the elevator silently continued its freefall. There was no sound of cables snapping or gears breaking. It had been as if some mysterious force had stopped the car at just the right place, held it there just long enough for everyone to exit, and then released it. The group looked around at each other, but eventually all eyes fell on Alex.

"C'mon!" Nick urged, as he started down the hall, toward the stairwell sign. The group followed, and before long they made their way to the top floor and out into the parking lot.

Now that the group had made it out of the building, Roger began to slow down, but Nick urged him to keep going. "We're not far enough yet!"

Roger shook his bald head and squinted his dark eyes. "What do you mean? We're out!"

"The blueprints to the place shows that the structure continues on for most of the parking lot!"

As the group raced to the edged of the lot, the building behind them began to collapse in on itself. At the fence, Nick and Roger panted as they gently sat Alex down and leaned him up against the chain link. They turned around just in time to see the entire building turn into a puff of smoke. At first it looked like some amazing magic trick that might have been preformed by David Copperfield or Doug Henning, but as the smoke began to clear it was obvious that the building hadn't vanished into thin air. The entire structure had caved in on top of itself. For just an instance the earth stopped shaking, and the group breathed a sigh of relief, but almost immediately it started back up. Whatever swallowed up the lab was now swallowing up the parking lot that surrounded it. The hole kept enlarging, bringing the edge ever closer to the group, and soon Mercedes and Lisa began to worry. Everyone quickly stood up and pushed their backs hard into the fence behind them as they watched the edge of the opening approach.

At that exact same moment a crowed had gathered across town to watch another bizarre event. The Trend Star building and its three companions were mysteriously shaking themselves apart. Just like at the Boris Lab, the quaking started at a single spot within the building and quickly spread outward. Mr. Davenport's bronze nameplate on top of his desk was the first to tremble. Within moments the trembling had grown so strong that the thick glass walls cornering his office shattered. In no time at all the entire building was quaking. Just as the foundation was about to give way the tremor had spread to the neighboring three buildings and they too, began to shake. As a matter of fact, crowds were gathering all over the city as many different structures, all owned by the Biotronics corporation, were falling victim to the strange and mysterious hit and miss earthquake. Although many commercial buildings were toppling over and caving in, only two residential homes found themselves affected. A small mansion, belonging to Mr. Jonathan Davenport of course and a beautiful but modest three-bedroom house, owned by none other than Henry Boris were just about to become a couple of piles of rubble.

Meanwhile, at the lab, the hole had devoured 90% of the parking lot and the gobbling edge had come within less than a meter before the quaking finally stopped. Everyone stood as still as humanly possible, even refraining from breathing, afraid that the slightest movement might somehow restart the earth-swallowing event.

Finally, Roger was the first to speak. He carefully whispered, "I think it's over." Mercedes and Lisa slowly began to relax, but his hope had come a bit too soon, for the moment the words left his lips the ground once again began to tremble. Immediately Mercedes and Lisa both stiffened back up and tightly gripped the chain link as they watched and waited for the hole to gobble them up. As the girls were getting ready to scale the fence, Nick was noticing something very different about this shaking. As he began to assess the situation, he realized that it wasn't the ground that was trembling. It was Alex.

He bent over and raised Alex's head. Alex's face was extremely pale. Dark and pus-filled flesh encircled bloodshot eyes, and his skin was cold and brittle.

Soon the group began to relax as they too realized that the shaking was only coming from Alex and unlike before, this time the ground wasn't copying him.

Then another strange thing happened. Alex's death-filled eyes began to go from person to person, and seemed to shine with recognition as they went.

First, he gazed up at Nick, and for just a moment it looked as if he just might smile. Then, he turned to Lisa, who had barely let go of the fence and was in the process of latching onto her father. As Alex peered at her, a tear found its way to the edge of one of his eyes. Finally, after a brief gaze in Roger's direction, Alex's eyes met Mercedes'.

He was wheezing and finding it hard to breathe, and his eyes had to work hard to stay open. It looked as if he wanted to speak, but before he could get anything out, he coughed. It was bad and seemed to go on forever. Several times he would spit up green mucus and looked as if he was about to vomit, but nothing would come up. Finally he cleared his throat and with a string of drool hanging from his chin, his voice crackled as he wheezed out her name.

"You remember me?" She replied, fearfully bewildered.

Alex coughed again as he shook his head. "No, but I can see the memories you have of me in your mind. You told me that I wasn't alone anymore," he hesitated as he coughed again and then continued, "and that no matter what happened we would face it together." His words were weak and soft.

Mercedes smiled happy-sad tears as he coughed once more.

"You kept your promise!" This time as he continued to cough, blood poured over his bottom lip.

Mercedes stopped smiling, straightened her face and she said, "We have to get him to a hospital."

Just as Nick and Roger were leaning over, getting ready to latch back onto Alex's arms, Alex protested, "No! There's no time. She wants you to know…"

Nick and Roger hesitated as Mercedes asked, "Who? Who wants me to know?"

"Not you." He wheezed, and then turned his gaze toward Nick. Nick's stomach began to sour as he realized just whom Alex was talking about.

"She wants *you* to know," Alex repeated as he stared into Nick's curious eyes.

Nick swallowed hard and although he knew the answer, still he asked the question, "Who? Who wants me to know?"

Alex coughed up more blood and latched onto Nick's leather jacket. "There's no time. She wants you to know! She wants you to know, now!" He pulled hard and Nick nearly fell on top of him. As Nick was bracing himself with his palm on the asphalt on the other side of Alex, Alex reached up with his free hand and grabbed Nick's face. At first, Nick instinctively began to struggle, but almost immediately he found himself once again back at the river.

This time however, he wasn't seeing things out of his own eyes, but rather he was seeing them through hers.

He found himself in her kayak, battling to get to shore, and then in a flash he was at the bank, trying to get out of the boat. However, something terrible happened and he slip. The next thing he knew he was beneath the rushing water, and his head was stuck between a couple of tree limbs. The current was strong—too strong—and no matter how hard he struggled he couldn't break free. He grabbed the branches with both hands and worked with all his might, but it was no use. Before long he began to run out of air, and then the strangest thing happened. All of his thinking began to center around a single thought. It was the most bizarre and absurd thought he could have possibly imagined, because the thought that he was thinking was of himself. All he could imagine, as his body swayed at the mercy of the rushing water, was his very own face. He felt sickeningly queer, as his dying hope was to feel his very own hands around him, to comfort him. Then, just as he was giving up hope, someone grabbed his hand. The mysterious person quickly moved in closer and latched on tight with both hands, then began to pull. Whoever it was, was strong—very strong—but still, the person couldn't break him free. Then suddenly, he realized that the person pulling on him was himself! And then he remembered this was her life. He wasn't really here. He was still in the parking lot, at the Boris lab. This was a memory—*her* memory. This must have been what they transferred into Alex, and now Alex was giving it to him.

As he felt himself tug, he began to fill up with peace, and then something inside him knew that he wasn't going to make it, but it didn't matter. All he had wanted—all she had wanted was to be next to her husband one last time, to feel his loving arms around her, to feel the love between them, and she did. Nick was surprised to find out that although she drowned, she died happy, and full of love. There was no fear, for the one she loved was with her. Then, just when it seemed as if it couldn't get any stranger, Nick became weightless and the river no longer had any control over him.

He gently floated up, out of the water and oddly hovered next to himself. As he watched the younger image of himself scream in torment he wondered: *how this could be part of her memory?* Wasn't her body beneath the water? And if this was her soul, then how did this memory get into Alex's head? Before he could figure out the answers or ever ponder the questions further, he began to sense a flood of emotions welling up within her.

Empathy. Nick had never felt so much empathy. She wanted to reach out to him. She wanted to tell him not to cry, that she was no longer in pain, but she was helpless to do so. Then suddenly, some peculiar force began to pull—or more accurately—call her away. Nick sensed her resist as she tried desperately to let him know how she felt. The time they had spent together was more than she could have ever wished for, more than she could have ever deserved.

The mysterious tugging began to grow and soon it would be impossible to resist. She had to let him know how she felt. With all of her might she reached out with her soul and tried to force a single feeling into his heart. "If by some strange miracle of God I would have been given the choice in advance to have either lived a long life without having ever known you, or to have lived the life that I did and suffer the ending I did, then there is no question. I wouldn't have traded a single moment of the time we shared for an extra hundred years or even more."

Finally, the calling became so strong that she could no longer resist it. He went with her as she slowly floated upward, away from the river, and as he did, he wondered just how long this *memory* was going to last. He kept going, and soon layers of clouds began to pass beneath him.

Then suddenly, there was a blinding flash of light, followed immediately by complete and utter darkness. For a while there were no sounds to be heard and no images to be see. The universe had gone completely still. Everything within it had vanished and time itself had come to a stop.

Then, ever so gradually, after the passing of what can only be thought of as eternity itself, he opened his eyes, or at least he thought he did, but instead of finding himself back on the asphalt with Lisa, Mercedes, and Roger, as he expected to, he found himself in a very strange place. At first what he was experiencing was incomprehensible. He could not tell exactly which of his senses were being stimulated, because the information that he was receiving was unlike anything he had ever experienced. To say that he was experiencing sight and sound would not be totally correct as his senses were far too limiting and couldn't possibly be interpreting the information that was coming to him now. There was no ground beneath him, and oddly no reason for one. There were no structures in the distance, and no movement at all. He couldn't tell whether he was flesh and blood or something more. The most peaceful and beautiful fog had wrapped itself around him and extended for as far as he could interpret. Confused, and unsure, and with something keener than eyes, he carefully studied his surroundings, and then he noticed her.

She was barely more than a faint silhouette, enveloped at the very edge of the fog, but he recognized her instantly.

He slowly moved closer through the haze and then expectantly asked, "Allie?" He was surprised to recognize his own words. It was as if he was talking and not talking, thinking and not thinking. He wasn't sure if he created the words or if they had been there for all of eternity, just waiting for him to acknowledge them.

As he moved closer and her silhouette took on a more defined shape, he could tell that she was facing away from him and holding onto something vaguely familiar. As he focused in on it, he recognized it to be a paper napkin.

"Remember this?" Even though she wasn't exactly speaking and he wasn't exactly hearing, he still could not believe that he was experiencing a voice that had been missing from his life for over eight years. He froze. "You gave it to me the night we met, the night you rescued me. Remember?"

For a moment he was silent, petrified, unable to respond. Somehow, someway, he was in the very presence of the only woman he had ever truly loved. How was this possible? Was he dead? Was this Heaven or was he just trapped in some dysfunctional synapse of Alex's mind? His soul felt as if it just might crumble and be squashed out of existence by the sheer weight of the situation. His mouth, if that's what it was, seemed to go completely dry. Finally, with a bit of effort, he managed to push a question out into the abyss. "Am I dead?" The question hung in front of him and seemed to be as real or more so, than he himself.

Then, suddenly, he was consumed with fear and wonder as she slowly turned to face him. He looked upon her with his new eyes and was instantly awestruck. He remembered her to be beautiful, certainly, but the person before him was so far beyond beautiful that the only way to describe her was to say that she was perfect. Is this what happens when a person dies? Do they become perfect? And if so, are they really the same person they were, or do they become something more?

"No, you're not dead. It's not your time. There is still so much for you to do." She came even closer. "I'm here to tell you something." As he gazed upon perfection he couldn't help but wonder whether Allie was still Allie or something else.

"Tell me something?" he repeated her question, barely able to push the words into the void as he pondered what it would be like to merge with God.

For a while she remained motionless and just held his gaze. Then, just as he was about to repeat himself she continued, "It wasn't your fault."

Confusion and fear crept into his soul as her words hung timeless in the void before him.

"None of it was your fault."

"What wasn't my fault?" he asked, but deep inside he knew.

"The accident."

Hopelessness hid at the very corner of his soul, and anger filled his heart. "I should have never taken you to the river that day!"

"You didn't force me to go," she replied sternly.

"I should have never taught you to kayak."

"That didn't kill me."

"I should have never helped you into that boat!"

"It wouldn't have mattered," she insisted, raising the impact of her words just slightly.

"No!" he protested. "No, if I wouldn't have done those things, then you wouldn't have been taken away from me." His words were powerful, but hung without conviction.

"That's not true, Nick. That's not the way it works. We don't get to choose when we die, or when our loved ones die. That's a decision that God alone makes. It wouldn't have mattered where I was or what I was doing. I died because it was my time to go."

He readied himself and began to object, but found no words waiting in the void. Somehow, deep inside, he knew she was right. It *hadn't been his fault*, but if not, then why had he blamed himself? Why would he put himself through so much pain for so many years? The instant the question ran through his mind he was awarded the answer, but for the moment it was more than he could handle. It was so powerful and so frightening that his soul immediately screamed in protest, "No!"

Turmoil filled his heart, and for an instant he was completely blinded by the answer. "No it's not true!" His words were hollow and hung violently in front of him. Before long he pushed the answer out of his mind and convinced himself that it had never come. As the turmoil dissipated he once again accepted a blame that was not his to accept. The accident *had* been his fault. Of course it had. He was just as much to blame for her death as the sinister tree limb that trapped her head beneath the water.

She went to him and warmly wrapped her love around his soul. "Nick, you *didn't* kill me."

"Maybe not, but I helped!" he insisted.

"No!" her words were simple and full of truth, "You didn't."

Why was she doing this? His thoughts shifted back and forth, as if trying to dodge tiny bullets of invisible truth as he searched for a way to respond, but found none. Suddenly, he no longer wanted to be here. He moved away from her and searched the nothingness, but there was nowhere to go.

"Nick, open your heart," she pleaded.

"No, I don't want to know this!"

"I know, but you must."

"Why? Why must I? It's bullshit. Just send me back. I want to go back." For just a moment he was half shocked to find the word *bullshit* floating there in what might have been heaven.

"You want to go back?"

"Yes!"

"To what, a life of lies? One where you can continue to hide behind false guilt?"

Then miraculously, for a split second in time she became one with the void and was everywhere at once. "YOU HAVE TO FACE THE TRUTH!" Her words rang out aggressively and duplicated themselves until they all but filled the abyss.

Nick shuddered beneath the force of the sentence and tried to respond, but couldn't, as there was only one word left hanging in the void, *truth*!

Suddenly, the words entering the void became so powerful and violent that Nick wasn't sure if they belonged to Allie or God himself. "The truth is that you did not cause the accident, and the reason you keep lying to yourself is because you're too afraid to let go!"

Nick wanted to respond, but cowered. The words dominated every inch of reality. They swirled around him as if blown by some powerful and invisible wind, and came at him from every direction.

"You're terrified to let go of the past because you know that if you do, then someone else might just sneak past your defenses and get close to you again."

Nick struggled to resist, but the words were too strong. Then unexpectedly, images of Mercedes entered his mind. There was the beautiful photo on her website, the image of her doing the splits on the floor at the motel, her face, her smile, her eyes. "This is what you're afraid of!" The sentence echoed loudly in the abyss, and then just hung there in front of him, completely made up of truth itself.

"No." Nick managed to push a single, meek word into the abyss, but it was empty and only hung faintly in the haze.

Finally, Allie and the void separated, and once again she was there beside him.

"Life is a fragile thing, and only God knows how long we have, but we can't stop loving because we're too afraid that we'll lose the person we love." Once again her words were soft and full of truth, but this time Nick didn't fight them.

"I don't think I can do it Allie, not again. It hurts too much."

Then a miracle happened. As he struggled with a pain that he could not comprehend, she once again wrapped her love around him and then reached out and touched his soul. Instantly, he was filled with an amazing peace and for a few incredible moments his pain completely went away. As he existed in the void filled with God's love, wisdom entered his heart and something inside him changed. When she let go, however, the pain rushed right back in, but somehow it didn't seem to be as bad now. Perhaps he *could* handle it. Perhaps he *could* love again.

Her soul smiled warmly as he pondered his new inner strength. "I don't know what to say." Then, without warning, as his words of gratitude hung in the abyss, everything dramatically changed. Reality itself blinked and the emptiness gave way to an endless sea of chaos. Suddenly, Nick was using his five senses again. He watched as a multitude of dark, sinister colors churned around him like demons circling their victim. Where had Heaven gone? In the distance, he could barely make out the pounding of a human heart, and somehow he knew it was his own. Although he still had a fuzzy impression of the heavenly abyss, it was fading and he was sure that he had never been there. For as long as he could remember, for all of time itself he had existed here, stuck in this never-ending swirl of madness.

"Daddy!" Lisa's scream broke through the chaos and entered his ears from every direction. He struggled to move, but found it nearly impossible, feeling somewhat like a fly stuck deep within a can of thick, wet, deadly paint. Then, just as quickly it had come, the chaos was gone and once again he found himself back in the void, with Allie. This place was so much more *real* than the chaos had been that he wasn't completely sure that reality had ever blinked at all. As a matter of fact it was as if he had simply imagined a fleeting feeling of chaos and had never really been there.

"There's nothing to say." Her smile brightened as she addressed his statement.

"Thank you." His words were soft and his heart was strong. Then it happened again. Reality blinked for a second time and chaos was everywhere! As he struggled against the sinister colors around him he could not tell whether he had actually been in the abyss with Allie or if he had just imagined it.

"Daddy, please!" Lisa's scream was louder this time, and Nick struggled with all his might, but couldn't get free.

Reality shifted once more and as before, chaos was nothing more than a faint feeling of something that never really happened.

"You must go." Her smile softened, and Nick began to see other silhouettes at the edge of the fog.

Then suddenly he was back in chaos, and the heartbeat grew louder.

"Nick!" The scream was ear piercing and this time came from Mercedes.

Flash. Back in perfection, and not even remembering that chaos existed. The silhouettes were coming closer and beginning to take shape. There seemed to be hundreds or even thousands of them.

"You must go now!" Allie urged.

Nick agreed and smiled goodbye, but just before he was whisked back to reality, three souls emerged out of the crowed.

One of them he knew, but couldn't quite place, however the other two were unmistakable, and his spirit overflowed with joy as he pushed a single question into the void, "Mom, Dad?"

Then, just as their souls lit up in warm smiles of love, Nick was once again slammed into chaos.

The heartbeat continued to pound and the presence of evil grew stronger, until it was utterly unbearable. On the verge of madness, Nick screamed and the dark colors took advantage of his opened mouth and flowed into his body. Then suddenly, new images came to his eyes.

Lisa was leaning over him, screaming frantically. "Daddy, please! Please! Don't go!"

It took a moment, but the instant she noticed that his stare was no longer blank and that his eyes were staring into hers, she stopped in mid sentence. Her face instantly changed, and new screaming began. "Daddy! You're alive! You're alive!"

He went to hug her, but found it nearly impossible to move his arms. They were heavy and felt like lead rods embedded in the asphalt. Eventually, with some bit of effort he slowly pulled them away from the ground and managed to wrap them around her. "Oh Daddy!"

As Lisa drew near, Nick looked over her shoulder and saw Mercedes standing above him. She also had a face full of tears, and although he had seen her many times before, somehow she looked different now. She seemed softer, prettier.

"We thought we lost you for a second there," Roger chimed in. Nick slowly turned his stiff neck and gazed up at the big man. "Your light was out man. I mean it was out!" Roger took his finger and slid it beneath his chin, from one side of his neck to the other.

Nick turned back toward Mercedes as Roger continued. "No pulse, no breathing, no nothing!"

Mercedes' eyes glistened as a soft smile found a way into her face.

Nick finished hugging Lisa and then, with Roger's help, worked his way to his feet. For a few seconds he just gazed into Mercedes' water-soaked eyes and just as she began to laugh with joy, he kissed her, and for the first time felt no guilt. The fist one was short and sweet, but it was so good that he leaned in and kissed her again. This one was longer. It was so long as a matter of fact that Roger began to worry that they just might pass out from lack of oxygen. Just as Roger was getting ready to give a snide remark, a familiar voice poured into the night. "Hey guys, need a ride?" Ernie Baxter was sitting behind the wheel of Roger's van, out on the street, less than 50 feet on the other side of the chain link.

Earlier, after the guards had busted into the van, and taken Ernie to the ground floor of the lab, they tried to reach Davenport to find out exactly what he wanted done with the electronic eavesdropper. Ernie was slammed down in an office chair and told to be silent as the guards tried many times, without success to reach Davenport. One guard in particular, a newly hired Russian named Hilda found Ernie to be rather attractive, and as the other guards huddled together across the room, to discuss Erie's fate she volunteered to keep her eye on him. After a few minutes they decided to go into the lower levels of the lab and try to find out what happened to Davenport. While they were gone, Hilda and Ernie got to know each other.

Ernie was the first to speak. He wasn't trying to make friends with her, only to calm some of his nerves. As she stood on the other side of the desk, staring at him and strumming her fingers on her belt, he glanced down at her guns and nervously asked, "So, you ever used those before?"

She kept raising her eyebrows and looking at Ernie in a very funny way. She would turn her head from side to side, revealing just how long and skinny her nose was and do something funny with her lips, and then wink.

Ernie began to feel uncomfortable and if he would have been wearing a tie to loosen, he would have done so. Ever so slowly, Hilda made her way around the desk and over to him, puckering her lips, winking her eyes and making strange noises as she went. Then just as she was planting a huge, wet, completely unwanted and totally unsolicited kiss smack on his lips the place began to shake. The kiss wasn't as bad as he thought it would be and as he felt the earth move he wondered if it was love, but as the quaking quickly grew worse he realized that they were in trouble. He struggled to get up, but she wouldn't let him, not so much because she had been appointed to guard him, but rather because he was right where she wanted him to be. Just as she was forcing another kiss on him and working her tongue through his stiffened lips one of the windows shattered, and a piece of glass flew through the room and sliced her arm. The cut wasn't bad, but it did give Ernie a chance to run. He quickly made it out of the building, but halfway across the parking lot he heard a loud explosion behind him, immediately followed by a cry for help. He didn't know what possessed him, but for a few short moments he just stopped and put his hands on his hips as he contemplated going back. Then as a second cry for help came out of the building, he turned around and started back for the lab.

Now out on the street, Ernie pressed on the horn. "C'mon guys, enough already."

Nick and Mercedes parted with a chuckle as Ernie got out of the van and carried a pair of bolt cutters to the fence. As Ernie was cutting the links, Nick looked down at Alex's body. "Is he...?"

"Yeah," Mercedes nodded sadly as sirens sounded faintly in the distance. "He's dead."

"Um, guys I think we should go now," Roger nudged as Ernie finished snipping the last of the chain link.

"Hurry up Buttercup!" A woman with a heavy Russian accent and a large square face poked her head out of the van window.

"Who in the world is that?" Mercedes asked.

"Oh, that's Hilda." Ernie snorted with a smile.

"Hilda?" Mercedes scrunched her face as she strained to get a better look at the woman.

"Yeah, she's one of the security guards. I think she likes me." Ernie's cheeks turned red as Roger cocked his head and raised a skeptical eyebrow.

As the sirens grew louder, Nick gazed down at the naked corpse one last time and then nodded as he said, "Yeah, yeah, we should go."

The team got to the van and pulled away just as a couple of cop cars and emergency vehicles rounded the corner at the far end of the block.

"What's that?" Mercedes asked while pointing at a piece of white material poking out from Nick's coat pocket.

"I don't know," Nick said as he pulled out a small paper napkin. Curiously, he unfolded it to reveal a drawing of a heart.

Water filled his eyes and a soft smile found his face as he whispered, "She gave it back."

"What did you say?"

"Nothing." Nick smiled confidently, nodded his head and re-pocketed the napkin.

CHAPTER THIRTY-THREE

One year later...

Nick and Mercedes stood at the foot of the grave with their hands together and their fingers interlaced. The West Virginia air was unusually dry and cool for noon on an August day, and a few of the trees had even begun to turn. "She's in a better place now," Mercedes encouraged as she squeezed his hand.

"I know," Nick spoke with confidence as he smiled at the marble headstone.

"I still miss her," Lisa said sadly as she knelt down and laid six long-stemmed roses on the grave.

"I know you do, peaches. I do too."

"I wish I could have met her," Mercedes said with a warm far away look in her eye."

"She was an amazing person!" Nick assured and then took a deep breath, filled his lungs with the clean mountain air and was happy to be alive.

"So, you think she approves?" Mercedes asked as she reached over with her free hand and fingered the engagement ring.

Nick turned to Mercedes and looked her over as if inspecting a piece of merchandise while he pondered the question. "I don't know. She was pretty particular about things."

"Oh Dad, she was not!" Lisa derailed her father with a teenage glare and then softly turned to Mercedes and said, "Aunt Dottie would have loved you."

As they walked back across the grass to the car, Mercedes' cell-phone rang. "Iceman Investigations, this is Mercedes...Oh, hi Ernie. How's the office? Oh really? That's great!" Mercedes covered up the bottom of the phone and spoke to Nick. "Ernie says the new marketing ideas are working like a charm. The phone is ringing off the hook."

Nick's face lit up with a proud smile as he popped in a Gummy Bear, pulled up on the handle and opened the car door.

"Well, we'll be back tomorrow," Mercedes continued as she stepped past her prince into the waiting car. "I'm sure you and Hilda can handle things 'til then."

Nick shut her door, put on his sunglasses and smiled as he walked around to the driver's side. A slight breeze picked up and blew past Martha Rodman's grave as the car pulled out of Sunset Memorial Park and into the distance.

CHAPTER THIRTY-FOUR

Somewhere in Southern California, a glass of milk waited on the table as one of the three chocolate chip cookies was picked up and neatly bitten into. A half opened duffle bag filled with various newspaper clippings sat on the booth beside him. Teddy picked up the current addition and glanced at the headlines. The main story was about a small plane that went down in the San Bernardino Mountains. The pilot and his four passengers weren't anyone Teddy knew. As he glanced through the paper, looking for any information on the two souls that he had helped *go home* just a couple of nights ago, he came across something shocking. It was a message from God, from God himself!

As he was flipping through the community section of the paper, he glimpsed a picture that jumped out at him like a demon from Hell. Teddy stopped and stared and could hardly believe his eyes. There in the middle of the paper was a picture of the demon that he had almost sent into oblivion just one year ago. Teddy grinned as he read the names beneath the engagement photos. Nicholas Chadwick and Mercedes Atwater.

Teddy could hardly believe the good fortune that God was giving to him. He reached into his duffle bag and retrieved a clipping titled, "God's wrath on Biotronics." The story was about a mysterious earthquake that had destroyed the company last year. The paper had published several photos of the event and many of the people that worked for the company. One of the photos was of the man who had tricked Teddy into believing that he was an angel. Teddy knew the truth now. Although the man may have been a warrior of God once, he was lured to the dark side and fell. Teddy had reasoned that everyone working with Biotronics were demons or pawns of the Devil. Until now, he had believed that God had destroyed them all, but he was wrong. God had left one for Teddy to take care of himself.

Teddy's eyes were bright and happy as he left the bakery and headed for his car.

***

Meanwhile, somewhere in the deep Midwest, after being on the road for hours, a familiar black van with government plates finally pulled up to a lonely gate labeled *No Trespassing*. An intelligent looking, dark-haired man in sunglasses, wearing a white polo shirt and gray slacks stepped out of the van and opened the gate. A few miles down the road, the van pulled up to an obscure military base, reportedly used for routine combat and tactical operations. After showing CIA identification, he proceeded to the elevator, where a retina scan and a voice evaluation were required. Twelve floors below the ground, the elevator stopped and the man stepped out into a long corridor with polished floors and featureless walls. His rubber soles made little noise as he walked, and moments later he entered a room where a man in military uniform waited.

"Hello Colonel," he said as he walked to a large white table in the center of the room.

"Matthew," The Colonel nodded as Matthew placed the container on the table.

"How's she doing?" Matthew asked as he opened box, releasing a small cloud of cold air.

"I don't know. She hasn't even blinked since you left, last night."

"She did rejuvenate though, right?"

"No." The Colonel shook his head and pondered.

"No at all?"

"Anh ah." The Colonel shook his head again and then asked, "Matthew, you sure it's not too soon to do this?"

"Too soon?" Matthew replied while retrieving a small glass jar full of an odd looking white substance from the container. "It may be too late already."

"But she's only been out of her coma for three days."

"And thank God she finally came out of it. I don't think we would have been able to keep these together another week." As he spoke he reached in and pulled out another glass jar. "Hell, as it is they're probably too far gone now. It's been a miracle we've kept their integrity for as long as we have."

"Tell me again why these memories are so important?" The Colonel asked.

"Because, my dear Colonel, these three brains belonged to Jonathan Davenport, Dr. Boris, and Gregory Patterson, the three men who were found underneath the rubble at the bottom of the Boris Lab the night that Hell broke loose on Biotronics. I've got to know what happened that night. I've got to know just what took down four skyscrapers and a half a dozen office buildings all across Southern California."

"We're ready for those now, sir." Another man entered the room and gestured toward the container on the table.

"Be very, very careful with these. If anything happens to them before the transfer's complete I'm holding you personally responsible," Matthew warned sternly as he handed over the container.

The man took the box down the hall and disappeared down a flight of stairs. Matthew and the colonel turned around and walked to the far glass wall that overlooked another room diagonally below. In the room, a somber-faced woman sat strapped in a chair. Several men in lab coats and various electronic devices surrounded her. Within moments the man carrying the container entered the room.

"Why did they call her Number Twelve?" The colonel asked.

"Because, Biotronics created several of them in a lab, and she was the twelfth one. They had to call her something. One day soon we'll have our own Number Twelve." As the doctors began the memory transfer on Number Twelve Matthew thought of the future and smiled.

Just two floors beneath him, in an area the size of a large warehouse, thousands of metal containers were fast at work cooking up the next generation of what he liked to call memory-transferring humans.

The End